THE OPENING CHASE

Also by Cap Daniels

THE
OPENING CHASE

CHASE FULTON NOVEL #1

CAP DANIELS

ANCHOR WATCH
PUBLISHING
** USA **

The Opening Chase, Chase Fulton Novel #1

13 Digit ISBN: 978-1-7323024-0-2
Library of Congress Control Number: 2018942866
Cover Design: German Creative
Printed in the United States of America

ANCHOR WATCH
PUBLISHING
** USA **

This book is dedicated to . . .

My lovely wife, Melissa,
without whose patience, support, tolerance of my writing addiction,
and her writer's block resolution program, this book would
have never been possible.

Special thanks to . . .

My Amazing Editor:
Sarah Flores, Write Down the Line, LLC
www.WriteDownTheLine.com
She is not only a talented editor, but also a wonderfully inspirational teacher, without whose touch my story would have been unreadable.

Medical Editor:
Judson Moore, MD, orthopedic surgeon extraordinaire

Inspiration:
Everyone who crossed my path in my five decades on Earth and provided the inspiration for countless characters who have been set free on the pages of this novel.

1
MVP

Omaha, Nebraska, June 1996

I'll never forget that day. It was damned hot. Especially beneath ten pounds of catcher's gear designed to protect me from any ninety-mile-per-hour fastball that found its way past my mitt. Having anything get past my mitt was unlikely since I'd been catching for almost a decade and earned a reputation of keeping things that could hurt me well out in front where I could control them. My somewhat obstructed view through my filthy face mask revealed runners on second and third, with a beast of a man digging into the batter's box in front of my right knee. I couldn't see the scoreboard through the sweat cascading into my eyes, but I didn't need to see it to know we were winning four to three with one out in the bottom of the ninth. If I could keep Bryan Payne from falling apart on the mound sixty feet and six inches away for a few more pitches, we'd win the 1996 College World Series and solidify our place in collegiate baseball history.

I expected Coach Woodley to make the call to put Goliath on first with an intentional walk, but his hand signals told me to call for the breaking ball. Putting him on base would bring up the all-time collegiate base-hitting record holder. Apparently, coach didn't want to pitch to him with bases loaded. At that moment, nothing on Earth mattered more than coming up with a plan to keep Goliath from crushing a hanging curveball into the parking lot and sending us back home as the second-place finishers . . . the runners up . . . the first losers. I reached back with my right hand, tapped the umpire's foot, and demanded, "Time!"

I sprang from my crouch, trotted toward the mound, and pulled off my mask. I didn't have anything meaningful to tell Bryan. I just wanted a reason to stand up, wipe the grime and to-bacco juice from my face, and let the puddles of sweat drain from behind my knees.

My God, it's hot.

I patted Bryan's hip, leaned in, and whispered something about how every cheerleader on Earth would be lining up at his door if he struck out just two more batters . . . starting with Goliath.

"Let's have some fun with Mongo up there at the plate," I said. "I think we can get him to dance a little, don't you?" I pat-ted Bryan on the hip once more and galloped back to my battle station.

The giant dug in again, kicking red clay and sand into the air as his spikes found purchase in the batter's box. Bryan leaned in, awaiting my first pitch call. With a flash of my fingers between my thighs, I called for his filthy slider down and in—way down and way in. It was a dangerous call. If it got past me, the runner from third would score easily and the game would be tied. If it actually hit Goliath, the bases would be loaded, but playing it safe is not what winners do. Bryan suppressed a grin and nod-ded, accepting the pitch I called as I crept toward the enormous left-handed batter.

"How are those knees, Mongo? Man, this is really gonna hurt."

The batter looked down at the top of my helmet as I edged ever closer to his feet. He lifted first one foot, then the other, softening his stance in fear of Bryan bouncing five-and-a-quarter ounces of cork, wool yarn, and cowhide off his twenty-year-old right knee. The ability to strike fear into the hearts and minds of batters with simple, not-so-subtle wordplay was one of the things I loved most about catching as a University of Georgia Bulldog.

Psychological warfare. That's what Dr. Richter called it. He was the most brilliantly deceptive and masterfully manipulative person I'd ever met, but most of all, he was the best psych professor in the world.

I'd just talked a supremely confident homerun hitter into losing his nerve. Instead of thinking about crushing a fastball over the right field wall, that two-hundred-thirty-pound beast was planning his escape route to protect his precious knees.

Dr. Richter would be so proud.

Bryan made that face—the one that meant he was about to throw hard. Every collegiate batter in the country knew that face, and most feared it, even if they wouldn't admit it. Goliath was no exception. The ball left Bryan's hand in a blur and began rotating and picking up speed. The contrasting red stitches against the brilliant white cowhide spun like a cyclone as the ball started to dive, and dive it did, right at Goliath's feet.

I drove my right knee into the ground behind his heels and forced my glove into the dirt, bracing for the impact of ball, glove, dirt, knees, and sweat. A cloud of sandy dust exploded as the ball plumaged into the dirt, squirming and twisting as it went. I felt the ball find its home in the webbing of my well-worn mitt, and my eyes darted down the third base line to see the runner coming in hard.

Goliath had swung in a mighty descending arc of swatting and clumsy self-defense, leaving himself stumbling backward out of the batter's box as the cloud of dust billowed between my knees. With the ball still wrapped tightly in my mitt—exactly where it belonged—I leapt from my crouch and spun to the right, pretending to frantically search for the ball that everyone on the field believed had escaped between my feet. The umpire galloped backward, determined not to interfere with my effort to recover the ball even he believed was loose and still alive.

My charade was working perfectly. Bryan broke into a sprint toward home plate as the determined runner thundered for home. He was, quite literally, playing right into my hand. It was time to stop the charade and play some full-contact baseball. The left fielder sprinted toward third to back up the throw I'd inevitably make . . . if I survived the collision at home plate.

The runner storming toward me, and his teammate plowing from second behind him, were just temporary obstacles. In my head, I was already drinking beer in the clubhouse and watching Bryan do the ESPN interview.

I turned and powered back toward home plate with reckless abandon and absolute determination in my eyes. That was the moment when everyone in the park, from the umpire to the hot dog boy, and especially the runner from third, realized I'd never lost the ball. It'd been firmly embedded in my mitt from a millisecond after it crashed into the dirt at Goliath's feet.

I saw it in his eyes when the runner made his decision to power through me and tie the game. I was about to break his heart . . . and perhaps a rib or two. Ten pounds of armor protected my two hundred pounds of muscle and determination. I wouldn't lose the imminent jousting match—fear of base runners was never an affliction from which I suffered. When the dust settled, I'd still be holding the ball and the runner would be lying in the dirt, trying to catch the breath I'd knocked from his lungs.

Home plate disappeared between my feet, and my spikes dug into the same dirt Goliath had kicked up only seconds earlier. With knees bent and shoulders lowered, I waited for the impact. My wait would be brief, and I secretly hoped the runner wouldn't disappoint me by chickening out and sliding instead of taking his shot. I wanted to feel his shoulder hit my chest pad and hear the sounds he made when I didn't surrender. To my delight, he didn't slow down, and he definitely didn't slide. My teeth rattled, and the explosive collision sent stars circling my head. Fortunately, I exhaled as he hit me, so my lungs were empty, but his were not. He'd been chugging down the third base line, sucking in air as fast as his lungs could take it, and fortunately for me, he'd just filled those lungs the instant his shoulder plowed into my chest.

I knocked more than the wind from his lungs. His ambition and pride went, too. I won't lie . . . it felt like I'd been hit by a dump truck, but I won, and more importantly, I didn't get tangled up with him after the wreck. Shaking off the crash, I leapt to my feet and positioned myself for the throw to third. Throwing with all of my might should've placed the ball in the third baseman's glove less than a second after leaving my right hand, but that's not what happened.

Instead of the ball rifling into his glove as it should've, it corkscrewed through the air like a broken Frisbee. Terrified, I watched the ball sail across the third baseman's head and into the grass. The disbelieving runner and the third base coach watched the ball flutter into the outfield. The coach windmilled his right arm, and the runner rounded the bag, heading straight for me.

The world moved in ultra-slow motion as I watched the play that should've already ended, continue to build.

Why did I make such a horrible throw?

My question was answered by a glance down at my right hand. Instead of a healthy, albeit filthy right hand, I saw a twisted mess of misshapen fingers pointing in every direction but where they should've been. As I glanced up to see the runner picking up speed with victory in his eyes, the left fielder twisted his lanky body into a throwing arc and launched the baseball— one hemisphere still covered in red clay—soaring past the runner's head and toward my chest.

Unable to resist one more glance back at my hand, I realized my broken fingers weren't the only problem. My wrist was bulging as if the bones were trying to force their way through the flesh. I looked back up to see the ball screaming through the air while the runner accelerated toward me for the second collision in one play. Not looking forward to the coming crash, I tucked what was left of my right hand behind my back and reached out with my mitt to receive the muddy missile now less than a tenth of a second away.

The ball and the runner arrived simultaneously. This time, I wasn't prepared for the impact. I hadn't exhaled nor planted my feet. I hadn't tucked my chin, and I hadn't lowered my shoulders. In fact, I'd done nothing right. Worst of all, I was standing on my heels instead of the balls of my feet. I remember the sound of the runner's gasping breath and the feeling of my lips exploding against my teeth as his shoulder met my face. I remember the sound of the back of my head hitting the ground and the agonizing feeling of my breath leaving my body in an explosive evacuation. That's when my lights went out.

When I came to, I wasn't on earth. I was several feet above the infield in Bryan Payne's arms, being hoisted higher and higher by every infielder on the team. Every player, coach, and manager whose uniform resembled mine came pouring out of the dugout with fists raised and shouts of victory bellowing from their lips. Although I had no memory of it happening, we had apparently won the game.

As fate—or luck—would have it, I still had the ball in my mitt after the catastrophe at the plate. Both runners were out. Goliath was confused, and the umpires were leaving the field. We'd just won the College World Series, and I was the MVP.

In less than six months during the following winter, I'd be twenty-two and a professional baseball player. I would be a Major League catcher. I'd never been so happy until I took another glance at what remained of my right hand dangling helplessly at the end of my arm. The adrenaline-charged high that had kept my pain at bay faded in an instant, and I yelled in agony, but the team kept lifting and tossing me about, drowning out my cries for help. I was badly injured with no way to express my dire need for assistance, so I tucked my destroyed hand behind my chest pad and held on for the ride. Sooner or later, my teammates would put me down. I was praying for sooner.

Finally, the celebration lost its steam as the reality of the victory overtook the elation of the moment. I was crying, but I wasn't alone. Almost every member of the team was crying, but theirs were tears of joy while mine were tears of agony. My whole body felt like it was on fire. A medical trainer ran toward me, his eyes filled with terror. He slid his hand up my chest and around my neck as he laid me on the grass and watched as my mind and body succumbed to the trauma.

When I awoke in the recovery room at the Nebraska Medical Center, I had no memory of the game, the victory, or the injury to my hand. I was confused, afraid, and groggy. My right arm was encased in a white cast from my hand to just above my elbow.

This has to be some bizarre dream. It can't be real. I'm twenty-one years old and the star of the University of Georgia baseball team. I'm going to catch for the Atlanta Braves. I can't be in a hospital with a broken arm.

A nurse with eyes like the ocean stood beside my bed with one hand on my chest and the other fiddling with an IV bag. Her efforts to smile at me were masked behind concern and perhaps even sadness.

When she spoke, her voice was kind and her tone sincere. "Mr. Fulton, your surgery went very well. The doctors were able to repair most of the damage to your hand. You're going to be all right. The surgeon will be in to tell you all about it as soon as the anesthesia wears off. Are you thirsty?"

What on Earth is she talking about? What damage to my hand? What surgery? What's happening to me?

As my confusion became apparent to the young nurse, her tone softened even more. "You don't remember the accident, do you?"

"No. What accident? What's happening?"

She patted my chest and leaned closer. "Mr. Fulton, you were injured in the game against Oklahoma State this afternoon. Your hand was badly broken, but the doctors were able to repair the broken bones, and they believe, most of the nerve damage. The surgeon will explain all of that to you very soon. Do you understand?"

Through my confusion, I mumbled, "Did we win?"

Her smile grew animated and sincere. "Yes, sir, you surely did." The Midwestern drawl was as cute as her dimples and deep blue eyes.

The grogginess hadn't fully worn off by the time the doctor came in.

"Well, Mr. Fulton, it's good to see you awake. I'm Doctor Goldman. I'm the orthopedic surgeon who led the team to perform the initial reconstruction of your hand. You suffered what is called a fracture dislocation of the wrist. You see, there are eight bones that make up the human wrist, and your accident essentially split those bones apart from the inside. You were quite fortunate it wasn't actually an open fracture. Had that been the case, you would've lost a lot of blood, and that alone could've made the overall injury much worse." He paused, I suppose expecting me to celebrate with him, but I didn't flinch.

With a glance at his clipboard, he continued. "In addition to the damage to your wrist, you managed to break all of your fingers. Your wrist and hand are remarkably complex structures. The damage you sustained in the accident was severe to say the least. You're quite fortunate we were able to get you into surgery literally within minutes of the accident. We've saved the hand, but you're going to require a number of additional surgeries and several months of physical therapy to regain any measure of normal use out of the hand. Were you right-handed, Mr. Fulton?"

My memory was returning in spontaneous flashes, but trying to piece the memory of the game and the accident together with the surgeon's words was overwhelming. "I'll still be able to play ball, though. Right, doc?"

He furrowed his brow. "Young man, you're lucky to still have any use of that hand at all." He looked down at me over the upper rim of his glasses. "I'm afraid your baseball days are over. You're going to have to focus on the rehabilitation that lies ahead. It's important you focus on the fact we've been able to save your hand and not worry about what you *can't* do in the future."

Does he expect me to thank him for telling me I'll never play ball again? That's not happening.

"Look, doc. I'm going to be a Major League ball player. It's just a few broken fingers. I'm young and in great shape. I'm going to be fine, right?"

He lifted his clipboard and frowned. "I'm afraid it's not that simple, Mr. Fulton. We'll be moving you up to your room in a few minutes, and your family will be able to see you then. If there's anything you need, the nurses will be checking on you regularly. You and I will talk again later this evening." With that, he patted my leg and disappeared through the curtains.

2

The Recruit

My mind was reeling, and my thoughts were a tornado of twisted confusion. I'd learned everything there was to know about the Kübler-Ross model in my psychology classes. The five stages of grief were pretty simple, but they clearly didn't apply to me.

The doctor is wrong. My hand's going to be fine.

Denial. Stage one.

Why me? This isn't fair! I'm too young and talented to have this happen. It's not right!

Ah, anger. Stage two.

I'm going to make the sacrifices necessary to regain full use of my hand. I'll just work harder than everyone else. I can do it. I can work harder and do everything right to use my hand and play ball again. It's just going to take some hard work. That's all.

There it is: bargaining. Stage three.

Then the tears came . . . and kept coming. I was alone, empty, hopeless, and every dream I had for my future lay in shambles. Nothing mattered since I couldn't play ball.

What was I going to do? It didn't matter. I didn't eat. I didn't talk. I barely slept. What I did was cry and wish I'd died on the field that day.

If I can't play professional baseball, there's nothing left for me.

Of course, depression. Stage four.

Stage five is acceptance. I never achieved stage five; instead, I channeled stages one through three with the intensity of a laser and the subtlety of a bulldozer.

I endured three more surgeries that were, more or less, successful in transforming what had been a healthy, strong, capable right hand into a somewhat responsive hunk of flesh, pins, screws, suture anchors and pain . . . a lot of pain. The physical therapy was agonizing. I spent hundreds of hours flexing and relaxing, stretching and rotating, pushing and pulling, screaming and cursing. I was young, strong, determined, and pissed off. That combination makes for a volatile and dangerous cocktail.

Realizing, but still refusing to accept that I would never again crouch behind home plate, I poured myself into the study of psychology in what remained of my senior year at UGA. I read every book I could beg, borrow, or steal. I attended every lecture given by anyone with a PhD. I even volunteered at Emory University Hospital's psych department. The determination and drive I'd poured onto the baseball field was now dumped enthusiastically into the study of the human mind and its frailties, departures from normalcy, and especially its resilience.

I spent every minute that he'd allow with my favorite psych professor, Dr. Robert Richter. He began to refer to me as his protégé, and I liked the moniker. I'd even begun calling him "Coach." I'd done it mistakenly at first, but I came to realize my mind had begun thinking of him as my coach. Mostly out of amusement, I think he actually enjoyed that revered title.

Twenty-one-year-old boys on the verge of becoming men need the influence of men of strong moral character in their lives. My father had been the epitome of character to me, but his life, and the lives of my mother and sister, were snuffed out in the middle of the night on the edge of the rainforest in Panama just before General Noriega's debacle in 1989.

My mother and father had been U.S. aid workers on a humanitarian mission to provide medical care, education, and general comfort to orphans of that country. They'd worked throughout the Caribbean, as well as Central and South America for as long as I could remember; in fact, I learned to play baseball in the Dominican Republic with hordes of other children whose lives were nothing like mine. They lived in abject poverty in the third world and didn't always know when they'd eat their next meal. I was, from their perspective, a child of privilege from America, but baseball erased those imaginary cultural and economic lines. Baseball made us all the same. That was fifteen years and a lifetime ago.

On one unusually warm Thursday evening in the library, I found myself surrounded by reference material, piles of notes, and stacks of audiotapes of interviews with psych patients. I simply couldn't absorb information quickly enough to satisfy my thirst for the understanding of the human psyche. I was so engulfed in my studies that I didn't notice Dr. Richter silently sliding his long, lanky frame into the oak chair across the table from me. I saw him only after he lifted my weighty primary reference book to read the spine. Startled, I looked up to see his sunken eyes peering through his professorial, wire-rimmed glasses.

His lips formed the words even though he made no sound. With unrepentant contempt, he read the spine of the oversized textbook. "Abnormal Psychology . . . ha! What other psychology is there?"

He removed his glasses and slid them into the ancient sleeve firmly attached inside the pocket of his threadbare, short-sleeved, button-down shirt, then he licked his thin lips and surveyed the room. "Mr. Fulton, my boy. What are you doing? You aren't going to learn the ways of the human mind in this compost heap of intellectual crap. We learn the ways of the mind by observing the behavior of its keeper."

I wondered two things about Dr. Richter. First, why didn't he ever call me Chase? He'd never called me by my first name—only Mr. Fulton. Second, why did he harbor such contempt for academia? He was, after all, an academic. He had, on far more occasions than I could remember, spoken of the weaknesses of academic study, instead, preferring listening and observing. He was not only unique in his physical appearance, but he was also alone among the staff of UGA in his poor opinion of the importance of classroom lectures. Before the dawn of another Monday, I would learn the answer to at least one of my questions.

"Mr. Fulton," he said, "you're bright, ambitious, strong, and not unlike I was a lifetime ago. You'll graduate from this fine Southern institution of higher learning on Saturday. Have you thought about how you're going to unleash your brilliance on the world come Monday?"

I'd given that question exactly zero thought. I'd been so consumed by my desire to learn that I had no idea what I'd do with all of that knowledge when I finally left school. It suddenly felt as if I'd already failed in my future before my future had actually begun.

Before I could stumble through any poorly delivered answer, he nodded and looked over each of his shoulders as if he was going to tell a dirty joke he didn't want anyone else to hear. I was intrigued.

He leaned forward and closed my book. "I have some people I'd like you to meet, Mr. Fulton. There are some things you should know about me, your parents, and especially about yourself, so let's go for a walk."

He pocketed the pile of plastic cassette tapes lying on the table and gathered my stack of notes.

What does he mean? What could he possibly know about my parents? He's never met them. Is he guessing, or is he playing one of his mind games designed to teach me yet another universal psychological truth that would never appear in any textbook?

I'd learned he was never without a surprise, and he was constantly teaching, even when he didn't intend to be doing so. I think that may be what made him such an incredible professor—and coach.

As we left the library, Dr. Richter winked at a middle-aged librarian who was looking through her bifocals at the card catalog and holding her chin at an angle that seemed painfully high. The demure librarian blushed and smiled coyly at Dr. Richter's flirtation.

I bumped his shoulder with mine. "You old dog, you."

"You have no idea, my boy. You have no idea."

Our walk continued down the aged stone steps and onto the sidewalk. We passed a few students who were obviously searching for any excuse to avoid studying.

Without looking at me, Dr. Richter spoke softly but confidently. "Mr. Fulton, things are almost never as they seem, and if they are, then we perceived them incorrectly. Take me, for example. I've not always been a professor. I spent the first thirty years of my adult life mostly overseas working for the government . . . sort of. It was a good life, Mr. Fulton, a life full of interesting people, places, and opportunities. It's not for everyone, but it was certainly right for me. I see in you the same things that made me very good at that sort of work. I see adaptability, intellect, natural curiosity, and an ability to see things that others cannot or will not see."

My confusion was compounding.

"I know none of this makes any sense right now, but it'll all come together this weekend. What's the use in going to a stuffy old graduation ceremony anyway? I'll pick you up tomorrow morning at six. Pack a bag for the weekend. Bring a nice shirt and a tie if you have one . . . and some boating clothes."

All I could muster was a confused, "Okay."

A car horn blasted and continued for several seconds. I reflexively turned to see what caused the driver to create such a commotion. It didn't take long to determine it was a lover's quarrel in a dark parking lot. I chose to ignore it and turned back to Dr. Richter, but he had vanished.

We were on a sidewalk, on the campus of the University of Georgia, over a hundred feet from any building, and this old, worn-out, mysterious man disappeared into thin air. I must've been watching the lover's quarrel longer than I realized. I tried to shake off the confusing gibberish Dr. Richter poured into my head, but I couldn't do it. Something told me my confusion had only just begun.

3
The Last Weekend of My Life

As rebellious as most people are between sixteen and twenty-four, there is still an inherent desire, even in those rebellious years, to please the people we love and respect. I was no different. I wasn't going to let my coach down, so I was packed and wide awake at five-thirty Friday morning. He arrived ten minutes before six in his VW Microbus. Prior to that moment, I had no idea what he drove, but I wasn't surprised. I climbed aboard the microbus and tried to imagine what mysteries the coming weekend would uncover.

I remembered him telling me he'd worked for the government before becoming a professor, but he was intentionally vague about what that meant. I was naïve and essentially clueless about how real life worked, so I assumed he'd been in the Army, or maybe the Navy. For some reason, he struck me as a Navy man.

There are moments in history when people have been famously wrong about things. When Napoleon believed he could win at Waterloo and when Julius Caesar thought meeting with Brutus in mid-March would be a good plan, they were only slightly more wrong than I was that particular morning.

Before I'd settled into the perch that Volkswagon calls a front seat, Dr. Richter offered me a cup of coffee, and I thankfully accepted. I usually didn't mind early mornings, but I'd gotten so little sleep the previous night that I was definitely in need of caffeine. My mind wouldn't stop churning over what the weekend would hold. I was excited and even a little nervous. Nothing my young mind could come up with remotely approached what I would soon learn about Dr. Richter— and about myself.

We drank our coffee and hardly spoke for the first fifteen minutes of our ride, but when we pulled into the Athens-Ben Epps Airport, my curiosity was piqued. We passed through a security gate that opened when Dr. Richter pressed the button on a small garage door opener hanging from the mirror. The gate closed behind us, and we pulled up to a hangar that looked like an enormous version of his microbus.

"Grab your gear and let's go."

I did as he said, shouldering my backpack as I followed him to the door. When we walked through the heavy steel door, I heard a metallic click, and an electric motor begin to whir as the massive hangar door rose. The light of the morning sun spilled into the hangar, and a silhouette of a P-51 Mustang slowly revealed itself. The plane glistened in the morning sun and appeared to be flying while motionless on the spotless hangar floor. Emblazoned across the right side of the fuselage in elegant script, I saw "Katerina's Heart" and a painting of a beautiful, fair-haired woman sitting seductively with her legs crossed. She was smiling as if she knew a secret she'd never tell.

"Isn't she breathtaking?"

"She certainly is," I answered. "It's a P-51, right?"

"Very good, my boy. That's exactly what she is. She's the reason the French aren't eating sauerkraut and speaking German. You're in for the ride of your life, Mr. Fulton."

Having never seen one up close, I stood in awe of the breathtaking warbird. "Is she yours?"

Instead of answering, he climbed aboard a small tractor attached to the tail wheel of the Mustang and pushed her out of the hangar into the bright morning sun. He returned the tractor back into the hangar and pulled his microbus in alongside it. As the door closed, he walked around the airplane, pulling and pushing, peering and feeling every inch of her. He watched her react to his touch and seemed to enjoy feeling the machine beneath his hands. After he'd finished inspecting every surface, we climbed aboard—me in the front and him in the rear.

The panel in front of me was a masterpiece of dials, screens, and instruments of every kind. I'd flown all over the western hemisphere with my parents, but never in anything like the Mustang. We donned headsets so we could hear each other when we spoke, and I was surprised at the clarity and ease of talking back and forth. Finally, after feeling the rudder pedals and control stick wiggle around for a few seconds, the engine roared to life. It was the most impressive sound I'd ever heard. It seemed to ooze raw power and yearned to fly.

Why has he never mentioned he was a pilot? What else will I learn about my mentor this weekend?

I listened as Dr. Richter spoke with the air traffic controllers in a language that was foreign to me. We taxied to the runway and waited for the controller to clear us for takeoff.

Finally, we rolled onto the runway and I got my first taste of the Mustang's power. The engine bellowed and roared, belching orange fire from the exhaust. Feeling the plane accelerate down the runway was breathtaking. It was clear the Mustang was no ordinary airplane. She was something special. As the tail wheel left the ground, I was rewarded with my first clear sight through the windshield. It was astonishing to see the sun gleaming off the propeller as the blades disappeared in their arc.

"So, this is what it's like to be a fighter pilot, huh?"

Dr. Richter chuckled. "No, Mr. Fulton. This is how it used to feel to be a fighter pilot. Today's jet jockeys are little more than computer operators. Thirty years before you were born, this is how real men ruled the skies over Europe, with two feet on real, metal rudder pedals, one hand on the stick, and one finger on the trigger."

As we climbed through the cool morning air, my fascination slowed down enough to take in the scenery and wonder of what was actually happening around me.

Unexpectedly, at least to me, the left wing fell out of sight and the world began to rotate around us. One second, the Earth was beneath us and disappearing. The next, it was above us and moving so fast I knew my coffee would come back up. Suddenly, the sky was up, and the Earth was down again. We'd done a barrel roll to the left in what seemed like a microsecond. Amazed, I twisted my head so sharply to look back at Dr. Richter that I swore I felt my spine crack. I could barely see him around the seat back and all the gadgets, but I made out his satisfied, crooked smile. He looked twenty years old. He was clearly in his element and completely alive.

I remembered the feeling of doing exactly what I was meant to do. I remembered how comfortable and exciting it was to pull my face mask down and feel my long legs curl up beneath me when I crouched behind home plate. I remembered how it felt to know exactly what the batter was thinking and how I could read the runners' intentions in the way they moved their feet. I remembered knowing precisely what was going to happen next when the pitcher started his stretch and the runners began to fidget. Yes, I knew exactly how Dr. Richter felt. He was at home and completely in control. I missed that feeling more than anything, and I wondered if I'd ever know that feeling again.

We leveled off at eleven thousand five hundred feet over eastern Georgia with the rising sun just off to the left, casting its yellow-orange glow over the seemingly endless fields of pine trees. Atlanta was off to the west, but there was no evidence of anything resembling a concrete jungle from where I sat. The world looked green and peaceful. It was beautiful in the way that only simplicity can be. It was too vast to understand or comprehend, but it was breathtaking. I knew we'd see the Atlantic Ocean before long, and I couldn't wait. I'd always loved the water—especially the ocean.

Dr. Richter hadn't said a word for fifteen minutes, and I wondered why he was so quiet.

Just then, his voice came through the headset. "What do you think, Mr. Fulton?"

"I think it's astonishing."

"Well said, my boy. Now that she's sufficiently impressed you, let me tell you a little about *Katerina's Heart*. As you properly identified her, she's a North American P-51D. We converted her to a two-seat model so I wouldn't be lonely. The boys at the Rolls-Royce plant built that big ol' twelve-cylinder Merlin engine out there. That thing makes almost eighteen hundred horsepower. The whole big, beautiful thing weighs about eleven thousand pounds when she's full of people and gas. I've had her do nearly four hundred and thirty miles per hour up high, but she's old like me, so I don't push her that hard. I'm good to her and she's extremely good to me. That little snap roll we did just after takeoff is one of the nasty characteristics these old girls developed when they started putting the bigger engines in them. They get a little squirrely on takeoff if you don't hold on to them. I did that one on purpose so you could see how nimble the old girl is, but they used to unexpectedly do that on a regular basis before some smart engineer-type decided he could reign that in with the addition of an aerodynamic fin. It worked, too, and it saved the lives of a lot of pilots and a bunch of airplanes. Without the P-51," he sighed, "well, my boy, I don't even like to think how the world would look today without the P-51. Ask any old bomber crew who their guardian angels were over Britain in nineteen forty-four and they'll tell you, without fail, it was the Mustangs. That was my war, son, and probably your grandfather's war too. Not this particular one, but I flew several of these old things over there. I don't know what became of the ones I flew, but I'm sure thankful to have one that'll never be shot out from under me again. It reminds me of the days when the Russians were our friends and it was okay to shoot first and ask questions later. Now we hate the Russians, or we used to hate them, but now we sort of like them again since Reagan had them knock down that wall they loved so much. Now we're afraid we'll hurt somebody's feelings if we flex our American muscle too hard."

I wasn't sure what his little speech was all about, but I enjoyed hearing the passion in his voice when he talked about the good ol' days. I was learning a lot of new things about my favorite professor.

I noticed he hadn't mentioned the nose art. "So, who's Katerina?"

"Look down there. That's Jekyll Island."

I took in the scenery of the barrier islands and noticed several yachts anchored in the river and an old building standing majestically against the lush green landscape.

Had he intentionally ignored my question about Katerina?

"What's that place, Coach?"

"That's the Jekyll Island Club Hotel. That's where we'll be staying tonight. The prime rib will melt in your mouth."

We kept descending and the runway came clearly into view beneath our left wing. I felt the landing gear come down and heard the noise of the engine noticeably change. We rolled gently to the left in a giant U-turn and rolled out precisely aligned with the runway. The strip was a lot shorter than the one back at Athens, and I remember thinking we might not be able to stop, but that was a wasted thought.

We touched the runway so gently I could barely tell when we stopped flying and started rolling. Soon the nose of the airplane filled the sky again and I was left, just as before, blind to the world in front of me. Little did I know I'd spent most of my life in exactly that condition: blind to the world in front of me.

4

Gentlemen

As we climbed out of the Mustang, three old guys who looked a lot like Dr. Richter pulled up in a stretched golf cart with three rows of seats.

Dr. Richter grinned from ear-to-ear as he embraced each of the old guys in turn. They patted backs, shook hands, and even playfully threw some pulled punches into each other's guts. For their ages, they certainly appeared to have kept themselves in shape. I stood silently by the wing and watched the geriatric reunion. I was growing accustomed to not having a clue what was going on around me, so whatever this was didn't surprise me a bit.

With the hugs, shakes, and fake punches complete, Dr. Richter turned to me and gestured with his open hand. "Gentlemen, meet Chase Fulton."

They looked me up and down as if I were a horse about to be sold at auction.

The oldest of the bunch—at least he appeared to be the oldest —approached and stuck out his hand. "Nice to meet you, Mr. Fulton. I'm Ace. This is Beater, and that decrepit old fart over there is Tuner." He motioned toward Dr. Richter with his head. "Clearly, you already know Rocket."

Did he just call Dr. Richter "Rocket"?

I cleared my throat. "It's nice to meet you, uh . . . gentlemen."

The man who'd introduced himself as Ace stared into my eyes as if he were looking into my soul, then turned to Dr. Richter. "He doesn't know why he's here, does he, Rocket?"

My favorite professor smiled. "No, not yet."

Ace, Tuner, and Beater erupted in laughter and plopped down in the golf cart. Dr. Richter put his arm around me and led me to the rear seat.

"What's going on, Coach?"

"All in due time, my boy . . . all in due time."

We tore out across the manicured lawn of the palatial grounds of the Jekyll Island Club like drunken frat boys. The weekend certainly wasn't going to be boring with these guys. Ace brought the cart to a screeching halt on the marbled patio behind the hotel, and the five of us poured out of the cart and into chairs that had to be a hundred years old. A waiter appeared with glasses, a bottle of something that looked like it probably cost more than Dr. Richter's microbus, and an elegantly carved wooden box of cigars. He began to pour glasses of whatever was in the bottle when Beater said, "Just leave it and get outta here."

The man obeyed and left the open bottle on the table.

Ace glared at Beater. "What's wrong with you, Beater? He's just doing his job. Give him a break."

Beater growled, "I'll give him a break. I'll break his scrawny neck if he don't leave us alone."

The four old friends roared with laughter . . . again.

I didn't know what kind of boys' club I'd stumbled into, but I had to admit these guys were still full of life.

Ace seemed to be the leader of the pack, or at least the most civilized at the moment. He opened the wooden box of cigars and peered inside, inspecting the contents. He pulled out five dark brown cigars and handed one to each of us. I was about to smoke the first cigar of my life, and I thought I was in pretty good company for my inaugural smoke.

Each man sniffed his cigar and then looked at it as if inspecting it for flaws. Not wanting to appear a novice, I did the same.

It smelled divine and looked flawless to me, but what did I know? They reached into their pockets and withdrew cigar punches. Of course I didn't have one. I closely watched each man puncture the round end of his cigar with the tool.

Dr. Richter, a.k.a. Rocket, leaned in close to my ear and handed me his punch. "Hold your cigar in your left hand and the punch in your right. Press the cigar to the punch firmly while twisting the cigar, letting the blade cut into the leaf."

I followed his instructions, and the tool slid easily into the dark brown tobacco. I withdrew the punch and admired the perfect hole I'd created. The scars on my wrist and hand reminded me of a time only months earlier when I would've had neither the strength nor dexterity to accomplish such a simple task. Thankfully, the months of almost unbearable physical therapy and my determination to be whole again had given me a hand that, except for the lingering scars, almost looked and felt normal.

Lighters were produced and flames ignited the ends of the cigars. Clouds of white, aromatic smoke filled the air. Of course, I didn't have a lighter, either, so Beater slid his across the table. I held the cigar in my fingertips and rolled the tip into the flame, trying to emulate the actions of my new friends. As I inhaled my first draw, my lungs convulsed, and I couldn't hold back the cough that instantly branded me a novice.

The old guys chuckled, but I was undaunted. I continued my quest for fire and finally managed to get my cigar lit without throwing up. After surviving the awkward first draw, I began to enjoy my first cigar.

I could get used to this.

I was out of my element, to say the least, but I was recognizing this was more than a social gathering. I was on the verge of something, but I had no way to know just how big that something was.

Ace, the spokesman for the group, said, "So, Rocket tells us you're one hell of a psychologist."

"Well, I'm not a psychologist yet. I haven't graduated. For now, I'm just a student of psychology."

Ace smiled. "So, you think you're only a psychologist after some stuffy, academic type hands you a piece of rolled-up parchment with a nice little ribbon around it? All that means is you sat still for a few years, wrote a few papers, and paid your tuition. Psychology is about understanding why the human mind makes us do stupid stuff, and Rocket says you're one of the best he's ever seen at predicting when people are about to do something dumb. Is that true?"

"Rocket said that about me?"

Beater pointed at Dr. Richter, caught his breath, and roared, "The kid called him Rocket. I love it!"

I was reaching my limit of just watching and listening, so after another coughing fit—this one less dramatic than the first—I said, "What's all this about? Who are you people, and why don't you have real names?"

There's nothing quite as deafening as pure silence. Even the birds seemed to shut up and tremble a little. Everyone looked at Ace. He took a long draw from his cigar then poured himself several fingers of whatever was in the bottle. I turned to Dr. Richter hoping for some help, but he stared down at his feet.

Ace broke the silence. "I'm going to tell you a story about a man who you believe was named James Alan Fulton."

That was my father's name. What does this old guy know about my father?

A tear formed in the corner of my eye, and I bit my lip to keep it from escaping. I don't know if I was sad or furious, but I held my tongue, at least for the moment.

Ace continued. "The man you know as James Alan Fulton, your father, was not a missionary. He was not an American aid worker. He was not a humanitarian. What he was, Chase, was a cold-blooded, ice-water-in-his-veins, communist-killing hero. He was the original badass, son. He and your mother were agents of the U.S. government, among other things. They traveled the world under the guise of missionaries and humanitarian aid workers in impoverished regions, gathering intelligence and killing enemies of democracy. They were heroes, plain and simple. You believe they died at the hands of guerillas in Panama, and you're partially correct. They died in Panama all right, but it wasn't at the hands of guerillas. It was at the hands of assassins who'd been pursuing them for a decade. Son, your family was killed by people who hate freedom and everything the United States holds dear. Now, I know this isn't easy to hear, and I know you don't believe a word of it yet, but you'll soon understand and believe. My name is . . . Hell, I have no idea what my name is. I've been Ace for so many years, I can't remember who I really am, but I'll never forget *what* I am. Like your mother and father, I'm a tool, an agent of democracy, a guardian of freedom, and a relic of the Cold War. I'm an old, dying, dried-up ghost, but what I am, and what these gentlemen you're smoking with truly are, can't die. We're washed up and done, but what drives us can never be allowed to die. What keeps us and America alive must be protected. You see, son, you're the next generation of what we were. You and people like you are the reason that normal, selfish, greedy people can sleep at night. You're part of us. You're the next generation of the best of us. The way you understand the human mind is what will make it possible for children to play baseball and families to go on picnics and pay their taxes, and all that Yankee-Doodle Dandy stuff we all take for granted. You're one of us. You're special, and you're different. You're going to be a Yankee-Doodle badass just like your daddy was . . . and your mother, too. Let's not forget about her."

My head was spinning, and I had a billion questions, but I couldn't make my mouth say a word. I turned to Dr. Richter and locked eyes with him. "You knew my father?"

They all nodded.

Ace said, "Yes, son, we all knew your father, and your mother as well. They were good people. They were dangerous, deadly people, and they loved you to your rotten little core. You're a lot

like your father. You're strong, brilliant, determined, and probably fearless. You just don't know it yet."

I turned to Dr. Richter again, and he returned my gaze with a
solemn, determined look that made my blood run cold. I'd just
stepped into a world I hadn't known existed. These old geezers
were spies or CIA agents. They were the real deal, and my parents had been part of whatever they were.

Everything was confusing and screwed up and perfectly clear
all at the same time. I put my cigar back in my mouth so I
wouldn't say something stupid. My heart was pounding, but I sat
in silence, tasting the tobacco smoke and trying to keep my
mind from exploding.

Just as I was swallowing a mouthful of cigar smoke and trying
to figure out what I was supposed to do next, Ace said, "So,
you're probably asking yourself what you're supposed to do next.
That's the reasonable question. What you should do now is relax,
enjoy your cigar, and have a glass of very good, very old scotch
with us. There's no need to talk. There's no need to even think
right now. Just enjoy the scotch and the cigar . . . and breathe."

So, that's what I did. I tried not to think, and I enjoyed the
cigar and the scotch.

5

What's in a Name?

No one spoke a word for what felt like an eternity. I didn't know if I was supposed to break the silence or just wait. Patience isn't a quality most twenty-somethings possess, and I was no exception. I simply couldn't wait any longer, so through a cloud of wafting white smoke, I said, "What's with the nicknames?"

Ace lifted his chin, and through his bifocals, looked at me with an amused frown. "Of all of the questions that must be swarming around in that head of yours, the first question out of your mouth is about our nicknames. Now that's interesting."

I didn't think it was particularly interesting. It was, in fact, a delaying tactic on my part. I wanted anyone other than me to talk while my brain whirled out of control. In retrospect, I suppose my decision to question their names was a significant psychological indication of how my mind worked. I *was* curious about their nicknames, and I *did* want to know what they meant, but the names weren't as important to me as most of the other questions I had. I could listen to the story of their nicknames while still sorting and sifting through the bevy of information my mind was processing.

Ace took another long draw from his cigar and washed it down with a mouthful of scotch. He looked around at the collection of characters and cleared his throat. "Well, let's start with Rocket Richter over there. You see, back in the early days of

high-speed flight testing that ultimately led to the immortaliza-
tion of Chuck Yeager, somebody had to be the first maniac to
volunteer to strap himself to a ten-thousand-pound bottle rocket
and go for a ride. Enter Rocket Richter."

I immediately began to see my beloved professor through a
whole new lens. "Are you telling me you were really the first guy
to break the sound barrier?"

Dr. Richter turned to his old friends and chuckled. The others
joined in, and it soon turned into a mighty crescendo of belly
laughs.

"Hell no, he didn't break the sound barrier," said Beater. "He
barely broke the speed of smell. It was the worst crash anybody
had ever survived. That rocket went about sixty feet, crapped its
pants, and fell out of the sky with good ol' Rocket Richter riding
it like a rodeo cowboy. The Nevada desert looked like the Dust
Bowl when all the pieces finally stopped moving. Ol' Rocket
there came wading out of the mayhem burnt to a crisp and wanting to know if there was another one he could ride since he was
already dirty."

The laughter grew, and Dr. Richter shook his head.

Ace went to work trying to regain control of the crowd. "So,
that's how your teacher became Rocket a long time before you
were born, Mr. Fulton."

"That's a great story," I said, "but what about you? How did
you become Ace?"

"Ah, my story isn't nearly as exciting as Rocket's. I just shot
down a few Germans over Europe a few decades ago. You know,
when you shoot down five krauts, they call you an Ace."

Beater shook his head. "That's kind of how the story goes,
kid, but it ain't the whole story. Ace is right. When you shoot
down five bad guys, they do call you an ace, but when you shoot
down five Germans on your very first day in combat, they call
you The Ace. Boy, sitting in front of you is the by God Ace of
Aces. Don't let him get away with being modest. He was the bad-
dest fighter pilot in the sky—before he got old, of course."

I looked at Ace, trying to imagine that old man as a fighter pilot.

He winked as a halo of billowing smoke encircled his head. "Ah, I just got lucky . . . a lot," he said.

Ace surveyed his glass as he swirled the liquor into a tiny tornado. "Now Beater over there, his story is a little less glamorous. He just likes to beat the pulp out of folks who get in the way. He was the heavyweight champion for three years running while he was supposed to be studying at the Naval Academy about a hundred years ago. After they finally kicked him out—or graduated him, whatever they do up there at Annapolis—he found out he was pretty good at getting people to talk when they thought they didn't want to talk. It never took long for a prisoner to spill his guts after Beater's fists showed up. Most of the intel that turned out to mean anything during the Cold War was extracted from captured agents by none other than our friend Beater. He never wrecked any rockets or shot down any Germans, but he sure did his part to save the world one black eye and one busted lip at a time."

It was clear that Beater had once been quite the brute. He still carried well over two hundred pounds, and most of it in his shoulders, chest, and arms. I caught myself looking at his huge hands, imagining them hurtling through the air at my head. I was sure I'd talk, too.

Beater looked embarrassed. "Ah, they've got it all wrong, kid. I'm just a big teddy bear. I wouldn't hurt a fly."

Ace smiled. "So, now I guess we're down to Tuner. Good ol' Tuner. You've probably noticed he doesn't say much. He just listens. That's what he's always done—listen. Tuner learned about fifty years ago that underwater, German submarines don't sound like American submarines. In fact, he figured out that German subs don't even sound like other German subs. To those ears, every sub sounds different, so he started cataloging how each one sounded. All of a sudden—well, maybe not all of a sudden—but soon thereafter, we had a catalog of every German submarine's unique acoustic signature. He decided if subs were so easy to distinguish by the way they sound, maybe everything else in the world sounded pretty unique, too. Our friend Tuner is the father of acoustic signature identification. He wrote the book—hell, he wrote all the books on the subject—and taught a few thousand people how to listen with purpose. Thanks to him and his magic ears, our Navy, and a few other services, within seconds, can now detect, classify, and identify almost any sound made on the planet. Son, you're in the company of greatness, and you didn't even know it. You just thought we were a bunch of old guys. Well, maybe you were right about that. We are a bunch of old guys, but we got old by learning to stay alive when everybody around us was dying. Now it's your turn to learn those skills and hopefully, one day, become an old guy yourself."

I was in awe. I never expected that the outrageous bunch of nicknames being thrown around would be historically significant. I thought these were old drinking buddies. I had no idea.

Dr. Richter tapped a knuckle on the table. "So, let's go have some lunch and see if we can find a boat that nobody's using for the afternoon."

Everyone rose from his seat and started for the dining room. I leaned forward to crush out my cigar, but before I could press it into the ashtray, Beater grabbed my wrist with his bear-trap hand. "Don't you dare put that out, boy. Smoke it 'til the hair burns off your hand, then eat the stump."

I quickly stuck the cigar back in my mouth and followed the crowd into the lobby. I thought someone would yell at us for smoking in the hotel, but nobody said a word as we wound our way through the old majestic building.

6
The Pitch

We ate for almost two hours, and during that time, my four new friends shared more stories about my parents. Those stories served to both remind me how much I loved my parents and to solidify my need to connect with what they were.

That was a brilliant psychological play. The old guys knew exactly what they were doing by appealing to the emotion surrounding the loss of my family. It was the perfect pitch without sounding like a pitch. Those guys were good. Very good.

After lunch, we found ourselves aboard a gorgeous Morgan 452 sailing yacht. Emblazoned across the back of the yacht, in elegant script, was the word *Aegis*. Having spent most of my childhood in the Caribbean, I was no stranger to sailboats, but that one was special. I'd launched more than a few Hobie catamarans through the air and across the waves, but a yacht of that size was definitely out of my league. I was fascinated by everything about the yacht. The masts looked like telephone poles, and the winches were the size of paint cans. As magnificent as Dr. Richter's airplane had been, to me, the Morgan was the more impressive machine.

We motored down the Mackay River, past the St. Simons Light, and into St. Simons Sound with Ace at the wheel. It was quiet as we watched the seabirds drift on the afternoon breeze.

"Come on up here, boy!"

I didn't hesitate. I took the wheel with confidence, determined to prove I wasn't as naïve on the water as they expected. The channel was well marked with red and green buoys that bobbed and cast ever-increasing wakes as the powerful current flowed past them. Even though I knew we were in no danger of running aground as long as we stayed between the buoys, I kept a close eye on the depth as we left the river and headed out into the Atlantic.

The wind instrument showed a constant sixteen knots from the northeast. I pulled the throttle back and felt the yacht slow beneath my feet. Before I could ask if we were going to continue motoring, Ace and Beater went to work hoisting the sails.

As the sails went up and the engine fell silent, the roar of the diesel engine gave way to the sounds of the wind in the rigging and the rush of water gliding past the hull. The yacht heeled over and felt light and graceful under my hand on the wheel. I hadn't sailed in years, but the old feelings came rushing back as I held the yacht into the wind with the sails close-hauled. I liked the feeling. We sailed for an hour or so, wandering about in the depths of the Atlantic with the east coast of Georgia only a few miles to the west, but somehow, it felt like we were a million miles from the rest of the world.

Dr. Richter put his hand on my shoulder. "You're a fine sailor, Mr. Fulton. Why don't you let Ace drive a while so you and I can have a chat?"

Ace took the wheel, and I followed Dr. Richter onto the foredeck and settled into a pair of teak chairs. We turned south, and the sails swung away from the centerline of the yacht. The heeling fell away as the boat rolled gently into a downwind run and the deck leveled beneath our feet. The wind fell to a light breeze, and our seats grew far more comfortable on the level deck.

"So," began Dr. Richter, "I'm sure all of this is a bit overwhelming for you. First you learn your parents aren't who and what you believed they were. Then you're introduced to a side of the world you probably never knew existed outside of a movie theater. Finally, while you're trying to absorb all of that, you're asked by four old guys you barely know to become something you don't understand. I'm sure you have more than a few questions, so now's the time to ask. I'll answer as honestly and completely as I can."

He leaned back and pretended to be comfortable. In reality, I'd never seen him more uncomfortable. I knew it wasn't possible to outthink him, but for the first time in my life, I felt I had some standing with Dr. Richter, and maybe, just maybe, I had something he wanted—perhaps even something he needed.

I decided at that moment to never again let anyone or anything make me feel like I was less than completely in command of everything in my world. At that moment, my days of being a student of academia ended, and I became a student of reality. Those two worlds have almost nothing in common. They sometimes collide, but they never collaborate. Academia and reality can never be bedfellows. I had questions by the bushel, but I had to decide which ones would come at that moment and which would be saved for later—many of them for much later.

I started where any rational party to an irrational negotiation would begin. "Just what is it you want me to do, Coach?"

When I first started learning how to crouch behind home plate and sit relatively still while another human threw baseballs at me as hard as he could, I learned there was nothing more important than having better balance than everyone else on the field. I learned when to lean forward on the balls of my feet and when to dig into the clay and make a stand to protect something worth protecting, be it home plate or my pitcher when an errant fastball brushed a little too close to a batter's head.

I decided that I would psychologically lean forward onto the balls of my feet and make it clear that I was not off-balance. Dr. Richter quickly recognized my posturing. Even though I may have appeared confident in that moment, in truth, I was terrified out of my young, arrogant head. I would soon learn to harness that fear and turn it into something deadly.

Dr. Richter looked up as if he were trying to decide how to form the words that would become his answer, but he didn't hesitate more than a few seconds. "Mr. Fulton, I want you to kill everybody on this planet who doesn't think freedom is the answer to everything that's evil."

I didn't expect that. I expected something patriotic, but nothing so blunt. He wanted me to kill people for him, and if not *for* him, for the same people he'd once served. Perhaps he was still their servant.

Before I could convince my mouth to form real words, he continued. "I know, I know. You're thinking you didn't expect me to be so frank, but this is no time to beat around the bush, Chase. This is the time to make some tough decisions. My answer to your question was overly simple. In reality, what I want is for you to agree to forget who you are and who you thought you'd be when you grew up. I want you to forget that you're a brilliant psychologist and that you lost a promising career as a Major League ball player. I want you to forget that you're an orphan, and stop believing you're alone in the world. I want you to become something invisible, invincible, and definitely and defiantly insane. I want you to volunteer to learn a set of skills that'll turn your body and mind into something humanity needs and deserves, but something humanity has no stomach for knowing. I want you to disappear for a year, or maybe longer, so you can be taught by some of the best clandestine operators on Earth. I want you to learn to shoot while you're bleeding, think while you're terrified, run when your body tells you you can't take another step, and most of all, Chase, I want you to learn to take the lives of other men who don't deserve to continue breathing."

I did my best to keep my composure. In a voice that I wanted to sound far more confident than it actually was, I asked, "And you want me to do this for the CIA or the FBI or for whom?"

"Oh, for God's sake, none of the above. You've got a lot to learn. The CIA and FBI don't have assassins. They have operators who are bound by ridiculous rules, laws, and regulations. No, my boy, rules, laws, and regulations are for people who allow their minds to be fettered by others who consider themselves morally superior. You won't get a badge or credentials that'll get you out of a speeding ticket. You'll work on the fringe of morality and legality. You'll be paid handsomely for what you'll learn to do. You'll die a very wealthy man. Unfortunately, that death may come far sooner than you'd like, but that's all part of the game we play. You see, you're the perfect cocktail of brilliance and insanity that makes the best assassin. By the way, I don't like that word, assassin. I prefer to think of people like us as problem solvers. The problems we solve are contrary attitudes and misguided beliefs. There are people on this Earth who'd take your freedom and that of every American and piss on it before breakfast every day if the opportunity presented itself. Those are the people we extinguish. Those are the ideologies we erase. It's the oldest, corniest story in the world, but we're the good guys, and for the good guys to prosper, there have to be people who are willing to do what others can't or won't do to protect the freedom under which we all bask in this great country. Look around. You're aboard a beautiful boat off the coast of one of the most beautiful islands of the greatest country that's ever existed. Almost one hundred percent of Americans lack the stomach for what we do. Almost one hundred percent of them have no idea we exist or that what we do is not only necessary, but crucial to the continuation of life as they know it."

He paused, lifted a glass I hadn't realized was in his hand, and took a long, appreciative swallow. Time stood still and simultaneously raced. I suddenly wished I had a drink.

"So, who will I be working for?" I asked.

"You'll be working for the American people," he said. "You'll be paid mostly by the U.S. Government out of funds that are set aside for, well, let's say less-than-usual situations. Occasionally, there are international pots of money floating around that need a place to land. A few especially interesting jobs pay a little more than others. You'll never really know, and honestly, it doesn't really matter."

His words were chosen carefully, but it was clear he wanted to tell me more, so I opened the door a little wider for him. "Okay, let's say I'm in. When do I start, and who's my boss?"

Before answering, he enjoyed another long swallow. "You've already started. As far as a boss is concerned, you'll be what most people call a contractor. You'll be asked to do certain unthinkable things from time to time by people you'll never meet. You'll do those things, and shortly thereafter, you'll be paid well. It's as simple as that."

I stammered a little. "But I don't have any training or skills like you're talking about. I've never broken the sound barrier. I've never beaten people up during interrogations. I've never listened for submarines. And I've certainly never shot down any Germans. What makes you think I can do any of this?"

He smiled. "There was a time when none of us had ever done any of those things, either, but we learned, and we excelled. Tell me one thing in your life at which you've ever failed. Tell me one time when you let anyone outperform you at anything. Tell me the last time someone expected more of you than you could deliver."

I thought about it, but before I could answer, he said, "Never. That's when. Never have any of those things happened. You aren't common or ordinary. You're elite, and you know it. You've known it all your life. It's in your blood, just like it was in your parents' blood."

At that moment, Beater came on deck with a carbon copy of whatever Dr. Richter was drinking. He offered it to me and said, "I figured by now you could use a drink. We're going to be coming about soon . . . whatever that means. Ace just wanted me to let you know."

I thankfully accepted the drink and savored the musty, oaky taste of the scotch as it warmed my tongue and melted its way down my throat. I looked up to see the main boom being centered. That meant we were about to gybe and head back north to St. Simons Island. I carefully looked through the wall of my tumbler at the honey-colored liquor swirling inside and whispered, "I'm in."

The boat turned to starboard and heeled as the genoa, the sail out front, crossed the foredeck and found its place on the opposite side. It was beautiful to watch the elegant boat behave so well under the experienced hands of Ace and Tuner. Beater just tried to stay out of the way.

As Dr. Richter and I made our way back to the cockpit, I asked, "What does the name of the boat mean?"

He grinned. "Aegis is from *The Iliad*, my boy. Most people believe it was Athena's battle shield, but a few of us think it's a protective force of incredible power that's rarely seen. That's what you'll soon become." He patted me on the shoulder. "Oh, and don't you go shooting down any Germans. They're our friends now."

7
Welcome to Hell

I assumed we'd spend the rest of the weekend smoking cigars, drinking scotch, and talking about what I'd be doing in the near future, but as assumptions tend to be, mine was dead wrong.

Nothing of the sort happened when we stepped from *Aegis* back onto the dock near the resort. Before my feet met the weather-beaten, warped planks, two guys who looked like linebackers flanked me. The larger of the two placed his beefy hand on my shoulder, and in a matter-of-fact tone, said, "Mr. Fulton, you'll be coming with us."

My mind raced.

Who and what are these guys? Are they cops? Other younger versions of my hosts?

Instead of resisting, I fell into lockstep with the linebackers and never looked back. They ushered me into the back of a black, ominous-looking Chevy Suburban, and each man found his place in the front.

In some ridiculous random thought, I blurted out, "Hey! What about my backpack and stuff?"

Silence.

Before I realized we'd left the island, we were merging onto I-95 North. We arrived less than an hour later at Hunter Army Airfield in Savannah. Had we done the speed limit, it would've taken nearly two hours to make the ninety-mile trip. My heart was pounding again, but I can't say I was afraid . . . perhaps just anxious.

After passing through the security gate manned by a young, imposing-looking military police officer, we continued deeper into the base, but our speed had greatly diminished. I guess speed limits on a military base meant more to those guys than limits on the highway. We drove onto the flight line and alongside a gorgeous blue and white Gulfstream jet.

I reached to open my door, only to discover there was no handle. As I reeled from the thought of being held captive in the back seat of the blacked-out Suburban, my door burst open, and there stood linebacker number one. He motioned for me to get out, so, unwilling to argue, I followed the unspoken order. As if materializing from thin air, linebacker number two appeared at my side, and once again in lockstep, we began our determined gait across the tarmac. They directed me toward the stairwell of the Gulfstream, and I wasted no time bounding up the stairs. Neither linebacker followed me, but the door closed before I could decide which plush leather seat to occupy.

I appeared to be the only living soul aboard the airplane, but that appearance was obviously misleading because the plane began to taxi before I was buckled in. As I was fumbling with the seatbelt, a voice filled the cabin. It could've been the voice of God for all I knew, and frankly, after the day I'd just experienced, it wouldn't have surprised me. The voice turned out to be far less divine. It belonged to one of the pilots.

"Mr. Fulton, please make yourself comfortable. We'll be on the ground again in a little over an hour. In the meantime, relax, and try to get some sleep. It may be the last good sleep you ever get. Enjoy the ride."

I tried to figure out how fast the Gulfstream would fly so I could come up with some reasonable guess as to where we might be going. I guessed it could go five hundred miles per hour. That could put us in East Texas, Oklahoma, Indiana, the Florida Keys, or maybe even Washington D.C. in a little over an hour.

As it turned out, D.C. wasn't a bad guess. I watched the Capitol pass beneath the wing as we descended into what must've been Virginia.

When the door of the Gulfstream opened, I felt a rush of cold, wet air pour into the airplane. Summer clearly hadn't made its way into Virginia yet. I pulled my sleeves down and turned my collar up against the cold as I descended the stairs.

When my feet hit the earth again, another beast of a man materialized in front of me, but that one was no linebacker. He was more like an aged oak tree. I'd never seen such a solidly built human. He carried himself with incredible confidence and looked fiftyish, but I suspected he was much younger than he appeared. It was clear he'd lived a rough life, most of it outside.

"Welcome to The Ranch, Mr. Fulton. My name is Grey. It'll be my job to get you settled in and make sure you're comfortable. I'm sure you have a lot of questions, but there will be time for those later. For now, let's get you out to your new home. It's a little damp, and the heating system is on the fritz, but you'll adapt."

We climbed into a pickup truck with no doors and a badly broken windshield and tore away from the airstrip nearly as fast as the linebacker twins on I-95. We broke out of a tree line on a narrow, winding road, and I spotted a huge, open body of water to my right, and a smaller, much less inviting pond to the left.

Grey shot a glance across the cap and barked, "Put on your seatbelt!"

I did as I was told just as the truck made an abrupt and violent turn to the left toward the dark, foreboding water. It was clear we were going into the water, and there was nothing I could do about it.

It's amazing what the mind is capable of imagining in highly stressful situations. My thoughts bounced around inside my skull like a pinball. I drove my foot into the floorboard with such force that I could feel the bones of my leg quiver in protest of my desperate, but futile attempt to press the imaginary brake pedal. I turned abruptly toward Grey, only to find he, much like my imaginary brake pedal, wasn't there. He'd vanished, leaving me alone and careening toward the nastiest water I'd ever seen.

I resolved that I'd soon be underwater and still securely belted in the front seat of what was left of a truck, somewhere in the wilds of northern Virginia. I didn't like my predicament, but I had to come up with a plan to deal with it, and quickly.

A wall of black water filled the air as the front bumper found the surface of the cesspool. I drew a full breath, thinking I may spend the next several minutes submerged, cold, and dying. As the energy of the truck was absorbed by the water, the seatbelt cut into my flesh and the muscles of my body absorbed the shock of the collision. I'll never forget how cold and dark the water was. I tried to relax and avoid panic, but that's much more easily thought than accomplished. Panic arose, but I somehow found the strength to suppress it.

Interestingly, the reality of riding a sinking vehicle into the murky depths is nothing like Hollywood wants us to believe. It's not peaceful, clear, and bubbly. It's terrifying, violent, and hellishly black. I clearly remember the feeling of the metallic buckle as I drove my thumb into what should've been the release button. It was sharp and immovable. I was going to have to find another way to escape the seatbelt. I opened one of my eyes and exhaled a small stream of bubbles, hoping to determine which way was up, but it was dark, and I could neither see nor feel the stream of bubbles pouring from my mouth. I was exhaling air my body was going to desperately need, so I promptly ceased my exhalation. In vain, I tried the buckle one last time, but it was hopeless. I tried sliding my body up and out of the seatbelt, but when my head hit the roof, I found myself bound and even more terrified than before. My heart pounded, and my mind churned, desperately searching for a solution.

I opened my eyes, and to my amazement, saw a light—a dim, foggy, perfectly motionless light. It seemed almost close enough to touch, but at the same time, immeasurably distant. I couldn't slow my mind enough to determine the position of the light or why it was there. I could even see bubbles escaping around the light, but I wasn't exhaling. I was still holding my precious breath in the ridiculous belief that holding air in my lungs would somehow keep me alive long enough to resolve my predicament. My lungs burned as panic overtook what was left of my logical mind. The light grew ever closer, and I felt myself blacking out. I resolved that I'd met my fate. I would drown in that filthy black pond in front of the ghostly, bubbling light. I made peace with it, exhaled, and opened my mouth to draw the murky water into my lungs and join my family in whatever was on the other side of that light.

I was surprisingly at peace with my impending demise. There was no panic, no terror, only acceptance and submission. I believed my death was imminent, but death didn't come. Instead, a pair of strong, quick hands appeared, cutting away the seatbelt and shoving the mouthpiece of a small air bottle between my lips. I was being rescued by a scuba diver in the blackest, coldest, nastiest water I'd ever known.

Where'd he come from? Why is he in the water with me?

I learned a powerful and painful lesson that day: sometimes it's impossible to tell the difference between being rescued and being captured. As my head broke the surface of the murky water, I spat the bottle from my mouth and gasped. My lungs ached but relished that first full breath. Although cold, scared, and still confused, I was happy to be alive. I remember thinking there was nothing more important than being and staying alive. That belief became the core philosophy of the rest of my life. No matter how bad things were, as long as I was alive, almost anything else could be resolved.

The celebration in my lungs was short-lived as I saw a figure in a black wetsuit, hood, mask, and gloves moving through the water toward me.

Where's Grey?

The diver pushed my head back beneath the surface of the water for what felt like an eternity. I fought against him, and my lungs ached again as panic consumed my body. Just as I thought I'd reached death's door for the second time, I chose to fight. I drove a strong left fist into the ribs of the diver and felt his body convulse. He backed away, allowing me to resurface. I filled my lungs just as the diver wrapped his right arm around my neck from behind. Dragging me backward, he pulled me from the water and across a muddy embankment. His hold around my neck made it nearly impossible to breathe, but I managed to twist my head far enough to open a small airway and keep myself alive for whatever would happen next.

Before I could get enough air in my lungs to ask what was going on, another figure appeared. Like the first man, he was also dressed in all black, but instead of a wetsuit, he was wearing cargo pants, a black sweatshirt, and a ski mask. The diver yanked me to my feet just as the masked man's fist landed squarely in my chest. I was familiar with the feeling of being hit in the chest, but I'd never been hit with a fist quite that hard. What little air was in my lungs exploded from my throat and left me gagging from the agony of the blow. I felt my body collapsing, but the diver wouldn't let me fall. He held me on my feet while the second man continued the punishment. Before I could gather the strength and breath to defend myself, a bag was pulled over my head and bound around my neck.

In what I assumed was an effort to further disorient me, the two men spun me around several times. The instant the spinning stopped, another powerful blow landed in my gut. That time, no one held me up, and I collapsed to the ground. My hands and feet were bound, and I was dragged by my feet through the mud. Occasionally, I was rolled over and dragged facedown. I felt twigs and rocks of every size tear at my skin. The experience was agonizing, but finally, the dragging stopped, and my feet fell to the ground. The distinct swoosh and click of a switchblade knife filled my ears, and I was horrified.

Why did they drag me through the woods just to kill me here? Why didn't they just let me drown?

Thankfully, the knife wasn't intended to kill me, yet. It was to free me from *some* of my bindings. They left my feet bound, presumably so I couldn't run, but they cut the tie from my neck, removed the bag, and cut my hands free. Freeing my hands seemed like a terrible decision on their part. The masked man was joined by another, and they yelled at me in some language I'd never heard. It wasn't Spanish. My Spanish was strong. It wasn't German. My mother spoke German, and I knew it was not what my mother had spoken. By their tone, it was clear they weren't my friends. They wanted something from me. That's when it occurred to me. This was all part of the mystery of my training. They wanted to see how I'd react to being captured, tortured, and questioned. It was a mind game. I knew a thing or two about mind games, so I decided to play along.

Well, that isn't entirely true. I decided I'd play along if I continued to believe it was a mind game. If it wasn't part of my training, I was in far more trouble than I could imagine.

"Look, guys. I want you to understand that if this is part of my training, that's fine. I get it. But if this is something else, I'm going to hurt, and possibly kill, at least one of you. I'm not exactly sure what's going to happen after that. If this is all part of the game, it would be a good idea to let me in on the secret."

The two masked men looked at each other with a look I couldn't identify, but I thought it might've been amusement. Neither said a word.

I was kneeling on the muddy ground with my feet tucked under my butt, a position in which I'd spent a great many hours behind home plate. I'd thrown a few thousand baseballs to second base from that position. Surveying my environment revealed two relatively round, large rocks well within my reach.

"I'm serious here, guys. If you understand English and you want to stay alive, now would be a really good time to speak up."

In the interest of being as fair as possible, I repeated my warning in both German and Spanish, just in case they didn't understand English. Neither man moved nor spoke. I'd given more than ample warning. Deciding to try a little visual misdirection, I quickly let my eyes jerk to a point behind both men. As I did, I let a look of fear and shock consume my face. I ducked quickly as if I believed I was going to be shot, and dived to my right, feigning fear and performing a dramatic reaction to a threat that didn't exist.

My gambit worked. Both men turned to identify my imaginary attacker. The distraction granted me the tiny window I needed to firmly grasp both rocks. Returning to my knees, I twisted at the waist and poised my hand behind my right ear with the baseball-shaped rock held firmly in my grasp. Seeing nothing in the trees, both men turned back to face me, knowing they'd fallen victim to my charade. Before either could react, I uncoiled my body and brought my arm forward in a rush of accelerating force, releasing the stone as my hand passed my temple. I followed through just as I'd been taught, but what came next wasn't in any catching lessons I'd ever endured. Using the energy of my throw to carry my body forward, I tucked my right shoulder beneath my chin and propelled my body into a roll that left me on my feet and less than four feet from my captors. I stood from my roll and watched the man with the knife recoil and collapse to the ground when my stone sank into his left eye and a curtain of blood filled the air. I lunged toward him with all of my strength and grabbed the switchblade from his hand while his body melted to the ground. I drove the blade between my feet, slicing the plastic binding holding my ankles together. The binding gave away, and for the first time in what felt like hours, I was completely free.

I stumbled but finally found my footing. When I focused, I discovered my second captor standing in front of me in a fighting stance with no fear in his eyes. He didn't care that I was free and armed with his partner's knife. He was ready to fight, but so was I. I suspected he was well trained and confident, but I was afraid and somewhat well armed with the switchblade.

The months I'd spent with my right hand and arm damaged, healing, and mostly useless, I'd learned to do almost everything with my left hand, including throwing a baseball. I tried one more misdirection and used the natural weapons that I actually had.

I hopped into a throwing stance with my right hand held high above my head, with the knife held firmly between my thumb and fingers. I'd never thrown a knife, but I was going to try. I stepped forward and brought my right hand downward, whipping the blade past my ear and releasing it into the air. It left my hand and tumbled through the air directly toward my opponent. Unfortunately, it wasn't flying toward his heart. It was descending in an arc that was clearly going to fall short of his feet. Stepping back, he watched the blade bounce across the leaf-covered ground. What he didn't see was my pivot that placed my right foot just in front of my left, and the forceful arc of my left hand cutting through the air. The stone left my palm and almost instantly found its target: the man's right ear. I heard the collision of stone, flesh, and bone as I watched his knees buckle and his mass fall limply to the earth.

Having no idea what to do next, I found myself at the mercy of instinct. I snatched the knife from the ground and began running back toward the water. I didn't know what I was going to do with the knife, but something inside me said possessing it was better than leaving it behind. Running with energy I'd never felt, I rounded the muddy edge of the filthy lake when I heard my name ringing in the air. I thought I knew the voice.

"Chase! Stop running!"

It was Grey, the former driver of the truck that almost became my watery coffin.

Still breathless and wet, I turned to Grey. "What was all that about?"

Instead of answering my question, he asked, "How did you escape?"

8
Operator?

I never got my answer. I would soon come to learn that life, especially life in my new line of work, rarely has answers, and almost never direct ones. Instead of answers, I was given a towel and some dry clothes—clothes that were almost identical to what my captors had been wearing. Without further inquisition, I climbed into a much nicer truck than the one that was now resting peacefully on the bottom of Lake Nasty.

After a short, bumpy ride, I found myself in a dreary office deep within an old concrete block building that had been painted so many times the walls appeared to be made of soft clay. The concrete floor was occasionally covered with pieces of carpeting that looked like they belonged in an abandoned library from the 1950s. Almost everyone in the building was dressed like me. They wore black, olive drab, or khaki cargo pants and tactical-looking, button-up shirts, with sleeves rolled up near the elbows. Everyone was busy at some task, and almost no one noticed me. Grey sat silently beside me in a metal folding chair that reminded me of chairs that might be found in the basement of an old church.

Through the door burst the most intimidating man I'd ever seen. I wasn't even sure that Beater could've taken that guy, even back in his glory days. The man was around six feet tall and two hundred pounds. He wore khaki cargo shorts and a skin-tight, black T-shirt with a logo of a lightning bolt crashing through a wreath. Beneath the logo were the words "Admit Nothing. Deny Everything. Make Counter Accusations."

His hair was closely cropped, and his skin was like tanned leather. Two days of stubble punctuated his chiseled features, and a pair of cold, steel-blue eyes sat deeply in his face beneath gray, bushy eyebrows. He wore green jungle boots with black laces over black socks that were rolled down to the tops of the boots.

He slammed the door hard enough that everything in the office appeared to shy away. With a callused and weather-beaten right hand, he grabbed my belt buckle and forced his left hand beneath my chin, jerking me from my chair. I thought he was close to sixty years old, but he had the strength and vitality of a much younger man. He shoved me into a huge metal filing cabinet with such force the cabinet shuddered at the impact. The man pressed his thumb so painfully into my neck that I considered trying to break his arm, but I doubted he'd be as easy to defeat as the two guys in the woods.

As he ground my head into the concrete block wall of the office, he roared with anger and disgust. "What is wrong inside that skull of yours? What made you think it was okay to kill one of my cadre and deafen another with your little rock-throwing demonstration earlier?"

Did I kill that guy? I didn't mean to kill him.

In a vain attempt to get him off me, I braced my left heel against the wall and threw a knee shot to his crotch. To my surprise, he blocked the blow by twisting at the waist and redirecting my knee into the filing cabinet. Before I could react to the pain, he released my throat and belt buckle simultaneously while sweeping my foot from beneath me. When I came to rest, I was folded like a pretzel in the crevice formed by the wall and the cabinet. His knee was pressing into the back of my neck and driving my face into the cold, damp wall.

What the man hadn't realized was that I was a little more flexible than most. I'd spent a few thousand hours kneeling behind home plate, so my predicament wasn't as uncomfortable as he likely wanted it to be. I could use my flexibility to a decided advantage. My plan was to hook his ankle with my foot and force him to lean back. This would get his knee off my neck and give me an opportunity to deliver an uppercut to the spot where my knee shot should've landed. Having been in more than my share of brawls on the baseball field, I'd never met a man who could stay on his feet following that particular shot.

My plan would've worked perfectly on most normal people, but there was nothing normal about that guy. The instant I extended my leg, he lifted his foot, sending even more of his weight down on my neck and shoulder. When his foot fell again, it landed on my ankle and sent bursts of pain exploding up my leg. If my ankle wasn't broken, he'd done some serious damage, but he wasn't finished. I reached for his boot, but he reacted with blinding speed. He thrust his Ka-Bar fighting knife only millimeters beneath my wrist and pierced my sleeve. When the knife came to rest, it was buried through the fabric of my sleeve and into the metal of the file cabinet. With a broken ankle and one hand anchored to the metal cabinet, I was pinned beneath his knee. There was no fight left in me.

I was defeated, but I refused to give him the pleasure of hearing me beg, so I tried to relax and stop resisting. He recognized my surrender and rolled his foot from my ankle, then quickly, but cautiously, stepped backward and held his fists defensively in front of his body. I didn't know what he expected me to do. There was no way I could get to my feet to fight him. I wasn't moving.

"Get him up, Grey," the man said in a voice that was ominously calm. He wasn't even breathing heavily.

Grey did as he was told and pulled me to my feet after kicking the knife free from the cabinet. I'd never seen a knife penetrate metal.

I was beginning to wish I'd never met Rocket Richter.

When I was finally deposited back into the uncomfortable metal chair, I discovered my attacker was sitting behind his desk with a cigar clenched between his teeth and a long wooden match ablaze between his fingers. Soon the room filled with aromatic smoke, and I found myself suddenly yearning for his cigar.

I risked a glance at my swollen ankle. It probably wasn't broken after all, but that didn't decrease the pain.

Grey took his seat in the corner of the small office, and the man behind the desk exhaled a cloud of smoke. "You're having one hell of a first day here, boy. Just what is it that makes you think I'm going to let you get away with showing up here and killing one of my training officers in your first fifteen minutes? Huh?"

"I told him twice and in three languages that I was going to kill him, and I gave him the chance to tell me if the whole thing was part of my training, but he didn't listen. So, if he's dead, he's dead because he underestimated me."

Before the sound of my words had time to cross the old, tattered desk, the man exploded from his chair and lunged for me. His powerful hands found my throat again, and I felt my chair collapse beneath me. Remembering the concrete wall less than three feet behind me, I braced for the impact my body would make when I stopped flying through the air. I don't remember the actual collision. My head hit the wall with such force the lights went out before my body stopped moving.

The concussion that followed left me unconscious for almost an hour, and when I finally awoke, I was lying facedown on a hospital gurney with the worst headache imaginable.

I saw Grey sitting in a chair across the room and grunted, "What was that about?"

He looked up, frowning. "Hey, kid. Welcome back. You got one humdinger of a knot on that noggin' of yours. Looks like it hurts."

"You've got quite a way with words. You know that, Grey?" I coughed and thought my head would explode, so I vowed to never cough again. I could only imagine what agony a sneeze would bring.

Grey rose from his perch and leaned through the doorway. "Hey, doc! The kid's awake in here."

He looked back at me and then strode out into whatever was beyond the doorway. There was no actual door, but I still couldn't see what lay beyond the opening because of my angle and limited ability to use my eyes for anything other than squinting.

A man came into the room with a stethoscope in one hand and a clipboard in the other. I had a flashback to the day I'd awakened in the hospital in Nebraska, but something told me this hospital wasn't quite as hospitable.

"Hey, Chase. I'm Doctor Hamilton. You sustained a pretty nasty bump on the back of your head. I stitched it up and shot some films of your skull and ankle. Your skull is fine, but it's going to hurt for a few days. Your ankle isn't broken, but it's a nasty sprain. I shot it full of cortisone and wrapped it up. It'll be okay in a few days, too. You were on my agenda for an initial physical exam later in the week, but it looks like you found a way to cause enough trouble to move to the front of the line."

I was beginning to feel like I'd fallen down the rabbit hole. I was in a makeshift hospital at some sort of training camp somewhere in Virginia where I'd been nearly drowned, taken captive, interrogated in a language I didn't understand, fought back, escaped, and taken to some maniac's office where I was attacked again and nearly beaten to death. I couldn't wait to see what day two was going to bring.

Before I could ask Dr. Hamilton any questions, he was gone and replaced by a guy who was a study in contrasts. From the waist up, he looked like a chemist. He wore a short lab coat with at least a dozen pens protruding from the breast pocket. Dangling awkwardly from his lab coat was a name tag that read "Fred." The chemist look ended at his waistline. Like everyone else, he wore cargo pants, except he must've cut them with a blunt pair of scissors. The left leg was at least six inches shorter than any shorts should ever be, and the right was oddly diagonal and touching his knee. He wore a pair of tattered leather sandals and had a pencil in his mouth and one behind each of his ears. Nothing about him made sense. He looked up at me in total surprise, as if he hadn't expected me to be there. I wanted to laugh, but I was terrified that laughing would hurt worse than coughing. I tried not to stare, but he was like a walking freak show. I just couldn't look away.

Shaking his head wildly from side to side, he said, "Hi, Mr. Fulton. I'm kind of like in charge here. I'm the psychiatrist, and it's my job to make sure you aren't too sane to be here. You see, sane people don't live long in this line of work, so it's really important that you be at least a little crazy like the rest of us. From the looks of you, it appears you're going to fit right in. Do you have any questions for me?"

I had far more questions than I had time left on Earth to ask, so I opened with the obvious. "What is going on?"

He looked at me in further astonishment, as if I'd asked him the meaning of life. "I'm sorry," he said, "but I don't know what you mean. You're here to train to be an operator, aren't you?"

Did he just say operator?

"Okay, now I'm completely lost. Please tell me what's going on. I've had a bad day, and I really need some answers that make sense."

"No, your day hasn't been bad at all," he said. "You're doing exceptionally well compared to most of the trainees who show up here. Usually, they spend the first several days being held captive, enduring torture, and being interrogated in Russian. You cut that exercise pretty short. Everyone's totally impressed. You're showing signs of being exceptional in every category so far. You've demonstrated you can stay calm when most people panic. You didn't freak out when the seatbelt wouldn't release while you were sinking. You displayed exceptional morality by warning your captors that you were going to kill them before you actually did. By the way, you only killed one of them. The other is going to have trouble hearing from one ear for a while, but he's alive. Sometimes being alive is what's most important. Oh, and by the way, that morality of yours is something we're going to have to work on. You can't be doing that in the field. You'll have to just kill them and not give them a chance to get away, but we'll deal with that later. You showed masterful environmental awareness by locating the rocks you used as weapons without our training officers recognizing what you were doing. You then held your own against Gunny. Nobody, and I mean nobody, comes out of that office in as good a shape as you. Even he was impressed. You're going to be a fine operator, Mr. Fulton."

So, I learned what I thought was the worst day of my life was, in Fred's opinion, not bad at all.

"Okay, slow down. So, you're telling me I'm doing well?"

"Yes! Yes! Very well, indeed," he insisted.

There was quite a chasm of misunderstanding between Fred and me. I still had almost no idea what I was doing in that place, and he seemed to think I fit right in. I needed to close the gap between our thinking.

"Okay, let's break this down," I said. "All I know is four old guys told me I was going to become some kind of secret agent, and the next thing I knew, I was drowning in that cesspool you people keep calling a lake. I'm a psych student, and I used to be a decent baseball player. That's the limit of what I know. Now, please fill in the rest for me."

He looked like a confused puppy with his head cocked sideways and his brow wrinkled. He looked down at his clipboard, perhaps for inspiration, or maybe for a delay to gather his thoughts. "Oh my," he said. "You are out of your element, aren't you? Here's how this works. You've been recruited to combine a set of natural skills you already possess, with an impressive set of skills you'll develop over the next several weeks, months, and years, to become a tool used by people you'll never meet, to accomplish things you'll never understand, for reasons that are bigger than we lowly servants could ever fathom."

I wasn't wise enough to grasp the weight of such a profound statement, but he was more correct than even he knew.

After consulting his trusty clipboard again, he continued. "So, what's going to happen is that you and I are going to spend some time together. I'm going to poke around in your head and make sure you aren't going to melt down under the extremes of what you're going to become. If we make it past that milestone, which I believe we will do quickly, I'll teach you things about the human mind that will terrify and thrill you. I'll teach you how to make people believe things that could never be true, and how to manipulate the perception of those around you to create realities of your own design. You see, I learned these things from your beloved Dr. Richter. He was my mentor long before you ever met him, Mr. Fulton. Now you'll learn those things from me."

He let his words hang in the air, and I was starting to like Fred, but I didn't know why. I should've listened more and talked less, but I had so many questions. I just couldn't be silent any longer.

Assuming it was a good place to start, I asked, "So should I call you Fred or Doctor or what?"

He looked thoroughly puzzled. "Why would you call me Fred?"

I glanced at the dangling name tag pinned to his lab coat. "That's what your name tag says."

He grinned. "See how easy it is to manipulate the reality of those around you? I never told you my name. I never suggested that I even had a name. You simply assumed I had a name and that I would wear it on my chest. To you, that imaginary name became your reality. You and I are going to have a lot of fun together."

9

So Much to Learn

I convinced Fred— I'd never stop calling him Fred—that I was sufficiently insane to survive in his world, and he blessed me with the stroke of his pen and sent me off to become an operator.

I learned killing an instructor on my first day was not the best move I could've made. That seemed to make every other instructor want to kill me, and they did their best, but I prevailed.

In the months following the surgeries to put my hand back together, I pushed myself beyond reasonable limits both mentally and physically. Physical therapy was a waste of time. They wanted me to stretch and flex and take my time regaining the use of my hand. I had no patience for such a pitiful pace. I ran a hundred miles a week and spent endless hours in the gym. When I arrived at The Ranch, I was in the best shape of my life, but when I left, I was in the best shape of anyone's life. I could run almost endlessly without even breathing hard. I could shoot any weapon that had ever been manufactured with more precision than most snipers. I could fight with lethal skill and efficiency. I could change my appearance at will and speak four new languages. I could fly anything with wings or rotors and run any boat that could float. Needless to say, I, along with the plethora of talent at The Ranch, had transformed myself into a remarkably sharp tool.

Fred and I spent countless hours together, learning to untangle the mysteries of the human mind, but more important than untangling them, he taught me to weave such intricate webs of deception in the minds of others that there were times when I questioned the reality I created. I learned that people are sheep. They want to believe the insane lies life tells them. They're hungry for meaning, even if that meaning is ridiculous. I learned to prey on that weakness by using my understanding of psychology like a modern-day alchemist, but instead of turning lead into gold, I could transform perception into reality.

When I wasn't learning to kill or confuse somebody, I was learning tradecraft, the art of applying intricate techniques into our operations in the field. I learned to evade surveillance, bypass security systems, pick locks, and other crucial skills that would keep me alive.

I had no way of knowing when my training would officially end and I'd be sent out to accomplish something meaningful, but occasionally, I'd leave The Ranch and interact with real people. Fred called them field trips, but I liked to think of them as vacations from Hell. One such field trip would change my life forever.

"Have you ever been to New York, kid?" That was the sound my alarm clock made at four a.m.—or at least I thought it was my alarm clock. As it turned out, it was Dutch, a seasoned operator who occasionally observed my training. He almost never interacted directly with me other than to critique something I'd done or to offer suggestions on how to do it better. I learned he was great at being invisible. He'd show up in post-training briefings and give detailed analyses on aspects of the day's activities. I was always amazed by how he could take in so much information from the world around him, process it, and spit out critiques so efficiently without ever being seen.

I remember running twelve miles, shooting three thousand rounds of ammunition at hundreds of targets one day, and seeing no one other than my trainers, but somehow, Dutch showed up and told me I'd jerked the trigger instead of squeezing it on my eight hundredth shot of the day when the fly landed on my nose.

"What?" I moaned and rubbed the sleep from my eyes.

"I said, have you ever been to New York?"

Still wondering what Dutch was doing at my bedside at that hour, I groggily replied, "No, I've never been to New York. Why?"

He yanked the cover from my bed and tossed me a backpack. "Let's go. I'll brief you on the way."

I landed on the cold floor, content to be doing anything other than running, shooting, or fighting for a change, and pulled on my T-shirt, cargo pants, and boots, and tried to keep up with Dutch.

In his gorgeous, brand-new BMW 5 Series, we headed north. I was curious about what fresh hell awaited me in New York. As it turned out, it was a real mission.

Dutch asked, "What do you know about horse racing?"

I shook my head and admitted, "Nothing."

"That's good," he said. "That way you don't have any preconceived notions of what's going on. Do you know what the Triple Crown is?"

I shook my head.

"The Triple Crown is horse racing's most coveted prize. Winning the Triple Crown means a horse wins the Preakness Stakes, the Kentucky Derby, and the Belmont Stakes all in the same year. The last Triple Crown winner was a horse named Affirmed back in seventy-eight."

Not giving him a chance to continue, I jumped in. "I remember that. I was just a kid, but I remember it being on TV."

Dutch continued, "So, needless to say, when a horse wins the Triple Crown, he instantly becomes the most valuable animal on the planet. This year, there's a horse named Silent Storm who's poised to be the next Triple Crown winner. He's owned by one Dmitri Barkov. Have you ever heard of him?"

I didn't know if he was asking if I'd ever heard of the horse or the owner, but the answer was the same to both questions. "No, I've never heard of him."

"He's a bad guy to say the least. Barkov is tied to the Russian mafia, and he's former KGB. He's rumored to have been the most corrupt agent in the history of the service. He made his fortune while everyone around him seemed to be begging for vodka and cabbage. Now he owns not only a healthy cut of the Russian black market, but also the horse who'll probably be the next Triple Crown winner. I don't know what you know about Russians, but they don't lose well. They aren't particularly good sports when it comes to second place."

"I know how they feel," I said.

"I thought you might. So, our friend Dmitri, as you might imagine, is particularly opposed to losing, and he has a lot of friends who'll do almost anything to make sure he keeps winning. At the Preakness three weeks ago, his horse Silent Storm wasn't the favorite. He was handicapped as number two behind a horse named Breaker's Folly. Breaker's Folly placed second at the Kentucky Derby two weeks prior, but he was coming on strong when Silent Storm beat him by a nose at the wire. At the Preakness, Breaker's Folly started strong and was leading for over half the race, but suddenly, the jockey's right foot slipped from the stirrup, sending him sliding off the horse. With the jockey hanging off his side, Breaker's Folly slowed down and drifted to the back of the pack."

"Wow. That sucks for him. I've never heard of a jockey falling off."

Dutch corrected my misunderstanding. "Oh, he didn't fall off. He just slipped. But *why* he slipped is what makes the story interesting. The stitching of his boot failed during the race. His boot literally fell apart while he was riding."

"Okay," I said. "Why does any of this matter to me?"

Dutch pursed his lips and thought for a moment. "Five hundred thousand dollars is why this matters to you. That's how much we're getting paid to make sure no more boots fall apart."

Silence filled the car as my brain tried to figure out what half a million dollars had to do with my ability to keep boots from falling apart. "How are we supposed to do that?"

Dutch seemed to expect the question and had an immediate explanation. "It isn't really as simple as boots. The truth is, the boots weren't really the issue. The issue was the people who had access to the boots before the race. You see, boots don't just fall apart—especially not jockeys' boots. We believe someone was paid handsomely by our friend Dmitri to apply a chemical agent to the stitching of the boots prior to the race. This would deteriorate the stitching to the point that it would give way under the stress of the ride, but not before."

I was fascinated that espionage existed in the world of horse racing. "What makes you believe it was a chemical? Why couldn't he have just cut the stitching?"

"Oh, my boy. You have oh so much to learn. Had he cut the stitching, that would've been blatantly obvious when we inspected the boots afterwards. It had to be something much subtler."

I sat quietly, considering what Dutch had said. I was still finding it difficult to believe someone would pay us half a million dollars to keep somebody from sabotaging a horse race. I wondered if all the horses had highly paid teams like us working on their behalf. I chalked it up to people having way too much money.

"So, how do we go about this job of ours?"

"*We* don't," he said. "*I* do. You're here to watch, listen, and learn. Trust me. You'll have nothing productive to add to any of this. You'll be introduced to several other people who were once just like you—bright-eyed and anxious to save the world, but they learned, as you soon will, that the world can't be saved. But you may, if you're lucky, make a small fortune from those people who believe otherwise. Wealthy racehorse owners are among that group of believers, young Chase."

We stopped for gas, coffee, and doughnuts. I was quite thankful for two of the three.

When we left the gas station, Dutch tossed me the key fob. "You drive. After all, it's your car."

"What?" I murmured as doughnut crumbs fell from my mouth and I struggled to catch the key fob. "What do you mean it's my car?"

He laughed at my clumsiness. "I thought you were some big-shot catcher. You look more like a juggler to me. Everyone gets a new car when they finish The Ranch. That one is yours."

I tried to remain calm and not show the excitement I was feeling. I simply glanced at the BMW. "Nope, no big shot here. Just a humble little guy with a brand-new car."

We pulled back onto I-95 and continued north. After we finished our doughnuts, he pulled a lockbox from the back seat and inserted a small key, releasing the top. Inside the box were a pair of Belmont Park ID badges on lanyards, a file folder, and a Walther PPK pistol in a well-worn leather holster. He slid the folder from beneath the other items, opened it up, and began to read silently.

After flipping through a few pages, he finally spoke. "Okay, here's what's happened so far. We've had a team of five operators in place for a little over two weeks. We're shadowing the trainers, handlers, veterinarians, groomers, and every other human who gets anywhere near Breaker's Folly. We even have a man with the training jockey, as well as with the jockey who'll actually ride at Belmont. We've become embedded, so to speak, with the handling staff. It'll appear to everyone outside our circle that our operators are just part of the crew. Believe it or not, we even have a little bitty dude working with the jockeys. If we'd put you in there, you would've stuck out like a sore thumb. Don't worry, though. On your next op, you'll be in the thick of things. This will be your last chance to sit back and watch."

I liked the sound of that. I was looking forward to getting my hands dirty. I'd been in training for so long, I was itching for some real action.

He tossed the ID badge into my lap. "Here. Wear this. Stay with me and don't speak. If anyone asks you anything, look at me, and I'll answer. Just pretend to be invisible and mute. Got it?"

I opened my mouth to say, "Got it," but I just nodded. It worked.

Dutch smirked. "Exactly."

He handed me the PPK in the holster. "Here. Conceal this, and do not pull it for any reason other than to shoot somebody who's trying to shoot me. Do you understand?"

"Got it."

We drove across the Verrazano Narrows Bridge on I-278 onto Long Island just after noon. Jamaica Bay was beautiful, but the city was not. I've never been impressed by cities, and the south side of Queens was no exception. I found it impossible to tell when one town ended, and another began. Everything ran together and was delineated only by signs. One of those signs announced we'd arrived in the town of Elmont, New York, home of Belmont Park.

After checking into the hotel and freshening up, we headed to the stables. As good tradecraft dictated, I wore the PPK on my left ankle, just as I'd been taught. Since I was, for all practical purposes, ambidextrous, I could shoot equally well with either hand, but operators wore their concealed weapon on the inside of their left ankle so other operators would know where to find a gun if they found themselves in a pile of dead operators. There were, of course, other practical reasons for the weapon placement, but that one was good enough for me.

I did exactly as I was told and followed closely behind Dutch. I listened to every word around me. I made mental notes of every detail of everything I saw and carefully seeded in my mind the name and importance of every person we met. Dutch would test me later, and I wasn't about to let him down. After all, he'd just given me a fifty-thousand-dollar BMW.

We met Judson Bennett, the majority owner of Breaker's Folly, and I wanted so badly to ask why he'd named his horse such a ridiculous name, but as instructed, I remained silent. Judson Bennett wore an absurd sport coat and an even more laughable ascot. His appearance immediately made me think of

Thurston Howell III from *Gilligan's Island.* It was going to be an enormous challenge for me not to call him Thurston.

We met trainers, jockeys, veterinarians, photographers, groomers, and handlers of every imaginable responsibility, but I couldn't get the veterinarians out of my head. I believed the best way to slow the horse would be through some difficult-to-detect injection of a substance that would slightly reduce Breaker's Folly's speed.

I actually caught a glimpse of Silent Storm on the practice track. He was a spectacular animal. If a more imposing figure existed, it had to be Silent Storm's owner, Dmitri Barkov.

Of course, there were no introductions, but Dutch directed me to watch Barkov through my binoculars and absorb every detail of the man. It was evident that Barkov was in charge of everything in his world, and no one questioned him. His orders seemed to be obeyed before they left his mouth.

He was a dark-haired, imposing figure who wore a perpetually furrowed brow. He appeared to be between sixty and seventy years old. His eyes were deep and dark. He was overweight, but not obese, and carried his two hundred fifty pounds mostly in his shoulders and chest, with only a slight bulge at the waistline. He wore a black suit and an open-collared shirt, but the most obvious feature of his wardrobe was a pair of silver-tipped, snakeskin cowboy boots. The contrast of his dark appearance, dark suit, and gaudy boots was impossible to forget. He smoked long black cigars almost constantly and never looked at the ground. He carried himself with such confidence that his eyes never left the horizon. He was a domineering and unforgettable figure.

"He's a dangerous man," said Dutch. "The type of man who fears nothing and will do absolutely anything to get what he wants. Men like him are rare, but when you encounter them, never underestimate them—especially not that one."

I didn't remove the binoculars from my eyes, but I didn't disregard his admonition.

Without looking up, I asked, "Why is this so important to him?"

Dutch thought for a long moment before answering. "He thrives on elite status. He's one of the wealthiest men in Russia, so more money isn't what he wants. He wants to be the only Russian to have ever owned a Triple Crown winner. The man has a long track record of getting exactly what he wants and crushing anyone or anything that stands in his way. Some twenty years ago, a woman named Katerina Burinkova told him her heart belonged to another man. Barkov immediately cut her heart out using a dagger he claims was once owned by Ivan the Terrible. He did it, so they say, to prove that her heart belonged only to him. If you ask me, I'd say he made his point."

10
And They're Off!

Race day was an exercise in both ceremony and pandemonium. It was a security nightmare. I couldn't imagine how all of the people coming and going could be screened, searched, and monitored. There were simply too many of them. I would never be a mass security expert. If I had an element, I was definitely out of it.

Following closely behind Dutch, I wore the white linen jacket he gave me in an attempt to fit in among the multi-millionaire owners and the hordes who pretended to be the elite. We met briefly with Judson Bennett, Breaker's Folly's owner, before heading to the prep stables. The meeting was no more than Dutch showing his face and reassuring Bennett the team was in place and his horse was in good hands.

To my surprise, Dutch assigned me a task other than being invisible. He handed me a set of binoculars and a credit-card-sized radio and earpiece. "Listen, Chase. You've done a good job over the last two days, listening, watching, and shutting up. I'm pleased, and the rest of the team has recognized you're valuable to this operation—as more than just a watcher. So, it's time for you to earn your keep."

I felt like a kid on Christmas morning, and I waited eagerly for his instructions.

"Here's what we need from you," Dutch began. "You're going to continue watching."

My heart sank, but to my relief, he wasn't finished.

"Unlike what you've been doing for two days, you're now going to talk, but only to me, and only using this radio. The radio sits in your shirt pocket, and the earpiece is wired under your jacket and behind your left ear. The mic is pinned just inside your cuff. You can talk to me without taking the binoculars from your eyes. Your job is to watch Barkov, and don't blink. If he does anything you don't expect, you immediately tell me. If he blinks too often, if he spits out his cigar, if he scratches his chin with the wrong hand, you tell me before you take your next breath. Got it?"

"Yes, I understand." I hoped I sounded more confident than I was.

I turned, immediately searching for the perfect vantage point from which to watch Dmitri Barkov, slid the radio into my shirt pocket, and routed the wiring as Dutch had instructed. The radio came to life at the touch of a button, and the comms check gave me faith in the gadget.

I scanned the park. "I think the infield is the best place to see Barkov in his owner's box, but I'm going to need some elevation."

Dutch nodded. "I agree. Get down there and dig in. Your pass will get you into the infield, but don't get caught acting like a spy."

I laughed. "But I am a spy."

Dutch smirked. "Indeed, you are, hotshot."

I made my way toward the infield, trying to act as if I belonged there. Fred taught me that perception is fact. If people perceived that I belonged in the infield, they wouldn't question me being there. I snatched up a clipboard and handheld walkie-talkie someone had abandoned. Using those as camouflage, I confidently strolled past the infield security and police officers mounted atop quarter horses in a world of thoroughbreds. No one gave me a second glance as I reconnoitered for a place to set up my observation point—O.P., as we called it in my new world.

I settled on a position near the start gate. All eyes would surely be on the horses when the gates opened and the race commenced, so no one would notice me blending into the background. As the race progressed, the tractor would pull the start gates off the track, and all eyes would still be on the horses. I could climb on top of the gate abandoned in the infield. From that vantage point, I would be able to put eyes on Barkov without being suspected of anything sinister, and most likely, without being noticed at all.

I took up my position as the horses made their way into the gates. The thoroughbreds pranced, postured, and snorted like the wild animals they were, beneath skilled jockeys perched lightly on their backs like gargoyles.

I scanned the owners' boxes and quickly found Barkov. His size didn't give him away as much as the cloud of billowing white cigar smoke around his head of thick, black hair.

"Dutch, this is Chase. I'm in position. I have eyes on the target."

"Roger," came the prompt reply. "You are six. I am one."

I keyed my small mic and simply responded, "Six."

I'd been taught proper radio procedures and discipline at length while at The Ranch, and the numeric call signs were almost always the standard.

Finally, all the horses were in the gate, and the crowd roared with excitement as the race began with the thundering of hooves and a cloud of dust.

I'd never seen a horse race in person. That wasn't going to change that day. I never glanced at the horses and kept my eyes firmly locked on Barkov as he chewed through his first cigar and let it fall to the floor, leaving a trail of gray ash on his black suit. He was watching his horse, Silent Storm, almost as intently as I was watching him.

Through the earpiece, I heard, "Six, report."

"One, Six . . . all normal."

"One," was the only reply.

I listened closely and was lured into the excitement by the animated tone of the track announcer. "And down the backstretch they come, with Silent Storm by half a length with Bay-man's Beauty and Breaker's Folly coming on strong. It's Silent Storm by a head and Bay-man's Beauty . . . no, it's Breaker's Folly now, then Bay-man's Beauty on the rail. It's Breaker's Folly closing the gap on Silent Storm as they enter the far turn. It's Silent Storm in a dead heat now with Breaker's Folly at the one-mile mark at just over a minute thirty-eight, as the dream of our first Triple Crown winner since Affirmed in seventy-eight may be on the verge of re-alization as they turn for home. It's . . . Silent Storm . . . no, it's Breaker's Folly by a nose as they open up down the homestretch. Here's the pack. It's Breaker's Folly, Silent Storm, Bay-man's Beauty, and Diamond Cutter outside in fourth. I Dream of Ge-nie in fifth now in his stride coming hard on the outside, but the race is upfront with Breaker's Folly and Silent Storm battling for the lead."

I tried not to get completely lost in the melodic chant of the announcer, and I watched as Barkov ripped his latest cigar from his lips and started mouthing something.

Excitedly, I keyed my microphone and almost yelled, "One, Six, target is agitated and saying something. I'm working on reading his lips."

Again, the reply came, "One."

I watched Barkov's beefy red mouth shape something that looked like, "Sterilize the lotion."

Sterilize the lotion? That doesn't make sense.

Then, realizing the obvious, I felt like an idiot. He's Russian. He's not saying, "Sterilize the lotion." He's saying, "*Strelyai v loshad!*"

I immediately keyed my mic and yelled, "He just said, 'Shoot the horse!'"

Barkov's head turned sharply to his right, and he appeared to be focusing far off to the east end of the track and away from the action of the race. He was clearly looking for something or some-one. Again, his lips formed the same words, but this time there was absolutely no hint of uncertainty.

Again, I keyed my mic. "He's got a sniper at the east end. He's going to shoot Breaker's Folly!"

"Find the sniper!" Dutch responded.

I turned my glasses from Barkov to follow his line of sight out of the race park and skyward toward the eastern horizon. I found a water tower with "Elmont—Home of the Belmont Stakes" painted in blue letters. On top of the water tower in a perfect sniper's position, poised behind a long black rifle, was . . .

A woman? What is a woman doing with a rifle on a water tower?

"Got him . . . or, I mean, her!" I yelled into my mic. "She's on the Elmont water tower with an unidentified rifle!"

The announcer's voice once again filled my head. "Now it's Breaker's Folly by a head with Silent Storm stretching out and gaining ground, but no, Breaker's Folly is pulling away, increasing to half a length now. Then it's Silent Storm and Diamond Cutter with Bay-man's Beauty falling out of the top three. I Dream of Genie still coming on strong, in his stretch now, but it's still Breaker's Folly out front with Silent Storm now almost a length behind. Dreams of the Triple Crown may be crumbling now with Breaker's Folly opening up an ever-increasing lead over Silent Storm."

Focusing on the sniper, I wanted to draw my pistol and fire at the water tower. I couldn't hit her from that distance, but maybe I could interrupt her concentration by bouncing a few rounds off the tower, hopefully making her blow the shot, but Dutch's admonition had been crystal clear—my gun stayed in its holster.

As I blinked, trying to bring the weapon into focus, I found myself mesmerized by the woman behind the rifle. She was thin and muscular with high-set cheekbones and captivating eyes. Her long blonde hair was pulled back into a ponytail protruding from a black baseball cap. Her shoulders rose and fell with every breath. Then it happened. Her breathing stopped, and her perfectly positioned body froze. She drew in one more full breath, let half of it out, and began the long trigger squeeze. I saw an instantaneous burst of red light from the rifle, but the sniper never flinched. There was no recoil from the rifle. There was no muzzle flash, no sound, nothing except a brief flash of red light. The recoil from a rifle of that size should've sent her body shuddering.

I yelled into my mic, "Shot!"

I saw the trigger pull and the flash, but there had been no actual shot. I was confounded and in disbelief. No matter how I tried to understand what I'd just witnessed, I couldn't make the scenario make any sense.

The announcer's excited tone heightened as he chanted, "Breaker's Folly has lost his stride. It's Breaker's Folly drifting to the outside and Silent Storm coming hard on the rail with Diamond Cutter less than half a length back. At the wire, it's a photo finish, but it's Silent Storm by half a nose over Diamond Cutter, with I Dream of Genie in third and Breaker's Folly in a disappointing fourth. Silent Storm has done it! Silent Storm has won the most coveted title in all of racing. The Triple Crown goes to Silent Storm and owner Dmitri Barkov. This is a historic day here at Belmont with Silent Storm, the first to win the coveted Triple Crown since Affirmed in nineteen seventy-eight. It's Silent Storm by half a nose. Silent Storm!"

I swept my glasses back to Barkov's box to see him hugging everyone in sight but still sending glances to the east. Turning back to the water tower, I watched the sniper toss a long black rope from her perch, rappel down the line, and shake out her ponytail. Her silhouette disappeared behind the tower, but the image of her elegant, graceful movement, and that face, that perfect, flawless face, burned itself into my mind.

I might've been the only person on Earth who'd actually seen what transpired.

Just like the Preakness, the Belmont Stakes had fallen victim to sabotage, only this time, there were no boots coming apart at the seams. Something far more daring had occurred, and unlike the Preakness, this time, there was an eyewitness to the sabotage . . . me.

11
Can You Keep a Secret?

Escaping the infield after Silent Storm caused the most excitement Belmont Park had ever seen was easier than I'd expected. People were everywhere laughing, screaming, celebrating, crying, and paying absolutely no attention to the linen-jacket-clad operator slipping through the throngs of horse-racing fanatics. I had to find Dutch so we could start building a narrative of exactly what happened only minutes before, but when I found him, he wasn't the receptive, mild-mannered professional I'd known for the past two days.

Instead of rushing me in to speak with Bennett to lay out what I'd seen, his eyes met mine in a stare that was something akin to the look a child gets when he's caught in a terrible lie. He was red-faced with clenched fists. He whipped his right index finger to his lips, signaling me to shut up.

Not only did I remain silent, but I also fell in step behind Dutch to watch, listen, and learn. I assumed Dutch would do a little verbal soft-shoe to shun as much responsibility for the attack on Breaker's Folly as possible and promise to get to the bottom of what happened.

Breaker's Folly was trotting sideways back to the stables, and Miguel Otero, Folly's jockey, was helped down from the thoroughbred by a handler who skillfully placed the five-foot-one-inch jockey on the ground.

The moment the jockey's feet hit the dirt, Judson Bennett grabbed the man with such force the jockey let out an audible groan that sounded like the dying cries of a wounded animal. Bennett shoved the jockey against the side of a trailer. Fortunately, Miguel hadn't removed his helmet; otherwise, he would've undoubtedly been knocked unconscious by the impact.

"What the hell was that?" Bennett yelled. "What did you do? Do you have any idea how much money you just cost me?"

Bennett released his hold on Miguel, allowing the jockey to fall to the ground. He stood over him, growing more furious by the second. Fearing Bennett may be on the verge of stomping the jockey to death, Dutch stepped between him and the cowering jockey and placed his hand in the center of Bennett's chest.

In the calmest voice imaginable, Dutch said, "Mr. Bennett, let me talk with Miguel, and I'll get to the bottom of this."

Bennett slapped Dutch's hand from his chest, glared into his eyes, and spoke in a breathy, rage-filled voice. "You damned well better get to the bottom of this. I paid you people half a million dollars to protect my horse, only to see this him throw it away two hundred feet before the wire. I want some answers, and I want them right now!"

Dutch knelt beside the jockey. "Are you all right, Miguel?"

He unfastened his helmet and laid it carefully in the dirt beside him. "*Sim, senhor. Eu estou bem. Obrigado. Obrigado,*" replied the terrified man.

"My Portuguese is terrible, Miguel. Can you speak English?"

Miguel drew in a deep, determined breath and replied in trembling, broken English, "*Sim* . . . ah, yes, a little, but is *difícil.* Uh, how you say . . . uh, hard, yes, hard. Ah, difficult. Is difficult when scared for me."

Dutch helped the jockey to his feet and led him to a pair of abandoned chairs. He helped dust off the jockey, who was covered in dirt from both the track and the ride Bennett had given him.

"Are you sure you're okay?"

"Yes, yes. I am okay. I . . . ah, how you say, *acidentado?*"

Dutch smiled again. "Yes, my friend, you are very *acidentado* . . . tough."

Miguel almost smiled. "Your Portuguese not so bad, *senhor.*"

"How's your Spanish?" asked Dutch.

"Better than English," Miguel said.

"Mine, too."

They continued their conversation in Spanish.

Dutch asked, "Can you tell me what happened to Breaker's Folly out there?"

The jockey calmed down and spoke in excellent Spanish. "I don't know, but I think something hit him in his eye. That's what it felt like to me. I've been riding horses all my life, and that's exactly how they behave when something hits them in the eye. You must tell the doctors to look in his eye. And please tell Mr. Bennett I didn't do it. I couldn't make Breaker's Folly do that if I wanted to. He got hit in the eye. I'm sure of it. Mr. Bennett is a rich man. He can make sure I never ride again, and I have to ride, mister, uh, I don't know your name."

"Just call me Dutch, Miguel. I'll talk with the veterinarians and with Mr. Bennett. He's just upset right now. He'll come to his senses. He knows you didn't do it. He just needed someone to blame while he was mad. Everything's going to be okay."

Dutch tried to reassure the frightened jockey, who likely felt his career going down in flames. They shook hands and parted ways. Miguel made his way to the shower as Dutch paced. Hundreds of boiling thoughts must've been going through his mind, and none of them were going to make the talk with Judson Bennett any easier.

Dutch assembled the team of operatives in the back of an RV we'd set up as a makeshift operations center. On the wall was a bank of monitors attached to some of the finest video playback equipment available.

I stood behind the seasoned operators and listened. Everyone had a theory, but no one was correct. They all had it wrong. Ev-

eryone heard my radio transmission about the sniper on the water tower, but all of them assumed Breaker's Folly had stumbled,
flinched, or was spooked by something, resulting in him faltering
before the sniper could get off a shot. I was the only one who
knew the truth. That wouldn't be the last time I was the only
person in the room who knew the truth. I liked the feeling of
power that accompanied such exclusive knowledge.

The team was buzzing with ideas and theories, but Dutch
called the room to order. "Okay, listen up! I have to brief Bennett, so get to work on the video. I want to know what happened, when it happened, and if it could've been prevented. You
have four minutes. Chase, you're with me. Let's go."

No one questioned his orders, and everyone went to work
scouring each second of video to find out what caused Breaker's
Folly to flinch and lose the race. Of course, I already knew what
was never going to be apparent on any of the video, but I still
wasn't sure if Dutch knew the truth.

He and I left the RV and climbed into the cab of an F-350
dually pickup. Dutch turned the key, and the big diesel engine
came to life with a roar. I started to speak, but Dutch held up a
finger. "Shh! Don't talk yet."

He scrolled through the radio stations until he found one with
a thumping bass beat and turned it up louder than a teenager
cruising the strip. Simultaneously, we drummed our fingers on the
windows of the truck. The extremely low-tech counter-surveillance
measures of the diesel engine, the radio, and the finger drumming
were designed to prevent anyone with a listening device from
hearing our voices or being able to record the vibrations of the
glass in the truck and turn them into usable audio.

"Okay, let's hear it. What did you see out there?"

I took a breath. "I saw Barkov become agitated when
Breaker's Folly took the lead. He told someone, in Russian,
'Shoot the horse!' Then, he looked to the east, so I followed his
line of sight and found the sniper on the water tower. She was
clearly well trained and had a rifle I couldn't identify. I watched

her shoulders rise and fall with her breathing, and finally, she held her breath and squeezed the trigger, but the rifle didn't fire —or at least there was no visible recoil. She never flinched, and by my estimation, she couldn't have weighed more than a buck twenty. Any thirty-caliber or better would've rattled her teeth, but she never wiggled. When she pulled the trigger, I caught a glimpse of a flash of light. It actually looked more like a reflection from something, but I can't be sure. After she pulled the trigger, I immediately followed her sight line back to the track and saw Breaker's Folly falling back and Silent Storm taking the lead. When I looked back at the sniper, she was rappelling from the water tower. Dutch, I think she temporarily blinded Breaker's Folly with some sort of laser. That explains the absence of recoil, and it jibes with what the jockey said. Something hit the horse in the eye."

Dutch considered my theory. "Did you get a good look at her? Could you pick her out of a crowd?"

The defining moment of my life was at hand. I was about to tell the biggest lie that would ever cross my lips, and it would forever change everything about my future.

"No," I mumbled.

Her face was in a shadow under her hat, but I think she had short dark hair, or at least dark hair that was tucked under her hat. She was thin, fit, and agile, but other than that, I couldn't say. Dutch, I'm sorry."

I felt my stomach implode with instant guilt. I didn't know why I'd lied, but there was nothing that could be done about it. I had to stick to my lie, regardless of the cost.

"Okay," he said. "You've got nothing to be sorry for. You did good, kid. I'm proud of you. Most new operators would've missed ninety percent of what you caught and remembered. You're going to be one hell of an operator, Chase. Keep it up. Now, listen closely. Tell no one what you saw today. Tell no one about our conversation. You saw a sniper pull the trigger on a rifle you couldn't identify, and the rifle clearly did not fire. The sniper's mission was a failure. Breaker's Folly took a rock to the eye or a bee sting or God knows what, but it doesn't matter. He wasn't shot. There was no bullet because there was no gunshot. You've done your job, and you'll get a nice little check to go along with your new car. Good job."

Dutch patted me on the back for lying to him, then he told me to wait for him to create the next lie that I'd tell. I was beginning to think my whole new world was based on lies.

* * *

"Come with me and don't say a word to anyone. Understand?"

We stepped from the truck and headed off to find Bennett.

When we finally found him in a private suite in the owner's club, he was still fuming, but his hands had stopped trembling. He held a phone pressed tightly to his ear with his left hand and a tumbler of whiskey in his right. A bevy of assistants, aides, and God-knows-who-else was orbiting him, awaiting instructions and praying they weren't going to be the victims of his next tirade.

Dutch waded through the crowd and leaned in closely to Bennett. "We need to talk . . . privately."

Bennett waved his assistants away with a brush of his hand. "Give us the room, now!"

The crowd dispersed, leaving the three of us alone in the lavish suite.

Without looking at me, Dutch pointed to the door. "You're on the door, Chase."

I posted beside the door and watched the scene unfold in front of me.

Dutch began his pitch. "Mr. Bennett, I know you want somebody to blame for this afternoon's results, but it's beginning to look like it was just a stroke of exceptionally bad luck. We've reviewed every second of video, and it's crystal clear that Breaker's Folly took something to the eye. Maybe it was a rock or some sand. I don't know, but the video shows his right eye fluttering and his head jerking abruptly. Miguel did absolutely nothing out of the ordinary in the seconds leading up to the flinch. I believe it was a freak accident, and the video agrees. This was clearly nothing sinister and certainly nothing criminal. It was just bad luck."

Bennett roared, "There's no such thing as luck, you idiot!"

He threw his highball glass across the room, and it exploded against the wall. The man turned back to Dutch with unequaled ire in his tone and disgust on his face. "So, you're telling me it was just bad luck that my horse got a rock kicked in his face at the exact moment that Russian's horse needed to win the Triple Crown? What kind of incompetent ass are you?"

Bennett crushed a lampshade that was probably worth more than my car. "Get out! Take your so-called team with you, and get out!"

Dutch started to protest, but Bennett lifted what was left of the lamp and hurled it through the air at his head. Instead of defending himself, Dutch let the lamp hit him squarely in the face. He could've easily blocked it or even sidestepped it, but for some reason, he just took the shot. Cupping his left eye in both hands, Dutch crushed a capsule of theatrical blood in his palm. The crimson liquid dripped through his fingers and down his jawline.

I knelt and drew my Walther from my ankle holster, prepared to defend Dutch if things continued to escalate.

The senior operator stared through Bennett. "You put out my eye, you son of a bitch. Your check better not bounce, or I'll sue you for every dime you'll ever have, and I'll tell the whole world you had to hire a 'so-called team' to protect your horse from your own paranoia. You're out of your league, Bennett."

As he stormed from the room with blood dripping from his face, Dutch said, "Shoot him if you want, Chase. Just make sure you kill him if you do."

I stared into Bennett's eyes with my pistol gripped firmly in my hand. "Let's wait 'til his check clears," I said. "We know where to find him."

12
Old Friends

The previous year of my life had been regimented beyond measure. I woke up before five every morning, ate everything I could find, then studied, trained, ran, learned something new, and perfected what I'd learned the day before. There was no formal graduation with caps and gowns, and certainly no diplomas for the education I'd earned. I was quickly learning that my education at The Ranch, no matter how good it was, had not prepared me for everything I'd learn in real-world operations.

I sat behind the wheel of a car in Elmont, New York, on a gorgeous spring afternoon, thinking about her, the mysterious sniper who moved like a cat. I pictured her lying on the water tower with her hair glistening in the afternoon sun, and her long, lean body stretched out with such elegance and confidence behind that rifle. The world around me faded away, and I was consumed with thoughts of her. I wanted to hear her voice. I wanted to look into her eyes, and I wanted to touch her skin. I wanted to know her name. And I could never tell Dutch.

He snapped his fingers. "Hey, kid! Wherever you are, come on back."

I shuddered. "Sorry, I was just . . ."

"It doesn't matter, kid. You've had a big day. You've earned a vacation. Let's drive into the city and celebrate. We just made half a million dollars."

He was clearly proud of himself for the ruse he'd pulled on Bennett.

"You didn't tell him about the sniper," I said.

"No, I didn't tell him. Why would I? The rifle didn't fire. The horse got a rock kicked up in his eye, and he flinched. It was just a fluke, a stroke of bad luck. We did our job. We protected the horse, and we got paid. Now, it's time to celebrate."

I was treading on thin ice since I was fresh from The Ranch, but I just had to poke the bear. "So, who do you think kicked that rock into Breaker's Folly's eye? He was in the lead, half a length ahead of Silent Storm, when this mystery rock got kicked into his eye. Who kicked that rock, Dutch? There were no horses in front of him."

Dutch cleared his throat and dismissed my question with a wave of his hand. "Who knows? Besides, what difference does it make?"

I accepted his voice of experience.

"Who was she, Dutch? Who was that girl on the water tower?"

His eyes met mine. "I don't know, kid. She's nobody. She's probably some low-level SVR corporal or something. Barkov probably borrowed her for the weekend. Who cares? The job's over, and we got paid. Now, it's time to party!"

We took the Long Island Expressway into Midtown Manhattan and the Four Seasons. Traffic was insane, and my dislike of big cities suddenly felt well-founded.

When we arrived, Dutch and I exited the car, leaving it in the capable hands of the overdressed valet who seemed anxious to relieve us of the burden of my BMW. He was courteous and welcomed us to the Four Seasons. The bellman, also overdressed, offered to take our bags, but Dutch slipped him a folded tip. "It's already taken care of, but thank you."

The bellman nodded. "Thank you, sir."

A man at the front desk was the first employee not overdressed. He wore a nice dark suit and tie, but certainly nothing as gaudy as the guys out front.

Before Dutch or I could start the conversation, the man said, "Ah, Mr. Fulton. Welcome to the Four Seasons. Your friends are waiting for you in the dining room, and your suite is ready. Your packages arrived earlier, and we had someone unpack for you. If there's anything you need while you're here, please don't hesitate to ask. We are at your service."

I turned to Dutch. "My friends? My suite? My packages? What's he talking about?"

Dutch formed a thin horizontal line with his lips. "Yes, Mr. Fulton. Do join your friends in the dining room. I'll catch up with you later. Oh, and nice job today, by the way. You done good, kid."

As I entered the dining room, the maître d' greeted me as if he'd been expecting me for days. "Welcome, Mr. Fulton. Let me show you to your table. Your friends are waiting."

He deposited me at what he referred to as *my* table, where I found a welcome surprise. Sitting around the table with open-collared shirts and dinner jackets were Beater, Tuner, and Dr. "Rocket" Richter. The trio wasted no time greeting me with boisterous enthusiasm and handshakes.

Dr. Richter clasped my shoulders and held me at arm's length. "I'm proud of you."

That was the first time he'd ever called me Chase.

"Thank you, Coach."

Dr. Richter said, "We've been hearing all about your exploits at The Ranch and on your field trips. It sounds as if you've already made quite an impression on the decision makers. I never had any doubts."

I wasn't sure what to say, so I simply offered a polite, "Thank you," and took a long sip of the scotch that had magically appeared in front of me.

I hadn't seen those guys for over a year, and for some reason, they felt like family to me since I no longer had a family of my own. It was good to see them.

"Where's Ace? It's not a party without him," I said.

The table fell silent until Tuner, the quiet one, said, "Ace passed about six months ago. It was the big C. Cancer gets all of us if we live long enough."

I found myself battling to keep a tear from escaping my eye, but I managed to raise my glass and choke out a toast.

"Here's to Ace. Let's hope he's not trying to shoot down any angels if they actually let him into Heaven."

"Here! Here!"

We drank, ate, laughed, and shared stories—some true, and some a little more creative.

"So, Chase, what've they had you doing since you finished up at The Ranch?"

I'd learned a great deal about operational security and the importance of keeping information limited to the need-to-know crowd, but I figured there wasn't anything classified about a horse race, so I told my story. "Well, you'll never believe it, but I've been at the Belmont Stakes for the past couple of days, protecting the fourth-place finisher."

"Protecting the fourth-place finisher sure sounds exciting," Beater said. "Did you get to shoot anybody?"

My old friends laughed.

"Go ahead. Laugh it up, guys. It's a long story, and in fact, I almost got to shoot a guy who wanted to kill Dutch. Speaking of Dutch . . . Where is he?"

"Dutch doesn't exist," Dr. Richter said. "He's a ghost. You may never see him again, or he may show up in your suitcase when you least expect it. He's a brilliant operator when he wants to be, but I think he's in it for the money now, and that's a shame."

A rumble of agreement came from around the table.

I learned from seasoned operators at The Ranch that the mindset of security and black ops had changed dramatically over the past few decades. When Dr. Richter, Ace, and the guys were hard-core operators during the Cold War, they did it for the love of freedom and to beat back the spread of communism. Since the Berlin Wall came down and most of Russia was, at least by outside appearances, democratic, the need to keep communism at bay had been depleted. The world faced new threats from tyrants in the Middle East and the like. The new operators referred to the Cold War–era operators as dinosaurs. I suppose the respect I had for the guys, Dr. Richter in particular, kept me from dismissing their attitudes and opinions as antiquated. Those guys still had so much to teach me about the basic tradecraft of covert operations. I would never be a military Special Forces operator, so I would never have the benefit of attending most of the military schools. I'd spend my life as a civilian covert operative, and as such, I'd have to learn everything I could from every source I could find. I couldn't imagine a better source than the guys who'd seen and done it all.

Dinner was perhaps the best meal I'd ever eaten. The courses kept coming, and the drinks kept flowing. I listened to old stories about Ace and the antics of the foursome through the years.

"Why don't we find somewhere in this fancy place to fire up a few good cigars before it's past our bedtime?" Beater asked.

"Great idea," Dr. Richter said.

In his typical style, Tuner silently nodded his agreement. I was coming to appreciate how he just listened when the rest of the world seemed to be producing more noise by the minute.

We found a cigar-friendly bar where Dr. Richter produced four Cuban Cohibas. He offered me his punch, but I proudly refused and produced my very own Xikar punch and lighter.

"Indeed," Dr. Richter said.

We spent the next hour enjoying the embargo cigars and a bottle of, what I learned was, excellent brandy.

I began to feel the effects of the alcohol and the cigar, and I placed my hand on Dr. Richter's shoulder. "I need to talk with you. I have some things I want to tell you, and I need your advice."

He looked at me, then checked his *Vostok Komandirskie* wristwatch. "Not here. Let's go upstairs."

It occurred to me in the elevator that I didn't know which room was mine. The deskman said my suite was ready, but he hadn't given me a key. The realization of my oversight made me feel like a rookie, but fortunately, Dr. Richter solved my dilemma. "Our rooms are in the same suite, so we can talk in yours while Tuner listens to Beater snore next door."

I followed him to our suite that looked more like a palace than a hotel room. I was amazed and overwhelmed. I'd spent the last year of my life sleeping on a surplus army cot—when I was lucky. On most nights, I got no sleep at all.

As we stepped into my room, Dr. Richter motioned for me to join him on the balcony overlooking Central Park. The view was breathtaking, and the spring night air was crisp. We made ourselves comfortable, and he poured two glasses of scotch.

"Don't get too used to this, Chase. Nights like this in places like this are rare. Treasure them. They'll make the nights you spend in cold, dark, wet holes more bearable. You've learned a lot and proved a lot in the last several months, but you still have a great deal to learn. Most of that can't be taught; it can only be experienced. Half of all new operators are killed in the first eighteen months out of The Ranch. Most of those who survive the first year and a half lose their minds or stomachs for this work and either kill themselves, walk away, or end up getting caught and going to prison in some godforsaken corner of the world. The few who remain go on to make a real difference in the world and make a good living at this. Then, there's that one in a thousand who lives long enough to enjoy the fruits of his labor. I believe that's you, Chase. You're something special. You're your father made over, only better, smarter, stronger, and with one advantage over him: you're alone. You don't have a wife and two kids to watch over, even if that wife was an operator, too. You see, when a man is burdened with the responsibility of a family, this job is doubly hard. He worries every second his children or wife are going to end up in the hands of someone who wants him to suffer, and that suffering will come through the torture of his family. A man doesn't need that kind of stress. You're free to pour yourself into your work without worrying about somebody feeding your little girl to a woodchipper somewhere. You have a huge leg up over your father. You're going to do great things, Chase Fulton."

I gave his speech some careful, cautious thought. I'd never considered how my father must've felt every time he left us home —wherever home happened to be at the time—to go out and do whatever it was he did. It must've terrified him to think that we could be vulnerable. What a hell that must've been.

"I know this probably sounds juvenile, but I don't have any-where to live, Coach. I don't have any money or any idea what's going to happen next. They taught me how to kill and disappear, but they left out the part about how to live from day to day be-tween the killing and disappearing. So, what do I do? Am I just supposed to stay here in this place and wait for the phone to ring?"

He gave me a long, thoughtful look. "You don't really think we'd spend all of that money and time on you and then throw you out on the street, do you? That's not how this works. You're going to be very well cared for. In fact, I have some things for you."

He left the balcony and returned a moment later with an alu-minum locking briefcase. He placed the case on my lap and re-turned to his chair, reclaiming his scotch. I pressed the releases on the latches, but nothing happened. There was a small set of combination locks for each latch.

He answered before I could ask. "It's the first three and the last three digits of the serial number on your pistol."

I had, of course, memorized the serial number, so I entered the numbers and felt the latches spring open.

I'd given up trying to guess what was behind door number three a long time before that night, so I had no preconceived no-tions of what might be inside the briefcase. The contents turned out to be Christmas and my birthday all rolled into one. Inside, I found four identities for myself. Each included a well-worn passport, driver's license, credit cards, and a brief history, called a leg-end, of each identity. I'd been taught I would have to become someone else on a regular basis, and to do so, I'd have to fully immerse myself into the history and identity of each character. I discovered that, with the contents of the briefcase, I could be a Canadian, Australian, German, or Italian. In addition to the four identities, I found a badge and credentials identifying me as a supervisory special agent with the U.S. Secret Service. I held up the credentials.

"My boy," Dr. Richter said, "I know enough about you to know you're going to occasionally get yourself into trouble that even you won't be able to talk your way out of, so those credentials will keep you out of jail when your wit can't. They'll also unlock a lot of doors and put inquisitive local cops at ease when you turn up snooping around where civilians shouldn't. You have to remember, though, to never, under any circumstances, allow yourself to be fingerprinted. We've gone to great lengths to ensure that you don't exist. When you get caught, and you will get caught, ensure that whoever catches you calls the number at Treasury inside that wallet before processing you. The person who answers the phone will get you out of the mess you created, but he or she will demand some answers from you about why you let yourself get caught. So, keep your head on straight. And for God's sake, don't store the identities together. Understand?"

The potential scenarios poured through my head like Niagara Falls. "I understand."

"Keep digging," he said.

I laid the previously discovered contents on the table between us and pulled at the corners of the lining of the case. It gave way, revealing another compartment holding a satellite phone, two more pistols, and a pair of credit cards—one with my real name and one with my Canadian alias.

Dr. Richter continued his lesson. "When you're paid, you'll be paid into an offshore numbered account. Both of those cards are drawn on that account. That's how you'll live. Keep plenty of cash on hand. Cash is a tool. You'll learn it's often more powerful than a bullet. Wherever you live, keep a high quality safe, and never have less than a hundred thousand in cash in it."

"A hundred thousand dollars! Where am I going to get a hundred thousand dollars in cash?"

"We'll give you all the tools you need, my boy. Where do you want to live for now?"

I'd matured a great deal since Rocket Richter flew me to the barrier islands off the Georgia coast, but I was still amazed when he asked questions like that.

All I could put together was, "I want to live someplace warm. I hate the cold."

He smirked. "When you get to Miami, go see David Shepherd at the Federal National Bank. Here's his card. He'll see that you have whatever you need down there, and he's expecting you."

"David Shepherd? Really? That's a little too biblical, don't you think?"

He lifted his glass. "We're doing God's work, my boy. So, what did you want to talk about? You said you need my advice."

I so badly wanted to know what I should do about the sniper. I wanted to tell him how I couldn't get her out of my mind. "Oh, nothing," I said. "I think you answered all of my questions."

13

The Good Shepherd

Two thoughts consumed my mind on the drive to Miami. The first was how much I loved my new car. If they never paid me another penny, at that moment, the car was enough. The second thought was a little heavier. I couldn't get the sniper out of my head. I had to know who she was. I spent four years at the University of Georgia, where there was certainly no shortage of beautiful girls, but none of them ever captured my attention the way the sniper had. Being a psychologist, I couldn't stop overanalyzing why she was so fascinating. Part of it had to be rooted in her capabilities. I watched her do everything right, from the position she was in behind the rifle, to how she controlled her breathing during the shot, or non-shot. It may have been the way she moved so gracefully, so catlike. Of course, there had to be an element of physical attraction in addition to the fascination I had for her skill. She was, after all, practically perfect physically.

In the few moments my thoughts weren't solidly on her, I wondered how many others there were like me. I met other operators while I was in training at The Ranch and on my field trips, but I had no idea how vast the network was. It also occurred to me that I really didn't know who I worked for. The more I thought about that, the more I realized it really didn't matter. Most young college graduates would kill for an opportunity to work for any major company and make ten percent of the money I would make. I actually laughed at the thought of my classmates being willing to kill. Not only was I willing, but I was also well trained, heavily equipped and financed, and even poised to do exactly that—kill. I wondered how many of my assignments would include the necessity of taking the life of another human. I remember thinking I could guard racehorses for the next twenty years and retire quite comfortably, but that wasn't what lay in my future.

* * *

When I arrived at the Federal National Bank in Miami, I asked to see Mr. David Shepherd and laughed to myself at that unfortunate name. I was immediately ushered into his office and told, "Mr. Shepherd is expecting you, and he'll be right in."

I sat and glanced around the office just as I'd been taught. I spotted a letter opener that would make a nice weapon. Resting on David's modest desk was a glass paperweight with a scorpion encased within its hemispheric dome. That would serve perfectly as a blunt weapon, but something else caught my attention: a baseball bat poised in a decorative mount on the wall with Hank Aaron's signature emblazoned across the barrel. That made me smile. Not only would the bat make a great weapon, but it was also an impressive piece of baseball history, and for that, I had great respect.

There's an old adage in the special operations community that says, "Be nice, professional, and courteous, but have a plan to kill everyone in the room." I didn't fear Mr. Shepherd would be a threat, but I did find myself analyzing my situation in his small office. There was only one exit that didn't involve breaking some relatively thick glass. Perhaps worse than that was the fact that there was no place in the office where I could sit that would give me the advantage of seeing him before he saw me. I didn't like that at all. Instead of surrendering to my disadvantage, I chose to eliminate the office from the equation by stepping outside the door and seeking out a water fountain. I spotted the fountain and spent considerable time pretending to drink from it while glancing beneath my arm to identify Mr. Shepherd before he identified me.

I was wearing jeans, an untucked T-shirt, an Atlanta Braves cap, and running shoes. I certainly didn't look the part of anyone who would be awaiting the arrival of the vice president of anything, let alone a bank, so I thought I might be able to hide in plain sight, but I was wrong.

As I arose from my final make-believe sip of water, a hand landed on my shoulder.

The booming voice of David Shepherd filled the air. "Mr. Fulton! I've been expecting you. I'm glad you made it. Let's step inside my office, and we'll take care of you."

He was not the diminutive Jewish banker I'd anticipated. He was enormous and towered over my greater-than-six-foot frame by several inches. His hands looked like dinner plates with fingers. I decided the letter opener and paperweight were useless against him. Honestly, I didn't have much faith in my chances with the bat, either. I just hoped he was one of the good guys.

He folded himself behind his desk. "I'd offer you something to drink, but you pretended to drink a gallon of water from the fountain while watching for me, so we'll forego that formality. I'm David Shepherd, and so there's no confusion, I know exactly who and what you are. We're on the same team. See?" He pointed toward Hank Aaron's bat. "I'm a Braves fan, too."

"It's nice to know I'm not alone." My level of discomfort must've been apparent.

"Relax, Chase. You're among friends. This bank and almost everyone in it work for the same people you do. Most of us have been through The Ranch and even spent some time in the field. Where you're the operations branch, we're the financial branch. It's my job to see that you have what you need to do your job. I know all of this is a little overwhelming, just like everything else in your life for the last year or so, but I promise you'll soon begin to see all of this as normal . . . and that should scare you, my friend."

I had to ask, "Why should that scare me?"

He opened one of his desk drawers and produced a bottle and two highball glasses. He poured each of us a drink, slid one to me, and offered up a toast. "Here's to knowing when to be afraid."

I touched the rim of my glass to his.

"Fear is an interesting thing," he said. "You see, men can grow accustomed to almost anything when exposed to it long enough. If you put a man in a pot of water and raise the heat slowly, you can boil his blood before he realizes he's dying. The trick, young Chase, is to never get too comfortable in anyone else's pot. Do you know what I mean?"

I wasted no time in answering. "I have no idea what you're talking about, Mr. Shepherd, but if you keep pouring that whiskey, I'll listen until it makes sense."

He poured another inch of the golden whiskey into my glass, then squinted his right eye and gave me a look. "I like you, Chase. You remind me a lot of . . . well, of no one I've ever met, and of everyone I've ever known. That's an excellent quality."

I wondered why he spoke in such riddles, but I listened, drank, and waited to see what would happen next. I didn't have to wait long.

Shepherd had apparently decided it was time to get down to business, so that's precisely what we did.

He swallowed the remaining whiskey from his glass, pulled a green ledger from a small safe behind his desk, and placed his glasses on his nose. "You are, of course, free to live anywhere you'd like, but there's someone else you should see before you make a decision. I think he may have exactly what you want. Here's his number."

He slid a business card across the desk, and I read it carefully. It said, "Dominic Fontana, Yacht Broker."

I pocketed the card as Mr. Shepherd opened the ledger, made some entries, then passed me a slip of thin paper with some cryptic note scribbled across it. "Hand this to the cashier, and she'll get you the money for your safe."

I tried to pretend I understood, but he obviously detected that I was quite uncomfortable.

"Look Chase, this is no big deal. Really. We do this sort of thing all the time. It'll get easier. Don't be afraid to ask me anything. Absolutely anything. I'm here to help. We'll get you some stash money, some walking-around cash, and a place to live. You have a car, right?"

"Oh, yeah. They gave me a BMW."

"Good," he said. "Enjoy it and your new life. Soon enough, you'll get a call and have to go to work. Living between jobs is important. You have to live. Never forget that. Call me anytime."

I shook his hand and took the slip of paper. I was beginning to feel a little more comfortable—until I met the teller.

I handed her the slip of paper, and she smiled. "I'll be right back, sir. Do you have a bag?"

I certainly didn't have a bag of any kind. "No, I don't have a bag."

She never missed a beat. "That's no problem, sir. I'll get you one."

She returned with a cart, another teller, and a beautiful leather attaché case. She counted out one hundred ninety thousand dollars, placed the bound stacks of bills inside the case, and slid it across the desk to me.

In a cheerful voice, she said, "If there's anything else you need, Mr. Fulton, just let us know."

"Thank you," I said as I slid the case from the desk. I was surprised how much one hundred ninety thousand dollars in cash weighed.

Before I made it to the door of the bank, Mr. Shepherd appeared and handed me a small, oddly shaped key.

I looked up at him, something I wasn't accustomed to doing. "What's this?"

"This is your key to your safe deposit box here in the bank. I would recommend making use of it before you find a permanent place to live and have a safe installed."

He glanced down at my attaché case and back at the safe deposit box key. He had an excellent point, so I followed him to the vault. He showed me how to work the box, then he left me alone. I counted out one hundred seventy thousand dollars and stacked the banded bills neatly into the box. In the bottom of the box was a small yellow envelope. I picked it up and pulled the card from inside.

Written on the card was: "Nothing good can come of what you're thinking. Forget about the sniper."

It was signed, "Rocket."

14

An Old Friend

How could Dr. Richter have known about her?

I'm not sure if I consciously chose to ignore Dr. Richter's admonition or if I was incapable of heeding it, but either way, I wasn't going to stop thinking about the sniper. He was, of course, correct. I should've banished the thought of her from my mind, but there was no chance of that happening.

I pulled the yacht broker's card from my pocket and found a pay phone.

"Good afternoon. Paradise Charters and Yacht Brokers," came the decidedly Hispanic voice on the other end of the line.

I imagined her sitting behind a curved desk, wearing high heels and a little red sundress, and long, dark hair falling across her shoulders.

Recovering from my little daydream, I said, "Hi, my name is Chase. My banker, David Shepherd, gave me Mr. Fontana's card, and—"

"Hello, Mr. Fulton. We've been expecting your call. Please hold one moment. Dominic will be right with you."

I hoped I'd be able to make a call or show up someplace in the near future without being expected. I was beginning to believe everyone around me knew more about my life than I did. That's when the phone came alive with the voice of a man who was way too happy.

"Chase! Dominic Fontana! I've been waiting for your call. How are you?"

"Fine," I lied. The truth was, I felt confused, anxious, and even a little anxiety over what the coming hours, days, and years of my life would hold.

"Good, good. That's good to hear. Listen, I have an old friend of yours here who'd love to see you. Why don't you come on down?"

"I'll be at your office in thirty minutes."

I couldn't imagine who he was calling an old friend of mine, but just like the rest of my life, I was sure it would be a surprise.

When I arrived at his office, the receptionist looked exactly as I'd imagined, except she was wearing glasses. I hadn't thought of that detail, but the glasses worked nicely for her. I doubted she'd been hired solely for her skill as a telephone operator, but she certainly made the lobby look good. She smiled as I walked through the door and introduced myself. Her lipstick was a little too bright, but outside of that, I couldn't find a flaw.

"Hi, I'm Chase. Is Dominic available?"

Realizing I was still dressed like a bum, I considered apologizing, but that would've sounded awkward and made me look even more ridiculous.

"Hi, Chase. I'm Maria. It's nice to meet you. Dominic's office is straight back. He's expecting you."

I'm not sure what was happening in Heaven the day God made Cuban girls, but He must've been in a very good mood.

When I found my way to Dominic Fontana's office, I knocked, and a gentle voice came from the other side.

"Please come in."

I wasn't expecting what awaited me when I opened the door. I'd expected Dominic to be the typical flashy, used-car-salesman type, but I thought I'd found his grandfather instead. The gentleman behind the door was no Sonny Crockett wannabe. He was a seventy-something, white-haired yacht skipper. He rose with the spry step of a much younger man and extended his tan, weathered right hand.

"Good afternoon, Mr. Fulton. I'm Dominic Fontana. It's nice to meet you. I've heard a lot about you."

Unlike the polished salesman tone he used on the phone, Dominic spoke in a smooth, Southern drawl, making me feel instantly comfortable and right at home.

I shook his offered hand and looked into his experienced eyes. "You're not exactly what I expected when we spoke on the phone."

"Be careful what you expect, Mr. Fulton. Reality is rarely what it appears to be. Now, let's go see that old friend of yours, shall we?"

I played along. "I can hardly wait."

My anxiety and impatience were going through the roof, and I couldn't imagine who he was talking about. I practiced a little self-control and waited patiently for the big surprise. We climbed into Dominic's Range Rover and headed for the marina. I tried to figure out what the afternoon would hold, and I couldn't resist asking about the earlier phone conversation.

"So, Dominic, who did I speak with on the phone earlier, and what was that all about?"

He continued his concentration on the road. "That was me on the phone earlier, Chase. We all have skill sets that make us valuable in unique ways. My skill sets are very much unlike yours. You have youth, strength, and the ability to look down a long black barrel and pull a trigger when most people would tremble in fear. I can't do that." He paused. "More correctly, I can't do that anymore. These days, I just pretend to be different personalities on the telephone to make people believe things that aren't true. I set people on edge or set them at ease depending on what the particular instance calls for. I'm what's called a voice man. I can whisper in your ear and convince you I'm a seventeen-year-old Guatemalan virgin, or I can be a ninety-year-old pervert—and almost anything in between. The day will come when you can't run and jump and dodge bullets anymore, and you'll have to refine your skill set into something a little less physical, but that's a lifetime away for you. Ah! Here we are. Do you remember her?"

When I looked out the windshield, I couldn't believe my eyes. Sitting there, atop a dozen metal stands with a gorgeous new paint job, was *Aegis*, the sailing yacht on which I'd been recruited into that crazy life almost two years before.

"That's Ace's boat." I did my best to hide my excitement.

"Ace isn't with us anymore, my friend. He loved being alive, but the things we love the most are the things that are the most difficult to hold on to. Before he passed, he told a few of us old dinosaurs he wanted you to have *Aegis*. Specifically, he told us, 'If that little son of a gun from Georgia makes it out of The Ranch, ask him if he'll take care of my boat, will ya?'"

I'd given up trying to hold back the tears. I remembered that day off the coast of Jekyll Island when he let me take the wheel. I never imagined I would ever see *Aegis* again, but there she was, sitting right in front of me.

I stepped from the Range Rover and stood in awe of the magnificent yacht. I found a ladder poised at her stern and started up as memories of that day poured over me like rain. Her lines were elegant, and she was welcoming, just like an old friend. I slid my palm against the wheel and almost felt the ship sigh at my touch. I slid back the companionway hatch and lowered myself down into the salon. It had been completely gutted. There was nothing inside, and I was astonished and disappointed. I don't know what I expected, but it certainly wasn't an empty space. As I turned to climb back into the cockpit, I saw Dominic standing there.

"Don't look so grim, my boy," he said in a British accent. "She's awaiting a refit under your direction. There are master carpenters and shipwrights hereabout who'll turn her into whatever you fancy. In my younger days, I was a naval architect for the Brits, you see, so I'll be at your service during the refit. You'll make the old girl a bloody-good skipper, I do say."

I laughed. We shook hands and climbed back down the ladder.

As we nestled back into the luxurious leather seats of his Range Rover, he said, "She's yours, of course, but the yard fees and the refit will have to be paid. I understand you've arranged with David Shepherd for the financing. Is that right?"

"Yes," I said. "I met with him earlier, and he made it clear that I would have whatever I needed. I'm confident he'll be more than willing to foot the bill to get her back in the water. Don't you think so?"

"Indeed, he will," he said with confidence. "I would think we can have the interior and the engine done in a matter of weeks, and she'll be back in the water before you know it."

* * *

The weeks passed quickly, and *Aegis* came together beautifully. Dominic turned out to be an astonishing wealth of knowledge and experience in the design and fitting of the new interior. We even included a nicely concealed safe aboard, as well as an impressive array of electronics. *Aegis* would be more capable of extended sailing than any vessel I'd ever seen. Even though I didn't know much about sailing yachts, it was easy to see she was something special. Her accessories included a desalinization system capable of producing thirty gallons of fresh water an hour, a massive collection of radio equipment allowing me to talk to almost anyone almost anywhere at almost any time. Her engine was a one hundred fifty horsepower Cummins diesel that would push her along at around eight knots in almost any conditions. She was impressive, to say the least.

The day we launched her was a day made in Heaven. The wind blew at twelve knots out of the east, and the sky was as glorious as a Renaissance painting. Beater, Tuner, and Dr. Richter showed up to watch the flag and sails go up again. They even agreed to serve as deckhands on her maiden voyage, under my command, of course. Well, everyone except Beater agreed to that. He agreed to drink, complain, and ride along.

I paid for the yard fee and refit with a cashier's check from David Shepherd, and the harbor master at the marina offered me a slip for a month at no charge, just in case she sprung a leak and had to be hauled back out of the water. I accepted his generous offer and finally moved everything I owned aboard my new home.

There were no leaks and no need to haul her back out, so when my free month reached its end, I fired up the diesel and motored out of the marina. My immediate destination was Key Largo. I would spend a few months there at the Anchorage Resort and Yacht Club on Jewfish Creek. I thought it would be best to stay relatively close to Miami for a while, at least until I was completely confident aboard *Aegis*.

When I reached Anchorage Resort after motoring down Jewfish Creek at high tide, I found my mooring ball and set *Aegis* to rest. I hadn't been at anchor more than ten minutes when my satellite phone chirped. I answered, and my peaceful life aboard my newly refit yacht came crashing down around me.

15

Enter the Gopher

I lifted the satellite phone, pressed the green activation key, and waited for the electronic tone before saying, "Chase."

The voice on the other end was dry and monotonous. Without preamble, the caller asked, "Are you alone?"

"Yes, I'm alone."

The voice responded, "Prepare to be boarded," and the connection went dead.

Although, by education, I'm a psychologist, I don't know why I stared at the phone after it went dead, but that's exactly what happened. I held the bright yellow plastic phone in my hand and bore holes through it with my eyes.

Prepare to be boarded.

Following the mysterious instructions, I left the salon and headed up on deck just as a dinghy with two men aboard motored alongside at *Aegis*'s stern.

I tossed them a line. "Come aboard, gentlemen."

The younger of the two caught the line and made it fast to a cleat on the bow of the small boat. The two men climbed aboard *Aegis*. The younger was clearly more comfortable on the water than the older of the two. I chuckled while watching the older one stumble up the ladder, and I secretly hoped he might end up in the drink.

We shook hands, I offered drinks, and they accepted. While I poured, one of them fired up the stereo and turned it up a little louder than I would've preferred. It occurred to me the purpose of the music was to shield our conversation from any ears that might be within range. I was learning, and at that moment, I was certain I'd never stop learning the craft.

We sat on deck, drinks in hand, and introductions were made. I'm confident they used names that weren't the ones their mothers had given them, but that didn't matter since I doubted the messengers would become fixtures in my life. When the cordials were over, they wasted no time getting to the point of their visit.

Not remembering their made-up names, I decided to label them Thing One and Thing Two in deference to Dr. Seuss.

Thing One, the older man, began the meat of our conversation. "Chase, it's time to go to work. We have an operation for you. Take a look at these."

He handed me a stack of photographs that were clearly taken from a significant distance with an excellent camera. In each of the pictures was a short-haired, thin, wiry, and extremely bucktoothed man in his thirties. In each of the photos, the man wore neither a frown nor a smile. I suppose the terribly unfortunate condition of his exposed front teeth kept him from producing any other expression. He just looked odd, like a cartoon character.

I handed the pictures back to Thing One. "Okay, so who's this character?"

They looked at each other and then back at me.

"He's no character," Thing Two said. "We don't know his real name, but he's known as Suslik."

I ran that name through my mind, trying to come up with its meaning, but it wasn't coming.

Thing Two cracked the first smile of the day. "I thought your Russian was good. Come on, Chase, dig deep. Really chew on it. It'll come to you."

But no matter how much I chewed on it, I couldn't figure it out, so I leapt into the salon and grabbed my Russian-to-English dictionary and thumbed to the S section. "Really, guys? You call this poor guy, Suslik . . . the gopher? That's just cruel."

I tossed the dictionary back on the table and climbed into the cockpit. "So, tell me about our friend, the gopher."

"He's far from our friend, Chase. He's a dangerous man. It's extremely rare to see him outside of Europe, but we've gotten lucky this time. We have intel putting him aboard a yacht in the mouth of the Rio Almendares. The Secret Service, in doing their advance work for the secretary of state's trip to Central America next week, picked up some chatter that Suslik had been contracted to take a shot at the secretary. You see, there's a little bit of bad blood there from the good ol' Cold War days."

"Okay," I said. "So is the Secret Service going to pick him up?"

Both Things smiled. "No, Chase. That's not how it works. The Secret Service doesn't just pick up people like Suslik and question them. Suslik doesn't let himself get picked up. He kills people who try. If he's under contract to shoot the secretary of state, he'll do it, or he'll die trying."

"So, what do we do about it?"

"We make him die trying," they said in unison.

Thing Two said, "Well, actually, *you* make him die trying, Chase. You're going to hop a freighter into the Port of Havana and make your way to an asset we have down there. This asset will take you via fishing boat into the mouth of Rio Almendares, where you'll find Suslik, positively identify him, kill him, and get out of Cuba before Castro gets his hands on you. Simple, right?"

"Oh, sure, simple," I said. "I'm going to sneak into a communist country, kill an assassin, and sneak out before anyone knows I was there. I'll be home in time for dinner."

Thing One handed me an envelope. "Inside this envelope, you'll find a photograph of your Cuban contact and his boat. You'll meet a helicopter at Homestead Air Force Base tomorrow morning at six. The chopper will take you to the Hondial Shanghai, a freighter bound for Havana. You'll make the Port of Havana some time late afternoon or early evening. After that, you're on your own. If you get caught . . . well, don't get caught."

Before I could ask any questions, they headed for the stern and back to their waiting dinghy.

I hurriedly asked, "So how do I get home?"

As Thing Two's head disappeared over the side, he said, "Just run home to Papa, Chase. We'll leave the light on for you."

What does that mean? I should be catching for the Braves, not sneaking into Cuba to kill a gopher.

I spent the next several hours scouring over detailed maps of Havana. I'd commit every detail of the area to memory before I let myself sleep. With my geography lesson complete, I crawled into bed and slept like a baby.

At exactly six o'clock the next morning, Homestead Air Force Base disappeared beneath my feet as the helicopter climbed and turned toward the south and out over the seemingly endless azure water of the Gulf Stream.

When fear and apprehension should've been consuming my mind, my training took over and allowed me to relax and enjoy the ride. I was playing through the upcoming night in my mind, planning as I progressed. There were so many unknowns and so many things that could go wrong. I packed one small backpack containing three liters of water, my dive knife, about a hundred feet of 550 cord, a pair of waterproof binoculars, a waterproof cigarette lighter, a compass, bug spray, and a few changes of clothes. I knew I'd be given provisions aboard the freighter, but my training taught me to be prepared to survive in case I never made it to the next provisioning point. I could survive in almost any temperate climate for a long time with that backpack full of goodies.

The freighter came into view on the horizon and the pilot said, "Three minutes, Chase."

I would soon watch the chopper disappear, leaving me to my own devices aboard the freighter.

"Thirty seconds," I heard through my headset as the pilot brought the helicopter to a hover above the freighter.

I removed my headset and slid the door fully open on its rails and locked it in place. Leaning out the door, I tried to estimate how high we were above the shipping containers. When I'd decided that we were between ten and fifteen feet above the huge metal boxes, I looked over my shoulder at the pilot who was giving me a thumbs-up. I tossed my backpack out the door and watched it land with a thud on a container. I wasn't looking forward to the landing, so I looked back at the pilot, and with a thumbs-down motion, asked if he could get me any lower. He shook his head and pointed out the door emphatically. I sat on the floor with my feet dangling outside the helicopter and pushed off with all my might. I watched the container rise to meet me, and I tucked my knees into my chest, performing a parachute landing fall just as I'd been trained. It worked, and I turned to signal to the pilot that I was all right, but he obviously didn't care. All that was left of the helicopter from my perspective was the tail rotor. He'd turned and flown away in the time it had taken me to reach the container and find my footing.

I slung my pack over one shoulder and climbed down the stack of shipping containers toward the deck of the freighter. When I made it to the deck, I was welcomed by Gunny, the instructor from The Ranch who'd beaten me to a pulp on my first day in training. Remembering how he'd left me pinned between a concrete wall and a filing cabinet, I was glad to be on the same team as him. I never wanted to fight him again.

Through the roar of the wind on the deck, he yelled, "Welcome aboard, Chase. Come on inside, and we'll get you geared up."

He led me through a hatch into the pilothouse and crew quarters, and into a tiny room with one small cot, two footlockers, and a desk. He pulled out a chair from the desk and motioned to the footlocker, so I took a seat. He slid a heavy, plastic Pelican case from beneath the cot and opened it on his lap. He handed me a worn Costa Rican passport with my picture and the name Jason Jones inked inside. The passport had been stamped two days before with a Cuban stamp.

This should come in handy.

"Don't get yourself caught, but if you do, this is your get-out-of-jail-free card," he said with a threatening tone. "Your contact on the ground is Domingo Cruz, a Cuban asset we have in place. You probably remember him as Grey, the truck driver who put you in my lake at The Ranch." A cruel smile crept across his face.

"Ah, yes, I remember him. I'll see if I can return the favor," I said.

"Training is over," he scolded. "We're all on the same team now. Remember that. Grey will keep you alive as long as you don't put him in a position to blow his cover or get him killed. So, here's how this works. You've been trained to do everything this mission will require. You're to verify Suslik is on that yacht. When you're sure it's him, you're to engage and eliminate him without being detected. Then, run like the world is on fire behind you. Trust me. You do not want to be in Cuba when Castro discovers Suslik is dead."

"It all sounds pretty simple right up until that running part. Where will I run? How am I supposed to get home?"

"Don't worry, Chase. We'll leave the light on for you."

Why does everyone keep saying that?

Gunny looked at his watch, then started unloading the Pelican case. He handed me a suppressed Makarov nine-millimeter pistol, a night-vision monocular, two military Meals Ready-to-Eat (MREs), a waterproof bag, and finally, a tiny plastic bag with a white pill inside.

I understood everything he'd given me except the white pill. I held it up and looked back at him.

He swallowed deliberately and looked down at the deck. "Chase, if Suslik or any of his people catch you, they're going to do far worse things to you than we ever did at The Ranch. They'll torture you until you tell them everything you know, and then they'll kill you. You will not escape. These people are pros at making certain of that. If they capture you, don't hesitate. Get this pill down your throat immediately. You'll be dead before they can get your hands tied up. I assure you that you do not want to go into the next life at the hands of those people."

For the first time, I realized the severity of my new reality. I was now an assassin and an expendable asset. That's when it occurred to me that none of this made any sense. I quickly locked eyes with Gunny and demanded, "Why me?"

"What?" he asked. "What do you mean, why you?"

"Why send me to do this? I mean, I'm just a rookie. So far, the only thing I've done is endure your training and watch a horse race. Why not send someone more experienced if this Suslik character is so deadly and important?"

"Grow up, Chase. You're trained for exactly this. You've endured some of the most grueling training on Earth and walked away smiling. Besides, nobody knows you yet. You're our invisible man. Every other operator in the service has a reputation and a picture. Nobody has ever seen you. You could stand in front of Mikhail Gorbachev himself, waving an American flag, and he wouldn't recognize you as a threat. Even if Suslik sees you, he'll run through his card catalog of operatives in his head and your picture won't be there."

He took a drink of coffee from a disgustingly stained cup, then continued. "You'll probably fail. Ninety percent of the operators on Earth would fail, but ninety percent of the operators on Earth would be recognized before they ever got within pistol-shot range of Suslik. We can hide you right under his nose."

I thought about what he said and decided to press the issue no further. "So, on the off chance that I do eliminate him and survive, I've never been to Cuba. How do I get home?"

He took another drink from the filthy cup and looked at the ceiling. "Chase, you don't have a home. You live wherever you are. If you get lucky and actually survive, run for the light. The good ol' Red, White, and Blue will get you out of there."

I was being left in a communist country to accomplish a job that was nearly impossible, with no egress strategy. That told me I was being sacrificed. Whoever was paying me to find, identify, and kill Suslik was expecting me to be captured or killed during the mission. Otherwise, there would be an extraction plan in place. I'd spent most of my childhood on islands and on boats in the Caribbean. I was not going to be a fish out of water. I was finally in my element.

I tossed all the gear he'd given me back into the Pelican case and closed it securely. "Is there anything else?" I asked. "I need to get some sleep before we get to Havana. I've got a long night ahead of me."

16
Catch of the Day

When I awoke from my nap, the sun was low in the western sky and Gunny was shaking my boot. "It's go-time, kid. Get your gear in the dry bag. It's time for you to go for a swim."

I rubbed the sleep from my eyes, stowed my gear in the dry bag, and followed him from the cabin. He led me down several sets of stairs, each darker and rustier than the last, until we reached a compartment near the front of the ship with an open hatch about twenty feet above the waterline.

"You're not scared of heights, are you, kid?" He laughed, then tied a gadget around my left bicep. "This is a locator transmitter. Try to keep it out of the water as much as possible. Grey will be along shortly to pick you up. Enjoy the swim. The sharks are pretty much friendly. Oh, I almost forgot. When you hit the water, kick away from the ship like your life depends on it. You don't want to get tangled up in those propellers."

He disappeared back up the stairs and left me standing there, twenty feet above the water a few miles off the coast of Cuba. I'd been well trained at The Ranch, but they never covered jumping off moving cargo ships. Not knowing what to expect, I stepped from the freighter and accelerated toward the water. With my chin tucked against my chest and my hands over my face to protect my nose and eyes, I hit the water like a missile. I pierced the surface as the dry bag was ripped from my hand, but I'd forgotten to deflate the bag before I leapt. My descent was finally ended by several forceful kicking strokes. I could hear the massive freighter plowing through the water just above me and feel the power of the wake billowing away from the monstrous hull. When my head broke the surface, my dry bag was floating like a cork only a few feet ahead of me.

Plowing through the water until my hand struck the bag, I quickly slid my arm through the sling and continued swimming away from the massive freighter. Having never been in the water in close proximity to a moving freighter, I didn't know what to expect, but I was too busy to be scared. When I finally stopped swimming, I was exhausted, breathless, and alone . . . drifting in the ocean with Havana Harbor only a few miles to the south. The freighter disappeared, and I began the long process of keeping myself calm, afloat, and alive while I waited for Grey's arrival.

Minutes passed like hours as I shivered in the water that had felt warm only minutes before. I'd been taught to survive for extended periods in the water, but even warm water rips heat from a body at a remarkable rate. Staying focused and avoiding my teeth chattering became increasingly difficult as I bobbed in the Florida Straits, using only my inflated dry bag for flotation.

Finally, just when I believed I was going to have to swim to Havana, the sounds of an approaching boat pulled me from my dread. I prayed it was Grey, or Domingo, as he was known in Cuba. When the boat came into view, it was a fishing trawler with nets and cables hanging from every inch of her. She was smoking like a locomotive and listing to starboard as if she were on the verge of rolling over. Although I was glad to see her, she didn't have the look of any boat I would call seaworthy.

The man at the helm was round, dressed in dirty coveralls, and wore a big straw hat. It was impossible to tell if it was Grey; in fact, it was impossible to tell if it was human. He never looked at me. He never reacted to my presence except for dropping a net directly on top of me as he motored past. I grabbed the net, wrapped myself once in the tattered fabric, rolled onto my back, and kept my head above water as much as possible. Just as I thought I might drown while being dragged through the ocean, the fabric of the net tightened, and my weight filled the sagging lines. The fisherman hoisted the net out of the water, and I collapsed onto the deck of the decrepit trawler with a thud, thankful to finally be out of the water.

Without looking at me, the man at the helm said, "Every time I see you, you're trying to drown yourself, kid. How've you been?"

The voice was Grey's, and I was happy to see him.

"Yeah, well, last time, you were the one trying to drown me, but this time, I'm sure glad you came along. It was starting to get a little nippy out there."

"That'll happen. Okay, no more English, gringo. Welcome to Havana," he said in extremely good Cuban Spanish.

I answered, trying to sound like I was from Costa Rica, but my Spanish was undeniably Panamanian, "*Sí señor. Gracias por pasar por mí.*"

He continued only in Spanish. "There's a towel in that box and coffee in the cabin. Dry off, and pour us some. While you're at it, throw that mannequin overboard. Now that you're here, we don't need him anymore."

I found the towel, stripped off my wet clothes, and stepped into the coveralls the mannequin had been wearing. I stuck my feet inside a pair of rubber boots and tossed the mannequin into the water. The air was much warmer than the water, so my shivering stopped, but I was still thankful for the towel and coffee.

I liked the piece of visual deception Grey pulled with the mannequin. If anyone had seen him leaving the port alone and returning with me aboard, he would've had a lot of questions to answer, but with the mannequin onboard, any prying eyes would be expecting him to return with his trusty sidekick.

Between sips of coffee, he said, "Please tell me you have a stamped passport."

I pulled the passport from my dry bag and tossed it to him.

He inspected it closely before tossing it back to me. "Good. Now pull those tarps off that stack."

I did as he instructed, and I was surprised to see hundreds of fish in huge, clear plastic bags lying on the deck.

"Now, spread out that net I caught you in, and roll those bags into the net."

Again, I did as he instructed, and he pulled the lever that operated the hoist, lifting the net back into the air and over the side of the boat. When the net was suspended alongside the boat, he leaned overboard with a huge machete and cut away the plastic bags, letting the water pour out and leaving the fish trapped in the net. He lowered the net back into the water and began to troll back toward Havana.

"Things are rarely as they appear," he said.

We found ourselves near two more fishing trawlers as Grey hauled up the net we already knew was full of fish. The fishermen aboard the other boats barely seemed to notice as we poured the contents of the net onto our deck. The fish went into the hold, and we headed for the mouth of the Rio Almendares.

As we motored into the river, Grey said, "Don't look, but the yacht anchored about a thousand yards to port is your target. The tide will come in tonight, and he'll swing around, bow to sea, and you'll be able to look right up his stern."

It took all of my willpower not to stare at the yacht, but I kept my eyes cast straight ahead and never acknowledged it.

When we tied up alongside the dock, Grey and I went to work unloading the day's catch into giant plastic tubs of ice under the watchful eye of two Cuban soldiers with AK-47s slung across their backs. I never so much as glanced at the soldiers, but I could feel their suspicious eyes burning into my back. I tried not to look like an American sent to kill a Russian assassin aboard a mega yacht less than half a mile away.

"*Toma lo que quieras y lo pagas*," ordered one of the soldiers.

A wrinkled, worn-down old man handed a wad of bills to Grey and pulled three of the best of the day's catch from the ice.

The soldiers then walked away as the tubs were loaded onto a waiting truck that must've been fifty years old.

Grey dragged a wooden dinghy from the dock and onto the deck of our boat, then instructed me to cast off the dock lines. With smoke billowing from the old diesel engine, we motored away from the dock and found Grey's mooring ball in the shallows, about eight hundred yards from the yacht that held my prey.

Grey lifted the dinghy overboard and let it splash into the water. As he climbed overboard into the boat, he said, "Keep your head down. Don't turn on any lights. Don't get caught spying. And for God's sake, don't be here when I show up in the morning." He rowed away, leaving me alone on the decrepit fishing boat.

The first of my MREs claimed to be ham loaf. The loaf part accurate, but there was no evidence of anything resembling ham. Although it tasted like cardboard, I needed the calories, and there was no way to know when I'd eat next.

Just as Grey predicted, the tide came in, turning the yacht on her mooring so the bow pointed out to sea, and the stern pointed up the river, directly toward me. Darkness fully consumed the sky, and thanks to a low, overcast cloud layer, there was little light from the moon. It was the perfect night for spying, and I had the perfect vantage point.

The sounds of the water were familiar, even though I'd never been to that particular spot on the planet. Fish broke the water as they breached in pursuit of floating insects, and crickets chirped in the nearby trees. In addition to all the familiar sounds, the halyards of a nearby sailboat slapped against its mast and made the sound that annoyed every cruiser within earshot who tried to sleep.

From the pilothouse of the aged trawler, I peered through my binoculars toward the yacht. When my eyes adjusted to the darkness and the magnification of the binoculars, four figures came into view on the stern deck. The first two figures were a pair of topless, dark-haired beauties. Their role was clearly to keep the drinks flowing, the cigars lit, and to provide as much affection as the remaining two figures desired.

The third figure was sitting perfectly erect in a deck chair. He wore a tank top that served to frame his bony shoulders and thin, muscular arms. His hair was cropped short, and what remained of a cigarette dangled from the corner of his mouth. A red cherry glowed at the end of the cigarette just before the man pulled the butt from his lips and flipped it overboard. Red sparks flew from the cigarette butt as it arced through the air and across the rail.

The thin man watched the two topless women dance to the rhythmic beat from the yacht's stereo, then he slid forward to the edge of his seat as the taller of the two women writhed seductively between his knees. The woman leaned toward him, giving him full access to her toned body. The man glanced over the woman's shoulder and smiled broadly. When he did so, his obscenely oversized two front teeth shone like a pair of beacons in the night. There was no doubt the man enjoying the lap dance was Suslik—the gopher, and my target.

My heart raced with excitement and anxiety. The first two phases of the four-phase plan were complete. I'd safely been smuggled into Cuba without being detected, and I'd positively identified the target. All that remained was to kill him and run like the wind.

Environmental and situational awareness was pounded into my head with such consistency and force at The Ranch that I knew my reconnaissance was far from complete. Suslik wasn't going anywhere. He was completely enthralled by the mostly naked stripper at his fingertips, so I continued scanning the deck of the yacht. When my gaze fell upon the other man, my heart stopped. I recognized him immediately as Dmitri Barkov, the owner of the most recent Triple Crown winner, Silent Storm.

What sort of coincidence could this possibly be?

No matter how hard I tried, I couldn't stop picturing him in the owner's box at Belmont Park. For a moment, I almost let my mind stray from the task at hand. I never expected to see Barkov again, but there he was, in the flesh, and in the company of the assassin, Suslik.

I immediately hatched a plan.

17

Best Laid Plans

My plan to get close enough to Suslik to take his life was beautiful, even if it was daring and replete with potential to fail. I remembered the sound of the halyard slapping against the mast of the sailboat at anchor in the mouth of the river, and I knew only a rookie sailor would leave his halyard untethered to slap and keep neighboring cruisers awake night after night. The owner of the slapping halyard was most likely ashore drinking and having a great time in Havana.

I scanned the water for drunken boat owners motoring their dinghies from shore to their rattling sailboats. I didn't have to wait long. One particularly intoxicated sailor in an overpowered dinghy bounced off the hulls of several anchored yachts in a clumsy, drunken display of a nautical identity crisis, and finally arrived alongside a forty-foot Beneteau. It appeared the drunkard had finally found his boat after several attempts to board the wrong one. He stumbled up the ladder before loosely tying the dinghy to a cleat at the stern of the Beneteau.

I cut pieces of the 550 cord into lengths of approximately twenty feet each and tied a lasso in two of them. I wound the remaining cord into a tight ball and stuffed my suppressed Makarov pistol and the cord into my dry bag. I crept down the companionway into the belly of Grey's rotten boat and found a set of scuba gear, just as I'd expected. My feet were at least two inches longer than his, so the fins were a poor fit, but I had to make do.

With a set of regulators attached to the tank that was already affixed to the buoyancy compensator, I turned on the air. Thankfully, the gauge showed just over three thousand pounds of air in the tank. I stuck the regulator in my mouth and drew in a breath just to make sure everything worked as it should. My dry bag suddenly seemed too bulky, so I placed my gun inside a bread wrapper, sucked the air from the bag, and tied the wrapper into a knot. The wrapped pistol fit nicely in my right-side pocket on the BCD, and the lengths of the 550 cord found a home on a D-ring on my vest. The ball of cord went into my pocket. With my dive mask snug against my face, the regulator in my mouth, and fins cutting into my feet, I slipped over the stern of the boat and into the black water.

Swimming around the boat, I took a compass bearing on the yacht before descending to the bottom of the river. The incoming tide was far too strong to fight on the surface. The only way I could reach the yacht was to swim or crawl as close to the bottom as possible. When my knees struck the sandy bottom only a few seconds after leaving the surface, I was pleased to feel the strength of the tidal current subside. With my dive light pressed tightly against the face of my compass and shielded by my body so no one on the surface could see, I counted out sixty seconds to let the light charge the luminescence of the compass face. Then I doused my light and tucked it away. Following the compass bearing, I counted kicks as I swam for the yacht.

When I thought I'd swum far enough to be beneath the yacht, I lay on the bottom, holding my breath, listening for the sound of the music and perhaps a generator aboard the luxurious vessel overhead. I thought I could faintly hear the thumping of the stereo, but I wasn't certain, so I decided the best plan would be to swim to a point I knew would be in front of the yacht, and then surface silently to get my bearings without being seen. The lights of the houses and shops in the mouth of the river would be behind the yacht, painting it in silhouette if I were on the ocean side of the vessel, so I continued to swim on my original course until I was confident I was well beyond the yacht's position. By cupping my hand over my compass, I deflected some of its light onto my depth gauge. It read seven feet. That didn't make any sense. I had to be deeper than seven feet. The yacht had to draft at least five or six feet, so if I was only seven feet deep, I would've run into the keel of the yacht. Then it hit me. The gauge was graduated in meters, not feet.

When will I stop making these rookie mistakes?

I pulled the deflator on the left side of my buoyancy compensator, sure to release any air still trapped inside. Any air that may have been trapped inside the BC would almost double in volume as I rose the seven meters to the surface, turning the BC into a cork and leaving me floating like a balloon. With all the air out of the BC, I gently pressed my fins into the soft bottom of the river and cautiously rose toward the surface. Exhaling steadily as I ascended was essential. A lung overexpansion injury would put a damper on my plans for the remainder of the evening.

My timing was perfect. As soon as I felt the top of my head break the surface of the water, I exhaled my last drop of air. I pulled the regulator from my mouth, making sure it didn't free flow and give away my position. With only the top half of my head above the water, I looked back up the river as my eyes adjusted to what little light there was on the surface. The beautiful sight of the bow of the yacht blossomed right in front of me.

Since there didn't appear to be a lookout on the bow of the yacht, I relaxed and let the incoming tide carry me back to the vessel rather than descending and using more of the air in the scuba tank.

When I drifted into the anchor chain, I descended down the chain until I reached the anchor that was nicely seated into the sandy bottom. I pulled the ball of 550 cord from my pocket and tied one end to the anchor chain just above the shackle with a bowline. Rigging lines and tying knots underwater with plenty of light is challenging enough, but in the dark, it's nearly impossible. I prayed I'd tied the bowline correctly by feel alone. Then I loosened the bolt on the shackle that connected the chain to the anchor until it was barely holding in place. I swam back to the belly of the yacht and wrapped the 550 cord around the propeller shaft several times before descending again to the anchor to loop the cord back through the anchor chain. I repeated the process until I'd exhausted my stash of cord, making several loops between the prop shaft and the anchor. I hoped the cord was strong enough to help accomplish my desired result.

With that done, I swam as hard as I could back to the bow of the yacht, then several more yards toward the open ocean. When I was confident I was far enough away, I surfaced again and took a compass bearing to the Beneteau holding the drunken sailor. With the bearing set on the compass, I descended back to the bottom and let the mild current carry me toward my destination.

Reaching the Beneteau, I surfaced and pulled myself aboard the dinghy still loosely tied to the stern. The inflatable dinghy was trailing behind the sailboat by seven or eight feet in the tide, but the tide was beginning to weaken. I lay as close to the floor of the inflatable dinghy as I could while removing my scuba gear, then pulled my Makarov out of the bread wrapper and stuck it under the edge of the plastic fuel tank. I pulled one of the lassos from the D-ring on the BC and tied the free end to a cleat on the bow of the dinghy. I then tucked the remaining lengths of cord through a belt loop on my pants for easy access.

I sat on the floor of the dinghy and caught my breath while I played the plan over in my mind. I had one chance to get it right. If everything didn't go perfectly, I would end up dead and adrift in the mouth of the Rio Almendares, less than ninety miles from America.

To my surprise, the painter line fell slack. The incoming tide had reached its high mark and would soon start back out, but until it did, the mouth of the river was at slack tide with almost no current. That was the perfect time to make my move. I tugged on the painter, pulling the dinghy toward the sailboat, then I slipped the line off the cleat and tossed it into the floor as I pushed off the hull of the Beneteau.

The outboard motor sprang to life on the first pull, and I immediately slid the motor into gear and opened the throttle, hoping, for the first time, to get the attention of everyone on Barkov's yacht. When I glanced toward the yacht, no one was looking my way, so I created a little more action. I flew between Grey's fishing boat and Barkov's yacht, and threw a rooster tail of water into the air behind the dinghy. At the last second, I turned the dinghy sharply toward Grey's boat and plowed into the side of the old trawler with more energy than intended, and the sudden stop threw me forward onto the bow of the dinghy. Fortunately, I didn't hit my head. That would've been a disaster.

At that moment, I remembered my old friend, the voice man in Miami, and I hatched a new addition to my plan. Trying my best to sound like a miserable, sleepy fisherman, I yelled in Spanish, "What's wrong with you?" I then answered myself, trying to sound as drunk as possible. I slurred, "I'm sorry, señor. I can't find my boat, and my wife's gonna kill me."

Stumbling back to the stern of the dinghy, I found the tiller and throttle with one hand and peeked over my shoulder at the huge yacht only a few hundred feet away. My act had done the trick. Everyone aboard the yacht was staring straight at me. Not only were they staring, but they were laughing uproariously at the drunken, wayward husband playing bumper boats. I had their full attention, so I turned the dinghy out to sea and headed out the mouth of the river as fast as the outboard would push me, roaring past the yacht and disappearing under its bow. When I believed Barkov and Suslik had time to return to their seats and have their glasses refilled, I roared around the bow of the yacht and down the starboard side, appearing to be completely out of control. I let my head slump down as if I were unconscious, but in reality, I was as rigid as I'd ever been. Every muscle in my body was tense, and I shoved my feet beneath the seat in front of me, preparing for what was about to happen.

When I was thirty yards behind the yacht, I thrust my body forward, pretending to have passed out over the controls, and shoved the tiller handle hard over until the dinghy was headed straight for the swim platform of the yacht. When the men aboard the yacht realized I was going to collide with their boat, they rose from their seats, shoved the women out of the way, and ran to the stern. Each man yelled in Russian, but I couldn't hear them over the scream of the outboard motor.

Just before the bow of the dinghy struck the swim platform, I shoved the motor into reverse, raised my pistol, aimed at Barkov, and yanked the trigger.

I'd fired well over a million rounds of ammunition in the past two years of my life by properly squeezing the trigger. I'd never yanked a trigger, but I'd never fired at a Russian mobster from a rubber dinghy in the middle of the night in Havana, either.

Barkov's left shoulder exploded as the round penetrated the flesh just outside of his collarbone. I hadn't killed him, but he was certainly incapable of putting up a fight with his shoulder blown apart. With one fluid motion, I retrained my pistol on the outboard motor of the yacht's dinghy hanging from davits above my head and fired two rounds through the motor, completely disabling it.

I scanned the rail of the yacht for more targets, and I was surprised to find no one else on deck other than the two terrified, half-naked girls, and Suslik. He reacted as he realized the whole charade was a ruse and lunged backward away from the rail, but I had the element of surprise on my side. I launched the lasso of the 550 cord high into the air just as the dinghy made contact with the yacht. Everything seemed to happen in slow motion. The lasso flew through the air and fell over Suslik's head as he powered backward, cursing in Russian.

The instant the lasso found its mark around his neck, I opened the throttle again with the motor in reverse. The slack in the line disappeared as the makeshift noose drew tight against the flesh of Suslik's neck. I thought for a moment the man's head might come off, but that didn't happen. He was faster and much more resourceful than I anticipated. In one explosive moment, he wound his arm around the cord and grasped the line in his bony grip. The flesh of his arm absorbed most of the force of the cord as the dinghy and I powered backward away from the yacht. Suslik soared over the rail of the yacht and flew through the air toward me.

I had the advantage for the moment, so I took an instant to scan the deck of the yacht one last time. Barkov stumbled through the door and into the interior of the yacht. Almost nothing was going as I'd planned. Suslik's head hadn't come off, Barkov was still alive, and the gopher was flying through the air toward my dinghy.

Suslik's body disappeared beneath the bow of my dinghy with a massive splash. It occurred to me that if he'd grasped the cord well enough, he might still be conscious and capable of pulling himself aboard the dinghy. An angry gopher was the last thing I needed in my boat, so I devised a new plan to quicken his soul's departure from his bucktoothed body.

Without reducing the throttle, I yanked the motor out of reverse and forced it into forward. The dinghy lunged forward with impressive agility, and the lasso cord come tight under the bow. I wondered if Suslik's body would create enough drag to pull the bow underwater and swamp the dinghy. I quickly did the math. The cord was about twenty feet long. A little less than two feet made up the noose. He'd probably wrapped at least a foot of the cord around his arm, and I'd tied at least a foot of the free end to the bow cleat. That left around sixteen feet of cord between Suslik and the bow of the dinghy. I estimated the rubber boat was twelve feet long, and the bow was almost two feet above the waterline. I smiled as I realized I'd accidentally cut exactly the correct length of cord to accomplish my kill. As my smile reached its zenith and the cord reached its limit, the propeller of the outboard motor struck something human. Despite his valiant effort to survive my attack, the propeller tore through Suslik's spine and left the pulverized remains of the legendary Russian assassin spewing into the mouth of the Rio Almendares.

Phase three was complete. Suslik was dead. I hoped I hadn't chipped the propeller on his buckteeth. All that remained was to run for home. I lunged forward with my dive knife firmly in my right hand and cut the cord from the bow cleat so the 550 cord wouldn't get wound around my propeller and kill the outboard. That little boat was my only hope for escape.

The engines of the yacht roared to life, and I watched the anchor chain start its rise from the murky water. When Barkov's hired captain shoved the transmission into gear to chase me, I knew my plan was going to work.

The multiple loops of 550 cord I rigged between the anchor chain and the propeller shaft of the yacht wrapped around the shaft at remarkable speed. As soon as the cord came taut, the shackle I'd sabotaged surrendered and set the chain free from its connection to the anchor. Without the additional weight of the buried anchor, the wrapping cord pulled the chain directly into the exposed shaft. When the cord had wound as tightly as it could, the bulky, whipping anchor chain began to wrap itself around the shaft and slap the hull of the yacht. It took no more than two seconds for the chain to shake the propeller shaft from its through-hull, water-tight bearings and tear several massive gashes into the hull. The yacht immediately took on water, flooding first the engine room, and then everything else below the waterline.

18
Run Like the Wind

With Suslik's corpse strewn about the mouth of the river, the time had come to accomplish phase four of my plan: run like the wind. I lay in the belly of the inflatable boat, as close to the deck as possible, and opened the throttle. The power of the outboard motor accelerated the dinghy across the smooth surface of the brackish harbor.

The surface of the water took on a light chop as I left the mouth of the river and entered the ocean. I hadn't actually given a great deal of thought to this phase of my plan. I had no idea where I was running, but I wanted to be as far away from Barkov's yacht as possible. My borrowed dinghy didn't have the fuel or tenacity to make the ninety-mile passage to Key West, but there were a lot of boats near Havana that could easily make it. As I bounced across the water, a plan began to form in my adrenaline-charged mind.

I'd expected my first actual kill to be far more psychologically challenging. Killing the instructor on my first day at The Ranch was different from what I'd done to Suslik. That had been an accident, and I was acting in what I believed was self-defense. My latest kill was malicious and intentional. I should've been experiencing some degree of guilt, but there was none. All I could feel was the desire to escape the waters of communist Cuba.

I headed southwest toward Marina Hemingway. "Run home to Papa" is what Thing Two said back in Key Largo.

There's only one Papa . . . Papa Hemingway.

I'd done it. Not only had I killed Suslik, but I'd also survived. All that remained was piecing together a getaway. I kept my head down and the throttle open as I roared down the shallow coastline, hoping to disappear before the sun rose. The mouth of the Rio Jaimanitas came into view, and Marina Hemingway was the next inlet. I powered on, but to my horror, a pair of patrol boats with spotlights slicing through the darkness came plowing out of the mouth of the river. One turned to the southwest, but the other turned directly toward me.

I should've panicked, but I didn't have time. I simply rolled off the throttle and let the inflatable come to rest, bobbing on the sea. If I hadn't stopped, the soldiers on the patrol boat would've cut me in half with the deck gun. I closed my eyes and whispered to whatever god hears the prayers of an assassin. I feared it might be Saint Murphy who heard my prayer because it was certainly time for something to go wrong, and the patrol boat unequivocally qualified as something going wrong.

I shielded my eyes with my hands against the cutting beam of the spotlight as the patrol boat approached and came to idle only feet from the bow of my dinghy. A voice come over a crackling loudspeaker, asking, "*¿Señor, has visto el accidente de avión?*"

I said a silent "thank you" to St. Murphy . . . or whomever. The soldier had just asked if I'd seen the plane crash.

In my best Spanish, I tried to sound disinterested. "No, sir. I'm just going to get my fishing boat. What plane crash?"

The soldiers never heard a word I said after "No." The man at the wheel forced the throttles full forward and powered around me, nearly swamping my trusty little borrowed dinghy. I kept her afloat and restarted the motor, but I was still blind from the spotlight. I kept my eyes squinted, almost shut, and continued southwestward toward the marina. Perhaps five minutes into my slow progress, I was able to pick out objects on the shoreline and even the silhouettes of a few boats on the water as my night vision slowly returned.

One boat in particular caught my attention as I motored ever closer. It appeared to be sitting still and pointed out to sea. A faint flashing light glowed a few feet above the waterline on the starboard side. The faint flashes were coming in patterns, sequences of short flashes followed by longer ones.

The flashes came—short-long-pause-short-pause-long-long-short-pause-short-short-pause-short-short-short—and then several seconds of nothing, followed by the same pattern again and again. It finally occurred to me that it was Morse code. I squinted and watched the flashes closely until I could finally put it all together. The signaler was saying, "*AEGIS*," the name of my boat back in Key Largo.

Having been trained to believe almost everything is a trap, I proceeded with extreme caution as I approached the signaling vessel. When I pulled within a hundred yards of her, I peered over the bow of my dinghy with my Makarov in my left hand and my right foot on the outboard tiller. I didn't want to give anyone on the vessel a broad target by exposing my head or body above the dinghy's inflatable sides. Suddenly, the signaling stopped, and the light went dark. A few seconds later, the light returned, but this time it was shielded by what appeared to be a cloth of some kind. It was blue, white, and red.

"Run for the light. The good ol' Red, White, and Blue will get you out of there," is what Gunny had said seconds before I stepped from the freighter. Thank you, Gunny!

I relaxed and took a deep breath for the first time in hours. The light was shining through a miniature American flag. I opened the throttle and powered toward the vessel. Before I came alongside, I closed the throttle to idle and watched carefully as Grey's round, tan face came peering over the rail.

From beneath his floppy straw hat, he whispered, "Get up here, gringo."

I tossed him a line and climbed aboard. Before my feet hit the deck, he asked, "Did you do it?"

His eyes were wide and expectant, so I started telling him the story of the past several hours, but he cut me off before I could start the second sentence.

"Did you do it or not?" he demanded.

"Yeah, I did it. Suslik is dead, and the fish in the mouth of the Rio Almendares are feasting on what's left of him."

He slapped me on the back. "Great job, Chase. Great job. Now, get up Elbow Cay. You'll meet some old friends there. They'll have a surprise for you. Go! Go!"

With that, he slipped the painter line and leapt over the rail, landing in my dinghy. He never looked back as he motored away into Marina Hemingway.

I took the helm of the cruiser and fired up the twin diesels. I checked my fuel quantities, oil pressure, and temperatures before gently pressing the throttles forward and feeling the boat accelerate.

I turned due north to put as much distance between me and the Cuban coastline as possible before turning northeast for Elbow Cay. Running without lights seemed to be the best plan. That would give me a couple of hours before the sun showed itself on the eastern horizon. If I'd done my nautical geography correctly, Elbow Cay was about a hundred twenty miles from Havana. That would take me between nine and ten hours at my current speed. Turning the GPS on before daybreak might illuminate the pilothouse with the light from the screen, so I motored on using only the compass. My watch reported just past one o'clock in the morning. I'd be on Elbow Cay before noon if I didn't get caught.

There isn't much to do at night at the helm of a powerboat in calm seas except scan for other boats. I locked the wheel in place and watched the ocean around me. Two cruise ships and eight freighters were all I saw in the five hours before the sun peeked over the horizon. I'd never been more thankful to see a sunrise.

The GPS came to life at the touch of a button, and it took several minutes for it to find enough satellites to determine where I was, but it finally depicted my location, first in extremely large scale. The coast of Cuba loomed to the south with the tip of Florida to the north. I found the zoom button and pressed it several times until I could no longer see either coastline, but what I could see was Elbow Cay. I'd committed an unforgivable sin of nautical navigation—I'd failed to consider wind and current in my speed calculation. The roaring current of the Florida Straits had hurled me northeastward at over twenty knots, leaving me less than an hour from my destination.

The hour passed peacefully except for the sounds of the engines and the water rushing past the hull. I loved both sounds, but as the adrenaline wore off, my body and mind demanded sleep. As I tried to shake the heaviness from my eyelids, the thought of money came to my mind. I wondered how much I'd be paid for what I'd done. I never asked, and no one had ever mentioned a number.

As I drew near Elbow Cay, the silhouettes of several motor yachts and sailboats at anchor a few hundred feet off the Cay came into sight. Motoring into the anchorage, I couldn't believe my eyes. Lying there, at anchor, with an American flag flying in the rigging, was *Aegis*. I pulled binoculars from their nest at the helm and seated them against my cheeks. As *Aegis*'s deck came into focus, I saw two men looking back at me through binoculars of their own. The younger of the two gave me a subtle thumbs-up sign, and I immediately recognized them as Thing One and Thing Two, the duo who'd delivered my assignment aboard my boat two days earlier.

I tossed three fenders over the starboard rail and gently nestled my temporary vessel alongside *Aegis*. I tossed a bowline and a stern line to Thing One, and he secured them to cleats. Protocol demanded that I ask for permission to come aboard, but *Aegis* was my boat, so I leapt the rail with ease and landed gently on the deck. Neither man said a word as they stepped across the rail and aboard my getaway ride. Before I could say anything, Thing Two pointed at the lines holding the two vessels together, so I cast off and tossed the lines aboard. As the lines landed on deck, the powerful diesels roared, and the pair motored away, disappearing to the southwest.

I wondered where they were going, but I suppose it didn't matter. I'd pulled off my first professional assignment without a hitch. The target was dead, and I'd escaped unscathed.

19
Island

My sleep was dreamless and perfect. I should've felt at least some degree of remorse for taking another human life for a price, but that remorse never came. The psychologist in me was concerned, and even a little frightened, that I had the capacity to be so cold. I tried to approach the self-analysis as if I were interviewing a patient and asked myself the same psychobabble questions.

"How did it make you feel when you shot a Russian mafia boss in the shoulder?"

In true schizophrenic fashion, I answered. "I wish I'd been a better shot and hit him in the face instead of the shoulder."

"But Barkov wasn't your target, so do you regret shooting him?"

"No, not at all. He may not have been my target, but he was an obstacle between my target and me, so I eliminated the obstacle."

"Interesting." Then I asked myself, "Do you think Barkov survived the shoulder wound?"

That's when I realized I'd made the worst possible mistake, short of getting caught or killed. I'd let a witness survive. Not only was he a witness, but he was an extremely powerful, vengeful, and wealthy witness who had no fear of the law and almost limitless resources. Barkov had surely survived the shoulder wound, and if he could identify me, he'd be coming after me with everything he had.

My self-psychotherapeutic counseling session ended abruptly, and I began to play the events of the previous night over in my mind.

Did Barkov see my face? Was he sober enough to identify me? Did I leave any evidence at the scene that could be used to identify me?

Other than Barkov seeing my face, I couldn't think of anything I'd done or overlooked that could make it possible for anyone to determine I'd been in Cuba.

Distance was my friend, so I fired up *Aegis*'s engine, weighed the anchor, and motored away from Elbow Cay as the evening sun was making its plunge into the sea behind me. The consistent southwesterly wind and the Gulf Stream would make for excellent conditions for sailing eastward toward The Bahamas. Other than distance from Havana, I had no particular destination in mind.

I slid an old Jimmy Buffett tape into the stereo and listened as "Island" began to play. I've always found it interesting how song writers are capable of writing lyrics that are so poignant and prophetic for so many people they'll never meet. I don't know if Jimmy smoked exactly the right amount of ganja or one lid too much, but with the lyrics of that song, he'd cracked open my skull and taken a peek inside.

I felt exactly like an island. I wondered if there were no other men on Earth exactly like me. Was I truly alone in the world? Mysterious people flashed into my life at unpredictable intervals and vanished just as quickly. My family was dead. My home was forty-five feet of teak and fiberglass that bobbed up and down at the will of the ocean. I was alone, but just as Jimmy said, unlike that island, heart and soul accompaniment seems to make me different. I wanted a hand to hold and a heart to love. I wanted to share my fears and doubts with someone who'd listen and care, even if she didn't understand. I wanted to do the same for her. I wanted to feel the delicate skin of a woman as we fell asleep every night. I longed to feel her breath on my shoulder as we slept. I yearned to taste her lips on mine when we could make the world disappear and get lost in each other's bodies and souls. Dr. Richter called a wife and family a burden in this line of work. Perhaps he was right, but that didn't diminish my desire to find a woman who could make me forget that I was just an expendable weapon for rent.

The lyrics of the old Buffett song warned of torn sails and broken oars and seemed to echo Dr. Richter's warning. Is that what would happen to me if I tried to approach a real relationship? I was beginning to think it might be worth risking a few torn sails and a broken oar to find out.

There had been no shortage of young coeds back at Georgia. I'd been a prominent athlete, so the rewards of staying in prime physical condition, hitting more than my share of homeruns, and wearing tight white pants on the baseball field were grand when measured by the standard of the average college student. Girls came and went, but my interest in the next girl tended to deplete my affection for the previous one, so in my four years at UGA, I never had an enduring, meaningful relationship.

The bonds I'd built with my teammates should've been bonds that lasted a lifetime, but I'd seen to the destruction of those after my accident. I couldn't bear the anxiety and angst associated with continuing relationships with the other members of the team. Watching those who were talented enough to be drafted to play professional baseball filled me with envious rage and left me to be an outsider. I wouldn't dare blame any of them for my exile. Any separation and isolation I experienced was entirely self-imposed. Sometimes the self-imposed punishments are the most brutal.

The deeper the feelings of loneliness ran, the more I dreamed of the sniper. I knew nothing about her beyond what I'd seen through my binoculars at Belmont Park, but I was drawn to her by some force, real or imagined, that pulled my soul toward her like the wind in *Aegis's* sails pulled me seaward. I had no idea how I would ever find her, or if I would ever see her again, but I prayed that fate, chance, dumb luck, or divine intervention would soon creep its way onto my island and deliver the beautiful blonde sniper into my arms.

20
Ghosts

Charlotte Amalie on the Island of St. Thomas would be my destination. It would give me a nice long voyage and plenty of time to think while also falling off the edge of the Earth for at least three weeks, as far as Dmitri Barkov was concerned. I would sail northeast around The Bahamas and Eleuthera Islands to put some ocean and a few rocks between Cuba and me before heading southeast for the Virgin Islands.

The voyage took a little longer than I expected. I blame rum and beach parties for the bulk of the delays, but in all honesty, I think it was the escape from the rest of the world I enjoyed most. I took my time, never got in a hurry, and enjoyed every mile of the journey. On the tenth day of my trip, I sent my passport with the Cuban immigration stamp, tied to a lead weight, to the bottom of the ocean in just over nine hundred feet of water. I couldn't afford to have it turn up. Small details like that can have a nasty bite when they show up at inopportune moments.

When I finally arrived in the anchorage off Charlotte Amelie, I set my anchor in twelve feet of clear blue water. I planned my final day of the journey so I'd arrive midmorning and at high tide. It was one of those postcard-perfect days. The wind was warm and consistent at just over ten knots, and the ocean was calm and welcoming. *Aegis* performed like a battleship and never offered a moment's trouble. My first solo mission was a success.

My first solo long-distance cruise was flawless. I feared it was time for a train wreck. Things just couldn't continue to flow as smoothly as they had over the past few weeks.

Since St. Thomas is a U.S. territory, I didn't have to check in with immigration. I was thankful for that little blessing, and made my way ashore to find a rum drink and a nice hammock in the shade. The rum drink was easy, but the hammock was a bit of a challenge. I opted, instead, for a wooden barstool in a small bamboo hut overlooking the sea. The rum flowed, and life couldn't get any better. That's when I caught my first glimpse of *her*.

The golden blonde hair glistened in the midday sun as she strolled along the shoreline with her sandals dangling loosely from her left hand. She was tall, perfectly toned, and graceful. She wore a flowing white cotton shirt draped off her shoulder and blowing lightly in the breeze. Beneath the open shirt was an orange bikini top that fit her toned figure as if it were part of her flawless skin. A pair of perfectly short cutoff blue jeans clung to her hips and offered the slightest hint of the curve of her bottom. Her jawline was sharp and her cheekbones exquisite. I watched as she slowly tilted her head skyward as if to soak in the warmth and beauty of the perfect Caribbean sun. The way her hair danced on the wind, and how her inviting smile shone perfectly on her face was more beautiful than words can describe. I was instantly mesmerized by her grace, and more than anything, her familiarity.

My heart pounded in my chest, and my mind raced with a million thoughts and one terrible fear. If the girl on the beach was the sniper from Belmont Park, she certainly wasn't there by accident. There's never been a coincidence that incredible. More likely, the girl on the beach bore a striking resemblance to the sniper I'd seen from a thousand yards away through the lenses of my binoculars, but it certainly couldn't be her. My mind was imploding as I tried to process the possibility of it actually being her. If she were the sniper, she'd been dispatched by Barkov to find, identify, and kill me—just like I had done to Suslik.

I was unable to look away. Every ounce of me was captivated by her, and I wished I hadn't had so many rum drinks. Maybe I could've thought more clearly and figured it out, or maybe if I were sober, I wouldn't have imagined some random blonde on the beach was the woman I'd been dreaming of for months. It had to be a case of hopeful mistaken identity.

As I turned back to the bar to order another drink, I was greeted by my second ghost of the day. Sitting beside me, in a Pineapple Willy's hat, tropical print shirt completely unbuttoned, cutoff cargo pants, and a pair of sandals was none other than Dutch. The implosion my mind was experiencing immediately became an explosion, and I shook my head in disbelief.

Before I could react, Dutch pounded on the bar. "Hey, I think my buddy here needs another drink. Fix him up, why don't you?" He turned to me as if he'd never seen me before. "Hey. My name's Scott. How you doin'? You look like you've just seen a ghost. Are you all right, partner?"

I tried to gather my wits and pretend to understand what was going on around me, but I did a miserable job of both. I stammered, "Uh, I'm ah . . . what are you—"

"I'm here on vacation, down from Panama City Beach. This place sure beats the heck out of the Redneck Riviera, if you know what I mean. How about you, fella? What brings you down here?"

I was still confused, and I questioned if the man sitting beside me really was Scott from Panama City.

Is it just a day of unthinkable coincidences, or am I suddenly believing everyone around me looks like mysterious and familiar characters from my not-so-distant past?

When the blender behind the bar came to life, belting out its grinding, whirring song, "Scott" leaned in close and whispered, "Relax, kid. Have another drink. Pretend you've never met me, and enjoy yourself. We've got a lot to talk about, but we'll get to that soon enough."

In time with his speech, the blender stopped whirring and another daiquiri landed on the bar in front of me. As soon as the drink came to rest on the bar, Scott said, "Hey, man. Set me up with one of those, and put his on my tab, will ya?"

"Sure thing, buddy," the bartender said. "Whatever you say. Wanna make it a double?"

Without hesitation, my new friend said, "Why not? Keep 'em coming."

Scott spun around on his barstool, leaned back, and placed his elbows on the bar. "Sure is a pretty place, ain't it?"

I swallowed a third of my drink and assumed the same pose. I reached into my pocket, produced a pair of Cuban Cohibas, and offered him one.

"Care for a cigar, Scott?"

"Don't mind if I do." He reached for the perfectly wrapped stogie, then pulled a golf tee from behind his ear and punched a hole in the end of the cigar while I pressed my Xikar punch into mine. He watched me work the punch into the leaf. "That sure is a fancy tool you got there for poking a hole in your cigar. My ten-cent golf tee seems to do the same job. How about a light?"

I produced my lighter, and he rolled the tip of his cigar into the flame with an expert hand. What an actor he was. I chuckled, reclaimed my lighter, and watched the flame kiss the wrapper of my Cohiba. As always, the cigar lit perfectly, and a cloud of white smoke rose around our heads.

After two deep draws, Scott inspected his cigar. "Not bad, kid. Not bad at all."

We sat drinking, smoking, and watching tourists for an hour without saying more than two dozen words to each other. Finally, when the Cohiba had become a nub, he ground it out against the leg of his stool and tossed the butt into the sand.

"Well," he said, "I reckon I'd better get back to the bungalow. Momma's gonna be wondering where I ran off to. You ought to stop by later for a drink. I'm in the green one with big red butterflies all over it. You can't miss it. Come on by."

It wasn't a cordial invitation. It was instructions, and perhaps even orders. I'd definitely be spending some time in the butterfly bungalow later, but before that, I'd be scouring the beach for my Russian sniper look-alike. If I couldn't have the real thing, I'd have to settle for an imposter.

* * *

My search for her was a complete failure, but I wasn't giving up hope. When I knocked on the door of Dutch's bungalow, it swung open about a foot, and I could hear the shower running and Dutch singing an old Michael McCloud song . . . badly. I made myself at home and poured a pair of drinks.

When he arrived in the front room of the bungalow, his hair was still wet, and his eyes were bloodshot—presumably from the soap, or perhaps not.

I handed him a drink. "So, how did you find me?"

He swallowed a long drink, then looked at the glass with curiosity. "Finding people is what I do, kid. You really messed up in Cuba. I guess you figured that out by now, huh?"

I hadn't wanted to accept that fact, but he was correct. Letting Barkov see me was nothing short of stupid, and I knew it. Now I was going to have to listen to Dutch beat me down for being such an idiot. I deserved the verbal lashing, but it didn't come; instead, he laid out a list of the things I'd done correctly.

With obvious pride, he said, "You did a hell of a job of thinking on your feet and adapting to a volatile environment. That thing you did with the anchor chain was a masterpiece. Even I wouldn't have thought of that one. And your decision to pulverize Suslik instead of shooting him? That was genius. Pure genius. You're definitely on the road to becoming a master in this little art of ours, but you did make one mistake."

"I know," I said, "I let Barkov see me, and I didn't kill him. I just winged him with a pretty terrible shot."

"No!" he said. "That's not it at all. Barkov was too drunk and too surprised by the muzzle flash to see you. It wasn't him. It was the hookers who saw you. I don't know where they were while you were shooting Barkov and trying to yank Suslik's head off, but they sure got a look at you. Oh, and Barkov didn't die, by the way, but I'm sure you already knew that."

I hadn't known, but I assumed he wouldn't die from a small-caliber shoulder wound.

"Okay, so the girls saw me, and Barkov is still alive. What does that mean to me?"

He headed for the kitchen. "You want another?"

"No, no. I'm good, thanks," I said as he refilled his glass. I wondered how bad things were going to get. Then, out of the blue, I said, "She's here, Dutch."

"What? Who's here? What are you talking about?" He looked at me as if I knew more than he wanted me to know.

I lowered my head. "The sniper from Belmont. The one who blinded the horse. She's here. I saw her on the beach today, just before you showed up at the bar."

"No way, kid." He swallowed a long drink. "You're just paranoid, and maybe a little horny. There's no way she's here. She was just some low-level nobody. She's no threat. You're seeing things. Besides, you told me you didn't get a good enough look to pick her out again. Have another drink. It ain't as bad as you think."

I started to protest, but he was probably right. I wanted to see her so badly that my eyes were fooled into believing the woman on the beach was the Russian sniper.

"Here's the deal, kid. You've been spotted, but the good news is it was dark, you were moving quickly, and shooting. Considering all of those factors, it would be almost impossible for anyone, especially two drunk, scared hookers, to put together an accurate composite sketch. The bad news is, they do have a rough idea of what you look like. Did you stand up at any point during the attack?"

I tried to put the pieces together in my head and remember everything I'd done, but I couldn't remember ever standing up. I had intentionally stayed low in the dinghy to not only keep my balance, but to provide less of a target if someone started shooting.

"No. I'm sure I never stood up."

"That's good," he said. "You're a tall guy. If they never saw you standing up, they have no way to know how tall you are. In the dark, there's nothing unique enough about you, other than your height, to distinguish you from a hundred other would-be Suslik killers. His list of enemies is long and distinguished. Oh, and let me tell you that you're a hero in their world. You pulled off an op on one of the top three assassins in the world. I gotta tell you, a lot of people were betting against you, but you showed 'em."

I tried not to react, but remaining stoic was becoming more and more challenging.

"So, here's what we're going to do. You surprised a lot of important people, so you're my boy now. I'm now your handler."

"What does that mean?" I asked.

"It means you work for me now. It means it's my job to get you the jobs that pay the best, and it's my job to keep you alive. You're gonna be a star, Chase."

I considered what he'd said and wondered if he'd assigned himself as my handler or if it had come from whoever we worked for. I remembered what Dr. Richter said about Dutch. *"He does it for the money now, and that's a shame."*

"So, about the money. How much did I make for killing Suslik?"

He looked at me, astonished, as if I'd said I was Hitler's grandson. "What do you mean how much did you make? Are you serious? You don't know?"

"No," I said. "I have no idea. Two guys just showed up on my boat, showed me some pictures, and told me to go kill the Russian. It never occurred to me to ask about the money."

He stood again and quickly headed into the kitchen, but he returned shortly with a bottle of rum, refilled my glass, and topped his off again.

"You're not going to believe this, kid, but there was a ten-million-dollar bounty on Suslik's head. That makes you a rich man, my friend. A very rich man, indeed."

My glass fell from my fingertips and crashed onto the floor of the bungalow. Shards of glass, crushed ice, and crystal-clear rum exploded at my feet, but I never heard a sound. He was right—I didn't believe him. There was no way I'd just earned ten million dollars for one night's work—work that I actually enjoyed.

I mumbled, "So, are you telling me I have ten million dollars now?"

He ignored the puddle of rum and glass on his floor. "No, don't be silly. It cost over a million bucks to pull it off, with all of the logistics, intelligence work, and equipment. You'll only get a little over eight. There's always expenses."

Only a little over eight million dollars?

I was twenty-four years old, living on a gorgeous sailboat, drinking rum with a spy in the Virgin Islands, and I was the world's newest multi-millionaire. It was all a little overwhelming.

Dutch wasted no time breaking my moment of silence. "You know, kid, most operators think they should share the wealth with the people who taught them the craft. You know what I'm saying?"

I decided to stick with my good old dependable response of a simple nod. It wasn't the response he wanted, but I think it made my point. I stood and pointed at the puddle on the floor.

"Oh, don't worry about that," he said. "The house girl will take care of it. Where are you going?"

"Back to my boat. I have a lot to think about."

"Okay," he said. "Find me tomorrow, or I'll find you."

As I pulled the door closed behind me, I couldn't get the sum of eight million dollars out of my head.

Is it possible he's right about the money, or is he playing one of his games?

I found my way back to my boat for a nap. Apparently, my mind was overwhelmed with incomprehensible information, so it needed to rest. I'd never slept so soundly in all my life. I slept so deeply, in fact, I never heard or felt the intruder climb aboard my boat.

When I was awakened by a sharp, open-handed slap across my face, I jerked abruptly and thought my spine would snap. As I formed a fist with my left hand and tried to power forward with a crushing blow to the head of my assailant, the thin wire binding my wrist cut into my flesh. I squirmed to build some distance between me and my attacker but discovered the same wire that bound my hands also secured my ankles to a locker. The harder I tugged at my restraints, the tighter they became. Blood seeped from my wrists as I struggled against the wires. I flexed my abdomen in an effort to sit up and perhaps lash out with a headbutt, only to feel the wire wound around my neck like a garrote. I was bound not only by hand and foot, but also tethered by the neck. I was not a fan of my new situation.

My vision was blurry from the depth of sleep, but my instinct to identify the threat was sharp. I picked out the outline of my captor as her golden blonde hair fell across her shoulders. She was good . . . Very good.

I was too shocked to be frightened, but when I opened my mouth to speak, the blade of her knife landed sharply on the surface of my tongue, and I froze. The taste of the steel blade and the blood filling my mouth was enough to transform my shock into terror.

In exquisite, Russian-accented English, she spoke calmly. "Who sent you to kill Dmitri Barkov?"

I'd imagined, and even fantasized, how her voice would sound, but in my dreams, it was under far less painful circumstances. She spoke in perfectly formed words that seemed to bite her lips as they left her mouth. Her tone was smooth, calculated, and calm. She was neither nervous nor frightened. That made me believe she had no intention of letting me leave my boat alive. Realizing that a lie was a waste of time, and possibly a death sentence, I opted for the truth.

With my tongue bleeding and my body exploding with pain from my bindings, I said, "I don't know."

She struck me again, but this time, she hit me with the bottom of her clenched fist like a hammer, the blunt steel handle of the knife protruding from her fist. The blow from the hard, solid steel of the knife left me dazed.

With her calm, smooth tone completely gone, she yelled in a voice that would make a grizzly bear tremble. "Liar! You know! Tell me now who sent you!"

Trying not to gag on the blood pouring from my tongue, I mumbled, "I'm telling you the truth. I don't know who sent me. I'm just a—"

The cold steel of her knife pierced the back of my right wrist and lodged against the steel pins and screws that lay beneath my skin where the bones of my wrist used to be. She pressed the blade with all of her weight, but it was no use. It wouldn't penetrate what the surgeons had spent hours building inside my arm. Her frustration rose, and she yanked the blade from my wrist and stuck it beneath my chin.

Her calm, measured tone returned, but when she spoke, it came out in far-less-polished English. "You will tell me who sent you, or I will gut you like pig!"

Ah, there's the Russian I expected.

I didn't believe she'd actually "gut me like pig" until she knew the answer to her question, so I stuck with my story, which happened to be the truth. "I'm telling you, I don't know who sent me. Two men showed up with a picture and instructions. I was simply doing as I was—"

A small-caliber pistol shot rang out from the galley of my boat. The mirror in the front of my cabin exploded, sending shards of glass hurling through the air and leaving my ears ringing as if I'd been inside a church bell when the clapper collided with the brass. I watched my attacker disappear through the hatch above my bed, followed closely by Dutch's bulky frame.

Dutch had a pistol in his right hand. His foot landed on my thigh and sent waves of pain through my already tortured body. His hips come to an abrupt halt as his bulk met the limits of my hatch. He was not only standing on my leg, but he was also solidly stuck in my hatch. Through the ringing in my head, I heard a faint splash as the Russian's long, graceful body slipped into the water beside *Aegis*'s hull.

21

How Many?

With blood pouring from his nose, Dutch finally wiggled his way down from the hatch, and the disgust and confusion on his face was unlike I'd ever seen from him. He'd always been the epitome of confidence and in full command of his environment. Had the situation not been so serious, I would've found his expression humorous. He clearly saw nothing funny about it.

"Who the hell was that?"

My tongue was on fire. "That's her. She's the sniper I saw at Belmont. She wanted me to tell her who sent me to kill Barkov."

His eyes shot wide. "What did you tell her?"

I motioned helplessly at my bindings. "Would you mind getting me out of these?"

He quickly cut me free, and I stuck my fingers into my mouth desperately trying to determine how badly I was cut. What I felt made me fear for the future of my tongue. My hand was almost instantly drenched in warm, thick blood.

I pointed to my tongue. "Do something about this, would you?"

Dutch spun around, searching for a medical kit. His clumsiness aboard my boat partially explained why he was unable to shoot my intruder from less than twenty feet away. He'd certainly not found his sea legs yet.

I pointed at the galley. "It's in there above the settee, beside the fire extinguisher."

He stumbled into the main salon and retrieved the medical kit. After staggering back into my berth, he yanked his glasses from his shirt pocket and perched them on his nose before grabbing what was left of my tongue with his left hand. I flinched and tried to pull away, but he wasn't letting go. With several wadded up four-by-four bandages, he dabbed at the surface of my tongue then made a face that terrified me.

"This is really going to hurt," he said while wincing.

He pulled on some rubber gloves and drew a syringe of anesthetic from a clear vial. I expected the pain to be excruciating, but I barely felt the needle pierce my tongue, and very quickly, the pain from the wound subsided under the influence of the anesthetic. I was thankful for the relief.

For twenty minutes, he stitched, glued, wiped, and manhandled my tongue until he either finished the task or ran out of patience. I was thankful to have his hands out of my mouth. He took a look at my bloody wrist and quickly threw five stitches in the flesh to close the small laceration. He forgot to administer the anesthetic, so I growled in pain as he finished the job.

Dutch removed his gloves and threw away the remnants of the medical procedure. "So, what did you tell her?"

"I told her the truth—that I didn't know who sent me. But that's not what's important. Her question is what's important. She didn't ask who sent me to kill Suslik. She asked who sent me to kill Barkov."

Realization consumed his face. "That's perfect! That means whoever she works for thinks you were after Barkov and not Suslik. They think this was a botched assassination attempt, when in reality, it was the epitome of success. You're a genius. Simply a genius!"

He grabbed my face in his hands and repeatedly kissed me on the forehead until I shoved him away. Then he calmed himself.

"Okay, okay, so tell me. How did she get the jump on you and get you hogtied without you waking up?"

Honestly, I had no idea how she'd been able to climb aboard my boat, evade the mousetraps, and tie me up with enough piano wire to build a dozen Steinway baby grands without waking me up. It was unthinkable. I hadn't been that drunk nor that tired.

That's when Dutch cocked his head and leaned toward me. I shoved him again, thinking he was about to continue his romance with my forehead, but he slapped my hands away and reached for my neck. He plucked a tiny dart from the flesh of my neck, about an inch below my hairline.

He held the dart up to the light and whispered, "Would you look at that? She shot you with a tranquilizer. Who is that girl?"

Instinctively, I rubbed my neck where the dart had been, but the puncture wound was so small I could barely feel it. "I have no idea who she is, but I'm going to find out. I'm most definitely going to find out, Dutch."

He stumbled his way to the galley and poured two drinks. I followed him through the companionway and up on deck. The anesthetic was wearing off, and the pain was returning. I thought a drink might help, so I graciously accepted what Dutch had poured and polished it off in short order. I handed the tumbler back to my surgeon and pointed back into the galley. He laughed, finished his drink, and promptly poured two more. This time, he brought the bottle.

With our fresh drinks in hand, Dutch asked, "So, what are you going to do now? You know you can't stay here."

My tongue throbbed and consumed all the free space in my mouth. "I'm not leaving this island until I find her, question her, and decide if I can let her live."

Blood trickled from my tongue, and I wondered if I'd ever be able to taste anything again.

"There's no way she'll come back tonight. I'm not sure if you hit her with your rootin' tootin' shootin' demonstration earlier, but I'm sure you scared her away, at least for tonight."

"Hey, I wouldn't have missed if it weren't for the nine thousand mousetraps on the floor. What's that about anyway?"

"It's not a floor, Dutch. It's a deck, and the mousetraps are my burglar alarm. Anyone who sneaks aboard while I'm sleeping will set off a few of the traps and make enough noise to wake me up. I borrowed the idea from Joshua Slocum, except he used carpet tacks in South America. He'd scatter a handful of tacks on deck every night before falling asleep, so any barefoot natives who decided his head would look good on their mantle would be in for quite a surprise. The tacks worked for Captain Slocum, but my mousetraps didn't do a thing to dissuade little miss blowgun from making herself right at home."

I downed my second drink and stared at him. "Dutch, whoever or whatever she is, she's very good. And definitely better than me."

"She ain't better than me, kid," he snorted.

"She made you miss a pistol shot from less than twenty feet, and then got you stuck in my hatch while she swam away. I'd say she bested both of us tonight."

He huffed and returned to his drink.

"So, do you have any suggestions on what to do next?"

He screwed up his face. "Yeah, I have a great idea of what to do next. You get this tub started and get out of here before she comes back and cuts your throat, which is exactly what she would've done if I hadn't shown up to save your tranquilized butt."

I wasn't so sure Dutch was correct. I wasn't convinced she was going to cut my throat, but I silently vowed the next time I saw her, she'd be at my mercy, not the other way around.

I asked, "So, how many of us are there?"

"It's just you and me, kid."

"No, I mean how many operators are there who do what we do?"

"Oh, I don't know. Maybe a hundred or so. I don't know all of them. Somebody's always getting dead, and somebody new is always coming up through The Ranch. I can't keep track. What difference does it make?"

"The difference it makes is that we could use a little help down here in paradise. Like my father used to say, 'If this ain't a mess, it'll sure do 'til one gets here.' I'd like to get some eyes on that girl and keep our thumb on her without her knowing we're watching. How soon can we get half a dozen operators down here to help us catch her?"

He lifted his drink and peered through the sweaty glass. "That's not how this works. We don't just call in reinforcements when things get screwed up. We deal with the problem, and we fix it. The fewer people who know what's going on down here, the better. If we get other people involved, they're going to want the credit for catching, interrogating, and maybe flipping this girl."

"What do you mean, flipping her?"

"Grow up," he said. "That's what we do when we aren't killing them. We flip them to work for us. Everybody has a weakness: sleep deprivation, hunger, torture, whatever it takes. We find out what scares or motivates them, and we exploit it until our captive spills his—or in this case, her—guts and tells us everything we want to know. Then, if we've not killed her, we put her to work as an asset for the good guys until she's found out and killed by her own people. That's how it's done, Chase. You should know that by now."

No matter how much I tried, I couldn't see me or anyone else flipping the sniper. She was cunning and fearless. Those aren't characteristics of a person with weaknesses. Even after she nearly cut my tongue in half and then tried to cut my hand off, I still wanted to know her name. I wanted to see her smile, and most of all, I wanted to hear her say my name. I didn't want to flip her. I wanted to hold her, smell her hair, and taste her lips . . . if my tongue ever healed.

"I'm going back to bed, and you're going back ashore," I said. "Thank you for shooting up my boat and sewing up my tongue. We'll talk tomorrow, then we'll find that girl."

"Since when did you start deciding what *we* were going to do, kid?"

"Get out of here, and let me get some sleep. She didn't get what she wanted from me tonight, so she'll be back. When she does, I won't be the one who gets interrogated."

22

My Deadly Mermaid

My mind wouldn't stop churning. I couldn't get her out of my head. I had to come up with a plan to find her and have a conversation without her cutting me, stabbing me, or tying me up again. I didn't understand why she felt so comfortable strolling along the beach in plain sight, but in the middle of the moonless night, it occurred to me she didn't know I'd ever seen her before then. She didn't know I was at Belmont. She didn't know I'd watched her on top of that water tower. She had no way of knowing that my thoughts had been consumed by her for months. I at least had that much of an advantage over her. She was clearly quite accomplished in her craft. She, or her support network, tracked me over a thousand miles through the islands of The Bahamas and the Caribbean and found me on St. Thomas.

I wrestled with that one for some time, but I couldn't conceive how they could've possibly tracked me. I'd made no purchases with anything other than cash. I'd bought no fuel, cleared no customs, made no telephone calls, and I'd done most of my navigation via dead reckoning since the weather had been so good, and I'd stayed within sight of the islands most of the voyage. Her ability to track me didn't make sense, but then again, Dutch had found me without any problem.

I had to find him before he vanished. I had to know how he was able to find me. A terrifying thought occurred to me . . .

What if Dutch intentionally missed his pistol shot? What if he's working with the Russian?

If, as Dr. Richter said, Dutch was in it for the money, my newfound wealth would make me an irresistible target for his greed. I didn't like the conspiratorial voyage my mind was taking. I wanted to trust Dutch. I thought back to the bank in Miami and the prophetic words of David Shepherd: *"Here's to knowing when to be afraid."*

Sleep wouldn't come. I inspected my throbbing tongue in the mirror and found it was twice its normal size. The stitches looked good, but the surface of my tongue was solid black from the bruising. My wrist was still oozing blood, but it didn't hurt. For the first time, I was thankful for the metallic hand the doctors built for me.

I tossed a towel, T-shirt, shorts, flip-flops, and my pistol into the dry bag, and grabbed my mask, fins, and snorkel. As quietly as possible, I slipped over the side of my boat and into the water that appeared inky black under the moonless Caribbean sky. I oriented myself toward a particularly dark cove and a secluded section of beach before setting off swimming.

Breathing past my bloated tongue proved more challenging than I expected. After what felt like half an hour swimming in the dark and gasping for air most of the way, I finally arrived on the beach, stripped off my wet shorts, dried off, and pulled on my dry clothes. I carefully hid my remaining gear under a pile of palm fronds, pocketed my pistol, and headed for Dutch's bungalow.

I not only didn't want Dutch or the Russian to spot me, I also didn't want a security guard to discover me lurking around with a pistol. As I approached Dutch's bungalow, I listened carefully for any sound. He would've set up at least some measure of perimeter security to warn him of anyone approaching. The closer I got to the bungalow, the emptier it appeared. There was no light coming from the windows and no sound coming through the thin walls. The most telling sign that the bungalow was empty was the absence of sand on the steps leading to the door. If anyone had entered after the steps had been swept, there would've been at least some trace of sand on the bowed, wooden planking. Clearly, he'd thoroughly cleaned the place before he left. His tradecraft skills were among the best on Earth. If he didn't want me to find him, I certainly didn't have the skill to flush him out.

If he were working with the Russian, it would be reasonable to assume his skill as a ghost would carry over to her, as well. Even if she were less skilled than him, he would ensure their tracks were well covered until they achieved their goal. For the moment, I was working under the assumption that their goal was my newly burgeoning bank account.

As I planned my entrance to Dutch's cabana, the world in front of me exploded with a blinding light. Shielding my eyes, I tried to peer around my fingertips to bring the source into focus. I knelt in the sand to shrink the size of the target I presented and squinted painfully against the light.

Dutch would never do anything to draw that much attention to himself in the middle of the night. Only a cop would be so clumsy. I was trained to think on my feet and avoid being arrested at all costs, so I hatched what I thought was a brilliant plan to not only avoid being arrested, but to get a look inside Dutch's bungalow.

I twisted my swollen tongue until I could feel one of the stitches between my teeth. I bit down on the stitch and yanked my tongue back as quickly as I could. The pain of the stitch tearing away from the flesh of my tongue was agonizing, but I held in the scream that wanted to explode from my throat. I let the blood seep across my lip and down my chin.

As I rehearsed the lines for my upcoming performance, a voice yelled out, "Don't move! Security! What are you doing out here sneaking around?"

I didn't have to exaggerate my inability to form coherent words. My bloated tongue did that for me. I held my hands to my mouth to emphasize the blood, and mumbled, "Two guys . . . attacked me . . . stole my wallet . . . ran in there, I think."

I pointed at Dutch's bungalow and watched the bright light jerk away from me and land squarely on the front door. I was still mostly blind from the light, so I made no effort to move. I sat down with a thud and covertly drove my pistol into the soft sand beneath my leg. When I regained the ability to pick out objects in my field of vision, I saw the outline of the security guard coming toward me.

He asked, "Are you okay, sir?"

I pointed to my mouth. "They hit me in the face and stole my wallet and passport. I didn't have much money, but I really need that passport."

I wasn't faking the pain associated with talking, but the pain was the only genuine thing about my performance.

The guard, clearly not interested in getting involved with my bloody mouth, backed away. "Okay, sir. Just stay right here. We're going to check inside the bungalow."

He turned and joined his partner and slowly approached the bungalow. With the barrel of his flashlight, the first security guard tapped the front door. "Security! Is anybody in there?"

When no answer came, he pounded more aggressively, this time with his fist. On the third or fourth blow, the door of the bungalow drifted open, just like it'd done when I knocked the previous day. The unarmed security guards shuffled through the door with their flashlights blazing a trail before them.

By that time, I mounted the top step behind the guards and began scanning the front room. My height permitted me a vantage point over their shoulders. When I saw the inky, semi-circular puddle a few feet inside the bungalow, my heart sank.

The guards noticed the pooling blood at the same moment I did. One of them crossed himself and whispered something that I suppose was intended for God's ears. Both men followed the blood with their flashlights until the white rings of light fell on Dutch's body. I leaned inward to get a glimpse. Dutch had been sliced from the tops of both kneecaps, up to his belt, with wounds so precise a surgeon would've been in awe. Above his belt line, he'd been gutted like a pig, but that wasn't the most disturbing wound. As I quickly surveyed his corpse, I noticed several small, cautious incisions around the base of his neck and a few inches down his shoulders. The wounds obviously weren't life threatening and hadn't produced much bleeding, but they were meticulous and unmistakably intentional.

I felt my stomach spasm as the reality of the scene overtook me, but I couldn't let the emotion of the experience overwhelm the necessity to disappear. I backed silently out the door, turned, and ran. I couldn't let myself get caught up in a murder investigation on St. Thomas, so I ran until the lights of the bungalows were no longer visible and I was completely breathless. I sprinted to the point where I hid my pistol and then snatched the Makarov from the sand. Having lost enough blood over the last several hours to drown a cat, I lacked my typical stamina. I finally collapsed on the beach where I'd stashed my gear under the palm fronds. When I was able to catch my breath, I reclaimed my dry bag, donned my mask, fins, and snorkel, and hurriedly threw my pistol into the bag before slinking back into the lagoon.

As my head sank beneath the water, I paused to adjust the snorkel in my bloody mouth and attach my dry bag to my belt loop. I pushed off the sandy bottom with my hands, and I thought I caught a glimpse of something sinking in front of me. I ignored whatever it was, and I gently kicked with my fins and felt my body move away from the beach. It didn't take long to realize what I had glimpsed was a thin rope, and it was drawing tightly around my torso, trapping my arms to my sides. At the same instant, a bony knee landed squarely between my shoulder blades, pinning me to the bottom.

My survival instinct joined forces with my mammalian reflex to find oxygen and sent my brain into near panic. There was nothing more important than getting air into my lungs, and there was no question whose knee was pressed between my shoulder blades, pinning me to the bottom of the lagoon. I was seconds away from being in the fight of my life.

I exhaled every ounce of air inside my lungs, preparing to inhale what might be my final breath. Just as I felt my lungs empty, I pumped my abdomen to draw in my next breath, but instead of air, salt water and sand poured into my mouth through the barrel of my snorkel. My situation had just become exponentially worse. Not only was I pinned to the bottom of the lagoon in less than three feet of water, but my arms were tied to my torso, and the deadliest woman I knew was kneeling on my back. As bad as all of those things were, the most troubling issue was the salt water and sand filling my lungs.

I was about to die with eight million dollars in the bank and the woman I so desperately wanted kneeling on my spine. After what I'd endured at The Ranch, and doing what only a handful of people on Earth could accomplish in Havana, I was going to die in mere inches of water.

I heard Ace's voice ringing in my head. "*You're something special. You're your father made over, only better.*"

I couldn't let them down—not Ace, and definitely not my father. What would Beater think if he knew I'd let a ballerina get the jump on me twice in one night?

I felt the hard metal frame of the Makarov pistol through the rubbery material of the dry bag pinned to my hip. I found the curve of the trigger guard and pressed my index finger against what I hoped was the trigger. If I got lucky, the barrel of the Makarov would be pointed toward the Russian, and the bullet would find enough flesh to get her off my back. When I felt the trigger collapse beneath the pressure of my finger and I heard the report of the pistol from within the dry bag, part of my brain expected to feel the heat of the bullet burn through my own flesh, but the burn didn't come. Before the echo of the shot could resound, I heard the Russian scream, and I felt her nimble body collapse beside me in the shallow lagoon.

Breathless and desperate, I rolled with all of my strength and sat upright, coughing and spraying sand and salt water from my mouth. I quickly scanned the horizon for security guards who had to have heard the shot, but no lights were approaching.

I squirmed and wiggled, flexing my arms until I freed myself from the lasso she'd draped over my body, and I saw the shadow of her body squirming and splashing at my side. She was a wounded animal and deadlier than ever, so I took two deep breaths before wrapping my arms around her thin frame and trapping her arms against her body in a bear hug from behind.

I liked how her body felt in my arms. I liked her strength and the taste of her wet hair. I didn't know how badly she was wounded, nor where I'd shot her, but she must've been in the worst pain of her life. It was time to play half psychologist and half professional wrestler.

Like an anaconda, I squeezed her powerful body until I felt the breath leave her lungs. She was bucking like a bull and trying desperately to strike my face with the back of her head as I squeezed her against my chest. Fantasies of the passion that boiled within her body flashed through my mind, but I couldn't let myself forget she was deadly. For the briefest moment, I considered plunging her into the water to get her to submit, but that was no good. She would simply exhaust herself fighting against me until she had no strength and no air. Then, she'd willfully inhale two lungs full of water and let herself die in my arms rather than become my prisoner. I wouldn't give her that option. I'd keep her alive, and I would subdue her no matter how long it took. I needed her to know how I felt about her, and I wanted her to feel my desire, but there was no way for any of that to happen until I got her calmed down. I was much stronger than her, and depending on where the bullet had struck, I was in far less pain. For the first time, I had the upper hand, and I wasn't going to lose it again. I sat there on the sandy bottom with my chin buried solidly into her neck and squeezed her tighter with every breath. Sooner or later, she would pass out from exhaustion or blood loss.

I finally felt her body relax. Her breaths came with marked brevity. She sobbed in agony and perhaps fear. I wanted to comfort her, but I couldn't let myself forget the danger she represented.

I talked to her in a slow, confident voice. "Just relax. I know you're hurt, but I'm not going to hurt you anymore. I want to talk to you. I can help you. I can give you the medical care you need. Relax. I'm not your enemy. I was not sent to kill Barkov. I wasn't there for him. He simply got in the way. He wasn't my target."

I felt her body relax even more when I said the words, "I wasn't sent to kill Barkov."

I'd found her trigger. That was the first time I believed one-hundred-thousand-dollars' worth of psychological education may have some practical use after all.

In breathless, gasping Russian, she cried, "What do you mean you were not there for Barkov?"

I relaxed my grip almost imperceptibly, but she detected the weakening and responded by twisting her thin, powerful body in my arms until we were face-to-face and only inches apart.

I could taste her breath and smell her blood. I could feel her heart beating against my chest, and I thought I detected the slightest softening of her expression as our eyes met. I savored the moment and treasured the closeness, but she was in the perfect position to drive her forehead into my nose. The pain I'd experience would be unbearable, and I'd be forced to release her.

If she rolled her head backward to build momentum to strike at my nose, I'd drive my forehead into her face as quickly as possible to hopefully stop the coming blow, but the blow that came was not a headbutt. It was something far more powerful and potentially deadly.

She didn't roll her head backward. Instead, she tilted her head to the right and slowly and deliberately pressed her lips to mine. With her legs wrapped around my waist, and her body pressed against mine, she kissed me.

The kiss was tender and delicate but felt sincere and powerful. For what felt like an eternity, I forgot that my tongue looked like an eggplant and felt like a broken arm. The woman I desired, dreamed of, and prayed for was in my arms, sitting on my lap with her lips on mine. Her pulse quickened, and her body quivered as the kiss continued. Apparently, neither of us wanted the moment to end.

Finally, she gasped and bit her lip. "Please get me to boat. I am bleeding to death. You shot me in foot."

I lifted her body from mine and sat her in the shallow water. She made no effort to escape or lash out, but I kept my eyes on hers, looking for any sign of aggression. She gave me no reason to believe she would fight or flee.

I slid my hand down her leg and found what was left of her shoe. In the dark, it was almost impossible to tell how badly she was wounded, so I slid the remnants of her shoe from her foot and removed my shirt. I tied my shirt around her foot, forming a field-expedient pressure dressing. She tried to smile as I finished tying the knot.

I reached for her body so I could pull her through the water as I swam back to my boat, but she flinched and pulled away.

"I'm not going to hurt you," I said. "I'm just going to swim you to the boat."

"No!" she said sharply. "I can swim. Is only flesh wound. Give to me fin. We will swim together."

Arguing with her would be wasted effort, so I surrendered, removed one of my fins, and handed it to her. She slid it on her good foot, rolled on her back, and began finning like a mermaid toward the sea. Her thin, muscular body continually tried to sink as she powered herself through the gentle waves, but she kept her head above the water enough to breathe jerky breaths.

We finally reached *Aegis*, and I climbed aboard before pulling her over the stern and laying her on one of the cockpit cushions. She looked at me with countless emotions pouring across her face and whispered, "*Spasibo, Amerikanec.*"

I smiled and whispered back, "You're welcome, Russian."

23
Welcome Aboard . . . Again

Water dripped from her long hair, and her gorgeous eyes gleamed, but she was obviously in pain. I regretted pulling the trigger and causing such pain, but I'd done it to save my life. Being alive is always the most important thing. I'd been trained to give no thought to the agony my target would endure, as there could be nothing more detrimental to the concentration my work required.

I'd not only been trained to avoid that catastrophic mistake, but I'd dedicated countless hours of self-exploration to the psychology of taking the lives of other humans. I developed an ability to focus on the necessity of moving through a target without letting him or her become human. Blindness to the humanity of my targets was essential. When I pulled the trigger minutes before, I believed I would die if I didn't take the shot.

Seeing her lying there, seemingly vulnerable and trembling in pain, I didn't want to believe she was capable and willing to take my life. I should've been doing everything in my power to flip her, but there were too many things to worry about at the moment to try talking her into joining the good guys.

I feared she hadn't softened; instead, she'd only become more patient than before. Her tradecraft was exquisite. She killed Dutch. Not only did she kill him, but she killed him in his own bungalow and left the site looking like it'd been professionally cleaned on her way out. Clearly, she was more seasoned, more skilled, and more violent than me.

I believed she was playing me. There's no way an assassin of her skill would surrender to physical attraction in the field. She saw how I looked at her. She recognized the desire in my eyes. It had, no doubt, been a familiar look for her. There could be no man capable of looking into her eyes without feeling her drawing his soul through his skin. She obviously used everything in her environment to her advantage. Her beauty and sensuality would be no exception. It was up to me to still myself against my desire, to find a way to be more cunning and smarter, and to remain one step ahead of the game she was playing. There may be nothing I'll ever do that was closer to impossible, but there were no other options.

"Welcome aboard *Aegis*," I said. "The last time you were here, you hadn't been invited, if I remember correctly."

She smiled. The last time I saw her smile was the day I'd unexpectedly met Dutch at the bar, and I watched her walking along the beach, staring into the sky, causing every man on the island to melt in his shoes.

"I have been on boat many times and you did not know. This is first time for being invited. I have been watching you. You drink too much, Chase Fulton."

How does she know my name?

I tried to hide my look of surprise and self-disappointment, but apparently, I did a poor job. She tilted her head, and several long strands of wet hair fell across her shoulder. Resisting her would not be possible. I didn't have whatever it would take to look at her without drowning in those eyes.

"Do not be hard on yourself. I am very good. Now, you must help my foot. You *did* shoot me, remember?"

Still reeling from the revelation that she not only knew my name, but she'd been watching me for some time, I bounced down the companionway to retrieve the medical bag Dutch had used to sew up my tongue only a few hours earlier. I would need to restock my med kit soon. Returning topside with a highball glass and a bottle of vodka in one hand, and my kit in the other, I poured three fingers of vodka and handed her the glass.

She accepted it and stared into the glass before drawing her wounded foot into her lap with the flexibility of a gymnast. She briefly glanced at me, then untied my bloody shirt from her foot and poured the vodka into her wound.

Uncertain of what to make of her unexpected use of the vodka, I looked into her eyes with what must've looked like confusion, and perhaps a little personal offense.

She furrowed her brow. "Is okay, Chase. You did not know."

"What didn't I know?"

"You did not know I am terrible Russian. I do not drink vodka. I detest cold, and I cannot eat caviar. Is terrible. I drink tea. Vodka makes my mind soft. I eat chocolate because it tastes better than fish egg. I rather chase you through Caribbean than build *snegovik* in Mother Russia."

Her command of English was impressive, but at times, her accent was strong. I chuckled to myself when she used the Russian word for snowman. She was testing me to determine how much Russian I knew, so I played along.

I asked, "*Snegovik*? Is that Russian for igloo?"

She laughed, "Yes, Chase. *Snegovik* is igloo if you say so."

I stared at her as if I were a schoolboy. She widened her eyes and pointed at her foot.

"Ah, I'm sorry," I said. "Let's take a look."

"No. Do not look, Chase Fulton. Do something! You shot off my toe, and it feels like leg is burning. Do something!"

I went to work on her foot. I had, indeed, shot her in the foot and left a nasty wound where her pinky toe used to be. One of the good things about gunshot wounds, if there are any good things about them, is that they're relatively clean until the bullet mushrooms as it starts striking bone. Fortunately, the bones in her missing toe were so small the bullet didn't have the inclination to mushroom. It cleanly cut off the toe and yanked a half-inch chunk of flesh from the outside of her foot. She'd made a good decision by pouring the vodka into the wound. What the saltwater hadn't cleaned, the vodka did.

I donned a pair of latex gloves, opened a fresh suture kit, and stuck a small flashlight in my mouth. I made several injections of anesthetic around and into the wound before suturing it closed and applying an awkward bandage. Even though I'd been taught to suture, I'd never been taught how to bandage a four-toed foot.

She laughed as I struggled with the swaddling. "You are not good doctor."

"No, I'm a terrible doctor, but I'm a decent sailor, and right now, that may be a more valuable skill. We really have to get off this island. Things are going to get hot around here when the sun comes up."

She cast a look toward the beach. "I agree. We must go."

I wasn't sure what would happen if I hauled up the anchor and hoisted a sail or two. Would the authorities on the island come after us? If they did, would she kill them? If they didn't, would she kill me?

There was only one way to know any of the answers to my questions, so I brought the engine to life and eased *Aegis* forward to weigh the anchor before turning for the mouth of the pro-tected anchorage. I locked the wheel and plowed ahead to rinse the anchor as it came aboard. As the anchor came to rest on the deck, I found a thin piece of line tied to the shackle. I pulled the line and found a heavy dry bag attached to the other end. My cu-riosity was piqued, but I didn't want to draw attention to our de-parture by turning on the deck lights, nor had I brought a flashlight with me on deck, so I returned to the cockpit with somebody else's dry bag in hand.

She looked up and smiled. "You want to know what is in bag, yes?"

"*Da.*"

She stared at the deck as if she were ashamed. "Is my tools and clothes. I was planning to take boat after I killed you on beach. I could not leave bag on boat, so I left on anchor."

Honesty is an interesting approach.

"Before I turn a Russian assassin loose on my boat with her bag of tools, I think I'll have a look inside, if you don't mind." I poured the contents of the bag onto the seat, and to my surprise, there was no pistol in the pile of clothes and personal items. "No gun?"

She looked offended. "I do not shoot."

"Actually," I said, "I've seen you shoot. So, now I've caught you in your first lie."

24
Svetlana?

At barely above idle, we motored out of the anchorage, and the night absorbed us. The receding tide made navigating the shallow waters even more challenging than the darkness alone. But when my depth sounder read eighteen feet, I relaxed enough to finally unfurl the headsail. The consistent breeze at just over ten knots out of the southwest was just enough to tug *Aegis* through the water at four knots. When I put up the mainsail, we'd likely make six knots. We weren't going anywhere quickly, but we were going.

I locked the wheel and turned to face my guest. The time had come to get her name. "Don't go anywhere, Svetlana. I'll be right back."

That was the first feminine Russian name that came to mind, so I decided to toss it into the wind and see if it garnered a reaction. It didn't. Either it *was* her name, and she was smart enough to avoid a reaction, or it *wasn't* her name, and she was smart enough to recognize that I was guessing. Either way, I was reminded she was probably smarter than me.

I strode down the stairs and set a kettle of water on the alcohol stove so I could make Katerina or Svetlana or Susie some tea since she obviously wasn't going to drink my vodka. I reached for my bottle of Jack Daniel's, but I remembered her admonition, "You drink too much, Chase." So, tea became the drink of the evening. I thought it might go a long way toward establishing some degree of trust.

Occasionally, I glanced back up the companionway, making sure she hadn't dived overboard again. I didn't want her to leave. I tried telling myself I wanted her to stay because she was a valuable intelligence asset, but in reality, I was already falling in love with her. My analytical psychologist's mind couldn't rationalize the idea, but trying to rationalize anything about my situation was a colossal waste of time.

When the kettle whistled, I pulled two tea bags and two mugs from the cupboard and headed back on deck with the steaming kettle in hand. I'd never tried to balance two mugs and a tea kettle on a pitching, heeling deck before, so I looked a lot like a drunk juggler.

Trying not to smile, my Russian took both mugs from my hand, pulled the teabag strings out of the mugs, and let them dangle over the rims. I braced my feet against the deck and poured the steaming water over the teabags. She never took her eyes off mine. She never once looked down at the mugs as I was pouring boiling water only inches from her fingers. I wondered if she realized what an overt demonstration of trust that was on her part.

"Would you like honey?" I asked.

She continued staring into my eyes. "Please."

I felt a bit uncomfortable under her gaze, and I wondered what sort of game she was playing.

My bear-shaped honey bottle made me feel silly, but I doubted a Russian spy would judge me for my choice of honey containers. She lifted the bear from my hand and drizzled honey into her mug before holding the ridiculous bear above my mug and looking questioningly at me.

I borrowed her line. "Please."

She let the golden honey pour into my tea, then wiped the opening with her index finger before closing the cap. She slipped the tip of her finger between her lips and seductively licked the honey from her skin.

I swallowed the puddle of saliva that had formed in my mouth and tried not to let her see the effect she had on me. There was no doubt in my mind she was well practiced in the art of seduction. I was certain she intended to use any means necessary to get me to pour everything in my mind into her waiting hands. I was questioning my ability, as well as my desire, to resist.

"So, Anastasia," I said, "why are you trying to kill me?"

The instant the name escaped my lips, her pupils exploded, and she swallowed hard. I'd guessed her name, but I showed no reaction and waited for her to answer.

She shook her head. "What? What did you say?"

I asked again, "Why are you trying to kill me, Anastasia?"

Confidence dripped from her tongue as she spoke. "If I wanted to kill you, I would have driven my knife into your back in water near beach. I do not want you dead . . . not yet. I have questions first. And do not call me that name again . . . not ever."

I took a sip of my tea. "In that case, thank you for not killing me . . . yet. And if I'm forbidden from using your name, what shall I call you?"

With an icy stare only Russians seem to pull off, she said, "You will call me Anya, but never again Anastasia."

She tilted her mug to her lips, and for the first time since our kiss, she closed her eyes. She seemed to embrace and savor the taste and feel of the hot tea on her tongue.

With my tongue resembling a grapefruit turned inside out, I couldn't taste anything, but I enjoyed the warmth of the tea and watching Anya enjoy hers.

"How's your foot?" I asked.

"Is painful. I would like aspirin, please."

There was no way this woman would swallow any pill I handed her. She was too smart for that. Basic tradecraft 101 dictates never ingest anything the enemy offers unless the enemy ingests it first. That's precisely why she'd made sure the honey went into my tea as well as hers. If I'd poisoned the honey, I would never have allowed her to put it in my tea. The aspirin would be an excellent chance to test my trust theory.

I reopened the med kit, poured two Motrin pills into the palm of my hand, and grabbed an unopened bottle of ibuprofen. I resealed the kit, sat the unopened bottle on the seat beside her, and offered the two white pills from my palm.

"Here, these are eight hundred milligram Motrin. They'll help quickly without making you drowsy. If you'd like, I have some morphine, but I remember you saying how much you dislike your mind being soft. The morphine will soften more than just your mind, but if you don't want these, there's a new bottle of ibuprofen. You may have whatever your little heart desires."

My speech was a carefully structured psychological experiment. There was no way she would take the Motrin from my palm. She hadn't seen the bottle, nor were there any markings on the pills to validate my claim that they were, in fact, Motrin. She was clearly in extreme pain, no matter how hard she tried to hide it, but I couldn't imagine her accepting the morphine. I expected her to take the sealed bottle of ibuprofen and swallow a handful of the two-hundred-milligram capsules.

She stared through my eyes and into my soul. "Give me your word you will not kill me while I sleep."

Curiosity bounced off the inside of my skull like a rubber ball, and I shook my head. "I'm not going to kill you. I have no reason to kill you."

She swallowed another mouthful of tea. "I will have morphine, please. It hurts badly."

My heart sank. I'd overestimated her ability to deal with extreme pain. She was in agony, but for her to ask for morphine that would render her completely defenseless was either the boldest display of trust imaginable, or it was just another step toward gaining my cooperation. At that point, I didn't care which. I was just glad she was willing to accept some relief from the pain.

I pulled a vial and syringe from the kit and drew out enough morphine to not only ease her pain, but also ensure she would have the best eight hours of sleep of her life. She turned slightly in the seat, offering me the delicate, smooth skin of her hip. I made the injection quickly but deeply enough for the drug to find its way into her tissue as fast as possible.

Anya didn't flinch. She simply placed her palm against my cheek and said, "*Spasibo*." She kissed me softly at the corner of my mouth, then pressed the two white pills into my palm. "I am sorry for tongue. You have Motrin."

She was testing my Motrin claim, so I quickly tossed the two horse pills into my mouth and swallowed them with my tea, demonstrating to her that the pills I'd offered were exactly what I said they were.

I held her delicate face in my hands and looked deeply into her hypnotic blue-gray eyes. "There will be things I can never tell you, but I will never lie to you, Anya . . . never."

"Take me to bed, Chase. For now, I will trust you. But only for now."

I lifted her into my arms and carried her down the companionway and into my berth. She closed her eyes, and I'll never forget how she looked and how I longed for both of us to have normal lives.

What might it be like if she were a schoolteacher and I were a banker, though no such reality would ever exist for us. We were assassins and vagabonds.

Back in the cockpit, I searched my chart for someplace to anchor. I was too tired to stay at the helm and watch for other boats all night. I needed to sleep, and I could only sleep when we were at anchor. A small island, not much more than a rock in the middle of the ocean, appeared beneath my finger. It was less than an hour away, so I set my course. Perhaps there would be some shallow water on its leeward side where we could drop the hook for a few hours until I was refreshed enough to sail on.

Thankfully, I found eleven feet of water in a small, protected cove on the northeast side of the island. I set the anchor and extinguished every light on the boat, although I was supposed to burn the anchor light at the top of the mast. I didn't want any attention. We were running and hiding, neither of which were easy to do in a slow, lumbering sailboat. I stood in the doorway of my berth for several minutes, watching the Russian sleep. I was mesmerized by her apparent innocence and almost childlike beauty as she lay there, breathing deeply, and making soft, gentle sleeping sounds. I wanted so badly to lie behind her and hold her in my arms, but instead, I chose to sleep in the main salon. It wasn't as comfortable as my berth, but it was adequate, and most importantly, I didn't disturb her much-needed sleep.

When I awoke, I started a pot of coffee, scrambled some eggs, and cut up a melon. I stood again in the doorway to my berth and listened to the sounds of her breathing and couldn't believe this breathtaking woman was asleep in my bed, on my boat, in the middle of the Caribbean. In spite of my efforts to remain silent, I must've made a sound she heard, or perhaps sensed. She opened her eyes, looked up at me, and smiled. I hadn't expect her to smile. It was a simple gesture that made my heart sing with delight. I expected her to be cold, and perhaps even cruel when she awoke, but thankfully, I was wrong.

In a raspy, but soft voice, she said, "*Dobroye utro.*"

"Good morning to you, too, Anya. How do you feel?"

"Am okay," she breathed. "Thank you for not killing me in sleep."

"You're welcome. I made breakfast. How do you take your coffee?"

She lifted her head from the pillow and looked into the galley. "You cook and sew." She pointed toward her bandaged foot. "How is it you have no wife?"

"I'm terrible in bed. That must be it."

Before she could respond, I headed back to the galley to make a plate for each of us. I chuckled quietly as I heard her fumbling with the head. "It's not like a regular toilet," I said. "You have to flip the black switch to the left, then pump the handle three times. That will fill the bowl. Then, flip the switch back to the right and pump again. That will empty it."

Based on the absence of cursing in either Russian or English, I assumed she'd overcome the mysteries of the marine head.

"Life on a boat is not like life ashore," I said. "It takes some getting used to."

She arrived in the galley wearing my shirt, and her long hair was pulled tightly into a ponytail. She picked a piece of melon from a bowl and placed it on her tongue. I couldn't tell if she was trying to be seductive or if she just really liked melon. I placed our plates on the table, poured two cups of coffee, and we ate in silence. I'm not sure either of us knew what to say. There we were, two assassins from two different worlds, having breakfast together miles from anywhere. I hoped it was the first of many breakfasts we'd share, but at that moment, neither of us knew what lay ahead.

"How's the foot?" I asked.

"It hurts, but is better. I cannot believe you shot me."

"You were trying to kill me," I reminded her. "I had to do something to get you off my back and get some air in my lungs."

She scoffed, "I told you, if I wanted to kill you, you would be dead. I let you live so we could talk . . . and maybe so you would make breakfast."

We laughed perhaps a little uncomfortably. I suppose that was the only thing either of us knew to do at that moment. We spoke little while we ate but caught each other staring too many times to count. I didn't know what she was thinking, but my mind was exploding with a billion questions, and I had no idea how to proceed.

I'd never really been trained to flip a foreign operative, but I had been trained to resist when one tried to flip me. Every time I looked at her, I feared more and more that I'd never be able to resist her.

When we finished breakfast, she gathered the plates, silverware, and mugs, and twisted her body past me toward the galley sink. Suddenly, it felt as if we were playing house.

"I'll take care of those. You sit and rest your foot."

She looked at me with that stern look of hers and demanded, "You sit. I will do this. You cook. I clean."

"Yes, ma'am." I pulled my coffee mug back from her hand. "But I want another cup of coffee."

She continued the stern stare as I poured another cup and gestured the pot toward her, but she turned away without a response. I climbed partially up the stairs toward the cockpit and sat in the companionway while she cleaned the dishes. Only twelve hours before, she and I had taken turns trying to kill each other, and now she was washing my dishes aboard my boat while wearing one of my shirts.

What a strange existence, this cloak-and-dagger life.

When she finished, she dried her hands on the small towel and limped toward me. She seemed to disapprove of me sitting in the companionway, or perhaps she didn't like being watched. As she drew nearer, I reached for her in the hope of holding her in my arms, if only for a moment before our peaceful morning turned into whatever the day was to become. But to my astonishment and great disappointment, she forcefully pushed my hands away and stepped back.

"Do not do that!" she said.

"I'm sorry. I only wanted to touch you. I didn't mean to—"

She interrupted before I could finish stumbling through my apology. "I like how you touch me, but not here. Not in doorway. Doorway is for going or coming. Nothing more."

I had a great deal to learn about the world, but I'd never met anyone who felt so strongly about doorways. My analytical mind tore into that one like a bulldog into a T-bone. I couldn't wrap my head around why she would be so insistent on not hugging me in the companionway. I tucked that one away with a plan to explore it more thoroughly later.

I finished the last of my coffee and stepped down into the galley to wash my mug. Before I reached the sink, she stepped in front of me, reached up, and slid her hands around my neck. I carelessly let my mug fall into the sink as I embraced her, timidly at first, but soon I was holding her tightly against my body and listening to her breathe. She loosened her embrace, then she pulled slightly away. Just as she had done in the lagoon the night before, she tilted her head and seductively licked her lips. When our lips met, the world disappeared. We could've been on top of the Eiffel Tower or at the bottom of the Grand Canyon, and I wouldn't have known the difference. The feeling of her lips on mine, and our bodies pressed together, made me forget everything in the world except how she felt.

Just when I thought our kiss was going to become something more, she sighed and opened her eyes. "I think we should go."

She was correct. We definitely should've gone, but all I wanted to do was continue with what was happening between us. I hoped there would be plenty of time for that later.

"You're right, but this is a lot more fun," I said, then turned and climbed into the cockpit.

There was almost no wind where we were anchored, but I could see ripples on the water around both ends of the small island. That meant the wind was definitely blowing outside the lee of the rock under which I had chosen to hide. I started the engine, then methodically eased the boat forward and engaged the windlass to haul the anchor from the sandy bottom. The anchor gave way and began to rise, so I pulled the transmission into reverse, locked the wheel, and bounded up on deck to clean the anchor as it came aboard. As it turned out, there was no reason to clean it. The sandy bottom left no residue on the anchor, so I kept it slowly ascending until it was seated firmly in its rest.

What I saw when I turned back toward the cockpit stopped my heart. Anya was standing at the helm with my pistol in one hand and my satellite phone in the other. I was terrified. She had that icy Russian look on her face again. I had yet to learn what that face meant, but so far, it was the one thing about her I hated.

She walked up on deck toward me, never taking her eyes from mine. Her graceful gait had been temporarily replaced by a painful limp. It was clear she was about to do one of two things. She was either going to call whoever she worked for with my sat-phone, then hold me at gunpoint until they arrived to either capture or kill me, or she was going to kill me first and then make the call. I couldn't decide which fate I preferred.

The boat was still idling in reverse and making less than one knot. If I could delay her call for only thirty more seconds, *Aegis* would be in the wind, and we'd start to turn and even roll in the gentle waves. Hopefully, her injured foot would make it impossible for her to stand on a rolling deck. I desperately needed time to speed up. I needed her to stumble. I could close the ten feet that separated us in less than three strides, but I would never survive the first stride if she were solidly on her feet. What she did next was the last thing I would've ever expected.

She turned gracefully and tossed the sat-phone through the air and over the starboard side. As the phone reached its zenith and began to fall toward the water, I heard the report of the pistol as she squeezed off one round.

The muzzle velocity on that particular pistol is well over the speed of sound, so if she had fired at me, I would've been dead before the sound reached my ears. I would've never heard the shot that killed me. Instead of a hollow-point round tearing through my chest, it tore through the plastic case of the falling sat-phone, tearing it into tiny pieces of electronics and plastic.

I watched the pieces rain down into the water before I cast my eyes back to her. In the time it had taken for me to redirect my gaze from the destroyed phone to her face, she'd fieldstripped the pistol into two pieces. The slide rested in her right hand and the frame in her left. Still staring through me like a stalking cat, she tossed the slide toward me in a gentle arc. Instinctively, I caught it and stood mesmerized.

Before I could ask what was happening, she said, "I *can* shoot. I choose mostly not to shoot. We should talk now."

25
Monkey's Ear

I wiped the sweat from my brow and followed her back to the cockpit. With the sails hoisted, we were underway, cruising at just over seven knots in the fresh morning breeze. When I joined Anya on the seat, she removed the bandage and began inspecting the wound.

"It doesn't look infected," I said, "but I have some antibiotics if you'd like them."

She smiled, so I took that to mean thank you.

I broke out the med kit again and handed her a yellow bottle of penicillin.

Instead of taking the bottle from my hand, she wrapped both of her hands around mine. "Thank you, Chase. You will give me one every day, yes?"

I wanted to believe her request meant she would stay with me aboard *Aegis* for at least several more days, but I feared it meant she was either going to leave soon and didn't want to take my only bottle of antibiotics, or she was simply trying to make me believe she was staying.

I was tired of second-guessing every word she spoke and every action she made. I wanted so badly to trust her. I'd told her I wouldn't lie to her, but she hadn't made the same promise to me. With that in mind, I went fishing—fishing for a promise of honesty.

"Listen, Anya. This whole situation is bizarre to me. Perhaps you're better at this than I am, but I'm still confused. I want to reassure you that I have no intention of lying to you about anything. I will honestly tell you everything you want to know as long as it doesn't violate the vow I made to my country. I will not desert my country, but I also will not lie to you. If I can't tell you the truth, I simply won't answer your question. That's fair. Don't you think?"

"It is fair. You want same, yes?"

I nodded.

Her smile dissolved into a thin, sharp line. "If I promise to tell only truth, but I have plan to lie, even my promise would be lie. So, you cannot know if I am telling truth or lie. You know I am smarter than you. More than smart. I have been doing this longer. That means I have experience you do not have. You have some skills . . . good stamina, strong, and smart. And almost smart enough to leave Cuba with not being followed."

That stung a little, but she was right. I didn't have her skill set, her experience, nor her amazing ability to track someone for thousands of miles through the ocean without being detected.

She looked at me with a stare that could cut steel. Her eyes were the most unique blue-gray color I'd ever seen. They could appear as cold as ice one moment and as warm and welcoming as the sky the next. Something about her eyes was so familiar and yet so new. Everything about her was a study in extreme dichotomy. She was physically striking but also deadly. She was intensely strong but could also be incredibly gentle and delicate. She was, without question, the most uniquely fascinating person imaginable. I feared her, adored her, and loved her all at the same time. It was impossible to separate the three emotions. They were intertwined like the silken strands of a spider's deadly web.

She wasted no time initiating the conversation. "You said you saw me shoot. I do not believe you."

Although that wasn't technically a question, she left it hanging as if she wanted a response, but I don't think she was prepared for what I was about to reveal.

"Yes," I said with confidence. "I watched you shoot a horse at Belmont Park in New York." I returned her stare and didn't blink.

She recoiled slightly and looked away. "I did not shoot horse. I only flashed laser in horse's eye so proper horse could win race."

"Is that so?"

Again, she didn't answer, but the realization that I'd actually seen her at Belmont must've overtaken her. "How did you see that? Why were you there? How do you know person there was me?"

For the first time, she was at least slightly shaken.

"I was hired to protect the horse you shot," I said. I realized I'd instantly given up the slight advantage I had.

Her smile returned with renewed enthusiasm. "That was first time I beat you."

I poked her arm with the tip of my finger. "You've never beaten me at anything."

She laughed. "I shot horse you were protecting. That is one. I tied you and cut tongue. That is two. I tied arms and could have drowned you. That is three. I think I beat you always."

She had three excellent points, but I *had* shot her toe off. That had to count for something, but playing that trump card didn't seem like a good idea at the time.

When she finally regained her composure after laughing, she asked, "So, if not to kill Dmitri Barkov, why were you in Cuba?"

It didn't take her long to get back to the question of who sent me to kill Barkov. I remembered her surprised reaction when I said I wasn't there for Barkov. I didn't think she was easily surprised, but it was clear she had no idea what my real mission was in Cuba.

I gave it a long moment's thought. I couldn't tell her the truth or refuse to tell her anything. I'd promised I wouldn't lie, so that was out of the question.

Before I came to a conclusion, she grabbed my leg with both hands. "Tell me, Chase. Why were you in Cuba?"

"Give me a minute. I have to decide if I can tell you."

"You can. You must. Why were you there, and who sent you?"

I took her face in my hands. "Okay. I'm going to tell you, but you aren't going to be satisfied with my answer. I wasn't there for Barkov. He just got in my way. I was there to kill Suslik."

She jolted upright in the seat. "What? You were there to kill Suslik, the gopher? If this is truth, you failed. You shot Dmitri Barkov in shoulder and scared two women for nothing. This does not make sense."

"I didn't fail," I said. "I pulled him from Barkov's boat with a piece of 550 cord around his neck and chopped him into fish food with the propeller of my outboard motor. I watched him die, Anya."

She looked at me, then at the deck, as if she were trying to process the information. It was clear nothing about what I was saying made any sense to her. I almost felt sorry for her, but she jolted back into the conversation as quickly as she'd looked away.

"I am confused. You were there to kill Suslik?"

"Yes."

"And to not kill Dmitri Barkov?"

"No."

"And you think Suslik was on boat with Barkov?"

"Yes."

"Who sent you?"

I sighed. "This is the part you aren't going to like. I don't know who sent me. I never know who sends me anywhere to do anything. I get a message and instructions to go someplace and do something. If I do it, I get paid."

"You get paid?"

"Yes," I said. "I get paid. Don't you get paid?"

She shook her head, "No. No, I do not get paid. Well, yes, I get paid, but I do what is my duty and I am paid a . . . uh . . . a *zarplata*. I do not know word in English."

"Salary?" I asked. "Now I'm the one who's confused. They pay you a salary to kill people and blind horses. Is that right?"

"Yes," she said. "Is my job. Just like your job is CIA, I am SVR."

I couldn't believe what I was hearing. A Russian SVR agent had just revealed herself right in front of me. That simply does not happen. Russian SVR officers don't reveal themselves to anyone, ever. I was more certain than ever she was going to kill me. There's no way she would've exposed herself to that degree and let me live. She had made at least one critical error, though. I was not CIA.

"You are CIA, yes?" she asked blatantly.

She was guessing, just like I'd guessed her name.

"No, Anya. I'm not CIA. I'm a contractor. The American CIA can't do what I do. We have laws."

"Yes, America's silly laws. Those are for people with small mind. Do not play games with me, Chase. We are not children. You promised you would not lie to me."

I liked how she almost never spoke in contractions. I found myself dissecting her intellect and personality and finding so many things about her to be thoroughly irresistible.

"I'm not lying to you, Anya. I do not work for the CIA . . . at least I don't think I do." After careful introspection, I said, "Anya, honestly, I don't know who I work for. I do what I'm asked to do, and then I'm paid well for doing it."

She smiled as if I'd revealed something of deep importance. "Chase, you are *nayemnik*. A mercenary. *Amerikanskiy nayemnik*."

She was correct. I was a soldier for hire, a weapon used by those who treasured plausible deniability. I was an expendable, deployable scalpel used for slicing microscopic, cancerous bits of humanity from the planet. She was making me see myself through her eyes. If it was a psychological tactic designed to weaken my resolve to resist her efforts to flip me, I feared it just might be working.

I didn't know what to say. There were so many questions I wanted to ask her, but I was engrossed in my own revelation of what I'd become. Perhaps she was a far better psychologist than me. I tried to return to the conversation and get as much information from her as possible, but I couldn't make my mouth produce any words.

"Is okay, Chase. You are not alone. There are many more like you all over world." Her tone softened, almost as if she were concerned about me. "Well, I do not think exactly like you. Inside, you are not like others."

I didn't know if she was being patronizing in an effort to garner my trust or if she was sincere.

"You don't know me," I said. "You don't know what I am inside." I tried to refocus.

"I know much of you, Chase. I know you are not killer without soul. You are man who has faith in much, but has also doubts. You are not—"

"How did you find me? I left no trail. I made no mistakes. How did you track me down?"

I was angry—angry with myself, and even a little angry for what my life had become. I was a professional killer who was being interviewed and recruited by a Russian spy on a boat in the middle of the Caribbean. Why wasn't I somewhere in south Florida in spring training with a farm team for the Braves?

She withdrew a small knife from her pocket. The morning sunlight played off the metallic blade as if it were a mirror. I should've been frightened, but nothing in her expression said she was going to hurt me. She had so many opportunities to take my life. As she said, if she wanted to kill me, she would've done it by now. With a tenderness in her eyes, she placed her left hand behind my head and pressed her fingertips firmly into the muscles of my neck and shoulders. She stopped about two inches below my hairline behind my left ear and pressed more aggressively.

She smiled a gentle, knowing smile, then sat cautiously on my lap with her legs draped around my waist. Last time we were in that position, we shared our first kiss. I hoped we were about to have a repeat performance, but I was soon to be disappointed.

She pressed her body against mine. "Hold me. This is going to feel not good, but you will like result."

Timidly, I wrapped my arms around her and enjoyed the feeling of her body pressed against mine.

She pulled my head tightly against her shoulder. "Take deep breath and hold. Do not move. Do not jump. And do not bite me."

I did as she instructed and drew in a deep breath. I closed my eyes and drank in her smell until I felt the blade of her knife puncture the flesh of my neck. Instinctually, I flexed every muscle in my body, but I tried not to flinch. At that moment, I understood why she'd instructed me not to bite her, because that's exactly what my mind was telling me to do.

As quickly as the blade entered my skin, she removed it. "Okay. You now can relax. I have it."

"You have what?"

As I leaned away from her, she presented a small, metallic capsule dripping with blood.

"What is that?"

"Is answer to your question. Is how your handler and I found you. It is state-of-art technology. They put this in neck while you were training in U.S. This is how CIA always knows where you are. I knew where you were because we have been able to track your people by . . . uh, what is word? Ah yes, piggybacking on your technology for many years. Do not tell me you think Cold War is over because your Ronald Reagan said so."

I was astonished and felt betrayed. The technology my country put inside my body made it possible for this Russian to find and kill Dutch, as well as track me down. I didn't like the way that tasted.

"So, is that why Dutch's neck was cut open? You were removing one of those from his neck, too?"

"Yes," she said. "But that is not why he is dead. He is dead because he did not trust me. Dutch has been working for Russia for very long time. He is hungry for money. He is how I know so much about you. I tried to remove device from him, but he fought with me. I tried to let him live, but he would not stop trying to kill me. I had no choice. I had to kill him. My people are going to be angry with me when they find out what I have done. I am afraid of what they will do to me. To them, he is valuable asset."

Genuine fear rose in her eyes. She wasn't fearless after all.

When she paused, the first question that came tumbling out of my mouth was, "What did you do with Dutch's tracker?"

She looked embarrassed. "I have with me."

"What does that mean?"

"I *really* have with me." She pointed toward her stomach. "I swallowed it. It does not work unless inside body. Is powered by chemistry of body."

It occurred to me that in a few days, Dutch's tracker would see the light of day again. I wondered if she had a plan for dealing with it at that point. The thought of her swallowing it again after its voyage through her digestive tract made me a little nauseous.

"Do you have one?" I asked.

She looked at me thoughtfully. "I think I do not."

"You think?"

She nodded. "I think I do not have one because we know how easy it is to, uh . . . piggyback. I do not think we would give you chance to track us like we track you."

She had a valid point, but I wasn't as convinced as she seemed to be. That idea needed to be explored.

"So, if you don't have one, how would your people know if you were killed on a mission? How would they know if I were to kill you and feed you to the sharks? I've heard stories of people being fed to sharks."

Her face took on a serious, even ominous look. "Chase, I am *raskhoduyemyy*, expendable just like you. If I die, there are hundred or thousand more girls waiting to become me. If you die, there are hundred or thousand boys waiting to become Yankee-Doodle badass."

That got my attention. "Where did you hear that phrase, Yankee-Doodle badass?"

She laughed. "That is how they recruit most of you Americans—just like your U.S. Marines are looking for few good men."

I was genuinely concerned. "How do you know so much about us?

"We listen," she said with a great deal of pride.

"So, what are we going to do with my tracker now that it's not inside my body?"

"We could put in your tongue since is already open."

She laughed until she was almost in tears. I suppose I didn't expect her to have a sense of humor, but I was wrong.

I could play her game. "I know someplace we could stick it, but Dutch's would shove it out when it finally made its escape."

She clearly didn't expect me to play along, and she pressed the palm of her hand into my chest. "You think you are funny. Let us see if you think this is funny."

She kissed me and wrapped her arms around me as if she were holding on for dear life. I loved the way she felt in my arms. I held her as we kissed for what felt like hours, and our hands explored each other's bodies. I was appreciative of her tenderness since my tongue still felt like it'd been run over by a truck. There's nothing like a mouthful of stitches and a swollen tongue to ruin an otherwise perfect kiss, but it didn't seem to discourage her. We kissed as if we'd been lovers our entire lives.

Her life was one of death, fear, and unimaginable danger, but when she was in my arms, it was like she let that world melt away. She felt vulnerable and soft when I held her, but inside her chest beat the heart of the deadliest woman I knew. I wanted to believe that heart was also capable of loving me.

Suddenly, she drove both of her hands into my chest. "I have idea!"

"That's quite a way to end a kiss," I said. "What's this earth-shattering idea of yours?"

"Dolphins! We can catch dolphin and put tracker under its skin. When it comes up to breathe, satellites will see, and whole world will think you and Dutch are together on boat wherever dolphin goes. Is brilliant idea, yes?"

"Yes, it's brilliant," I said. "All of it except the part about catching a dolphin. I don't know how to catch a dolphin. Do you?"

"That part is up to you. You are big strong American, and I am just silly girl."

"You are neither silly, nor a girl," I retorted. "You are a dangerous, mortally serious, and astonishing woman."

She smiled. I loved her smile. I think I loved everything about her. Well, everything except her cutting my tongue in half and that icy Russian face she made.

"I do like the basis of your idea, though. Do you still have any of those poison darts you shot me with?"

"Maybe," she said shyly.

"Every island within three hundred miles of here is littered with monkeys. What if we shoot a couple of them with your tranquilizers, shove the trackers in their ears, then make our escape?"

We laughed, enjoying the silliness we were able to bring to a moment so serious.

When we'd gathered our wits, she tossed my tracking device onto her tongue and swallowed it. "There," she said. "If your cooking does not kill me first, we will not have to worry about that for few more days."

26
Lemonade Sunset

The wind picked up to twenty knots, and *Aegis* heeled nearly twenty-five degrees. Anya had gone below to do whatever women do when they go below, and I found myself at the wheel, leaning as my boat cut through the waves like a sleek racing yacht. She was not built to sail on her side like the racing boats that thrived on heeling forty-five degrees or more.

Aegis was an easy boat to sail, but she could become a handful in high wind. Bonaire was my tentative destination, but the southwesterly wind would make for a long and uncomfortable cruise. I stood at the wheel with one knee on the seat, deliberating over other possible destinations, when Anya peered up through the companionway.

"We are flipping over, no?"

I chuckled. "I certainly hope not."

She looked uncomfortable. "Can you make it not do that? I do not like being tilted over like this."

"It's called heeling," I said. "It's one of the things sailboats do. You'll get used to it. I promise."

She looked up at me with eyes that were impossible to resist. "Please. I do not like this."

Little did she know, with those words, she plotted our new course.

Thoughts of shore-diving off Bonaire vanished. "Have you ever been to Anguilla?"

Her answer was perfect. "Not yet."

I brought *Aegis* to port and eased the sheets, allowing both sails to swing well out over the side, bringing us onto a broad reach with the wind blowing across the deck.

As we turned eastward, the big boat left its side, and the mast pointed straight up toward the heavens.

Anya mouthed, "Thank you," and disappeared back into the bowels of my boat.

Downwind sailing is boring and hot, but seeing my favorite Russian happy and comfortable was worth the cost. I pulled out my chart, even though I had a perfectly good GPS chart plotter onboard. I loved the look and feel of paper nautical charts, and somehow, sailing with them instead of electronic gadgets made the experience richer and more fulfilling. I plotted a course for Virgin Gorda. There was a perfect anchorage there where we could spend the night watching shooting stars, and sleep through the next day so we could make the seventy-five-mile sail to Anguilla the following night. Arriving in a new anchorage is always best done at daybreak. There's almost nothing more beautiful than sailing at night. Feeling the miles drift beneath the keel with a billion stars twinkling overhead is something magical that words can't adequately describe.

When I reached my limit of sailing flat under the midday sun, it was time for a drink. I stepped through the companionway and down the ladder into the galley. As my foot landed on the first step, a dishtowel exploded in my face. I didn't expect to suffer an attack from a dishtowel, so I was a little surprised.

"Get out!" she exclaimed. "If I wanted you down here, I would call for you. Now, get back up there and do boat captain things. I am busy."

"But I want a drink," I protested.

With hands on hips and a scowl on her determined face, she said, "I will bring for you drink. Just go."

I didn't know much about how real life worked, but I was smart enough to know following her instructions was the best possible decision I could make at that moment, so I obeyed and returned to the cockpit.

I had no sooner nestled into my seat under the canopy, when Anya came through the companionway with a pair of perfectly yellow drinks in her hands.

"Is lemonade, I think. Is first time for me making and for drinking, so do not complain. Just drink."

Again, I obeyed, and again, I was rewarded. The lemonade was the best I'd ever tasted.

I stroked her hair. "I'm really glad you're here, and I love your lemonade."

A frown consumed her smile. "I am glad I am here, too, but I do not know how long I can stay. They are going to come for you. They are going to try and kill you."

"Who?" I asked. "I'm not that easy to kill."

"Chase, you are very easy to kill. I could have killed you many times. Do not get feelings hurt. I am good at killing, but I am not best. There are many more who are better. They will come if what you say about Suslik is true. If you killed him, some powerful people will pay large price for your head."

Her words chiseled their way into my confidence. "If what you say is true, why haven't you killed me yet?"

She looked at me as if she had no understanding of why I would ask such a question. "I was not sent to kill you. That is not my job . . . yet. I work for Dmitri Barkov for now. He is wealthy and powerful man. He is *oprichnik*. You know this word, yes?"

"Yes, I know what *oprichnina* means. I'm sure my understanding is less thorough than yours, but I seem to remember that *oprichnina* was an elite group of individuals commissioned by Tsar Ivan IV—Ivan the Terrible to some—to carry out his will with complete abandon. *Oprichnina* ultimately became the *Komitet Gosudarstvennoy Bezopasnosti*, or KGB, four hundred years after good ol' Ivan met his demise. Then, after things began to turn friendly over there, the KGB evolved into the *Sluzhba Vneshney Razvedki*, or SVR, of which you claim to be an officer."

"Not bad. That is not exactly what happened, but is close enough. Okay, so Dmitri Barkov is descendent of *oprichnina* and former KGB. He is wealthy man and gets whatever he wants. Well, almost whatever he wants, but not always everything." She paused long enough to take a sip of lemonade, then looked into her glass. "Is this how it should taste?"

"It is," I said. "In fact, I think it's the best lemonade I've ever had."

"I do not know. Is sweet and sour at same time. This confuses my tongue, and right now, I have only good tongue on boat." She took another sip and continued. "So, when I became SVR officer and proved I was good at everything, Barkov insisted I come to work for him. I do not know why he chose me or how he knew about me. I am *sirota*—orphan. My mother died when I was young girl, and I believe my father was war hero and died before I was born, so without parents, I was nothing. I was educated by State and trained to be what I am. Russia is my family."

She sat stoically, showing no emotion while telling her story. The psychology of such a childhood fascinated me, but I didn't see her as a case study. To me, she was strong and impressive. Not only was I falling in love with her, but I was also becoming more impressed with everything about her.

"We are going to Anguilla, yes?"

"Yes, we are, but not today. Today we're going to Virgin Gorda. There's an anchorage where we can spend twenty-four hours without checking in with customs and immigration. Then, tomorrow night, we'll set sail for Anguilla. It's only about seventy miles from Virgin Gorda to Anguilla. If the wind holds, we can make that in less than ten hours. We'll be there for the sunrise. How does that sound?"

Instead of answering, she placed two fingers on my lips and spread them apart. She looked into my mouth with obvious concern. "Is getting better. How does it feel?"

"It feels much better today. I think it'll be back in kissing condition in another day or two."

"Oh, I think is in fine kissing condition already, but I cannot wait to know how it feels when you are back to perfect." She playfully kissed me on the tip of my nose before hopping up and heading back toward the galley.

"What are you doing down there?"

"I am cooking for you. Is that not what American women do for their men?"

I laughed. "I have no idea what American women do for their men. I've never been an American woman's man. Our line of work tends to be hard on relationships."

She tilted her head. "It does not have to be."

* * *

We arrived in the anchorage off Virgin Gorda about an hour before sunset. When I finished anchoring in sixteen feet of water, I shut down the engine and bagged the sails. As if she'd planned the timing to the minute, Anya came up with two steaming bowls of something that smelled heavenly, a loaf of French bread, and two bottled beers on a bamboo tray.

"It smells amazing. What is it?"

"It is simple stew. You had fish and potatoes, so I cook what you have. You have been so kind to me, except for shooting me, I thought you would like for me to cook for you."

I'd never known a woman of such extremes. She could kill a man in the blink of an eye, yet she still sought to please me by cooking for me.

Has she ever been shown kindness beyond general courtesy? Has anyone ever truly loved her?

I wanted to be the first man who saw past her deadly persona and found tenderness and true beauty behind her stunning exterior. I wanted to show her more than physical desire. I longed to touch her heart and taste her soul.

Would she invite me inside and allow me to experience the magic she kept hidden away deep within?

Perhaps it wasn't wonder on my part. Perhaps it was hope.

We ate her stew and drank our beer. My tongue had healed enough that I could taste the incredible flavors. The stew was full of pepper and bold flavors I couldn't identify, but I loved every bite.

When the last drop disappeared from my bowl and my bottle was empty, I laid my hand on her leg. "Thank you. That was magnificent. Just like you."

"You are welcome. I am happy I pleased you."

I placed my hand beneath her ear and held her perfect face in the palm of my hand. She closed her eyes and let me caress her neck and play with her long, flowing hair. She made soft, warm sounds that made me never want to let her go, but that was beyond all hope.

She licked her lips and drew in a long, full breath. "I will be right back." She gathered our dishes and returned to the galley.

When she came back on deck, she was wearing the same flowing, white cotton shirt as when I'd seen her on the beach in St. Thomas, and she had a silky wraparound skirt bound loosely about her hips and falling lightly across her thighs.

She turned around slowly, just beyond my reach. "You like?"

"I do," I said, reaching for her hand.

She placed her hand in mine and joined me on the cushion. We watched the sun sink into the ocean and the stars fill the night sky. She sat between my legs, reclined against my chest, and her hair danced in my face on the gentle evening breeze. I never wanted the moment to end, and I silently thanked God for the angel He'd placed in my arms.

As the stars made their timeless trek across the night sky, we lay in each other's arms, sharing ourselves in wordless expression, while the rest of the world drifted away.

Finally, she kissed me just below my ear. "*Ya ves' tvoya, Chasechka.*"

"And I am yours, my darling Anya."

I felt her breath grow deep and rhythmic as her body relaxed. I held her as the stars made their timeless journey across the sky, and she slept peacefully, safe in my embrace. If I never lived to see another sunset, I would die knowing that no woman could make me feel the beauty, the passion, and the submission I felt in the arms of a woman who should've been my enemy.

27

A Guest

When I awoke, the sun was already high in the bright blue, cloudless sky, and I stretched and yawned, trying not to disturb Anya as she slept at my side. Her skin shone with breathtaking radiance as the morning sun beamed through the hatch above her head. I slipped from the bed and left her to sleep.

I stood on deck and enjoyed a cup of coffee while watching the sea birds soar overhead. Occasionally, one would dive into the crystal-clear water and emerge victorious with a fish clenched in its beak. I laughed at how the less successful birds attacked the one with the fish. I couldn't help comparing that phenomenon to humanity. It always seemed those without fish were pestering the ones who had worked hard to capture a meal. Apparently, the concept of greed without willingness to sacrifice wasn't limited to the human species alone.

When Anya arrived on deck, she was wearing a pair of my boxer shorts drawn tightly around her waist, and one of my T-shirts was falling off her tanned shoulder.

"There is more coffee, yes?" she asked in a sleepy voice.

"There is. It's on the stove. I'll be happy to get it for you if you'd like."

"Thank you, but I am closer. I will get. More for you?"

I offered my cup. "Yes, please."

She brought the pot on deck, refilled my cup, then poured hers. We sat together on a long blue cushion. She was drawn to the antics of the sea birds, just as I had been. We sat silently drinking our coffee and watching the birds until she finally spoke.

"Last night was perfect."

Her tone was soft and self-assured. Her confidence was alluring without being arrogant.

"Yes, it was," I said, unable to keep from smiling.

Seductively, she said, "Perhaps we will have many nights like that, and perhaps some nights better."

I doubted I was capable of surviving many more nights like that, but I was absolutely willing to try. The only words that would come from my mouth were, "I certainly hope so."

A small, inflatable dinghy hummed in the distance across the calm water of the anchorage. As the boat approached, the figure of a single bearded man at the controls appeared. He stared intently at my boat and managed the outboard motor with practiced skill. He waved and smiled broadly as he drew ever closer.

Anya noticed him as well and couldn't seem to look away. Her instincts were so well-honed that almost nothing happened without her noticing.

I whispered, "Do you know that guy?"

She stared at the oncoming stranger. "I do not think so, but I cannot be sure. Do you know him?"

"No, I don't," I whispered, "but he wants us to think he knows us."

She leaned in close. "Keep him busy, and do not let him come aboard."

Not surprisingly, she'd taken control of the situation. Her skill and experience only added to her beauty. She slipped away from my side and through the companionway while the man in the dinghy continued his approach. He stood with his knees bent in a practiced pose that would make a perfect fighting stance, but I might've been reading too much into the situation. The stance was also perfect for standing in a small, unstable boat. Perhaps he'd been trained to stand that way, or maybe he'd learned it by falling out of a few too many dinghies.

"Mike? Is that you?" the man yelled over the rumbling sound of his outboard motor.

I stood, looking down at him and trying to determine if he was just a fellow cruiser who wanted to say hello or someone trying to get close enough to identify and kill me.

He looked back and forth between my eyes and his outboard and chuckled before yelling, "Ah, you probably can't hear me over the engine." He leaned down to press the kill switch, but instead of the engine falling silent and the man standing to introduce himself, he raised a suppressed pistol from beside the engine cowling and brought it to bear on my chest.

I dived to the deck and waited to hear the whisper of the bullet as it left the suppressor. The sound I'd expected came, but it came with a sound I hadn't anticipated. An instant before he pulled the trigger, the man emitted something between a grunt and a startled yell.

The small caliber bullet tore through the Bimini top of my boat, and I pieced together the scene unfolding in front of me. Anya's arm appeared from the surface of the water behind the gunman, and grasped firmly in her hand was an aluminum boat hook. My nine-toed assassin and lover used the boat hook to drive the gunman's firing arm upward just as he pulled the trigger. She then hooked his mouth with the tool and yanked him into the water with her.

With no time for hesitation, I dived into the water and found Anya with her left arm locked firmly under the gunman's chin and her left hand holding her right arm in a perfect choke hold. The man was not going to escape her grasp. If she didn't drown him, he'd soon pass out from the choke and be deadweight in her arms.

As he flailed in a wasted effort to break free of Anya's grasp, I drove my knee into his crotch and followed with a second knee strike to his gut. I wanted to pound every ounce of air from his lungs to increase the effectiveness of Anya's choke hold, and it worked. The man's eyes rolled back in his head, and his tongue hung loosely from his mouth.

Before Anya released her hold on the gunman, I drove my right pinky finger up his nose with as much force as I could produce while treading water. A finger shoved up a person's nose is impossible to ignore. If the man had been faking unconsciousness, he would've reacted to the intrusive finger, but he didn't flinch. He was out cold.

I killed the outboard and tied the dinghy to *Aegis* while Anya dragged his limp body through the water. I helped her heft his weight onto the swim platform, then followed her aboard.

We wasted no time getting him hogtied in the main salon, and I waved a small pack of smelling salts under his bloody nose. When he coughed and gagged himself back to consciousness, we listened closely for the first sounds leaving his mouth. Most often, when a person has been unconscious, the first words he speaks when he returns to the land of the living will be spoken in the first language he learned as a child. That tidbit would give us a pretty good idea of where to start our interrogation.

I was not expecting what came out of his mouth. He muttered, "What in tarnation was that?"

He sounded like he was from Dump Truck County, Alabama. There was no question he was American—Southern American.

Why was this guy trying to kill me?

I shoved my foot into his shoulder and rolled him onto his side. It was impossible for him to lie on his back with his hands and feet bound together behind him. Tying people up was definitely one of Anya's strengths. He grunted in agony when I pinned him to the floor with the muzzle of my Makarov pressed into his left eye. I wasn't certain how much pressure the human eye could withstand without bursting, but I had to be approaching that threshold.

"*Ubei ego!*" The words left Anya's lips with ease and confidence.

Her words were a test and not an order. She'd told me to "kill him" in unmistakable Russian. Our guest didn't flinch, so she repeated the command in angry, Russian-accented Spanish. His body stiffened, and terror filled his eyes. Well, terror filled one of his eyes; the other was still full of the muzzle of my pistol.

So, we'd learned our American friend understood Spanish but not Russian. We'd asked no questions, but we already knew more about him than he knew about us. I was certain he knew there was no chance he'd leave my boat alive.

"So, now that we have your attention," I said. "It's time to establish some ground rules."

I stuck out my damaged tongue for him to see. "Do you see this?"

He displayed every sign of confusion, and that was exactly what I wanted.

I returned my battered tongue into my mouth and paused for dramatic effect. "She did that to me when she thought I was lying to her. She loves me. She already hates you, so imagine what she'll do if she even *thinks* you might be lying to us."

His one-eyed gaze shifted to Anya as she made that angry Russian look she did so well. It even frightened me a little, and I believed she was on my team . . . at least for the moment. What she did next would've made me laugh had we not been interrogating the man who tried to kill me.

She pulled her dripping-wet shoe from her foot, along with the soggy bandage. She rested her heel on the man's forehead, giving him a front-row seat from which to enjoy the mangled flesh where her toe had once been.

When she was certain he'd fully absorbed the spectacle, she pointed at me. "He did this to me when I would not give him what he wanted. He loves me. He detests you. Are you understanding?"

The man spat saliva and blood at my hand as I continued to press the pistol into his eye. In impressive defiance, he said, "Go to hell, both of you!"

Anya grabbed her wet shoe and slapped the man with the sole. The sound echoed through the cabin. She shoved the shoe into his mouth, heel first, and quickly tied the laces around his neck, making it impossible for him to spit it out. She pulled out a half-gallon metal can of cooking alcohol from the locker beneath the galley sink. It was the alcohol that fueled our stove. Whatever she was about to do wasn't going to be much fun for our guest.

She poured the alcohol from the can into the shoe that had become our new friend's mouthpiece. The alcohol gushed out of the can, soaking the shoe and his face. Anya placed the can on the deck beside the man and calmly said, "Chew on that until you are ready to be nice."

The man shook his head violently and yelled unintelligible obscenities through the canvas of the soaked shoe. He bucked and shook like a trapped animal. Had he not tried to shoot me earlier, I would've felt sorry for him, but I was all out of pity.

Anya watched as if she were bored as he writhed and then turned to me. "We have how much time?"

I checked my watch. "I'm in no hurry. We'll stay as long as it takes to get him to talk."

"Good. I was afraid we would have to hurt him quickly, but we have time to make it fun and go slow."

I hoped our guest understood what Anya said while he was screaming and jerking around. I couldn't imagine the feeling of the alcohol in his mouth, nose, and eyes.

When he settled down enough to talk, Anya untied the strings, removed the shoe from his mouth, and asked, "Okay, are we going to be nice?"

He spat and roared in continued defiance.

She shrugged and reinserted the shoe. Against the violent shaking and thrashing, she patiently retied the laces around his head. She lifted the can of alcohol and deliberately poured it onto the shoe, letting plenty of the liquid puddle in his eyes and nose. When the can was empty, she set it on the side of his face as he lay on his side. He shook the can from his face and watched it bounce across the deck. Anya patiently lifted the can and pulled a Zippo lighter from beside the stove.

With unequalled patience, she held the can by its handle, and slapped the man with its long flat side. "You will be still."

She opened the lighter and rolled the flint wheel until a blue flame danced from the wick. She carefully placed the burning lighter on top of the alcohol can and stood the can back on the man's face.

With absolutely no emotion in her voice, she said, "Move, and can will fall. Then, I don't know. Maybe fire goes out, but maybe not. Women are mean when men burn shoes. Do not make me mean."

The man froze, proving Anya had his attention.

"Good boy," she said, patting his head. "We now watch. This is first time for me to try this. I think is working."

For the first time since we'd awakened the mysterious gunman, he was deathly silent and perfectly still. She'd found his weakness, and it had only taken minutes. He was afraid of fire. Most people are, but most people aren't professional hit men. At our core, all of us, even hit men, are afraid of something.

I wasn't a fan of an open flame in the cabin of my boat. There's nothing more devastating than a fire at sea, but I wasn't going to interrupt Anya's technique in the name of seamanship.

After we believed sufficient time had passed, and the man trembled from the tensed muscles in his neck, I lifted the lighter from the metal can and snapped it closed.

He didn't continue his rage; instead, he relaxed the muscles of his neck and let his head fall to the cabin sole. I learned at The Ranch that an operator will sometimes employ a tactic known as feigned submission. The captive will pretend to submit to the will of the interrogator and feed them a heaping helping of lies in order to stall the interrogation long enough to come up with a plan to escape. I feared that might be what the gunman was doing, and if it was, he deserved an Academy Award for best actor.

"Both of you are insane." The would-be shooter exhaled the words as if they might be the last he ever spoke.

I trained my pistol on the bridge of his nose. "We're not the ones who tried to motor up next to a big sailboat and kill the two assassins onboard. That would be insane."

He furrowed his brow and glared at Anya. "I'm not here to kill her. I don't even know who she is, but I'll tell you one thing. She's going to kill both of us before this is over, boy."

Anya showed no reaction to the man's attempt to divide and conquer. How could a woman of such intense passion be so cold and stoic in situations like this? She showed determined resolve to accomplish the mission that had fallen into our lap.

"Who sent you to kill him?" she asked.

The man spat and blinked as the sting from the alcohol became unbearable. He stared at Anya through his blood-red eyes. "Look, you little red commie, why don't you scoot on back to Moscow and let us men handle our business?"

The words had barely left his lips before the heel of my right foot landed across his nose, sending blood, snot, and spit spraying from his face. The sound of a wounded animal escaped his mouth, and he shook his head, trying to shake off the pain of having his nose crushed beneath my heel.

When he gathered his wits, he said, "Touched a nerve there, did I, boy? So, now it's all coming together for me. The grown-up spy over here has fallen in love with Red Sonja, who's here to seduce him and get him to spill his guts so she can get another medal from the Kremlin, or whatever they give characters like her for screwing American agents. You're a sucker, boy. She's doing the same thing to you that she's doing to me. The only difference is that you're getting to taste a little of her red commie candy before she puts a bullet in your brain."

Anya knelt beside the man and whispered into his ear, "I am not good interrogator. Is not what I do. I tear souls out of men like you and send them to Hell. Do not forget this. You have now one try to answer question. If you tell truth, I will kill you quickly. If you tell lie, I will have fun turning your insides into outsides, and I will watch you die slowly while I have my red commie tea. You understand, yes?"

By the look on what was left of the man's face, he understood completely.

He begged me, "Dude, she's crazy. Shoot her in the head, and I'll get you someplace safe. Otherwise, if she doesn't kill you, they'll never stop coming for you. I came, and there will be more. You screwed up when you killed Dutch. We all knew he was a traitor, but you should be smart enough to know you can't just go on a killing spree of your own accord. You're a wild card, kid, and you're too easy to track."

Anya gave me a look and then turned back to the gunman. "What else do you want him to tell you? I will make him talk for you."

I shook my head. "I think that pretty much covers everything we need to know, don't you?"

"*Da*," she said with ice-cold resolve. She plunged a syringe into the gunman's neck and watched him drift off to sleep.

Few have what it takes to do what she and I did professionally, but watching her kill with such efficiency and indifference left my stomach turning.

She bent the needle and tossed it into the trash. "Help me put him to bed."

"What? What do you mean, put him to bed?"

She laughed. "I did not kill him. He is still alive, but he is taking nap. When he wakes up, I will poop trackers, and we can put them in him and send him away."

She was brilliant. I had so much to learn from her. We moved the gunman to a bunk and tied him in place, just in case the drugs wore off before we expected.

We ate and watched the seabirds dive into the placid water in search of their midday meal.

"So, all of that stuff he said about you . . . I know it isn't true," I said.

She stared into the sky. Instead of reassuring me that she wasn't just waiting to flip or kill me, she looked up at me like a frightened little girl.

"What is it?" I asked.

She took a long, deep breath. "I do not want to do this anymore, Chase. I am tired of killing and games we play. I do not like it. Is not what I want. Is not what I want to be. Is not what I am . . . not really. Is only what I do. I want to run away from all of it, but I do not know how."

She cast her gaze back to the deck, as if unable to face me after admitting she wanted out of the life her country had chosen for her. Unlike me, she'd never known the freedom to choose for herself. I knew so little about her, yet she was opening up to me and sharing her deepest, most intimate desire: her desire to be free.

I took her face in my palms. She felt so fragile in my hands, but behind those hypnotic eyes was the mind and soul of one of the world's most dangerous women. She could tear my body apart before I could blink, and she could destroy my heart quicker than that. I fell in love with her so quickly, and so easily. I didn't choose to be, but I was completely lost in my desire for her. I longed to know her gentleness and kindness, and my body yearned to know her passion without end. I couldn't walk away from her now, even if I wanted to.

"Listen to me, Anastasia," I said softly.

Her gaze consumed mine almost instantly. "I told you to never call me this name."

"Why? Why can't I call you by your name?"

"You will think I am silly child. You will not understand."

Her words first came with anger, but quickly gave way to surrender. Her resolve melted away.

I stroked her cheek with the backs of my fingers, tracing the elegant, graceful curve of her face, and I fell more deeply in love with her as every second passed.

"I may not understand, but I want to."

Sincerity and perhaps the dawning of trust shone in her eyes. A tear filled the corner of her eye and ran down her cheek. She licked her lips, swallowed slowly, and pressed her head into the curve of my shoulder. I wrapped my arms around her as her body surrendered against mine. I so hoped it wasn't an act. I'd been taught that foreign agents would use unparalleled tactics of deception and feigned emotion to earn my trust, but I didn't believe Anya was doing that. I believed she'd finally found someone she could trust, and someone with whom she could be vulnerable and honest—at least that's what I hoped.

When she finally spoke, her words came softly and slowly. "Anastasia is name my mother called me. That was her name for me—only hers. After she died, no one has ever called me by this name."

She looked at me with eyes so wet I could barely see her pupils. "I told you my father died in war before I was born, but that is not truth. I lied only about that, Chase, nothing else. My father gave me name Anastasia before he died. My mother said he was brave, strong, and best man in all of world. She told me he would sing songs to me when I was falling asleep. I do not remember him, but sometimes, I can hear him sing to me when I am alone and afraid. I do not know how old I was when my mother died. I think maybe three or maybe four. Things are different in Russia for orphans."

She fell silent for a long moment. There was nothing I could say that would make her feel any better. She needed to be held and loved, but I had so many questions. I wanted to know about her mother. I wanted to know about her childhood, her education, and her training. I wanted to hear how she'd grown up and how she'd become a woman.

She didn't sob. She just breathed deeply and seemed to enjoy the feeling of being wrapped in my arms. I liked her willingness to share such intimacy with me.

She leaned back, away from my chest, and looked up with the tender, injured eyes of a child. "*Spasibo, Amerikanets. Spasibo.*"

She kissed me so tenderly that my lips barely felt hers.

"I have money," I said.

"What?"

"I have money. I have a lot of money, in fact. I have enough money for both of us to disappear for the rest of our lives. They paid me over eight million dollars to kill Suslik."

Her eyes widened. I thought she was astonished by the balance of my bank account, but that wasn't it at all.

Her tone quickly shifted from that of a frightened child to the voice of a confident, seasoned killer. "Where is money now, Chase?"

"It's in a bank in the Caymans. It's very safe. No one can get to it."

"You are wrong!" she insisted. "The people who put money in account know everything about you. They know account numbers, passwords, and what breakfast you had. When you do not answer phone I killed, they will think you are dead, and they will take money back. You must move money now. You must."

She looked fearfully into my eyes. "The man you call Suslik is not dead."

I didn't know her well, but I knew the tone she was using was more serious and sincere than anything she'd said to me up to that point, so I didn't react. The first two thoughts that came to my head arrived simultaneously.

Of course he's dead. I killed him. How could she possibly know he wasn't dead?

She must've recognized my doubtful expression. "Chase, you do not understand. Man you call Suslik is not man. He is cat, or ghost of cat with more lives than cat. I cannot explain this to you, but you must trust me. Move your money now before they know Suslik cannot be killed and before they think you are dead."

I sat wordlessly, pondering what she said. I had yet to decide if I was being played, or if she was sincerely as taken by me as I was by her. I didn't want to believe she was playing a game, yet I found it almost impossible to believe a woman like her could possibly care for me.

"I need you to promise you will move money, Chase."

"I will, Anya. I promise."

I took both of her hands in mine and squeezed them reassuringly. "Tell me what you want."

She wore a puzzled expression. "What I want does not matter. I do not have choices. I am not free to choose for me. I must do as I am told. It is not simple like you think. I cannot just walk away. My world is not like yours. I am not mercenary. I am soldier. You choose to go or do not go. I do not choose. I go. This is all. I go."

I continued holding her hands. "It doesn't have to be that way. I have enough money for us to live anywhere we want. You can choose right now. You can choose to stay with me."

"If it were simple, I would stay with you, Chase. I would love you. I would have babies with you, and I would have you love me."

"Listen to me, Anya—"

She pressed her finger to my lips. "No, you listen. You have shown me kindness with no agenda. I have only known such kindness once in my life. I want to believe I remember being loved by my mother when I was baby. Because she died when I was so young, I think my memories are not real."

My heart was breaking for her. "Anya, listen to me. The memories of your mother and the feelings you have for her are wonderful and perfectly normal. Don't push them away. They're—"

She stopped me again. "I need for you to listen to me and to not stop me, please. It does not matter if how I feel for my mother is real, because the way you look at me—the way you make me feel—is what is real now. I know it is, and I love it."

"Of course it's real. I do love you."

"I will not spy for you, Chase. I will not betray what I have been trained to protect, and I will not ask you to betray what you love. I know you think I am trying to seduce you to have you share what you know with me, but is not truth. I should be doing this, but I cannot. I know this is my duty to have you like putty in hands and take everything from your mind, but I feel for you. I feel honesty and need and trust for you. I do not trust anyone, but I trust you, and I do not know why. I know you are trained to lie to me and to get me to tell you everything, but you do not do that. You are sincere when you kiss me and when you make love to me. You are kind. That is new feeling for me. I want to be kind to you. I do not know feeling Americans call love. I know respect, fear, and lust, but I do not know love. I am, for first time, feeling something that frightens and excites me. I am feeling something with you that is foreign to me. None of this is easy for me. I cannot stay with you right now, Chase, but I will come back. I will."

She had to see the horror in my eyes when she told me she couldn't stay. I was at a loss for words, so I said the dumbest thing that could've possibly come out of my mouth. "How do you know Suslik isn't dead?"

I saw the pain in her eyes. I'd taken a tender, vulnerable moment, and turned it into a selfish question. I hated myself for being so stupid. I tried to take it back, but it was too late. The damage was done.

Her expression hardened, and she pulled her hands from mine. "Chase, I am leaving tonight. I will find you soon, but you must go home. You must move money, and you must go home. Listen to me. Do not try to find me. Nothing could be more dangerous for you. I will find you. I swear to you, I will find you."

I opened my mouth to speak, but she shook her head, stood, and disappeared below deck. I wanted to kick myself for my stupidity. Anya had poured her soul into my hands, and I let it fall to the deck. I was disgusted with my insensitivity.

Anya's head appeared in the companionway. "Our friend is still sleeping, and I think you should do same. You have sailing tonight."

She disappeared again. She was right, of course. I did need to rest before our long night of sailing, but she said she was leaving, and I didn't want to miss spending one moment with her.

Moments later, she appeared on deck with two drinks in her hands and sat beside me.

She half-smiled. "I think how we feel about each other is new feeling for you, too. We are to learn together, in time, but not now. I am going to make it for you easy. You take nap. I will wake you before sun goes down, and we will sail to Anguilla tonight. We will take care of our guest, then we will make plan to find each other again. Yes?"

I smiled, "Yes, of course, that's okay with me. I think it's a wonderful idea. Now, listen, I'm very sorry about the question—"

She shushed me and handed me a glass. "Never be sorry."

It was her perfect lemonade again. The tangy sweetness made me smile, and I emptied the drink in two long swallows. She placed her fingers against my bottom lip and pulled my mouth open as she peered at my swollen tongue. "It looks better, but is still too big. It will be okay in few days. I am sorry—"

"Never be sorry," I said as I pressed my lips to hers.

Her hands in my hair and her body against mine felt like Heaven had descended upon me. My eyes grew heavy, and my body melted into her arms. There was absolutely nothing I could do. I was powerless to resist the coming sleep.

28
Rude Awakening

The sun was still visible, but just barely, when I finally pried my eyes open. I felt as if I'd been hit by a bus. My head ached, and my limbs felt like they weighed a thousand pounds. I shook my head and squinted, trying to remember what happened for the past twelve hours.

Small pieces of the day came together, and I tried to focus on the things I knew for sure. Anya checked on our guest and declared him to be breathing. She'd made lemonade again and had a glass with me in the cockpit. I vaguely remember kissing her just before my lights went out.

The lemonade! How could I have fallen for such deception? Anya and her tranquilizers. . . .

Standing on trembling knees, I took inventory of my senses and surroundings. I was groggy. My boat was still well at anchor, but something was missing. It was the gunman's dinghy.

This can't be good.

But the dinghy wasn't the only thing missing. The gunman, Anya, and every drop of evidence that either were ever aboard had vanished. I called for her, but the only response came from the seagulls drifting lazily overhead.

My stomach felt like it was going to implode. I was abandoned and alone. I'd grown accustomed to feeling Anya's movement aboard the boat. I'd come to love her scent when we passed on deck and the feeling of her hair caressing my skin when we sat together in the cockpit. Now, she and every hint of her were gone from both my boat and my life.

She told me she'd be leaving and that she'd make it as easy as possible for me, but I didn't expect her to simply vanish. I don't know what I thought was going to happen, but none of it mattered. I was a long way from home—if I had a home—and even further from a plan.

My mouth felt like the desert, but my head was clearing. I pulled my favorite plastic cup from the cupboard and reached for the faucet in the galley. Living aboard a boat tends to create habits landlubbers don't understand. Creatures of all sizes tend to congregate aboard boats, and they like to take naps in nice cool places like inside plastic cups. The first mouthful of an unidentifiable bug taught me to always shake the cup upside down and take a quick peek inside before filling it with anything meant to end up in my mouth. The shake-n-peek had become an unconscious habit. When I reflexively performed the habitual motion, a small, curled piece of paper fell from the cup and onto the cutting board. I placed the cup in the sink, picked up the slip of paper, and examined it carefully. When I unrolled the paper, I couldn't believe my eyes. Written in delicate freehand script was:

Chase,

First, it is important for you to know I am sorry for going away while you slept, but I know you understand why it had to be. Second, move your money now. Third, I will find you, I promise. Fourth, stop being predictable and drink from different cup sometimes. We really have to work on what you Americans call tradecraft. Finally, I know how you feel about me, and I feel same for you. We will find a way.

Instead of a signature, the bottom of the note was adorned with a sketch of two skinny human feet. One had all five toes and the other only had four. I laughed aloud as I read the note a dozen times. I even lifted it to my nose on the off chance that her faint scent might still be lingering on the paper. I slid the note inside my copy of *Practical Navigation for Yachtsmen* and set about plotting a course for Georgetown on Grand Cayman. I needed to see a banker about moving a little cash.

Georgetown lay just over a thousand miles west with Puerto Rico, Haiti, and Jamaica sprinkled nicely along the route. Anya would've enjoyed seeing those places. The prevailing wind was nice and strong from the southwest, which would make for thirty degrees of heel. I laughed, remembering how Anya had unknowingly chosen an easterly course with her dislike of heeling as we beat into the wind. Considering my westerly course, everything about the coming night meant I was getting farther away from the unforgettable Russian.

With my course plotted, I weighed anchor and set sail into the fifteen-knot southwesterly wind. *Aegis* heeled and settled into the sea just as I knew she would. For the first several hours, I sat or stood with my hand on the wheel, feeling every twitch of the rudder and savoring the beauty and ease with which my fifteen tons of freedom cut through the wind and waves. I finally surrendered her to the autopilot and headed for the galley.

I did the shake-n-peek with every cup, hoping to find another note, but the search was disappointingly fruitless.

* * *

My journey, as is true of most of life's journeys, proved to be far more than a change in scenery. The seventeen degrees of longitude separating Virgin Gorda and Georgetown meant one hundred eighty degrees of life-changing distance in the days to come.

So many decisions were made without my permission, and so much life had been stolen from me in the previous two years. My childhood as the son of spies—who I thought were missionaries —left me both blessed and cursed with a headful of lies and mysterious truths that were impossible to separate. Physical injury

tore me from my future as a major leaguer. My friendship and respect for an eccentric psychology professor led me to becoming
what my father had been: a killer. I made none of those decisions. They were made for me, yet they were the defining events
of my life so far.

As the sun rose and set on my journey, it was time to make
some decisions for myself. Anya was correct. I had to move my
money someplace only I could find it. I had to talk face-to-face
with Dr. Richter about what happened, and specifically about
Anya. He was the closest thing I had to a father. More importantly, he was one of the few living souls left on Earth I could
trust.

* * *

The banking business in Georgetown was a life lesson for me.
I learned a million dollars in cash won't fit in most briefcases, but
it will fit in a gym bag, and it weighs around twenty-five pounds
in hundred-dollar bills.

I also learned I couldn't just walk out of a bank with eight
million dollars in cash. Besides weighing two hundred pounds
and taking up as much space as a beanbag chair, banks don't keep
that much cash on hand. I didn't know any of those things before my afternoon of embarrassing questions. I left the bank with
just over a million dollars in cash, seven checks, and a stack of
bearer bonds.

There could be no worse idea than to place that much perish-
able value aboard a sinkable sailboat in the Caribbean Sea. Instead of bedding down my fortune aboard *Aegis*, I chose to open
a few numbered accounts and spread it around. That part turned
out to be quite easy, and I ended the day with a stack of credit
cards drawn against five accounts. Remembering David Shepherd's instruction, I kept a nice little stack of hundreds as walking-around money.

* * *

Dr. Richter arrived on a chartered flight just as the sun was setting on one of those perfect Caribbean evenings that look so good on postcards. When I picked him up at Owen Roberts International Airport, I was surprised to see he wasn't alone. The man with Dr. Richter carried himself with the confidence of an operator but the look of a politician. It was an odd combination. He was fit and observant like a good field agent, but he wore the fake smile of a governor who wanted to be a senator. There was a dichotomy about him that was impossible to overlook.

Perhaps the other man's presence would make sense as the evening progressed, but at that moment, I was a little disappointed Dr. Richter hadn't come alone. When I called him, I made it clear that I needed to speak with him privately. I needed not only professional guidance, but also an old, trusted friend. I had a lot on my mind. I honestly felt a little betrayed that he brought a new character into my already crumbling world.

As Dr. Richter and the other man stepped from the plane and started across the tarmac, I left the terminal building to greet them. The man never took his eyes off me. I was tempted to not let him know I recognized his blatant stare, but I decided to play alpha male. Surprisingly, he blinked first. I didn't expect that. After he blinked, that politician's smile smeared across the lower half of his face disappeared. He wore khaki slacks, a blue button-down shirt, and a navy jacket. Dr. Richter, on the other hand, wore his typical professorial attire. His ragged shirt looked like it should've been thrown into a ragbag in the seventies. Some things never change.

I shook Dr. Richter's hand and embraced him as if he were my long-lost brother. He returned my hug, but not with the same measure of excitement. Something was making him uncomfortable.

When we parted, he turned to the man. "Chase, this is Michael Pennant. Michael, meet Chase Fulton."

The man extended his hand, and I shook it with confidence, just as my father had taught me.

"It's a pleasure to meet you, Mr. Pennant. Your name sounds familiar, but I don't recall meeting you before."

He smiled warmly. "I get that a lot. Most people who hear my name never actually meet me."

I was intrigued by his cryptic response, but I'd be patient and let it all play out in time, rather than rushing the situation with awkward questions.

"I haven't made any reservations for you," I said. "I'm on the boat. You're welcome to join me aboard, but I get the feeling you may not be accustomed to sleeping in a tiny bunk on a rolling boat, Mr. Pennant."

I watched him for a reaction, but none came. I kept playing the name Michael Pennant over in my head. I knew the name, but not the face, and Dr. Richter was no help.

Before Pennant could respond to my comment about where they'd sleep, Dr. Richter said, "Let's get some dinner."

"Great idea," I said. "There's a great little place right on the beach that has the best grilled snapper you'll ever eat."

"Sounds great to me," Pennant said.

We headed for my borrowed SUV. The manager of one of the banks where I'd made a sizable deposit earlier in the day had insisted that I use his Land Rover while I was on the island, so I took him up on his generous offer. The vehicle was comfortable, roomy, and even a little luxurious. I liked the ride and feel of the substantial car.

When we reached the Land Rover, Dr. Richter opened the rear door for Pennant. The man slid inside as if he were accustomed to being driven, and Dr. Richter closed the door behind him before hopping in the front passenger's seat. The servant role was not typical of Rocket Richter, so I was even more intrigued than before about who Pennant actually was.

We left the airport and drove along the sea on the southwest side of the island. It was a perfect night. The wind blew lightly, and the golden sun sank across the western horizon.

Pennant kicked off the conversation. "So, Chase, I've been hearing a lot of very impressive things about you and the work you're doing. You should be proud of yourself."

He left that statement floating in the air like a hanging curveball just begging to be driven out of the park, but I didn't swing.

"I don't know what you're talking about, Mr. Pennant. I just sail and fish. There's not much to be proud of about that, unless you're talking about that mahi-mahi I bagged this morning. She was a beauty!"

Dr. Richter put on his knowing smile. "It's okay, Chase. Michael is the deputy director of operations for the CIA. He knows more about you than you know about you."

So, that's why his name sounded familiar. Michael Pennant had been one of the most brilliant field agents the CIA had ever produced. He was a legend among operators, the world over. Now, he was in the back seat of my borrowed Land Rover showering me with compliments.

I tried to appear unimpressed. "The DDO, huh? How about that? What brings you to the Caymans, Mr. Pennant?"

"You, Chase," he said almost as if I should've been expecting him. "Your work in Cuba caused quite a stir on the international stage. We have a lot to discuss about how you were able to get so close to Suslik when nobody else on Earth seemed to be able to get it done."

I looked around nervously, unable to believe he'd just said that in a car that hadn't been swept for bugs, and after having only met me ten minutes before.

I looked around as if confused. "I'm sorry, but you must have me confused with somebody else. As I said, I'm just a sailor and a fisherman. I'm an American. Americans can't go to Cuba, and I don't even know what a Suslik is."

With raised eyebrows, I glared at him in the rearview mirror. "Isn't this borrowed car nice? I don't know who actually owns it, but I think it belongs to a bank here on the island. They're just letting me use it for a few days."

Pennant's eyes widened as he realized the Land Rover wasn't an asset of the Agency. He'd spoken out of turn and far too freely before he'd ascertained the level of security.

He said, "Beautiful evening, isn't it?"

We arrived at the beachside grill and spent two hours drinking island beer and eating every fish the cook would send out. The conversation was meaningless, but we had a few laughs as we tried to guess the occupations and hometowns of tourists in floral shirts with sunburned noses.

We finally made our way aboard *Aegis* where we could speak freely about almost anything. The speakers that had been installed around the deck pointed outward to muffle any conversation aboard. Sounds travel impressively well across the water, so the noise of the stereo made for an excellent curtain of audio security.

It didn't take long for Pennant to continue the discussion he began in the Land Rover. "So, Chase, tell me about the Cuban op."

I looked to Dr. Richter for any indication that I shouldn't proceed, but it didn't come, so I started talking. I told Pennant how everything had gone down, from the helicopter ride, to the freighter, and finally, to the run for my life after the mission was complete.

"I'm impressed, Chase. This kind of work is clearly in your blood. We made a good decision in recruiting you."

In a moment of confidence, I asked, "Do I work for you, Mr. Pennant?"

He looked at me, lifted his glass, and took a long, slow swallow. "No, you don't work for me. At least not yet." He swallowed the last of his drink. "Thank you for the hospitality, Chase. I'm going to call it a night, but I'm sure we'll talk again soon. I have a feeling you and I have a lot in common, and it was a pleasure to finally meet you. You remind me a lot of your father."

I tried not to react to the obvious uppercut, and I stood and shook his hand.

He pressed a business card into my palm. "Give me a call if you ever need anything or just want to chat."

I watched him walk away with his confident stride and step into the back of a black Chevy Suburban. It had been parked near the entrance to the marina the entire time we were aboard *Aegis*. Before sliding it into my pocket, I glanced at the card. It was plain white with a telephone number written in blue ink—nothing else. I returned to my seat and handed Dr. Richter another drink and a Cuban Cohiba. He produced a punch and lighter and soon had the cigar glowing cherry red.

"What was that all about?" I asked.

He examined his cigar. "That, my boy, was a debrief and a job interview."

"I don't need a job, and I'm pretty sure he already knew everything I told him tonight." I drew a long draw of sweet smoke and let it slowly escape my lips.

Dr. Richter looked sternly at me. "We always need another job, but I think you're correct about Pennant already knowing what happened in Cuba."

I didn't necessarily agree that I always needed another job, but I chose to let that bit of wisdom linger for the moment. I had too many other things I needed to discuss before we talked about future work.

I watch Pennant's Suburban drive out of sight. "What was that crap about knowing my father?"

Dr. Richter looked at the taillights and shrugged.

"Listen, Coach. I need to tell you some things, and then I need some advice. I can't promise I'll take the advice, but I want to hear what you have to say. Okay?"

Dr. Richter drew in another mouthful of some of the finest tobacco smoke on Earth. "I already know most of what you're going to tell me, and I probably know what you're going to ask. I'm sure there's nothing happening in your head that hasn't happened to almost every man who came before you, including me, but I'll listen, and I'll give you the best advice I can. I didn't always take the advice of those older and wiser than me, so I know you probably won't take mine. That's just the way of things."

There was no way he could know what I was about to tell him. I was confident my situation was entirely unique.

"So, you already know what happened in Cuba. It was a train wreck in a swamp in many ways, but ultimately, I think I accomplished what I was sent there to do."

"Actually, Chase, you didn't."

Those words echoed through the night air like thunder. Dr. Richter was telling me I'd failed, and that left me speechless.

"You see, you weren't actually sent there to kill Suslik. You were sent there to flush him out and muck up his plan to assassinate the secretary of state. No one expected you to get close enough to kill him. Everyone believed you'd stumble around and find Suslik, but they expected him to see you coming a mile away and scamper back to Europe rather than risk an encounter with American intelligence operatives. You were a pawn, Chase. Everyone at your level is a pawn. Don't let it get under your skin. You surprised everyone. Even me."

I couldn't believe I'd been sent to Cuba to risk my life, just to bird-dog one of the world's foremost assassins and send him scurrying back home. It *did* upset met. If I'd been told to scare him away, I would've done that, but I was told to kill him. Everything in my training had taught me to accomplish the mission. I didn't need to be misled. I would do what I was told without the necessity for deception. I started to protest, but Dr. Richter cut me off.

"Don't get upset, Chase. Again, it's just the way of things. You live in a world of deception now. You aren't always going to know the whole truth; in fact, most of the time, you aren't going to know any of the truth. You're an implement of policy, a sharp tool in a huge toolbox. People like you and me exist so people like Pennant will have the instruments at their disposal to accomplish the big-picture plan. It has to be that way. I know it's hard to understand, and it'll never make sense, but we just have to learn to swallow it."

His pep talk didn't go far towards making me feel better, but I did understand his point. As angry as I was about the deception, it was only a small part of what I needed to discuss with him.

"Okay, whatever. I understand I'm a low-level nobody, but none of that matters right now."

"No, Chase. You *were* a low-level nobody, but what you accomplished has catapulted you well toward the top of the totem pole in D.C. Extremely important and influential people are impressed. You're most certainly not nobody anymore. You're the prize pig at the state fair. Operators have been trying to find and kill Suslik for over a decade. He's proven to be one of the most elusive foreign agents in history. It's almost like he was a ghost. You caught and killed a poltergeist, my boy."

The word *ghost* rang in my ears like a church bell. It was exactly what Anya had called Suslik when she told me he wasn't dead.

"Coach, I have a lot to tell you, so I'm going to try to make it as simple as possible. You know about the sniper I saw at Belmont."

He looked at his feet. "Chase, trust me. Nothing good can come of that. I know better than anyone what happens when operators get involved with foreign agents. It never ends well for anyone. You have to get that girl out of your head."

"No, Coach, you don't understand. It's not like that. I saw her again. I mean, I did more than just see her. She came after me. She chased me for three weeks across a dozen islands and a couple thousand miles of ocean. She found me in St. Thomas with Dutch."

Dr. Richter's eyes came to life. "You saw Dutch in St. Thomas?"

"Yes. He actually found me there the same day I saw Anya on the beach."

"Wait a minute. Dutch found you?"

"Yes. He found me at a tiki bar on the beach in Charlotte Amalie. I was having a drink and watching Anya on the beach."

"Who is Anya?"

"Anya . . . Anastasia, the sniper from Belmont. She's actually SVR and not a sniper at all. She prefers edged weapons. I mean, she *can* shoot, but she just doesn't like to shoot."

Dr. Richter shook his head, "Slow down, boy. What are you talking about? How do you know all of this about her, and how do you know her name, for God's sake? And wait a minute. Anya isn't short for Anastasia."

I didn't know how to make him understand. If he didn't stop interrupting me, it was going to take two weeks to explain it all.

"That's what I'm trying to tell you. Dutch found me. We talked. Anya snuck aboard *Aegis*, drugged me, tied me up, and cut my tongue in half."

I stuck out my tongue to show him the scar. Thankfully, it had healed nicely, but a mark ran the length of my tongue as proof I'd survived Anya's knife.

"I'm going to need another drink," he said as he lifted the bottle from the deck and poured his glass well past half full.

I lifted my glass toward him, and he poured at least as much in mine. "It's going to be an interesting night," I said.

He raised his glass. "It certainly is. Now, go on. Make me understand what all of this is about."

"Okay," I continued. "So, she wanted to know why I'd tried to kill Dmitri Barkov and who sent me. She didn't believe I wasn't sent to kill Barkov. Oh, as it turns out, he's a pretty bad dude, too, but we'll talk more about him later."

An ominous look consumed Dr. Richter's face. He set his glass down and leaned toward me with a glare that looked like fear tempered with hatred. "Don't mess around with Dmitri Barkov, Chase. Don't get tangled up with him. There are none worse than him. He eats the souls of everyone around him."

I was confused and frustrated. I had no plans of getting tangled up with Barkov. I didn't know anything about him except he had a thing for racehorses, and he was some kind of big shot in the Russian mafia.

"We're getting way off track," I said. "I'm trying to tell you about Anya. She sort of works for Barkov."

That got his attention. "Wait a minute!" he said. "I thought you said she was SVR."

"Yes, she is SVR, but she also works for Barkov, I think. I don't really understand it yet, but that's not what's important."

"That's the only thing that's important! Slow down, and make sure you're telling me exactly what you know. This Russian SVR agent named Anastasia, who you call Anya, works for Dmitri Barkov, the Russian mafia kingpin? Is that what you're telling me?"

"Yes, but that's not what this is about. This is about the fact that she thought I was sent to kill him instead of Suslik. But it gets even weirder. She doesn't believe he's dead."

"She doesn't believe who is dead?"

"Suslik! She doesn't think he's dead. In fact, she said he can't be killed because he's a ghost, or actually, the ghost of a cat or something. That's the same thing you said about him. Why does everyone keep calling him a ghost?"

Dr. Richter sat back against the coaming of my boat and looked skyward. "This is getting hard to follow, so let's slow it down. First, I'll tell you about Suslik. Then, you have to tell me what happened to Dutch. No one has heard from him in over two weeks. Then, we'll talk more about this Anastasia, but we have to talk about Barkov, too."

I sat back, ready to listen.

He said, "Okay, Suslik is a ghost because he has an unearthly ability to be in several places at once. We'll have an agent photographing him in The Hague while another is watching him kill a diamond broker in South Africa. He can be on opposite sides of the globe within hours of a confirmed sighting. Thanks to you, we know for sure he's graveyard dead and making his way through the stomachs of some happy sharks off Havana."

I considered what he told me. "None of that makes sense. There was nothing ghostly about him when I yanked him from Barkov's yacht. He died just like any other man would've died, but I just can't get over how much Anya, and now you, seem to think he was something supernatural."

Dr. Richter squirmed, obviously uncomfortable. "It's about time you get used to things not making sense. This is not a world of working nine-to-five and making sales calls. We don't live in the same world as everyone else. Our world is almost entirely made up of characters who are far more than they appear. That includes you. Speaking of ghosts, when did you last see Dutch?"

"Dutch is dead," I said matter-of-factly. "Anya killed him in his bungalow on St. Thomas. He was working for the Russians, Coach. Somebody had flipped him, and he was getting paid. Remember when I told you Anya drugged me and tied me up?"

He listened intently.

"Well, Dutch snuck aboard *Aegis* while Anya was interrogating me, and he shot at her, but she escaped through the hatch without a scratch."

Dr. Richter looked doubtful. "Are you saying he shot at her but didn't hit her?"

"Yes, that's part of the problem. It doesn't make sense that he wouldn't have shot her in the head from less than fifteen feet away, but he didn't even graze her. That's part of why I know he'd been flipped. A drunken monkey could've made that shot, but Dutch missed. I just don't buy it."

"Neither do I," he said.

It was clear he was trying to process the whole scene in his mind, but it wasn't coming together for him. I had lived it, and it didn't make sense to me, so I could only imagine how confusing it was for him.

"Anyway, Anya killed Dutch in his bungalow because . . . ah, I don't really know why. Why isn't important. But she killed him and then tried to drown me in the lagoon. I shot her in the foot, and then we kissed."

He dropped his highball glass as his jaw fell open. "Wait a minute!" he roared. "She killed Dutch? Our Dutch? But you were able to shoot her in the foot while she was trying to drown you?"

"Yes, precisely. She was holding me on the bottom of the lagoon, and she stuffed my snorkel full of sand and salt water after lassoing me. I was barely able to get my finger on the trigger through the skin of my dry bag, but I got off one shot, and it took off her little toe. I had no choice. I was going to be dead in a few more seconds. I had to do something."

"Yeah, yeah, I get that. You had to shoot her. But why would you kiss her after she tried to kill you and after you shot off her toe?"

"It just happened. She was on top of me, and we kissed. It was one of those bizarre things that just happens. I can't explain it. I took her back to the boat and sewed up her foot. We spent the next several days together, and now she wants to quit, Coach. She wants to defect."

"No way! She's playing you, boy. She's trying to recruit you. Don't let it happen, or you'll end up like Dutch . . . or worse."

I wanted to protest, but from his perspective, there was no other way to see it. It didn't matter how I felt about her. To Dr. Richter, she was just an SVR agent and I was her mark—nothing more.

I finished the story, including the part about the American who'd been sent to kill me, but he seemed most interested when I described Anya.

"You can't imagine how beautiful her eyes are. They're unforgettable. There's something so familiar, yet so unique about them. Her mother was killed when she was a child, and she never really knew her father. She didn't actually say how her mother died, but it was clearly painful for her to talk about her childhood."

Dr. Richter stared at me until it became uncomfortable. When he finally spoke, he did so in a soft, almost timid tone. "Tell me about her eyes again. Look at me, and tell me about her eyes." His tone was troubled and haunted.

I didn't know where the conversation was going.

"Tell me again about her eyes. It's crucial."

"I already told you. They're like the eyes of a cat. It's as if she can look into my soul. They're sometimes blue and sometimes gray, but sometimes, they're both. And she stares with such intensity. It's impossible to look away from her, Dr. Richter. She's simply perfect."

"What exactly did she tell you about her name?" he asked.

"She told me to call her Anya. Apparently, her real name is Anastasia, but it infuriated her when I called her that name. She said only her mother called her Anastasia, and no one else. I know Anya isn't traditionally short for Anastasia, but maybe that's just the name she uses. I don't know. Maybe that's the name they gave her when she became an SVR officer. Do you think she was lying to me about her name?"

"No, I don't think she was lying to you. How about her last name? What's her last name, Chase?"

I looked at him as if he'd asked me how many rocks were on the moon. I didn't know what her last name was or if Anastasia was her real first name. It occurred to me that I knew almost nothing about her, but every little thing I did know made me want to know more.

"I don't know," I said. "I don't think she ever told me her last name. She knew mine, though. She knew all about me, in fact."

"That's okay. Listen to me, Chase. Listen very carefully. That girl is the most dangerous thing you'll ever encounter. She can kill you without a thought, or she can take your body and mind places you never imagined going. If you let her, she'll become your greatest weakness and your undoing. There are some things in life that are more important than everything else. It's up to you to determine the difference between what makes you alive and what simply makes you keep breathing. Those are two vastly different things. Do you understand?"

"I'm sorry, but I'm lost."

He smiled for the first time in over an hour. "It's okay, my boy. It'll all come to you in time."

I wanted to shake him and tell him I wasn't Daniel-san and he wasn't Mr. Myagi, but I wasn't sure he'd get the *Karate Kid* reference. I said, "You're welcome to stay on the boat with me tonight if you want."

He politely declined the invitation, then he looked up at the star-filled sky. "So, you killed Suslik, then your handler got dead at the hands of a Russian SVR agent who you then shot in the foot before she screwed your brains out. Does that about cover the last month of your life?"

"Well," I said, "I think I'd include a few more details, but you hit the high points."

"I have a way of reducing minutia to its core and summing things up," he laughed. "Get your butt back home. There's work for you to do. Now that Pennant thinks you're the newest American James Bond, he'll be throwing assignments at you like candy."

I grimaced. "I don't think I like the sound of that. I'm not interested in being his errand boy. Besides, I don't work for him."

Dr. Richter looked over his glasses. "No, you certainly don't work for him, my boy. Don't be afraid to say no. You can always say no." He stood and patted me on the shoulder. "Thanks for the cigar and the drinks. I'm proud of you." He looked at me with the same expression from earlier that made me so uneasy. "Protect her, Chase. . . . Especially from you."

29
Commandments

I lay awake trying to piece together the puzzle my life had become. It seemed the more I learned about my new life, the less I understood. Why would I warrant a visit from the deputy director of operations for the CIA? If it was Pennant's intention to make me his private one-man army, I wasn't interested. I would've preferred to remain anonymous. I feared Dr. Richter had just delivered me into the hands of the man who could become my greatest ally, or perhaps my albatross.

Dr. Richter had always been mysterious, but his dramatic change of position on my feelings for Anya baffled me. Why would he tell me to protect her? A woman like her needed no protection from someone like me. She was far more capable of taking care of herself than I could ever be.

Watching the stars wink over my head, for some reason, made me want to go home, wherever home was. The closest thing I had to a home was an anchorage off Jewfish Creek in Key Largo, so that was the next sandy bottom my anchor would taste. I would have seven hundred fifty sailing miles to ponder all the questions I may never be able to answer.

I'd been at sea for several weeks, but in many ways, it felt like only days. The passing of time on the ocean is a concept only perceived by humans. The sea has no clock other than what she feels when the moon pulls at her as it makes its nightly circumnavigation. I imagined the creatures in the ocean who lived their entire lives, be that days or decades, without ever seeing a human or man-made object, or even a speck of dry land. For those creatures, was there any time? Are we humans the only creatures insane enough to try to measure the passage of time, to measure something that doesn't truly exist? Perhaps I'd been at sea too long. I was turning into some sort of nautical philosopher. Had other men of the sea had such thoughts?

Are there other men like me? Is Dr. Richter like me? Was my father like me?

As the evening sun kissed the western horizon, I sailed from Georgetown, Grand Cayman, and set my course toward the Yucatan Peninsula. Watching billions of stars in their predictable and timeless journey gave me something dependable to believe in.

My father taught me about a great and mighty God who loved me and who created everything that exists. He taught me about the responsibilities God placed on us to care for and love each other. I think he believed those things. I think his heart was the purest heart ever carried by a man. Throughout my childhood, I watched him and my mother care for sick, dying, and starving people all over the Caribbean. Knowing what my father actually was—a killer—made me believe he needed his faith in God to deal with the unthinkable acts he committed in the name of freedom.

Will I ever have such faith? Will I ever possess the character my father had? Would my family still be alive if he'd only been a missionary?

Most men probably have philosophical moments of self-doubt when they find themselves alone and hundreds of miles from home. How would the rest of my life look? How many missions would I accept? When would I accept a mission that would ultimately be my last? No one lives forever, especially not in my profession. I was far wealthier than I ever imagined being, and I was free to come and go as I pleased, with the exception of the times I spent serving my masters. There was no reason I shouldn't enjoy the spoils of victory. Besides, I'd earned every penny I had scattered across half a dozen Cayman banks.

* * *

The wind shifted to the south southeast, and that suited me fine. Had it kept blowing from the southwest, I would've been on a downwind run all the way back to the Florida Keys. Downwind sailing is miserable. The boat lumbers along with its sails flapping and the main boom threatening to come violently roaring across the deck in an accidental gybe, stressing the rigging and scaring the crap out of me. I rigged boom preventers, lines running from the end of the main boom to the bow, to keep that from happening, but I somehow felt that was cheating. Instead of practicing good seamanship and keeping *Aegis* on course, I was relying on lines to protect me from my inattention. That didn't seem like something a real sailor would do. Fortunately, none of that mattered with the wind blowing from the south southeast. I would sail home on a beam reach with the sails trimmed off the port side and the wind blowing nicely across the deck. It looked like the remaining ride home would be close to perfect.

I was correct. The trip was something straight out of a Jimmy Buffett song. The wind blew exactly as I would've ordered if I had some direct line to the weather gods. More importantly, no armed patrol boats raced out of Havana Harbor to greet me when I skirted the northwest coast of Cuba by less than forty miles.

Four days of cruising put me off Tavernier Key, northeast of Islamorada. Having grown more homesick than expected, I bypassed Key West and continued homeward. I finally let the anchor fall in at Point Lowe, a protected anchorage off Tavernier, just as the sun was dissolving into the ocean.

I've never felt a real sense of home anywhere on Earth. As a child, my family moved around so much, we always felt like refugees. The four years I spent at UGA were the longest I'd ever spent in one place. To say Jewfish Creek was my home wasn't accurate, but it was close enough. I looked forward to motoring into the anchorage on Blackwater Sound the next day, but I wasn't willing to risk navigating Jewfish Creek in the dark, even if it was my temporary home.

I fell asleep within minutes of feeling the big Danforth anchor set itself firmly in the sand in just over eleven feet of water. I put out sixty feet of chain, so there was almost no chance *Aegis* would do anything other than sit right there until I wanted her to move.

I awoke with the morning sun and a feeling of excitement that didn't make sense. I would be back in the shallow water up Jewfish Creek in less than two hours, but there would be no one waiting for me there. There was no house, no dog to come wagging his tail and licking my face when I arrived, no mailbox to check, no grass to mow, and no one to welcome me, but in spite of all of that, I was still happy to be home. I'd drive my car, eat a Quarter Pounder, and for the first time in weeks, I'd drink a Coke that tasted like American Coke. Home, as it turns out, is much more a feeling than an address.

I motored gently over the anchor and hauled it back aboard. I was pleasantly surprised to see it come up perfectly clean. There are few things worse than some of the muddy filth from the bottom of the sea that rides an anchor. As I stood on deck with the water hose in my hand, ready to spray the anchor clean, I realized I was beginning to view the world as a morally filthy place, and cleanliness was becoming the exception rather than the rule.

I secured the anchor and stowed the water hose. The wind was light as the sun made its appearance over the eastern horizon. Seagulls screeched through the morning sky, and a pair of dolphins played just off my starboard bow as I motored from the anchorage and headed northeast. I watched dive boats heading for one of the most beautiful coral reefs in the world, and it occurred to me that I hadn't been diving for fun in so long that I'd almost forgotten how much I loved being underwater. I promised myself to go diving as soon as possible.

The tide was rising as I motored up Jewfish Creek. I dropped the hook in thirteen feet of water at high tide and patted *Aegis*'s wheel as I quietly thanked her for bringing me home. We'd put about three thousand miles beneath us in the last few weeks, and she made every mile like a warrior. *Aegis* had been the one thing in my life I understood. I didn't know if I was becoming part of her, or if it was the other way around, but either way, I liked how I felt at her wheel.

* * *

"Thou shall have no other gods before me." That was the first commandment God handed down to the Israelites when they wandered around in the desert a few thousand years ago. I remember my father, the humanitarian, the missionary, teaching me what God expected of his children. Was I still one of those children, or had I let eight million dollars become my god?

"Thou shall not make unto thee any graven image." I was never sure about that one. I seem to remember that it was number two, but that whole graven image thing was never clear to me.

"Thou shall not take the name of the Lord thy God in vain." I had that one covered. I'd never been a fan of hearing people do that. I didn't think twice about chopping bad guys into little pieces with boat engines, but I tried to leave God out of it.

"Remember the Sabbath day to keep it holy." I blew that one at least once a week. I talked to God every day, but I never really remembered what day it was. *Sabbath* is one of those words like *graven*. Who says it can't be on Tuesday?

"Honor thy father and thy mother." I missed my family, especially my little sister. I thought there was no better way to honor them than to live the life I'd been given. I doubted my father would've chosen it for me, but when I thought of how he loved me and the sacrifices he made for his family, I think maybe, just maybe, he might've been proud of me.

"Thou shall not kill." That's where it gets a little tricky. My father said it actually meant "commit no murder." I liked that better than "thou shall not kill," but that's not what it said, regardless of how my father interpreted it.

Adultery, stealing, bearing false witness, and coveting finished the list, if I remembered correctly. I was good on those four, but I'd have to think about the graven images and the killing. Man, I really missed my dad.

30
Yuri and Boris

The Earth kept spinning, the sun kept rising and setting, and the moon traversed the night sky as it had for millennia, but I was stuck on the thoughts of Michael Pennant, the ghost of Suslik, Dmitri Barkov, and Anya, the alluring Russian assassin.

I'd been hanging on the hook in Jewfish Creek for a few weeks, fishing, drinking, relaxing, and thinking. Occasionally, I'd take the dinghy ashore and spend some time on Key Largo. There were a few good seafood places that would cook whatever I caught and let me drink their beer while I was waiting. The psychologist in me liked watching the tourists and listening to their accents, but every twenty-five-year-old blonde made me yearn for Anya. Each time I saw a ponytail, I hoped it was hers. After all, she promised she'd find me. I knew little about her, but I believed she was a woman who kept her promises.

I was sitting at a concrete picnic table outside the Fish House one Friday evening, listening to the cars fly by on the Overseas Highway, when a voice behind me cut through the night like a lightning bolt.

Hearing Spanish in the Keys is pretty common. I could tell the difference between Cuban Spanish and Mexican Spanish within the time it took the speaker to spit out two or three words, but hearing Russian in Key Largo was like seeing a sumo wrestler at Sunday brunch—impossible to ignore. I suppose it

238 · CAP DANIELS

has something to do with our fight-or-flight reflex that makes us capable of blocking out everything in our environment that isn't directly related to what we perceive as a threat. Cavemen probably got pretty focused when a saber-toothed tiger showed up in the entrance of their cave.

My current saber-toothed tigers were a pair of Russian-speaking men sitting behind me and talking quietly about one of the few Russians I knew.

In painfully informal Russian, and in a dialect I didn't recognize, one of the men said, "It does not matter why. When Barkov wants someone found, we find her. No questions."

Why are two Russians in Key Largo talking about finding a woman for Dmitri Barkov?

My pulse raced, but I tried to stay calm. I was wearing one of those boater's hats with the long flap down the back to protect my neck from the sun. My back was to the Russians, and they couldn't identify me unless, of course, they'd been following me.

It was time to play a little cat and mouse with Yuri and Boris. I didn't know what their names were, but those were the first Russian-sounding names that came to mind. I feigned looking at my watch, then stood with my back still to their table and walked toward the parking lot. I listened for either or both of them to follow. The area was covered with gravel, so hearing footsteps would've been easy if it weren't for the traffic on the highway twenty feet away.

My caveman fight-or-flight senses calmed me as I got my mind under control. Every time either of my feet hit the ground, the unmistakable crunch of gravel was obvious. That meant I could probably hear either of the Russians if they chose to follow me. As I lifted my left foot to take a stride, I froze in midair. There was no way the Russians could anticipate I'd stop with my foot raised, and they'd continue their stride. That would allow me to hear their feet hit the ground the same time my foot would've hit if I had continued walking. The crunch didn't come. Either they were mind readers, or they weren't following me.

I continued my walk toward the parking lot and around the building, using car windows as mirrors to check for a tail. I entered the building through the kitchen and made my way into the dining room so I could peer through the front windows of the Fish House to get a good look at the Russians. Thankfully, they hadn't moved.

Yuri was lean and fit with a few days' growth of stubble. His hair was exactly the same length as his beard, so he probably shaved his face and head at the same time. I'd keep that in mind.

Boris was heavier, but not fat. He was thick through the chest like a man who spends a lot of time doing bench presses. His hair was dark and longer than Yuri's. Yuri wore an oversized button-down shirt over cargo pants, and brown boots. He was smoking an unfiltered cigarette and letting the ashes fall into his lap. Boris wore a tight black T-shirt tucked into his cargo pants, which were tucked neatly into the tops of his boots. The pockets of his pants were pressed tightly against his muscled legs. He had no place to conceal a weapon, although at his size, he could probably handle most men without the need for a gun or knife.

Yuri, on the other hand, was scrawny and had plenty of places in his baggy clothes to hide a collection of weapons. I was far more afraid of Yuri than Boris. Even the biggest and strongest men are vulnerable at their knees, eyes, throat, and groin. It was impossible to protect all four places simultaneously. I could deal with Boris hand-to-hand, but Yuri was small and nervous-looking. Guys like that tend to be unpredictable and quick to draw a gun. I didn't mind a little fisticuffs, but I had no desire to get into a gunfight in front of the Fish House.

Clearly, the two men weren't following me since they didn't notice I'd left the table. I asked the hostess if I could have a table by the front window instead of sitting outside. She quickly accommodated my request with a flirtatious smile. I placed my right hand behind her left arm and pulled her gently toward me, catching sight of her name tag. She gave no resistance and leaned in, placing her ear close to my mouth.

"Your name is Angie, right?"

She nodded and held her breath.

"I thought so. Look at those two men sitting right out there, Angie. Have you ever seen them before?"

She leaned in even closer and placed her hand on my thigh to brace herself as she peered through the window. Her level of comfort with me was going to make this easier than I'd expected.

"No, I don't think so. They don't look familiar. I'm sure they aren't local." She whispered as if she knew she was part of my scheme.

"Do me a favor, will you?"

Her eyes widened, apparently thrilled to be a player in my conspiracy. She was cute in that Florida windblown way that women get when they live in one hundred percent humidity and ninety-five-degree heat. I liked the look, and Angie wore it well.

"What do you want me to do?" she asked.

I said, "I took those guys and their girlfriends sailing yesterday, and some money came up missing from my boat. When they pay their bill, I need to know if they pay in cash or with a credit card. If they pay in cash, I want you to bring it to me, and I'll exchange it with mine. I think I'll be able to tell if it's the cash they stole from my boat. Can you do that, Angie?"

She took on a conspiratorial look. "Yeah, I can do that. No problem."

I knew she was hooked.

"By the way, I'm Chase."

She giggled. "I know who you are. This is a small island, and you're the new boy in town."

I pretended to blush. "I'm flattered. What time do you get off, Angie?"

"Around eleven. Maybe a little earlier."

She giggled again and looked back over her shoulder twice as she waltzed back to the hostess stand. I saw her recruiting a tall, dark-haired waitress into our plan. She leaned in close to Angie, looked outside at Yuri and Boris, then looked at me and smiled. I winked. Then, the waitress disappeared through the swinging doors and into the kitchen.

My red fish and rice arrived with a fresh cold beer. I enjoyed the meal while I watched the two Russians demolish a pair of fish sandwiches and fries. Just as I had hoped, when their check arrived, Yuri pulled out a crisp, clean roll of hundred-dollar bills and peeled one off. He placed it on the check and tucked it neatly beneath the edge of his plate to keep it from blowing away. The tall, dark-haired waitress folded the check around the c-note without touching it and tucked it into her apron. I was impressed. She hadn't touched the bill, so the last set of fingerprints on it would be Yuri's. I liked her. She had the makings of a spy.

When the waitress came through the front door, Angie reached to take the bill and money from her, but the waitress shook her head and turned toward my table.

Angie's face turned red, and she stage-whispered, "Crystal, no!"

Crystal pirouetted and smiled at Angie as she continued toward my table. She slid into the booth beside me until her leg was touching mine.

She retrieved the bill from her apron and slid it under my hand. "Angie said you're like a cop or something and you need to see those weird guys' money, so here it is. I didn't touch it so you could, like, get some fingerprints or whatever, okay?"

I discreetly took the ticket and used it to slip the one-hundred-dollar bill into my shirt pocket. I pulled two one hundred-dollar bills from my wallet and handed them to Crystal. "Thank you," I said. "You did great. Please tell Angie I'll see her at eleven."

Crystal snatched up the two hundred dollars from my hand and stomped away. She wasn't going to pass my message to Angie.

I left the Fish House and headed north on the Overseas Highway toward Miami and David Shepherd's office. When I walked into the bank, he greeted me warmly and ushered me into his office.

"It's great to see you, Chase. What brings you to Miami?" he asked with a little nervousness in his voice.

"Do you have any tweezers?" I asked.

David wrinkled his brow and pulled open his desk drawer, withdrawing a pair of chrome tweezers with an Atlanta Braves emblem on the butt. David really was die-hard, not just a fair-weather Braves fan.

I took the tweezers and lifted the hundred-dollar bill from my shirt pocket. I placed the bill on the center of his desk and watched it curl at the ends, trying to return to the shape it had known in the roll in Yuri's pocket.

David stared at the bill then looked up at me. "Where did you get this?"

I didn't answer. He was nervous about it for some reason, and I was going to find out why.

"Tell me what you know about that bill, David."

He reached for it, but I pushed his hand away before he could touch it.

"Don't touch it," I demanded. "The last fingerprints on it belong to someone I need to ID."

"Where did you get this bill?" His tone was more insistent this time.

I shook my head. "You first, David. Tell me what you know about the bill. There's clearly something about it that makes you nervous. I'll tell you where I got it after you tell me everything you know about it."

David stood, and his large frame cast a shadow over his desk and me. In two strides, he covered the distance to his office door. It would've taken a normal man four steps to cover that distance, but David was no normal man. He closed and locked the door, then closed the blinds. He returned to his desk and lifted the bill carefully with the tweezers as he pulled a magnifying glass from his desk and closely examined both sides of the bill.

I was anxious to hear what he had to say, but he was in no hurry to show his hand. He grabbed a roll of clear film from his desk drawer and placed it on his blotter before putting the bill in the center of the film. He carefully dusted the bill with a chalky black powder and lifted two crystal-clear fingerprints. He placed the tape containing Yuri's fingerprints on a white index card and made a small note in the corner, then slid it into a yellow envelope and sealed it.

David grabbed the bill with both hands before I could stop him. He squeezed and slid it between his fingertips and sniffed it. Then he held it close to his ear and listened while he rolled it between his fingers. Finally, he tossed the bill back onto his desk, leaned back in his chair, and pulled the bottom desk drawer open. He produced two tumblers and a bottle of Glenlivit eighteen-year-old scotch. He poured three fingers for each of us and slid mine across the desk. I graciously accepted and lifted mine in a silent toast.

"Talk, David," I said just before touching the rim of the glass to my lips.

The scotch was warm and creamy with just the right amount of bite. It tasted perfect, exactly as the distiller intended.

David took a long swallow and sighed as he placed the tumbler on his desk. "Okay. Obviously, you know the bill is counterfeit, so there's probably not much I can tell you that you don't already know."

I didn't know it was counterfeit. I hadn't even suspected it might be, but I wasn't going to show my hand just yet. "Obviously, but there's more to it than it simply being counterfeit, isn't there?"

He stared into the golden liquid. "Yes, Chase, there certainly is. Not only is it counterfeit, but it's a great counterfeit. In fact, it's one of the best counterfeits in the world. We believe there to be about half a billion dollars' worth of these floating around the world. They were produced in Moscow with plates that were stolen from the Bureau of Engraving and Printing."

I was stunned, but it appeared David didn't know how lost I was. I tried to feign boredom.

He continued, "About fifteen years ago, an employee of the Bureau stole the plates and sold them to a Russian intelligence officer for five million dollars. Then he disappeared." David took another drink. "The thief's body washed up in France beside the English Channel a few weeks later. He had a bullet hole in his head, and we never recovered the plates. It's impossible to know exactly how many bills the Russians printed using our plates, but needless to say, with so many bills of that series in circulation, it would be a Herculean task to sort out the real bills from the fakes —even if we had every bill of that series in our possession. When it comes to counterfeiting, it's one of the most horrific events to have ever occurred in the American financial system."

Something about the whole scenario made David obviously nervous. I wanted to know what was going on inside his giant head.

"Okay," I said. "We both know it's counterfeit. You know where it was printed. What I want to know is why that makes you so nervous."

David withdrew the bottle from his drawer again and refilled his glass. He leaned the bottle toward me, offering a refill, but I shook my head.

"It's not the counterfeit bill that makes me nervous, Chase. It's the fact that you showed up here unannounced with it after hiding eight million dollars that I placed in your account in the Caymans."

Ah, so that's it. He doesn't care about the counterfeit. He cares about the eight million bucks he can no longer control. Anya was right. Moving my money was the best possible thing I could've done.

It was my turn to kill a little time while coming up with something to say, so I swirled the remaining whiskey in my glass. "Come on, David. You know I couldn't leave all that money in one place. Only an idiot would do that. I know I'm still a rookie, but I'm not completely naïve. Leaving that money in an account you and who knows who else has access to would be childish and foolish. David, David, David. You know I'm neither a child nor a fool."

He peered through the tiny slits between the window blinds. "Chase, you know you're making a lot of people nervous. You got lucky on your first big job, and you got a big paycheck, but there are a lot of people who are upset you aren't back in the field working after all the time, money, and effort we put into training you."

"I don't care who's upset that I'm the one getting shot at, getting his tongue cut in half, and getting chased all over the ocean by God knows who. Everywhere I go, it seems some mystery man is waiting there to tell me some cryptic gobbledygook that I'm supposed to figure out. The whole world seems to know where I've been and where I'm going long before I know. Let them be upset. I'm the guy who finished the job no one else was able to accomplish."

David didn't respond as I expected. Instead of being taken aback, he grimaced and crossed his arms. He looked as if he were about to tell me my dog had died. "Well, some of what you just said is true, but there's something you need to know."

I didn't know what was coming next, but I knew what I'd been through already. I'd been shot at, stabbed, had my tongue filleted, been pursued all over the Caribbean, and most importantly, I'd killed Suslik and chopped him into shark food in Havana Harbor.

"Chase, Suslik was spotted in Gibraltar and Zurich after you allegedly killed him in Havana."

I was stunned. There'd been no doubt I'd dragged Suslik from the deck of Barkov's yacht and watched his body disintegrate in the propeller of the dinghy. He was dead—graveyard dead, as my father used to say. My mind raced through that night's events with the whole scene playing in my head as if it were happening on a movie screen. It was perfectly clear. Nothing had gone wrong. Well, almost nothing. I should've killed everyone on the boat. But without a shred of doubt, I knew I'd killed Suslik, the feared Russian assassin.

"That's not possible," I said. "David, I watched him die. Dmitri Barkov and two hookers watched him die. He's dead. That's all there is to it."

"I know, Chase. I know. Suslik isn't human. He's some kind of ghost."

"Why does everyone keep saying that? There are no ghosts. He was just a man, and now he's a dead man."

"It isn't that simple. We have confirmed sightings of him after your night in Cuba, but that's not all. Two of the sightings happened within an hour of each other over a thousand miles apart. I'm telling you, he's a ghost, and you can't kill a ghost."

I sat in stunned anger and disbelief while I tried to make sense of what David was telling me. It was impossible to believe.

"When and where were the last four sightings?" I asked.

David suddenly looked concerned and confused. "I have no idea. I'm not in that loop. I'm just a banker. What are you thinking? Don't make things worse by doing something crazy."

I stood up and placed two fists on the edge of David's desk. "I'll call you in two days, and you'll tell me whose fingerprints those are on that bill. Thanks for the scotch."

31
Three of a Kind

After landing at Dulles International, I took a taxi to CIA head-quarters in Langley, Virginia. When I checked in with security, it appeared that getting in to see Michael Pennant wasn't going to be as easy as I'd hoped.

"My name is Chase Fulton, and I'm here to see Michael Pennant. He's expecting me."

The security officer looked me over. I stood motionless, staring back at him.

"Please have a seat, Mr. Fulton. I'll notify my supervisor that you're here."

The guard was commanding, but I wasn't willing to yield. "I'll just stand right here while you make that call."

His gaze sharpened. "Sit down, sir. Someone will be with you shortly."

I placed my palms firmly on the countertop. "Look. I know you have no idea who I am, and you have no way to know that Mr. Pennant is waiting to see me, but let me make this clear to you. If you like your job and want to keep it, you will find a way to get someone on that phone who has the authority to get me through Michael Pennant's door. I'm really good at making a scene. If it comes to that, Director Pennant will know, without any doubt, that it was you who kept me from seeing him. I don't know how much money you make, but it's considerably more than you'll be making when you're flipping burgers at the diner around the corner. I'll stand right here while you dial that phone."

He glared back at me, but I didn't blink. He picked up the phone and dialed a combination of numbers. "This is Pierce. I have a guy down here who claims to be Chase Fulton, and he's demanding that DDO Pennant is expecting him."

He waited impatiently while something happened on the other end of the line. He said, "Yes, sir . . . Yes, sir, but . . . Yes, sir." He placed the receiver back in the cradle. "Someone will be with you soon, Mr. Fulton."

Soon wasn't soon enough for me, so I pushed my luck a little further. I checked my watch and paced back and forth for less than a minute. The guard never took his eyes off me, but it was time to make him more nervous than he already was.

I pulled out the card Pennant had given me in the Caymans and hopped up onto the counter. I reached across the desk and grabbed the phone. The guard reacted, but I redirected his grasp, causing him to stumble into the counter. I pressed the heel of my left hand into the back of his neck and held his face against the countertop in an awkward and painful-looking position. I didn't envy his predicament.

I dialed the handwritten numbers from the card into the phone and pressed the speaker button.

The phone rang once, and a voice came on the line. "Michael Pennant."

I released the security officer and let him stand in silent disbelief. "Michael, Chase Fulton here."

There was a brief pause before Pennant replied, "Mr. Fulton, it's good to hear your voice. How are you, and what can I do for you today?"

"Well, I'm down here at the security station waiting to see you, and this security guard doesn't want to let me get past Checkpoint Alpha. His name tag says Officer Pierce. Do you know Officer Pierce, Michael?"

"Put Officer Pierce on the line," came Pennant's brisk reply.

"Oh, he can hear you. You're on speaker," I said.

"Okay," said Pennant. "Look, Officer, Mr. Fulton is a personal friend of mine. I'll send an escort for him immediately. You are to discontinue any action you may have initiated to the contrary. Are we clear?"

The dumbfounded security officer stammered, "Yes, sir."

"See ya soon, Michael." With that, I pressed the button to disconnect the call and patted Pierce on the arm. "No hard feelings, huh?"

He glared at me as he wiped the blood from his lip where the countertop had made quite an impression.

I chuckled. "Repeat after me, Pierce. Would you like fries with that, sir?"

He showed me a finger just as a sharply dressed young man appeared with his hand outstretched.

"Mr. Fulton, please come with me. Director Pennant is waiting for you." The suit shook my hand with confidence and led me through the doorway.

I said, "That Pierce is a nice guy. Do you know him?"

The agent smirked. He deposited me in the office of the DDO in less than two minutes, and I was surprised to see how meager the surroundings were. I don't know what I expected, but I certainly thought he would've had wraparound windows with a view of something spectacular, as if there was anything spectacular to see in Langley, Virginia.

"Chase, how good it is to see you. What brings you to D.C.?" Pennant asked with more than a hint of suspicion in his tone.

I motioned to a chair. "Do you mind if I have a seat? We have a lot to discuss."

"Of course, of course. Please, sit down. Can I get you anything?"

Without answering, I sat in the offered chair. It was far more comfortable than the airline seat in which I'd spent the last four hours of my life.

"Mr. Pennant," I began, "I recently learned the man I killed in Cuba has been spotted in Switzerland and Gibraltar. I also understand those confirmed sightings took place less than an hour apart. I want you to know there's no way that's the same man I encountered in Havana. My man has long passed through the digestive system of a thousand sea creatures by now. I know you've been briefed on the mission, and I know I made a few mistakes, but leaving Suslik alive was not one of those mistakes. I should've killed Dmitri Barkov and the two hookers who spotted me, but I tried to stay within the operational parameters of the mission and kill only my target. I watched his body get torn to bloody shreds beneath the propeller of the boat I was using, so I'm certain he's dead."

Pennant cleared his throat. "I know, Chase. I know all about the op and the things you left undone. That doesn't concern me. What concerns me is the fact that you were paid handsomely for a job that is now under close scrutiny. There's no question Suslik has been seen, photographed, and even audiotaped on numerous occasions since your visit to Cuba. This isn't the first time he's appeared to be a ghost."

"Ghosts don't exist," I said. "The only reasonable explanation for any of this is that Suslik is a twin, at least, and more likely a triplet. How better to strike fear in the hearts and minds of enemies than to have three identical deadly assassins who show up randomly and simultaneously around the globe?"

Pennant replied, "Of course, you're correct, Chase. That's the only explanation, but that doesn't negate the fact that you were hired to eliminate Suslik, regardless of how many of him there are. As we discussed in Georgetown, you don't work for me, yet, so that means I can't arbitrarily send you hopping all over the globe with guns blazing at anyone who looks like a bucktoothed Russian. That's not how this works."

"I'm not suggesting that you send me anywhere. I'm not here for permission or orders. I'm here to gather every ounce of intelligence you have on Suslik. After I'm confident you've shown every tidbit of knowledge you have about him— or them—I'll disappear, and I'll send you pieces of his body until you believe you've gotten your money's worth."

"You can't just waltz in here and demand to be read in on things like this. That's not how we operate here."

"Look. I'm going after him. I don't need or want your blessing. What you want is to erase Suslik from the planet. I've proven I'm the man who can do that. Now, you can either help by giving me the information I need, or you can sit back and let me stumble around in the dark for the next few years until I figure out how to kill all of them. Now, Michael, which will it be?"

He picked up his phone and pressed a button near the top. Seconds later, he spoke softly into the handset. "Bring the Anatoly Parchinkov file."

Almost before he returned the handset to its cradle, through the office door came a perfectly divine woman of perhaps thirty-five. She carried herself with poise and grace. I was smitten, but she ignored me. I watched her come in, place the file in Michael's hand, and disappear. It was almost as if she were an apparition, floating when she walked.

Pennant placed the classified file into an innocuous, manila pouch, and tossed it onto my lap. I let it land on my thighs without moving my hands. Learning to avoid reacting to my environment was one of the most difficult skills I'd mastered, but it turned out to be incredibly valuable.

"There you go, Chase. That's everything we know about Anatoly Parchinkov, a.k.a. Suslik. You can read it in my conference room just through that door, but that file cannot leave this building."

Pennant pointed toward a door that looked like an entrance to a broom closet. I lifted the thick file from my lap, and without a word, I rose from my chair to begin learning everything I could about my prey.

When I opened the file, I found two dozen photographs tucked inside an envelope. I spread the photographs out on the table and scrutinized every image, searching for minuscule differences in the shape of his chin, the distance between his eyes, the size and precise location of his ears, and any other detail that might give away the fact that Suslik was actually more than one man.

Most of the photographs had been taken from a great distance with a long lens, but three were taken by an arms dealer who was once a CIA asset. Those three photographs were taken with a good camera, directly in front of Suslik. I rummaged through the conference room in search of a magnifying glass, but I found nothing that resembled one until I saw the cut decanter and set of eight etched whiskey tumblers on a silver tray.

I grabbed three heavy glass tumblers and returned to the table. I placed a tumbler over each of the three close-up frontal shots of Suslik and stood over them, staring through the bottoms of the glasses. The thick, heavy bottoms of each glass made excellent magnifying glasses and offered me a look into the soul of the man I'd sent to the afterlife.

I remembered his sunken, dark eyes. I remembered how they peered at me with disdain and emptiness that night in the tropics. I would never forget those eyes. In the first two pictures, the eyes peering back at me through the tumblers were clearly those of the man I'd faced and killed. But there was something about the third picture that wasn't right. The eyes were the same, but the left eye was cast ever so slightly inward. I compared the three photographs in excruciating detail, but I couldn't convince myself the difference was real.

Finally, I grabbed the three pictures and slammed them against the westward-facing wall of windows of the conference room. The afternoon sun was beating through the glass and made a perfect light table. I overlaid one picture on top of another and carefully aligned the eyes. They were identical. The size and shape of the pupils were the same. When I placed the third photograph over the others, the inward gaze of that left eye became a beacon.

Bingo!

I knew Suslik had been spotted over a thousand miles apart, with less than an hour between sightings, long after I'd killed him in Havana. He wasn't a ghost; he was triplets.

Suslik number one was shark food. Number two was hanging out in Zurich. And number three had been in Gibraltar. I'd already killed one, so I only had two to go.

32
Russian Grammar Lessons

When I finished poring over the file and committing every detail to memory, I tucked the pictures back into the envelope and closed the thick worn file just as it had been when Pennant dropped it on my lap. Satisfied with what I'd learned, and even more satisfied with how I'd muscled my way into the DDO's office and gotten exactly what I wanted, I headed for the door back into Pennant's office, but it was gone. The door had vanished.

That doesn't make sense.

I'd been patting myself on the back and celebrating my skill and brilliance, when I should've been smart enough to realize that, of course, there would be no doorknob on this side. It wasn't meant to be an access to Pennant's office. It was meant only to be an entrance to the conference room.

I banged on the wall where the door should've been, but no one answered. I yelled for Pennant. No response. I considered putting my foot through the wall when the door at the opposite end of the conference room swung slowly inward. Through the doorway came a young lady of perhaps twenty-five, in a navy-blue dress that fit her exactly as it should have. Her long, well-sculpted legs extended from the hem of the dress and were punctuated with a pair of black heels that could make a dominatrix blush. In her arms was a stack of files that must've weighed thirty pounds. She was managing the load with practiced skill and impressive balance.

"Hello," I said, as she approached the conference table.

The elegant beauty immediately turned into a baby giraffe trying to take her first steps. Files were airborne, one heel broke off with a loud snap, and she let out a squeal that likely deafened most dogs within a mile. Her reaction to her terror as she saw me for the first time, while unexpected, was quite impressive. She swiftly pulled a high-backed chair in front of her for cover, lifted the hem of her dress, and pulled a Walther PPK from a well-concealed holster on the inside of her left thigh.

I'd been taught to defend myself in almost every imaginable scenario, but I must've skipped class the day they taught self-defense against a gun-wielding CIA secretary. In what I perceived to be my best shot at survival, I immediately knelt, placed my hands with fingers interlocked on top of my head, and calmly but firmly declared, or perhaps begged, "Don't shoot. I'm unarmed, and I'm on your side."

In the confident tone of a highly trained intelligence officer, she said, "Who are you, and what are you doing in here?"

"My name is Chase Fulton. I'm a guest of Director Pennant. He put me in this conference room about an hour ago."

"Don't move while I check out your story."

I did exactly as she directed. While never taking her eyes, or her gunsight off me, she lifted the handset from a telephone on the table, and with her shoulder pressing it to her face, dialed a series of numbers. "There's a white male, age twenty-five to thirty, over six feet, approximately two hundred pounds in the DDO conference room. He claims to be Chase Fulton, unarmed, and a guest of the DDO. No one is scheduled in this room for another hour. Confirm ID and dispatch security. I'm in position two. Subject is in nine."

With her composure fully recovered, she didn't wait for a response, and she replaced the handset in the cradle. She continued covering me and sidestepped to her left, putting more of the conference table between herself and me. "Lie down with your arms and legs spread wide," she ordered.

I obeyed. I had no doubt she would pull the trigger if I gave her any excuse. I hated to admit it, even to myself, but I was both embarrassed and impressed. I'd killed one of the world's deadliest and most feared assassins on a mission that should've never succeeded, yet there I was, pinned down by a secretary.

I considered talking her into believing my story, but that would've been an utter waste of words, so I just lay there, embarrassed, and praying it wouldn't be Officer Pierce who came bursting through the door. He owed me a bloody nose, at least.

Thankfully, it wasn't Pierce who came to my rescue. I heard the invisible door open behind me, but I didn't dare risk turning my head to see who was there.

"It's okay, Grace. He's with me."

Those were the best possible words I could've heard coming out of Pennant's mouth. I watched Grace, name apropos, re-holster the Walther and collect the folders that took flight when I startled her moments before.

I leapt to my feet and tried to regain some semblance of dignity, but I certainly didn't feel like James Bond at that moment. I nodded a silent expression of appreciation when I met Pennant's gaze, then turned to apologize to Grace. I cautiously approached her and offered my hand. "I really am Chase Fulton, and I'm very sorry for startling you."

She planted her shooting hand firmly in mine and looked me squarely in the eye. "I almost killed you, Chase Fulton."

I smiled. She did not.

Pennant led the way back into his office. "Chase, what are you going to do with this information?"

Instead of an answer, I said, "Thanks for not letting your secretary shoot me in the face."

The look on his face made it clear he was in no mood to play games. "She's no secretary. She's a quite competent field agent who came to us very much the same way you did. Honestly, I'm surprised she didn't shoot you in the face. Believe it or not, she's one of the few people in this building more dangerous than you."

I was intrigued. I wanted to know more about Grace, the competent field agent. Not being the most dangerous human in a building didn't sit well with me, but if I had to be outgunned, it might as well be by someone who looked like her.

"I'm serious, Chase. I want to know what you're going to do with this information now that you have it."

I faced Pennant as if he were my enemy. "Mr. Pennant, you and I both know I can't tell you what I'm going to do next. You not only don't want to know, but you can't know. You need to have that plausible deniability people like you love so much. I'm going to take some time off and maybe do some traveling. That's all you need or want to know. Thanks for letting me stop by. I'll be in touch . . . or maybe not." I turned to leave his office.

"Chase, stop!"

I stopped just as Pennant ordered. When I turned to face him again, he was laughing.

"You can't just walk around in CIA headquarters without an escort. This isn't Walmart, you know. Just wait here, and I'll get someone to walk you out."

I still had a lot to learn about what I considered to be the corporate intelligence business. What little experience I had was in the real world with real bullets and real bad guys. It had been my experience that there were no escorts or visitor's badges in a gunfight.

I looked at my watch to express that I had more important things to do than wait for Pennant's escort, but in the end, I had no choice but to wait. I had no interest in risking another encounter with Officer Pierce.

"Have a seat. It'll only be a moment," Pennant said, pointing to his sofa.

I settled onto his sofa somewhat impatiently, but I didn't wait long.

Pennant pressed a button on his desk phone. "Will you escort Mr. Fulton out, please?"

A pleasant voice responded, "Of course, sir. I'll be right there."

Grace strolled through the door, and I quickly rose to join her. I'd spent the last minute I ever wanted to spend inside that building. Grace led the way through the maze of corridors, and we finally arrived back at Officer Pierce's station. We'd made the entire trek without speaking a word, so I expected her to discard me at the door and disappear back into the hall of spies while leaving me to my own devices.

She followed me through the door and onto the street, walking in lockstep with my every stride. I turned and offered a look, making it clear I wanted to know what she was doing. She grabbed my arm and encouraged me to keep walking.

When we were finally clear of the building, she said, "Listen, and do not react. Do you understand?"

I continued walking and acting like I hadn't heard her say a word.

"Excellent," she said. "I wasn't sure what to think when you cowered like a scared little girl when I drew on you in the conference room. It's nice to know you can actually follow instructions."

Ouch.

Again, I didn't react. I kept walking.

"I know who and what you are. We all know who you are, Chase, but not everyone knows what you're about to do. Before you do anything else, though, you need to know a few things about what just happened in there. You think you made a bunch of demands and got everything you wanted, but nothing could be further from the truth. You were played. Director Pennant wants nothing more than for you to go chasing Suslik all over the world and kill him—all of them."

My ability not to react had reached its bitter end. I gritted my teeth, trying to control my anger. "What are you talking about? Pennant didn't even know I was coming here."

"Oh, come on. You can't be that naïve. Do you really think you can do anything without us knowing?" She stopped and placed her hands firmly on my forearms. "Open your eyes. You know Director Pennant can't send an agent to hunt down Suslik, but what he can do is open a few gates, drop a few hints, then watch you go bounding through that open gate, guns blazing."

How could I be so arrogant to think I could bully my way into CIA headquarters, get exactly what I want, and think I wasn't being played?

"Why are you telling me this, Grace?"

She turned nervously and glanced back at CIA headquarters. "Where's your car?"

Reflexively, I also looked back at the building. "My car is a thousand miles from here at the Miami airport. Why do you care?"

She threw her hand into the air and hailed a cab. When it stopped in front of us, she yanked the door open, shoved me in the back seat, and slid in beside me. She slammed the door. "Driver, take us to Dulles, and don't hurry. We have some things to discuss."

The cabbie mumbled something about Dulles, but nothing else that came out of his mouth was remotely understandable. I was glad his English probably wasn't strong enough to understand what was about to be discussed in the back seat of his car.

Grace stared out the rear window of the taxi, presumably in search of someone following us. I couldn't imagine why any living soul would be following us, but I chose not to interrupt her little cloak-and-dagger, grown-up spy routine.

"Okay, listen. It's far simpler and so much more complex than you know, but what's important right now is that you trust me."

People who can be trusted rarely say, "Trust me." Even though I wasn't willing to trust her yet, I was willing to listen to what she had to say.

"You walked into a perfectly crafted trap," she began. "You talked yourself into doing exactly what Director Pennant wants you to do. He can't launch a worldwide manhunt for the Susliks. He knew once you figured out that Suslik was more than just the one man you killed in Cuba, you wouldn't be able to stop until you found and killed all of them, or until one of them killed you."

"Susliki," I said.

"What?"

I said, "Adding an *s* to Suslik doesn't make it plural in Russian. Adding an *i* does. Susliki."

She was obviously in no mood for sarcasm or a Russian grammar lesson, so she grabbed my shirt with both hands and pulled me to within an inch of her face. She was one of those rare women who was more beautiful the closer you got to her. That she had a Walther strapped to the inside of her left thigh, and knew how to use it, made her even sexier.

With our noses almost touching, she said, "If you go off on your own, without support, all you're going to get is dead. You may get lucky and find him, or one of them, but you can't just stumble all over Europe by yourself and expect to survive an encounter with people like Suslik. Think about it. How many people and how much planning went into the Cuban mission? You would've never been able to pull that off without massive support and a huge budget. Your success down there made it clear that you're good in the field, but no one is good enough to do what you're planning by himself—not even you, Chase Fulton."

What she said was important, but what she didn't say was even more meaningful. She warned me against chasing Suslik through Europe all by myself. She didn't offer up a support staff and massive budget. It was clear she was just trying to talk me out of going after Suslik.

"Okay," I said. "I won't go alone. I'll find another operator to come with me. I'll convince someone who's just as insane as me to come along for the ride. Would that make you happy?"

She looked through the back window again and finally released my shirt. "No. That doesn't make me happy. I'm going with you."

"Ha!" I laughed with exaggerated disgust. "So, you're going to tuck your CIA credentials into your bra and hop on a plane with me to go chasing the deadliest assassin on the planet across Europe. Is that what this is?"

"No, that's not what this is. I spent over three hundred days in the field last year, survived seven gunfights, caught a mole, and for all that, I made just over seventy thousand dollars. You went on one mission and made just over eight million in two days. You can afford to double my salary when I resign, but what you can't afford is to go without me."

Does she really think I'm going to take a CIA agent with me on an illegal, international manhunt?

Before I could put up a reasonable argument against her tagging along, she said, "I'm coming with you, Chase. It's that simple. To stop me, you'll have to shoot me, and I'm the only one in this car with a gun."

33
Our Boat

I called David Shepherd as soon as we landed in Miami.

"Whose fingerprints were on that bill, David?"

"Chase! How are you?" He sounded cheerful.

"I don't have time for small talk, David. Tell me whose finger-prints were on that bill."

My patience was growing thinner by the moment. I don't know what bothered me more: the fact that I'd been blindly suckered in by Michael Pennant, or the fact that there were two Russians running around the Florida Keys, looking for a woman on the orders of Dmitri Barkov.

He must've sensed my impatience. "The prints belong to Boris Novikoff, a mid-level bounty hunter type for the Russian mafia. He's dangerous, crafty, and fearless. He's a freelancer, but rumor has it he's been working for Dmitri Barkov lately. If you lifted that bill from him and he's in the States, there's a better-than-good chance that he's looking for you. Take my advice, Chase—"

I hung up before he could offer his advice. I knew exactly why Boris Novikoff was in Key Largo. He was looking for Anya, and by extension, for me. The thought of Anya possibly being in the Keys made it impossible to focus on anything other than seeing her again.

We found my car, and Grace immediately wanted to know what I'd learned from Shepherd. "What did he say?" Her impatience seemed to be running a close second to my own.

Trying in vain to get Anya out of my mind, I forced myself to focus on Grace. "He said the prints on the bill belong to a bounty hunter named Boris Novikoff. Does that name ring any agency bells for you?"

She tilted her head, obviously thumbing through her mental Rolodex. "No, I don't think so. Should it?"

"No, probably not. He's here looking for an SVR agent who works for Dmitri Barkov."

"What's his name?"

"What's whose name?"

"Focus, Chase. What's the name of the SVR agent Novikoff is chasing?"

"The agent's name is Anastasia, and she's a very long story. I'll explain later. What you need to know is we can't let Novikoff find her before we do. Actually, we aren't going to find her, either. She'll find us. That's sort of her thing."

Grace sat in the passenger seat of my BMW, watching the mangroves pass by at sixty miles per hour. I had to tell her about Anya, but I wasn't looking forward to confessing how I'd fallen in love with a Russian assassin. If there was a rule that came before rule number one in the spy handbook, it would be to never fall in love with the enemy. Perhaps I wasn't suffering from a lack of judgment. Perhaps I had a perception problem. I just couldn't let myself see Anya as my enemy. I was going to need a drink before opening that can of worms with my new partner.

I broke the silence as we turned onto Card Sound Road. "I live on a boat, you know. I had my boat moved up to the Ocean Reef Club. The security there's a little tighter, and it'll be better than being out in the open, so that's where we're headed."

As if she were bored, Grace mumbled, "Okay."

"I have a lot to tell you when we get to the boat."

"I know," she said.

* * *

I welcomed her aboard *Aegis* and poured cocktails for each of us. I silently wrestled with myself, trying to decide if I should tell Grace everything, or leave out the part about Anya and me getting a little cozier than we should have.

Grace took my glass and went into the cabin. While she was below, I scanned the horizon for anything that didn't look like it should be there. I was actually looking for anything that looked like a beautiful blonde Russian, but there was nothing to see except mangroves and seagulls.

Grace stumbled back on deck with my glass nearly full. She was a long way from finding her sea legs, but she didn't spill a drop. When she handed me the tumbler, her delicate hand lingered against mine a little longer than it should have. As *Aegis* unexpectedly rolled ever so slightly to starboard, Grace stumbled again and almost fell onto my lap. Her hand landed on my shoulder, and I found her face only inches from mine. I didn't move, but after the briefest hesitation, she did. She pressed her lips to mine, slid her hand across my shoulder, and let it come to rest on the back of my neck. Her embrace was firm but tender, and her kiss was passionate. It was impossible to avoid being attracted to her. She was stunning and smart, but I wouldn't surrender. I placed my glass on the seat beside me and leaned back. I pulled my lips from hers and held her face in my hands.

"We can't do this, Grace. I can't do this. You're fascinating, but there's a lot you don't know yet." I breathed the words more than spoke them as I tried to imagine what caused the boat to make that little roll. It must've been a manatee brushing against the hull.

Grace didn't show the signs I expected a woman to show after being rejected. She sat down next to me and took a drink. "Okay, Chase. Tell me about her."

I swallowed half of the scotch in my tumbler and felt my heart race. I'd put it off long enough. It was time for confession.

"So, you know about the op in Cuba, but before that op, I was on a job in New York at Belmont Park where I watched a sniper shoot a horse."

I saw the disbelief in Grace's eyes.

"Wait a minute," I said. "That's not what I meant. She didn't really shoot a horse. She flashed a laser in its eye. But that's not important. What's important is I watched her do it, and I'm the only one who saw it. She got away, but that's also not particularly important. After I killed Suslik in Cuba, I ran like the wind and wound up on St. Thomas, where I found Dutch. Do you know about Dutch?"

Her look of disbelief was replaced by intrigue. She was now hanging on my every word. "Yes, yes, I know about Dutch. Go on."

I tried to rein in my rambling narrative. "I found Dutch, or more accurately, he found me. The sniper was there, too. She was chasing me. You see, she works for Dmitri Barkov, and she was there to find out who sent me to kill him. It took me a long time to make her understand I hadn't been sent for Barkov. It's a very long story, but she cut my tongue in half, killed Dutch, cut a tracker out of my neck, and I shot off one of her toes while she was trying to drown me in a lagoon."

I realized how ridiculous my story sounded, and I paused for another drink.

Grace looked lost. "What are you talking about?"

"I know. I'm going to try to put it all together for you, but this is where it really gets weird."

She stood up. "Now I'm the one who needs another drink. If it's just getting to the weird part, I'm not sure I can handle the rest of this story without more alcohol."

I once again scanned the water around *Aegis* in the hope of seeing Anya approaching, but there was nothing except a coast guard patrol boat doing whatever it is they do.

Grace returned with her drink, but instead of sitting beside me, she sat across from me in the cockpit and waited for me to continue my ridiculous story. I glanced over her shoulder at the patrol boat making its way out to sea. For a moment, I wished I were aboard that boat. I wasn't looking forward to telling the rest of my story, but I was in too deeply to stop.

"I know none of this is making sense yet, but for you to understand what happened next, you have to know the history. After all of that, the sniper and I wound up on my boat, this boat, and . . . well, I really don't know how to explain what happened next."

"Stop stalling, Chase. Just tell me what happened."

She left me no choice but to continue. "I'm in love with her." The words exploded from my mouth before I knew I'd said them. The admission was an enormous weight lifted from my chest. I didn't know how Grace would react, but I didn't care. Nothing she could say would change how I felt about Anya.

Instead of explaining how dangerous, reckless, irresponsible, and stupid it was to fall for a Russian SVR agent, she knelt at my feet, crossed her hands over my knees, and placed her chin on top of her hands. She looked up at me. "I understand. Let's get some sleep, and tomorrow we'll decide how to find and eliminate your gopher . . . or *gopheri*."

Grace slept in the aft cabin, and I spent the night tossing and turning in my bed in the forward berth. My brain didn't want to sleep. It wanted to think about Anya and wonder when and where she would show up.

I thumbed the radio on and stretched my arms above my head, trying to wake myself from what little sleep I had. As the radio came to life, I heard, ". . . and in a bizarre story from Key Largo, the bodies of two Russian nationals were discovered early this morning in their motel room at the Seaside Motor Lodge. The two had apparently been bound with piano wire prior to their deaths. Police suspect drug trafficking to be at the core of this brutal murder, but as of yet, they have no suspects in this gruesome crime. Up next is the day's weather with Heather and sports with Garcia Murano."

The instant my feet hit the deck beside my bed, a forceful hand landed firmly below my throat and drove me backward. Before my head came to rest against the mattress, out of pure instinct, I retrieved and raised my pistol between me and my attacker. I was halfway through my trigger squeeze when the attacker's left hand grasped the slide of my Makarov, and with practiced dexterity, thumbed the safety into place. As my mind exploded in an effort to identify my aggressor and devise a plan to foil the attack, Anya's long blonde hair fell across my face, and her body rested on mine. The kiss that followed was more passionate than any we'd shared before.

As we parted, I opened my eyes and started to tell her how much I missed her, but she pressed her finger to my lips. "Who the hell is other woman sleeping on our boat?"

34
Tree Pee

"That's a long story," I said. "Her name is Grace. She's CIA, and she's going to help me find Suslik."

"See? I told you Suslik was not dead, but you did not believe me."

"Yes, Anya, you told me, but you weren't completely correct. Suslik isn't just one man. You and everyone else on Earth kept telling me he was a ghost, but that's not true, either. He's a triplet. That's why he can be in several places at once, like a ghost."

She gave me thoughtful look. "I think American saying is, 'You are late to party.' Of course Suslik is three."

It was my turn to ask some questions. "When did you get here? Where have you been? How did you get aboard? Did you kill Boris and his buddy?"

She smiled that wry smile that was so uniquely hers. "Slow down, *Chasechka.* I like kissing you with tongue healed. I am here three days. I was in water last night when CIA woman kissed you and you made her stop. Good boy. Very good boy. I kicked, uh, I do not know, *rul' napravleniya,* to make you look into water, but you did not look."

I smiled, recognizing the Russian word for rudder. "That was you?"

"Yes, was me. You are getting, uh, *nebrezhnyy.* I am still better than you."

I laughed. "You may be better at sneaking up on me, but your English is getting *nebrezhnyy*. The word you're looking for is *sloppy*."

I wrapped my arms around her and pulled her against me. We kissed while the first rays of the morning sun beamed through the portlights. Anya turned and looked from my cabin into the main salon. "I am to meet your CIA agent now."

She was declaring rather than asking, so I pulled on a T-shirt and a pair of swim trunks just before she tugged me through the cabin doorway. She stomped her foot onto the cabin sole and watched for Grace to stir. When she didn't, Anya dropped a small skillet into the stainless-steel sink, sending a clanging racket through the cabin. That did the trick. Grace opened her eyes abruptly and tried to focus on the figures standing only a few feet away.

Uncertain what was about to happen, I took control of the moment. "Grace, this is Anya. Anya, this is Grace."

Grace rubbed the sleep from her eyes. "Hi. When did you get here?"

In Russian, Anya said, "She has pig nose, and her eyes are too close together. She is not beautiful. And she does not speak Russian, or she would have tried to shoot me with her unloaded gun when I said she had pig nose."

I tried not to laugh when I saw the bullets from Grace's pistol standing on their ends and arranged like little soldiers on the first companionway step.

Before I could speak, Anya turned to Grace and said in English, "Is nice to meet you. I am Chase's . . ." She paused, obviously trying to think of the correct English word to describe what she was to me. Instead of finding the word, she said, "Yes, I am Chase's."

Grace didn't show any reaction to Anya's declaration, so I broke the silence. "I told you she'd find us."

Women, in some ways, are like wild animals. Animals will urinate on trees to mark their territory. Anya, in doing a little tree peeing of her own, took my hand and led me back into my cabin. She made no effort to muffle her expressions of ecstasy, making certain the remaining occupant of our boat could hear every sigh.

* * *

When we emerged from my cabin, we found Grace in the cockpit, sipping coffee. My bottle of twelve-year-old scotch, with its lid suspiciously missing, was resting on the countertop just beside the coffee maker.

I made breakfast of scrambled eggs, bacon, and toast. Anya returned from the shower and quickly made herself at home, devouring the contents of her plate. Grace sat across from Anya and me at the small table, and I wondered who would be the first to speak. The psychologist in me was intrigued, but the man in me was terrified.

It was Grace who spoke first. "So, Anya, forgive me, but aren't you an SVR officer?"

Anya swallowed a healthy mouthful of coffee and looked at me mischievously. "No," she whispered. "Not anymore."

I tried to appear calm, but my curiosity prevailed. "What do you mean, not anymore?"

"I want to work with you to find Susliki and then do what you said we could do . . . disappear together forever." Her words were crisp, and her English was good.

I was speechless, and Grace seemed flabbergasted.

From my days as a catcher on the baseball field, my mind could digest an enormous volume of information and process it down to the most important elements. That's what was happening at that moment. I was absorbing an overwhelming statement from Anya, and processing how it would mesh with the remainder of my life, but one thought kept pouring to the forefront of my churning mind: I had to talk to Dr. Richter.

"There's someone you have to meet," I said. "He's my mentor and the closest thing I have to a father. Anya, you have to meet him today."

I looked at Grace, trying to make her understand what was unfolding. "Stay here, Grace. Stay here on the boat. We'll be back tomorrow or the next day, and we'll go from there, but don't leave. We need you. You're crucial to what comes next."

She agreed.

With Anya by my side and Grace organizing the operation, we could not only find every Suslik on Earth, but we could also drive them into the ground in shattered pieces.

"Anya," I said, "you and I have a little trip to make. Have you ever been to Georgia?"

"Which one?"

"The American one."

"Not yet," she admitted, "but I will go with you anywhere."

I believed her, but I wondered if she'd feel the same after Dr. Richter spent the afternoon trying to talk us out of . . . everything.

35
Reunion

I had befriended Hank, the manager at the private airport at the Ocean Reef Club. As fate would have it, he'd flown with Dr. Richter in the war and still considered him a brother-in-arms. He owned a Bonanza he could no longer fly because of his failing health and what he called "that dad-blasted flight surgeon."

Hank essentially handed me the keys to the Bonanza to fly anytime I wanted. He believed "watching her die on the ramp was just too much to swallow." I didn't abuse his generosity, but I flew the airplane enough to keep her from dying on the ramp.

I introduced Anya to Hank and asked if he'd mind if we took the Bonanza to Athens to see his old friend. Anya's accent made Hank raise an eyebrow and shoot me a knowing wink.

"Sure, you can take my airplane anytime you want, Chase. You know that. Consider it yours. Just don't let that old coot, Rocket Richter, fly her. There's no telling what he'd do to the old girl. It's nice to meet you, Anya. Good luck with this one. He's a pistol."

Once we were in the air and climbing out over the Everglades into the brilliant blue sky, Anya said, "I did not know you could fly airplane, and why did that man call you pistol?"

"It's just an American saying. I think he likes you."

She smiled. "Yes, of course he likes me. Everybody likes me until I kill them."

I smiled, and she blinked sweetly, reminding me that underneath the exterior of that deadly killing machine lay a heart of tenderness yearning to be loved.

We reached our cruising altitude, and I offered the controls to Anya. "Put your hand on the yoke like this," I said, demonstrating how to hold the controls lightly. "Good. Now turn left and right, just like driving a car."

She made some gentle turns, and I watched her initial reluctance give way to excitement and sheer pleasure. She laughed as she guided the plane through ever-increasing turns. I showed her how to coordinate the turns with the rudder pedals and to change altitude with a gentle push or pull of the yoke and minor throttle adjustments. Soon, she was handling the Bonanza as if she'd been flying for years.

After half an hour, I took back the controls. "Anya, I want to tell you about the man we're going to meet."

She reluctantly surrendered the controls and turned to face me.

"Dr. Richter was one of my psychology professors at the University of Georgia where I went to school. He's an amazing teacher, but he's so much more than that. He's also a pilot and flew during the war. After the war, he went to work for the government, and he knew my parents. He's a very important man to me, Anya. He's much like a father to me now that my parents are gone. He actually recruited me into this work, so if I'd never met him, I would've never met you. I know you'll like him. And he'll love you."

I leaned toward her, but instead of the gentle kiss I'd anticipated, our microphones bumped and pressed into our lips. We laughed, pushed the mics out of the way, and pecked at each other's lips.

"Your Dr. Richter sounds wonderful. I must thank him for sending you to me."

As we flew our approach into the Athens airport, I clenched my teeth with anxiety. I was determined to grease the landing, and I couldn't have Anya laughing at me for bouncing.

My determination paid off, and I made the landing of my life. I nonchalantly taxied the Bonanza to the transient line and parked her in a well-marked spot. The lineman helped me tie her down and asked if we needed fuel and how long we'd be staying. I asked him to top off the tanks and told him we'd be leaving in a day or two.

"I have never been to this Georgia. It does not look like Georgia in Soviet Union." She looked like a tourist as she spun around on the tarmac, taking in the scenery of endless pine trees.

"I've never seen your Georgia," I said, "but I went to school not far from here, and that's where I played baseball."

She slipped her hand into mine as we walked across the parking ramp and past a dozen other parked airplanes. That was the first time she and I had ever walked while holding hands. We'd never done anything normal like typical young lovers, but our relationship wasn't the same as most people in their twenties.

I saw Dr. Richer emerge from the mirrored glass door and stroll onto the tarmac. It was a great feeling to see him again, but I couldn't decipher the look on his face. He was staring directly at Anya with both hands cupped over his mouth and tears streaming from his eyes. I couldn't imagine what could be wrong with him. I'd never seen him show any emotion, especially not tears. He never glanced at me. His eyes were locked on Anya.

Anya noticed him and froze in her tracks. She gripped my hand. "What is wrong with that man? Why is he looking at me like this? You have gun, yes?"

Dr. Richter approached with his chin trembling, and he reached to touch Anya's face. She stepped back and assumed a fighting stance with her fists raised in defense against the stranger.

"Anya, this is Dr. Richter," I said. "I don't know what's wrong with him."

His mouth hung agape, and tears poured down his cheeks. He reached for Anya again and took her delicate face in his palms.

She spread her feet, strengthening her stance, and glared at me from the corner of her eye. "Chase, what is happening?"

"My God, those eyes . . . and those cheeks. You are your mother a thousand times over. I can't believe it!"

Anya's eyes glistened, and she took a step backward. "How do you know I look like my mother? Is not possible you know my mother. She is dead for many years."

Dr. Richter wiped the tears from his eyes. "You must come with me. There's something you have to see."

He reached for Anya's hand, and to my utter disbelief, she placed her hand in his and let him lead her across the tarmac. All I could do was follow. Anya glanced at me several times as we walked. I don't know if she was looking for reassurance or an exit strategy, but I had neither. The man I trusted more than anyone, and the woman I loved were walking hand-in-hand toward some unknown destination.

We stopped in front of Dr. Richter's hangar, and he turned the key, unlocking the door. Anya and I followed him through the heavy steel door, neither of us saying a word. As the lights came to life inside the hangar, we stood beside the gleaming P-51 Mustang. Dr. Richter had the palms of his hands pressed firmly against the fuselage behind the propeller blades. The painting of the woman with irresistible eyes and delicately crossed legs adorned the side of the plane above the script "Katerina's Heart."

Dr. Richter admiringly looked up at the painting and then at Anya. "This is your mother . . . Katerina Burinkova. I've loved her since the first time I saw her over thirty years ago, and you, Anastasia Burinkova . . . you are my daughter."

Anya's knees lost the strength to hold her, and she clung to me. Tears trailed down her face as she stared at the painting of her mother on the nose of the Mustang. "This cannot be. What is happening? This cannot be true. I cannot be this man's daughter. My father is dead. My father was Russian soldier. This cannot be." Her body shuddered as she sobbed and gasped in my arms.

Dr. Righter led us across the hangar floor to a sofa and knelt on the hard, cold floor at Anya's feet. He wept like a child as he held her hands. I watched the two of them stare at each other, speechless, and overwhelmed with emotion until I finally noticed he had the same smoky blue-gray eyes as Anya. I saw the way her nose tapered at the tip, just like his. It was unmistakable. She was his daughter, and he was her father.

I never imagined seeing Anya so vulnerable. Her tears of disbelief seemed to give way to tears of acceptance, and she collapsed into his arms. Breathlessly, she pleaded, "Tell me about my mother."

Dr. Richter wiped his nose and cleared his throat. "Wait here. I promise I'll be right back."

Anya melted into the sofa and watched her father bound up the wooden stairs of the hangar and disappear into a doorway. She never took her eyes off his path until he returned with a tattered shoebox under his arm. He pulled a small table from beside the sofa and dumped the contents of the shoebox onto it. From the box cascaded dozens of envelopes with jaggedly torn tops and delicate notepapers exposed from each. Alongside the envelopes came a stack of photographs banded together with an aged rubber band that was nearly shredded.

Anya reached for the stack of pictures, and the rubber band crumbled at her touch. She held each picture in her hands so gently that the slightest breath would've blown them from her grasp. Through puffy eyes, she pored over the pictures. Occasionally, she'd hold up a picture and compare the man beside her mother to the face of Dr. Richter.

Watching the two of them cling to each other was an unimaginable scene for me, and both of them in tears was beyond my comprehension.

Anya pulled each letter from its envelope and read every word. It appeared most of the letters were written in Russian, but a few were in a combination of Russian and attempts at English. She closed her eyes and held each letter to her face, seemingly trying to recall her mother's scent through the worn pages. She carefully returned each letter to its envelope and placed it back in the tattered box.

After two hours of tears, letters, and photographs, Dr. Richter finally turned to me. "Chase, my son, this is the greatest gift anyone could've ever given an old man. I love you, my boy." He pulled me into his arms and hugged me as if I'd just saved his life.

When we parted, he clenched my shoulders in his powerful grip. "Chase, never let her go. Never. She is your life's treasure and your salvation . . . and maybe mine. You are to never let her go. Do you understand me?"

I had to come clean. "Look, Dr. Richter, I had no idea Anya was your daughter. I brought her here to meet you and to ask for your advice. She's the woman I told you about."

"There's no way you could've known. Only God and fate knew. I could never thank you enough for bringing her to me."

I'd never been good at anything emotional. I knew how to catch a baseball, land an airplane, trim sails, and kill people. That was the extent of my useful knowledge. I wasn't sure how to react or behave in the midst of such an emotional experience for the two most important people in my life.

"Coach," I said, "Suslik is a triplet. I killed only one of them. There's at least one more and probably two. I'm going to find him, or them, and kill them . . . or him. Anya wants to defect and help me do it."

He patted me on the shoulder. "Slow down, Chase. First, of course Suslik is a twin or triplet. We all knew that. You're a little late coming to that party. Second,"—he paused and looked at Anya—"she cannot defect."

"Yes, of course she can. You know exactly how to make that happen. You know everything we need to do. You have to help us."

"She can't defect because she's my daughter, and I'm an American. Her American citizenship is just a formality. Defection isn't necessary. It's in an obscure old document. I think it's called The Constitution. Don't be fooled, boy. It isn't going to be easy, but we can do it. Pennant will get her a temporary visa, and we'll go to work getting her naturalized. Very soon, Anastasia will have an American passport and maybe even a birth certificate."

Dr. Richter was planning every detail of turning his daughter, my Russian SVR agent, into an American. It had been my intention to introduce Anya and Dr. Richter, have a pleasant dinner, discuss the Suslik operation, and return to Florida. That should've taken less than eighteen hours, but that's not at all what happened.

Instead of building the operational plan with Grace back in Key Largo, we found ourselves at Dr. Richter's house, where I sat idly by as he and Anya, father and daughter, pieced together the past thirty years. He told her endless stories of how he and her mother met, fell in love, and were forced apart by a great number of things, including Dmitri Barkov.

Sometimes they laughed. Sometimes they cried. And sometimes they spoke conspiratorially. Occasionally, one or both of them would turn to make sure I wasn't within earshot before the whispering resumed. I wasn't afraid of anything they'd tell each other, but I was curious about what was so secretive.

When two full days passed, I insisted that we return to Florida to start planning the operation. Instead of protesting when I made the declaration, Dr. Richter stormed from the room, then returned moments later with a backpack slung over his left shoulder and an ancient leather case in his right hand. It would be a waste of time and effort to try to convince him not to come with us, so I made no such attempt.

Anya smiled. "Look at me. I am newest American girl, and I am going to Florida with my two favorite spies."

As if rehearsed, Dr. Richter and I replied in unison, "We're not spies!"

We climbed into Dr. Richter's VW Microbus and headed for the airport. When we arrived, he thumbed the button, and we drove through the sliding gate and onto the tarmac. We rolled to a stop beside my borrowed Bonanza.

"Anya and I will meet you at the Ocean Reef Club," said Dr. Richter. "I'm quite sure you won't be able to keep up. Now, get out . . . out! You're going to need all the head start you can get."

I kissed Anya and slid from the seat. I wasn't looking forward to the long flight alone.

Dr. Richter was right. I heard Jacksonville Center hand off North American 555, Dr. Richter's P-51, to Miami Center on the radio. That meant he and Anya had passed me in his much faster airplane and would be waiting for me on the ground.

When I landed at the private airport at the Ocean Reef Club, the Mustang was already tied down and covered with her custom canvas cockpit and wing covers. Katerina was still visible on the nose.

I parked the Bonanza and checked in with my friend, the manager. He told me that my "girlfriend and that old scoundrel, Richter" had landed over an hour ago, and they'd meet me on the boat.

What have I gotten myself into?

36

Some Things Never Change

I didn't expect the scene I found when I made it back aboard *Aegis*. Dr. Richter and Grace were sitting in the cockpit with half a dozen maps spread out in front of them. They had notepads, pencils, and calculators scattered about the deck, but Anya was nowhere to be seen.

Instead of a snide remark about how much faster his airplane was than my borrowed Bonanza, Dr. Richter took me by the arm and led me onto the foredeck. "Chase, I had to tell Anastasia about her mother's death. She's spent the past twenty years wanting the truth, and as terrible as the truth is, she deserved to know."

I stared into the water. "I know, Coach. You had to tell her. I just wish you would've waited until I was here. I'm going to check on her."

What I saw in my cabin tore my heart into pieces. Anya, the strongest woman I knew, was curled in a ball on my bed, her shoulders rising and falling in a sobbing, sickening cry. I felt like I was being gut-punched over and over. My insignificant pain couldn't compare to Anya's agony.

I lay down behind her and took her in my arms. She wrapped her arms around mine and pulled my hands close against her convulsing chest. I burned with the desire to ask how I could help, but sometimes not asking offers more empathy. I held the woman I loved and waited until she was ready to speak.

When her weeping finally gave way to deep breathing, she turned to me. Her face was streaked with tear stains, and her eyes were blood red. Seeing her in so much pain left me feeling powerless but aching to do anything to soften the unthinkable blow she'd endured. I brushed a strand of hair from her face and tried to wordlessly reassure her that I'd never let her go.

"He killed my mother. That bastard cut out her heart so she could not give it to man she loved—my father. Dmitri Barkov murdered my mother, and now I will cut his heart out of his chest and hold it in my hands while he dies at my feet. I swear it to your God and to my mother."

I knew Dmitri Barkov had killed Katerina, Dr. Richter's love, but until two days before, I didn't know Katerina was Anya's mother. The irony was inconceivable. Any attempt I would make to talk Anya out of avenging her mother would be futile. I would never try to stop her, but I *would* try to delay her. I needed her help to find Suslik, and I needed her to be focused and on her game. I prayed she'd be capable and willing to find and eliminate Suslik before we set out after Barkov.

I held her until her breathing became deeper and more regular, and she fell asleep in my arms, surrendering to the exhaustion of her emotions. Unwilling to move and risk waking her, I drifted off, joining her in slumber.

* * *

Before the sun rose above the banyan trees, I heard pots and pans rattling in the galley and smelled the wafting scent of coffee brewing. Anya kissed me lightly and slipped from the bed, quietly making her way to the shower. I joined Dr. Richter in the galley and accepted an offered mug of coffee.

"Is she okay?" he asked.

"No, but she will be. She's going to kill Barkov."

"Yeah, I know, but it wasn't right to keep the truth from her any longer."

"You're right," I said, "but it must've been terrible having to be the one to tell her."

He took a long drink of the dark coffee. "I'm the only one who could ever tell her. It had to be me."

I placed my hand on his forearm and looked into his smoky eyes. "When did you know she was your daughter, Coach?"

He looked to make sure Anya was still in the shower. "I suspected it when you described her to me and told me how Barkov had taken her under his wing. He wants to believe that she's his daughter, but he would never tell her that. He's filled her head with lies about who her father was and kept his thumb on her since she became an SVR agent. Her mother was KGB and one of the best operators I ever met. She could tear a man's throat out with one hand while smiling and whispering in his ear. She was mesmerizing and deadly. Her beauty made her almost invisible. She could walk into any room and catch the attention of every man there, but when seven of those men ended up gutted and dying on the floor, no one seemed to remember the Russian who had floated through the room with such grace. She was the most remarkable woman, Chase. You can't imagine."

I smiled as Anya walked silently into the galley in a T-shirt and a tiny pair of shorts. Droplets of water from her wet hair ran down her back. She brushed her hand across my shoulder and down my arm.

"Yeah, Coach, I think I know exactly what you mean."

He smiled his crooked smile. "Yeah, son, I suppose you do."

Anya leaned against Dr. Richter's shoulder and kissed him gently on the forehead. "*Dobroye utro, otets.*"

He kissed her cheek. "Good morning, my beautiful daughter. Sit here with Chase and have coffee. I'll finish making breakfast."

"No, father. You sit. I will cook."

She looked about the cabin. "Where is Grace?"

Dr. Richter answered, "She's gone for a run and swim. She'll be back soon."

"Ha, a run and swim," Anya murmured as she turned to the stove.

Breakfast was delicious. It seemed to be some sort of fried sweet cake with syrup and blobs of something brown. I decided not to question her about it. Anya and Dr. Richter spoke mostly in Russian, so I was able to decipher most of it, but there were many details I missed. Grace returned and spent the meal looking at me as if I should translate.

Anya reached across the table and took both of my hands in hers. "Chase, I want you to know I am focused on finding Suslik and killing him with you, but when this is done, I will find Dmitri Barkov, and I will gut him like pig. You understand?"

I definitely understood. I appreciated her willingness to prioritize the missions and focus on Suslik first. I couldn't stop her from going after Barkov, but I could certainly make sure she didn't go alone. I would do everything in my power to see that she never had to do anything dangerous alone ever again.

Grace said, "Okay, so here's what I'm doing. I've put out some feelers for intel on Suslik throughout Europe. I've pieced together that there have been no mysterious double sightings for the last six weeks. This leads me to believe that there's only one left and diminishes the potential that he may have been a triplet. I don't think it's safe to completely rule out that possibility, but for now, I think we should proceed under the general assumption that we have one target." Grace tapped her fingers against her lips and seemed reluctant to share a secret.

The three of us echoed, "What?"

"I know I'm not an analyst, but I have a theory," she said.

We gave her our full attention.

"Okay, this is just a theory, and it's not really based on anything other than what's going on in my head. Obviously, somebody sent Boris and his comrade to find Anastasia."

Anya immediately cut her off. "You will not call me Anastasia. That is my name only for my mother, and now my father, but never for you. You will call me Anya and nothing more."

"I'm sorry, Anya. I didn't know. I'm really sorry," Grace said with obvious sincerity.

"Is fine. Continue."

"Okay, so I think it's safe to assume the two Russians were sent here to either kill her or bring her home. Do all of you agree?"

Dr. Richter and I nodded, but Anya sat stoically. "No. They were not here to kill me. They are what you call in this country bounty hunters. They are not assassins. So, you are wrong. There is no probability of them being here to kill—only to bring me back."

I found it childishly amusing that Anya was jealous of Grace and took verbal jabs at her, even when she agreed with Grace's theory. I just wrote it off as more tree pee.

Unfazed, Grace continued. "Okay, so we all agree the guys were here to nab Anya and take her back to Russia to face someone. So, who do we think that someone might be?"

Dr. Richter and I believed it was Barkov, but without hesitation, Anya said, "Tornovich."

"Who's Tornovich?"

"I reported to Victor Tornovich before I deserted," Anya said. "He is SVR colonel. If I were taken back to Russia, I would have to answer to Tornovich. He would determine my fate."

"I thought you worked for Barkov," I questioned.

"Yes, I do. I mean . . . I did most times work for Barkov, but officially, I report to Tornovich . . . or I did report to Tornovich. It will be a time before I can stop saying in present and say in past, yes?"

I said, "It's important that you know how grateful I am to have you on my side. I'm still afraid of you, even though you're one of the good guys now, but I was terrified of you when you were my enemy."

Anya looked at me with what appeared to be disappointment. What came out of her mouth was both prophetic and definitive, but to her it was simply the truth. With her head tilted slightly, she said, "Chase, I was never your enemy. It was, at a time, my duty to kill you, but it was never my wish. I watched you for very long time, and in me . . . uh, the person in me . . . chose not duty but to be a person. I am sorry. That does not make sense to you probably."

"Yes, Anya. It makes perfect sense. It was my duty to flip you, but it was so hard for me to see you as an operative when, as you said, the person in me wanted to be your person."

Grace, obviously impatient, put the kibosh on our moment. "Yeah, yeah, okay. You two can write love letters later. We have an op to plan."

She was right. There was no time to get sidetracked.

"Okay," Grace said, "the bounty hunters were here to bring Anya back to Russia. They failed because she's obviously much better at what she does than they are. The key here is that they knew where to look for her. That's both good and bad. It's bad because they—whoever they are—know where to look for Anya. It's good because if they don't already know, they will soon know that their men failed and were killed. Everyone here knows more about the Russians than I do, but I think it's a good bet that they'll send others who are more capable than Moe and Larry."

"Wait!" shouted Anya. "I did not kill Moe and Larry. I do not know who that is. I killed Boris Novikoff and a, uh, *novichok*, whose name I do not know, but I do not think he was this Moe or Larry."

Dr. Richter chuckled.

Grace said, "I'm sorry. That was an American TV reference, but what's a *novichok*?"

Anya wasted no time seizing the opportunity. "*Novichok* is what you are, Grace, a person with not much experience."

"At least I still have all of my toes," Grace retorted.

"Focus," Dr. Richter said.

I wondered how long the petty nipping at each other would continue. I feared it might become a tactical issue if I didn't do something to quash it. I'm not afraid of men with guns, but snippy women are an entirely different animal. So, based primarily on my fear, I chose to let it play out and hope for the best.

"Anya," Grace said, "you're the only one of us who knows how soon Moscow will know of Boris's failure and when we can expect the next pair of bounty hunters, so we have to rely on you for the next decision."

I perceived that as an olive branch.

Was Grace pandering to Anya or actually being sincere?

Anya looked skyward and seemed to consider the tactical aspects of what would happen next. "Boris, and as you say, Moe and Larry, were low level. They would make report to superior every day. I killed them at two in morning, so we must assume they would be required to make report within twenty-four hours. That was four days ago, so Barkov knows they are dead. I am not so important to risk more lives to find me right away, but there is one more thing we must consider." She tapped her finger on her chin. "Hmm. If they believe I have come here to find Chase and help him, that is very different thing. They know I did not kill him when I was required to. They know also his mission was to kill Parchinkov, the man you call Suslik, not Barkov. If they think I am now helping Chase, they will send not bounty hunters next time. They will send *ubiytsa* . . . and not just for me."

By Grace's reaction, it was obvious she knew the Russian word for assassin.

Anya continued, "They will send Anatoly Parchinkov, who you call Suslik. They probably already have."

"Excellent," said Dr. Richter. "That's exactly what we want. Right, Chase?" He raised his eyebrows at me.

"Precisely, Coach. If we know Suslik is looking for us, we can not only be prepared, but we can also bait the trap for him."

"Is not so easy, Chase," Anya said. "He is very dangerous, and he does not fall into traps."

"His brother did," I said confidently.

"Yes, but now he knows you are tricky, and he will not be so easy as his brother."

"Of course, you're right, Anya. This time will be much more challenging, but this time, I'm not alone. I have the three of you.

Here's what I think we should do. If we anchor out aboard *Aegis*, say half a mile or so offshore, we can post a watch around the clock and see any threat approaching in time to mount a defense. There will be no way for Suslik to sneak up on us. We can—"

Anya didn't let me finish detailing my plan. She looked at me with disappointment. "Do not be naïve. Suslik will shoot each of us from two kilometers away when we show our heads on deck, or he will sink our boat from beneath and kill us as we try to swim away. Putting ourselves in middle of water would be perfect trap and would please Suslik. We must stop him where he does not believe we can. We must think five steps ahead of him because he is thinking at least four steps ahead of us." She closed her eyes, pursed her lips, and let out a long, heavy sigh.

Each of us sat silently, digesting what she said.

Anya obviously sensed that the rest of us didn't know what to say, so she continued. "So, here is what we know. Anatoly knows where we are. He knows also who we are, mostly. He probably does not know about my father and about her." She cast her eyes toward Grace.

Grace rolled her eyes. "Grace. My name is Grace. I don't like being called *her*."

With the cold emptiness Russians, especially female Russians, seem to master so early in their lives, Anya said, "I know you want me to believe your name is Grace, but I do not know yet if is your true name. I will know soon, and if is your name, I will call you Grace. We will see, but until then, you are *her*."

"Enough!" I slammed my palm onto the table and sent everything flying to the deck. "Enough is enough! We're all on the same team, and it's time we start behaving that way. Anya, you and I are here because we have a common enemy and common threat to our lives. Dr. Richter is here because he loves his daughter. Grace is here because she wants to do what's right and find and kill Suslik. Now, there's no reason to be acting like schoolgirls in a pissing contest. We're never going to get anywhere like this!"

Dr. Richter stared at Grace with sincere interest. I was steaming with frustration. Anya sat stoically, completely devoid of emotion, as if she were waiting for me to finish my rant. Grace narrowed her eyes and clenched her teeth.

Before Grace could explode, Anya said calmly, "You are right, Chase. My father is here because he loves me and also you. You are, to him, son in many ways. You and I are here because Anatoly wants you dead and me captured. About all of that, you are correct, but you may not be so correct in what you believe about her. She is here because she has made you believe she wants same things as us. She is CIA. Is her job to lie, to deceive, and to make her way into situations where she should not be so she can make report back to CIA. She is spy. She can never trust me. I am Russian SVR agent. She will never trust you. You are *nayemnik*. She will never trust my father because she believes is relic of Cold War. She is here only to spy on you, on us. Why else?"

Part of me wanted Grace to defend herself. Anya had a point. Grace had made a great effort to mole her way into my operation, and so far, there had been no effort on the part of the CIA to get her back. I was a fool for having not recognized that Grace may have, in fact, been a plant whose mission was to report back to Pennant on my every move.

Maybe Anya's right.

"There is more." In her native Russian, Anya said, "I think she may be more than a mole for the CIA. I think she might be a traitor, working with Suslik and man who killed my mother."

"I'm no traitor, you communist bitch!" Grace roared as she sprang from her seat and drew her pistol from its holster at the inside of her left thigh.

Grace leveled her pistol with Anya's ear and cocked the hammer, but Anya didn't blink. Instead, she turned, glared directly into Grace's eyes, and hissed in perfect Russian, "I thought you did not understand Russian, traitor."

I was blindsided, but Dr. Richter wasn't. The muzzle of his

government model 1911 Colt .45 pistol came to rest against the flesh beneath Grace's left eye.

Calmly, Dr. Richter said, "Put your gun on the table in the next half second, or I'll blow most of your head overboard."

Grace ignored Dr. Richter and chose to fight. She spun around and struck the back of Dr. Richter's gun hand, knocking the 1911 from his grip. She continued her rotation and made perfect use of her momentum when she wound Dr. Richter's arm around his own neck, pulled his body against hers, and rested her pistol at his temple.

Grace's eyes met mine. "If you pull your gun, he dies," she said.

Without drawing my Makarov, I said, "If he dies, I swear to you that you will be dead before he hits the deck."

She never heard my threat.

In a fraction of the second it took Grace to lock eyes with me and make her demand, Anya sprang from her seat and launched herself through the air toward Grace. Anya's palm struck Grace just above her lips, driving the cartilage of her nose upward and into her brain. Grace's head snapped backward, and blood exploded into the air as her agonizing cry echoed across the water. The debilitating blow dissolved Grace's grasp on Dr. Richter.

The Russian's momentum carried her and Grace's corpse across the gunwale and into the water. I expected Anya to emerge seconds after disappearing below the surface, but she didn't. After nearly a full minute without her resurfacing, I kicked off my shoes and prepared to search for her in the darkening water.

Before I could leap over the side, Dr. Richter placed his hand on my forearm. "Wait. Just be patient and wait. If she isn't back in forty-five seconds, I'll let you go."

Patience was never my strong suit, but I tried to heed his words. I grew more anxious with every passing second. Dr. Richter released my arm just as Anya slid across the coaming and back into the cockpit.

My hands shook as I asked, "Are you all right?"

Anya coiled her legs beneath her body and wiped the water from her face. "Yes, Chase. I am fine. Are you all right?"

I nodded, and she immediately turned to Dr. Richter. "And you, Father, are you hurt?"

"No, my child. I'm not hurt. What have you done with Grace?"

"I put her between the propeller shaft and hull of boat for now until we can find better place. She was going to kill me and probably you, too, Father. She had to be stopped."

I'd never seen this side of Anya. She was, for the first time, explaining her actions. I'd only seen the Anya who'd gone about her work with cold, emotionless precision. It appeared as if she were almost apologizing for killing Grace, or at the very least, rationalizing her action.

"Yes, yes, I know," Dr. Richter said. "You had no choice. You saved my life, and in the long run, you probably saved Chase's life, as well. That girl was clearly working two sides, and perhaps even three. I was on the verge of questioning her loyalty, but you saw through her façade more quickly than me. Your mother would be so proud of you."

The mention of her mother impacted Anya more than Dr. Richter probably expected. She hung her head and fell silent. I looked at him, and he pointed his chin toward Anya, indicating that I should go to her. He'd never steered me wrong, so I followed his subtle suggestion and reached for Anya. I grabbed a towel and wrapped it around her cold body, warming and comforting her by rubbing her back.

"*Spasibo*, Chase. *Spasibo*."

"You're welcome, my angel. Thank you for saving our lives. Are you sure you aren't hurt?"

She held my face in her hands, grinned, then made her way to the cabin.

Dr. Richter put his hand on my shoulder. "My boy. What a life you lead. You have a soaking wet Russian SVR officer changing clothes in your bedroom, a dead CIA agent stuck beneath your boat, and at least one Russian assassin waiting for you to walk into his crosshairs."

I laughed. "I'm living the dream, Coach."

"Indeed, you are."

Anya returned on deck with a look of terror on her face. "The radio says someone has stolen police boat off Key Largo. I do not think that is common. Do you?"

Dr. Richter and I stared at each other. "Suslik."

"Yes, it has to be him," Anya said.

My tactical mind roared into overdrive as I began planning and strategizing. "We have to get Grace's body back aboard. We can make it to Bimini overnight. It's less than seventy miles, but we have to go now."

Anya leapt into the water and reappeared thirty seconds later with Grace's dead body in tow. Dr. Richter started the engine and waited at the wheel. I leaned over the gunwale and tried to haul Grace's body aboard. Her wet, lifeless body was heavier than I expected. I finally wrestled her aboard as Anya climbed over the rail. Before I could catch my breath, Dr. Richter had *Aegis* motoring out of the marina through Dispatch Creek. We would soon be in the Gulf Stream, riding the current and southwesterly wind toward Bimini less than seventy miles to the northeast.

Anya and I hefted Grace's body into a locker aft of the cockpit. We couldn't have a dead body lying on deck if the coast guard stopped by for a visit. I wondered what I would do if we were approached by a Marine Patrol. *Aegis* couldn't outrun her own shadow, let alone an overpowered pursuit boat like most of the law enforcement vessels in the area. I also had to devise a plan to deal with Suslik if he approached us while we were underway.

Anya and I returned on deck after drying off. Dr. Richter had us well on our way to Bimini with sails aloft and *Aegis* clipping along at just over eleven knots in the roaring Gulf Stream.

When the wind is from the north, the waters of the Straits of Florida are deadly, but with the southwesterly wind, the Gulf Stream had suddenly become our friend.

"Nice job, Coach," I said as I took his place at the helm. "It's almost as if you've done this before."

Over the rush of wind and waves, he said, "As a matter of fact, this isn't the first time a female Russian agent and I have run from Russian assassins and American agents. Some things never change." Dr. Richter winked at Anya, then turned back toward the uncertain horizon.

37
Confessions

"How deep is water here?" Anya asked.

"Only a few hundred feet, but it'll be half a mile deep in another twenty or thirty miles. Why do you ask?"

She motioned toward the locker containing Grace's body. "We must do something with her. We cannot explain dead American in box on our boat. I think is best to sink her to bottom in very deep water and forget her."

There was the SVR agent I knew. I'd been waiting for her to show up.

"As much as I don't like the thought of sinking the body of a dead CIA agent, I can't think of a better option at the moment," I said.

Dr. Richter looked at the locker. "I don't think we have many choices at this point. I'll take care of the dirty work while the two of you start planning what we're going to do when we find Suslik, or more likely, when he finds us."

I set the chart plotter to alarm when the depth reached two hundred fathoms. I wasn't certain that my sonar was capable of reading twelve hundred feet, but if not, I thought it would probably alarm when it reached its limit.

I found Anya at the chart table with her head in her hands, and I brushed her hair back across her shoulders. "Are you okay?" I asked.

"I do not make mistakes. I know every way to kill a person, and I know how to strike without killing, but I did not, uh, *sderzhivat*. I do not know the English word. *YA ne smog vazderzhatsa, kogda nado bylo.*"

"It's okay," I said. "We all go further than we should sometimes . . . all of us. You're no different."

"Yes, I am different! I am better. I should have knocked her out, but I should have not killed her. I did not think. I only reacted to protect you and my father. I do not like emotion commanding me. I am better than that."

I knelt at her feet and placed my hands on her arms, squeezing them gently. "Anya, if you hadn't acted, at least one of us would've died before Grace could've been stopped. I've never seen anyone move as quickly as you did. What you did back there was the best possible reaction. Grace was going to shoot. Your father believes she was working with Suslik. He also agrees that she may have been working with DDO Pennant to keep an eye on us—and especially on me. I should've been smart enough to see that, but I was naïve and believed she sincerely wanted to help find and kill Suslik. She wasn't one of the good guys, Anya. She wasn't on our side. We're on our own, and we can't trust anyone who isn't on this boat right now. Despite being alone, we still have to finish what we've started. We have no other choice. We have to find and kill Suslik before he finds and kills us."

Anya covered her face with her hands then pressed her fingers into her temples. "Okay. I know some things I have not told you. You should sit for this. You must listen carefully."

I obeyed, as the moment I'd been waiting for had finally arrived. When she lived her life on both sides of the Iron Curtain, her loyalties remained firmly on the cold side, but all of that changed when she abandoned her home to be with me.

Learning Dr. Richter was her father only served to solidify her newfound alliance. Sooner or later, she'd come clean about everything I needed to know to catch and kill Suslik. She was about to spill her guts, and I hoped I had the courage and intellect to keep up.

"Chase, there were things I could not tell you before now. I need for you to know I did not like keeping information from you, but I did not have choice. Please tell me you understand at least little bit." Anya tried with great effort to look into my eyes.

I knew she needed me to understand. I took her hands in mine. "Anya, I understand more than you can know. Of course you had to keep things from me, but that's no longer necessary. You can tell me anything. Nothing you can tell me will change how I feel about you."

She pulled her hands away from me, obviously needing physical and psychological separation while she said what was on her mind. "This is not easy for me, and will not be everything, but is start. I will tell you what you need to know now, and I will always in future tell you everything."

"I understand. Please go on."

She looked toward my cabin and blew out a long breath. "Chase, the things I do with you in there are things I was taught to make men tell me everything they know. You must understand you are first man I have done those things with because I wanted to please him, and not because I wanted him to talk. You are first sincere man I have known. That is why I am here. I am not here because I hate my country. I do not. I am not here because I was doing wrong. I do not believe I did wrong. I am here with you because I feel with you some things I have never before felt. I turned from everything I know because you are something I have never known. I choose you, Chase, because being your person feels better than anything I have ever been. That is only reason. Do you understand?"

"No, of course I don't understand, but I believe you, Anya. I learned from my father that belief is far more important than understanding."

"Okay," she said. "That is all about that, okay?"

"Yes."

She said, "Now, I will tell you about Suslik. There were three of him. He was triplets—*identichnyye brat'ya*. You killed one in Cuba. I killed one in Gibraltar. I will tell you about that later. One is left, and he is trying now to kill both of us. He is, uh, I think English word is *rogue*. He is out of control and very dangerous. It was not safe for me to tell you this when Grace could hear." Anya stared coldly at the locker containing the corpse.

"Are you certain there are only three?" I asked.

"Yes, I am certain."

"Does he have a support network?" I tried to avoid sounding like I was interrogating her, but I needed to know some things for which she was my only source.

She seemed to understand my plight. She seemed to understand so many things I did not.

"He did have strong network, but no more. He has gone mad. He is like angry bear now. He is not thinking. He is acting only in passion and anger. He is now unpredictable and more dangerous than you can know." She sighed. "I promise I will tell you everything you want to know when there is time, but now, you know what you must know to finish and stay alive." She placed her hands on my cheeks. "I love you, my *Chasechka*."

Before I could respond, she stood, pulled her pistol from a small bag on the chart table, and slid it into her waistband. Then she went into my cabin and returned with her sniper rifle that seemed to fit perfectly in her hands. I followed her through the companionway and into the cockpit where we both froze in place at the horrifying sight in front of us.

Dr. Richter was lying across the seat, desperately holding his right shoulder as blood poured through his fingers. Anya struck me hard with her hand, pushing me back through the companionway and down into the galley. She grabbed her father under the armpits and dragged him into the cabin where she went to work inspecting his wound.

I saw the fear in her eyes as she applied a pressure dressing and tried to get the bleeding under control. The next few moments of our lives would feel like hours, and it would be a long time before we could get Dr. Richter to the medical care he desperately needed.

"Father . . . " she spoke reassuringly. "Is not bad. Stay down. You will be okay."

Anya curled her lips and growled. "He tried to kill my father. Now I will send him to Hell."

38

Comrade Colonel

Any thought we had of being the predator in this deadly game had vanished. We'd become the prey. Dr. Richter's gunshot wound was a chilling omen of the danger that lay across the waves. The determination on Anya's face told me she was devising a plan to drag Suslik into his own private Hell.

"Chase, you must start engine. I do not know what boat Anatoly is using, but I know is not sailing boat. I know we cannot go faster than him, so we must think faster."

I grabbed a pair of binoculars from a locker and shoved them into Anya's hands. "I'm going outside to get us under power and get the sails down. I'll turn us through a full circle. You find him!"

My words sounded more like an order and less like a plan, but Anya offered no objection as she pressed the binoculars to her eyes and took her place at a starboard porthole.

I slithered through the companionway and onto the deck of the cockpit. I pressed the starter switch and heard the diesel purr to life. We'd been sailing on a beam reach with the sails flying over the port side, so I turned the wheel to the right. As the bow passed through the wind, the sails luffed and howled their protest at being blown in line with the centerline of the boat and losing their ability to produce lift. I opened the halyard clutches, allowing both the main and jib to fall to the deck. I continued pulling

Aegis through the turn, determined to give Anya a complete three-hundred-sixty-degree view of the water around us. It was my hope she'd spot Suslik before he could get off another shot at us. I certainly didn't need rifle rounds bouncing around my boat.

I couldn't resist quick-peeking over the coaming as we continued our slow, lumbering turn. Anya was much safer down below with ample concealment, but her vision was limited by the combination of binoculars and the small porthole. During one of my peeks over the coaming, I caught a glimpse of a black silhouette that appeared to be powering directly for us.

Just then, I heard Anya start issuing orders through the companionway. "Stop turning, now!"

I rotated the wheel, bringing the rudder amidships, and stopping our turn. We rolled out on a steady course broadside to the wind, waves, and the oncoming vessel. It was not only the worst possible position to place a sailboat for stability, but it also presented a massive target for our aggressor. Anya obviously had a plan, and I had to trust her.

I couldn't resist poking my head over the coaming just once more to see how bad our situation had become. As my eyes rose clear of the fiberglass, I heard the cracking report of Anya's rifle from the cabin down below. Anya had opened fire on the oncoming boat, so I locked the wheel and dived headfirst through the companionway, landing at her feet. I rolled onto my back and looked up at her, but she was not looking back at me.

Her feet were planted like stones on the cabin sole, and her eyes were focused ahead. Her right eye glared through the scope, and her left scanned across the top of her rifle through the open porthole. She cycled the bolt, and the spent .308-caliber shell casing bounced across the cabin deck, smoking and rolling as *Aegis* wallowed on the waves.

"Tell me what you're doing!"

Without changing her position, she replied, "I want him to turn so I can shoot engine."

The rifle roared again, and the recoil drove Anya's body several inches backward, but she was unfazed by the jolt. As the barrel rose and fell powerfully in the porthole, she cycled the bolt with practiced precision. Just as the rifle came to rest, she squeezed the trigger and again absorbed the pounding recoil. This time, she didn't cycle the bolt, and instead kept her eye focused through the scope.

Without celebration, she said, "I did it. You must quickly turn toward him so we can be smaller target. His boat is dead. Now Anatoly will fight."

I ran up through the companionway and quickly freed the wheel lock. I turned hard over to bring us bow-on toward Suslik's crippled boat, and Anya scampered out of the cabin and crawled forward, burying herself in the head sail that was piled on the foredeck. She took up a perfect firing position inside the concealment of the sail, but she had no cover. The sail wouldn't stop any bullet Suslik would inevitably fire at us.

I tried to keep my head as low as possible and keep us pointed directly at Suslik. The instant I turned slightly to see the bobbing vessel, I heard something whistle past my head. I turned to watch the flying object land in the water in my wake.

The list of things the missile could've been was extremely short, so it didn't take me long to settle on the terrifying fact that it was a fired grenade. Before I could come up with a plan to react to the next incomer, I heard Anya yell, "*Granatomyot!*"

In any language, "grenade launcher" sounds ominous.

Grenadiers use a technique not unlike the tactics of larger artillery gunners. They carefully observe the first fired round and adjust the following rounds to correct the first miss. Gunners referred to this technique as walking in.

I watched the second grenade splash harmlessly abeam our starboard side less than ten feet away. The next round would be anything but harmless.

In a desperate attempt to disrupt his walking in, I pulled the power back on the diesel and forced the transmission into reverse. I opened the throttle and felt my heavy boat bleed off forward momentum. Suslik would calculate his next shot based on our previous speed, so if I could get *Aegis* stopped, or even better, moving backward, his next round would fall short of our bow. That would give Anya another few seconds to put some more lead into Suslik's lap. She was firing relentlessly and still yelling at me between the bellows of the rifle.

I couldn't understand most of what she was yelling, but I did hear what I thought was the best possible idea. She yelled, "Put raft in water!"

I left the wheel and dived for the davits where the dinghy was hanging. I grabbed the painter and secured it to a stern cleat.

Anya yelled, "*YA udaril yego!*"

Did she say she hit him?

Unsure if I'd heard her correctly, I freed the lines securing the dinghy to the davits and heard the small boat splash into the water at *Aegis*'s stern. I didn't watch the dinghy fall, and I lunged back to the wheel to continue my clumsy, lumbering maneuvers to avoid the next grenade. Instead of hearing another incoming grenade, I saw Anya walking backward toward me with her rifle still trained on the bobbing boat in front of us. I *had* heard her correctly. She hit him, but she was clearly concerned that the fight may not be over.

She stepped down into the cockpit and handed me the rifle. "Watch him closely. I am going to check on Father."

I shouldered the rifle and took cover behind the main mast. The optics of Anya's scope were much better than my binoculars, and I saw Suslik's body sprawled awkwardly across the gunwale of the powerboat. If he wasn't dead, he was doing a great impersonation of a dead bad guy. I watched for his chest to rise and fall, but he lay there motionless. I stomped my foot on the deck, and Anya stuck her head through a hatch.

"You hit him, all right. He's definitely dead, you little sniper."

She pulled herself upwards through the hatch, exposing her

head and shoulders, and peered across the bow toward Suslik's boat. "I told you I could shoot."

She went back through the hatch and reappeared in the cockpit with her father close behind. His eyes were bloodshot, and his face was deathly pale, but he was walking and appeared to be in good spirits.

"He needs doctor," she said, pointing toward the badly wounded shoulder.

Dr. Richter protested, "There's no time for doctors right now. We have work to do. We have to do something that should've been done a long time ago."

We were going after Dmitri Barkov.

"I have plan, but you will not like." Anya surveyed *Aegis*. "I have plan to bring Barkov to me, to us, but you must give up your home, Chase."

No matter what her plan was, I was onboard, despite the cost.

"Bring guns, knives, ropes, and blankets, and get in raft." She was going to call the dinghy a raft no matter how much I opposed.

I followed her direction and climbed into the dinghy with her and Dr. Richter. He started the engine and piloted one-handed toward Suslik's boat. As we approached, Anya lay over the bow with her pistol pointed cautiously toward the gopher's dead body.

She finally accepted that he was dead, lowered her pistol, and knelt on the gunwale as we came alongside the much larger powerboat. She tied the dinghy to a cleat, and the three of us leapt aboard Suslik's stolen powerboat with Marine Patrol markings emblazoned along each side of the hull.

She wasted no time grabbing Suslik by his hair and lifting his head from the deck. His dead eyes were still open. He looked identical to the man I killed in Havana, and no doubt, exactly like the man Anya killed in Gibraltar.

She pressed her pistol to the right shoulder of Suslik's corpse. In terrifyingly cold Russian, she whispered, "You shot my father in his shoulder, and now you will spend your death wearing same wound."

She pulled the trigger twice, and watched flesh, bone, and blood fill the air as the dead man's body rolled slowly into the dinghy. She untied the painter and let the dinghy drift away. Dr. Richter and I were helpless to do anything besides play our roles —whatever they were—in Anya's plan.

She took a seat on the deck and motioned for us to join her as low as possible.

"Anastasia, you must tell us what you're doing," Dr. Richter said.

"We are waiting, Father. We must wait for Barkov. He will come when he sees fire."

She lifted Suslik's grenade launcher from the deck and loaded an incendiary grenade into the tube. She frowned painfully and looked up at me. "I am sorry, Chase. There is no other way." She pulled the trigger, and the grenade left the tube with the tell-tale thump. I watched its arcing trail through the air and felt my stomach turn as the grenade pierced the deck of my boat. The incendiary grenade ignited a fire that consumed my home in orange flames, and I watched as smoke billowed from my beloved *Aegis*.

Dr. Richter watched what had been Ace's boat, and my home, reduced to black smoke that must've been visible for a hundred miles.

"I am so sorry, Chase," Anya said again. "Now we must set trap."

Her plan was becoming clear, and it was going to work if she was correct about Barkov being close enough to see the smoke.

"You must sit here, Father." She helped place him in the seat behind the wheel, then leaned him forward across the console with the grenade launcher perched precariously in his arms. "Your body is same shape and size as Anatoly. You must make Barkov believe you are Suslik." Anya stepped back and looked at her father. "Yes, will work. Now, we must hide."

She and I lay beneath a pile of canvas and fenders near the bow of the boat and pulled a blanket across us. We didn't have to wait long.

Dr. Richter whispered, "There's a boat coming. A big boat. And it's definitely not the coast guard."

I snuck a peek across the gunwale, and what I saw made me shake my head in amazement at Anya's ability to predict Barkov's moves. Coming toward us with impressive speed was a luxury yacht nearly identical to the one I'd assaulted in Havana. It could be none other than Dmitri Barkov.

The yacht came alongside, and Dr. Richter began his charade. He moaned and lifted his head just as a wounded Suslik would've done.

At that moment, the unmistakable voice of Dmitri Barkov filled the air. "*Anatoliy, ty v poryadke?*"

Dr. Richter stood up, faced Barkov, and leveled his pistol at the Russian's barrel chest. "Surprise, Dmitri. I'm not Anatoly, and Anatoly is definitely not all right. In fact, he's burning in Hell right now, and you'll soon be joining him."

Barkov froze as Anya and I sprang from our concealment with pistols drawn. We leapt aboard the yacht, and Anya wasted no time. She locked her heel behind Barkov's knee and drove him into a deck chair. I helped her tie him in place as he bellowed for help. Anya drove her elbow into his face, crushing his lips against his teeth. Blood gushed from his mouth, and his yelling ceased.

Dr. Richter climbed aboard with his bandaged shoulder still oozing blood. "You two go secure the rest of the boat. I'll keep my old friend company until you get back."

As Anya and I left the stern deck of the yacht, I heard Barkov say, "Comrade Colonel Richter, so you are still alive."

We cleared the remainder of the yacht, finding only a skeleton crew and staff. We ushered each of them overboard and into the crippled powerboat. Certain no one was left aboard other than Dr. Richter and Barkov, Anya and I returned to the stern.

In angry Russian, Barkov barked, "What have you done, Anya? Why have you brought this to me? I gave to you everything. I made you what you are. Without me, you would be a peasant, an orphan."

Anya stared stoically into Barkov's eyes. In Russian, she said, "No, you made me an orphan when you cut out my mother's heart. You killed my mother, Katerina Burinkova, so she could not give her heart to my father—to this man. You turned me into this thing I am—this thing that until now has only known killing and following orders. Your orders. You made me what I am, and now I will show you how deadly your creation has become."

She drew her knife and stepped toward Barkov. I sprang toward her as Dr. Richter yelled, "No, Anastasia! Don't do it!"

But we were too late. Her blade pierced Barkov's chest, and she drove it to the hilt with all of her weight sinking into his beating heart. She stared into his terrified eyes and watched the life leave his wilting body.

Through bared teeth, she whispered, "*YA serdtse Katereny.*"

I am Katerina's Heart.

About the Author

Cap Daniels

Cap Daniels is a former sailing charter captain, scuba and sailing instructor, pilot, Air Force combat veteran, and civil servant of the U.S. Department of Defense. Raised far from the ocean in rural East Tennessee, his early infatuation with salt water was sparked by the fascinating, and sometimes true, sea stories told by his father, a retired Navy Chief Petty Officer. Those stories of adventure on the high seas sent Cap in search of adventure of his own, which eventually landed him on Florida's Gulf Coast where he spends as much time as possible on, in, and under the waters of the Emerald Coast.

With a headful of larger-than-life characters and their thrilling exploits, Cap pours his love of adventure and passion for the ocean onto the pages of The Chase Fulton Novels series.

Visit www.CapDaniels.com to join the mailing list to receive newsletter and release updates.

Connect with Cap Daniels

Facebook: www.Facebook.com/WriterCapDaniels
Instagram: https://www.instagram.com/authorcapdaniels/
BookBub: https://www.bookbub.com/profile/cap-daniels